FOG HEART

FOG HEART

Thomas Tessier

VICTOR GOLLANCZ

LONDON

First published in Great Britain 1997
by Victor Gollancz
An imprint of the Cassell Group
Wellington House, 125 Strand, London WC2R 0BB

© Thomas Tessier 1997

The right of Thomas Tessier to be identified as author of
this work has been asserted by him in accordance with
the Copyright, Designs and Patents Act, 1988.

A catalogue record for this book is
available from the British Library.

ISBN 0 575 06452 8

Typeset by CentraCet, Cambridge
Printed in Great Britain by
St Edmundsbury Press Ltd, Bury St Edmunds, Suffolk

97 98 99 5 4 3 2 1

for Veronica

and in memory of
our friend
John Goodchild
1937–1990

Fog land have I seen
Fog heart have I eaten
Ingeborg Bachmann

Stranded

Oona didn't think of it as suicide, exactly. She wondered what it would be like to drift away and never come back. This time make it real. Water lapped gently around her ankles. Was there a tide, a current that would take her?

She wondered where she would go, what would happen. Would her thin little body wash all the way down Long Island Sound to New York City, bobbing in oily refuse? Perhaps she would thump against a gleaming yacht at the Greenwich marina. It might be best if she only floated a short distance, to the middle of the Sound, and then sank to the bottom of the channel, to rest there in silence. Silence – yes, that would do.

The water was cool but not unpleasant. Still, most of the people stayed on the beach, content to take in the sun and enjoy the fresh air. It was quite warm, in fact, and the air had a familiar marine tang. But the people. There were too many of them. There always were. They didn't particularly bother her, at the moment.

Oona waded a few yards, dragging her feet through the sand. She glanced back at the beach and spotted Roz in the crowd. She was still sitting on that colourful towel, her feet crossed at the ankles, arms propped straight behind her, sunglasses on, her dark auburn hair hanging loose. A model, nearly.

Beside Roz, the red and white cooler containing bottles of cranberry lemonade, the holdalls with their clothes, tapes, snacks, Oona's copy of *The Heart of Mid-Lothian*, sunblock, skin cleanser, combs, brushes, flip-flops, a rumpled *Register*, an old Walkman with a new battery, everything as it was. So many things to be counted and forgotten.

Roz saw Oona looking at her, and quickly flashed one hand.

Oona wriggled her fingers in return. Dear Roz, I'm writing this to say . . . I don't know what to say.

Oona slipped into the water and began a lazy crawl, but soon rolled over onto her back and floated. She steered herself to get in position so that she could see only the sky. Funny how you begin to see things that aren't there as soon as you look up at the empty sky on a day when it's such a brilliant blue. With no hint of land, no clouds. You see odd shapes and weird things, images that exist only in your eyes and head.

Water, flow into me.

This is the Atlantic, Oona reminded herself. An arm of the Atlantic, anyway. Like the North Sea, like the Firth.

You'd never make Leith from here. Why would you want to, anyway? There's nothing for you there. You brought it all with you, long ago. Scene of the crimes, real or fanciful. It would be of no use. How little is!

> In the bonny cells of Bedlam,
> Ere I was ane and twenty,
> I had hempen bracelets strong,
> And merry whips, ding-dong,
> And prayer and fasting plenty.

Oona rubbed her arm. Her skin was pale and burned easily, so she'd put on plenty of lotion. She could still feel it, slick as slime. Meet your new skin. It had the feel of something that had settled into the pores for the duration, like guilt.

She swung her feet down: they barely touched sand but Oona could tread water. The water didn't scare her, though she never felt at home in it. She was an adequate swimmer at best. There were so many people. One thing about them, they were easier to take at a distance. You're just not a people person, Oona.

Ah, but she is, you see.

She kept expecting to drift into a current that would carry her away, but she felt nothing. Just chilly water, no pull. She would have to do all the work, if it was going to be done. Think of it as making love. That would be a first. You want to do it gladly, if at all. Think of it as going home. But what on earth is *home*?

The people looked a bit smaller, she thought, but not small enough. Roz was still visible on the towel. There was something about the way Roz sat that suggested alertness. Lie down, girl, do us a favour. Close your eyes and daydream. That was what Oona wanted to do, at sea.

– A man's hands around her neck –

No, not again, no more, never. Kill me, for a change. Make it real this time, make it real, make it real.

By moving slowly, casually, by swinging around this way and that in lazy arcs, Oona was able to put a lot of distance between herself and the shore without causing alarm. At least, she heard no whistles or shouts. She heard nothing at all, and that was very nice indeed. The crowd was beginning to blur.

Roz at the water's edge, waving.

Oona righted herself and waved back, trying to make it look as if she were happy and relaxed. She wagged her head, splashed water, and then did a quick surface dive. She came up a few yards away, further out, and flopped onto her back. She floated nonchalantly, trying to make it look as if she were in complete control and didn't have a care in the world. As if she actually knew what she was doing.

You do, don't you?

The crowd was a narrow band of mixed colours and shapes, with no definition any more. Good, but don't look any closer or you'll see something you don't want to see. And that was it, of course. The thought itself was more than sufficient. Oona suddenly *knew* that Roz was swimming towards her now, that Roz wanted to catch up with her and make sure that everything really was all right, and take her back to this miserable land.

Oona turned away and cut into the water. She swam hard. She cupped her hands, digging into the waves and kicking her feet as forcefully as she could. Such a puny creature am I. There was a sensation of steady movement, but not of speed. The sea wants to take me, and I want to go. Let it happen.

Her strength disappeared quickly. Her arms began to burn

at the shoulders, her fingers splashed rather than scooped, and her feet began to slap weakly behind her. I want to sink, my body is ready, let me sink like sinking into exquisite sleep.

She caught a glimpse of the shore, the people, and all of it seemed far enough away at last. No, don't bother to say goodbye. The hardest part was to make your body let go, to allow the water in without fighting it. Hard, but worth it.

Greyness invaded her. Oona gagged.

Her body resisted, and that made her feel angry and useless. She began to cry as she choked, tears lost in seawater, still caught at the surface, her body refusing to sink, to yield to the sweetness she so dearly wanted. It was as if she could feel her fingertips brush against it, but could not take hold of it. What does it take to make death take you?

A presence near her. Oona tried to force herself down into the depths, but it was no use. Roz's arm looped around her neck and locked her chin in the crook of the elbow.

'No,' she sputtered feebly.

'It's okay,' Roz said, sounding very calm. 'Don't worry, I have you. You'll be all right now.'

'I'll never.'

'Sure you will. Don't try to talk.'

Now – oh, sure, *now* – Oona's body relented completely, and Roz towed her along easily like an inflated toy. Always too far, never far enough. Living doesn't work, dying doesn't work. A moment later Oona felt the sand beneath her. Her stomach hurt and her mouth tasted awful. She spat several times.

Roz draped an arm around her shoulders and steered her to their beach towel. Oona crossed her arms on top of her knees and rested her forehead on them. Her breathing was still ragged; her body trembled and occasionally shuddered with a gasp. Maybe she had come closer than she thought.

'Do you want to go to the ladies' room?'

'No.'

'You sure?'

'I'll be all right.'

Oona sipped a little juice. She lit a cigarette with some

difficulty, her hand shaking. She coughed sharply a couple of times and couldn't inhale deeply, but as always the smoke was a vague comfort. Roz placed a dry towel around her shoulders and stroked her back soothingly. 'Poor thing, you must've been terrified.'

Oona looked up at her. 'No,' she said. 'Not in the least. I wanted it to happen.'

When she saw the tremor of pain in Roz's face she was almost sorry she'd said it. But Roz understood. Had to.

'Oona.'

'I mean it,' Oona said, a bit loud.

Roz sat close to her, holding her, speaking in a low voice. 'But, darling, why?'

'You know well enough.'

'You can't just turn your back on it and give up.'

'I can try.'

'You can't do it,' Roz insisted, her voice almost regretful. Oona put her head down and began to cry again, silently, still shivering. Roz gave her a hug and rocked her comfortingly. 'Look, never mind about that now. Do you want to go home? We'll put our feet up and have a drink. What do you say?'

Oona nodded. 'Yes.' Sounding every bit as small and frail and miserable as she looked and felt.

'Sounds good to me, too.'

They gathered their things, wandered back to the car and got on the highway for New Haven. Oona found a Mozart violin sonata on the FM. She clutched her book tightly in her hands and tried to let the music fill her head. It was perhaps as dark as Mozart ever got, and it seemed to help.

At home, Roz put her in a warm shower, gave her a shampoo, towelled her down and carefully combed the snarls out of her hair. Oona had masses of long black hair, and it took a while. But Roz always had time for things like that. She could be the perfect attendant, a lady's lady. Oona sipped icy vodka from a crystal tumbler, and smoked long cigarettes. The acceptable vices. She felt better now, like a pouty child who is being over-compensated for a minor deprivation. She would let herself enjoy it.

'Oona.'

'Mm?'

'Did you see – '

'No.'

' – anything?'

'No.'

'You weren't in any real danger, then.'

'I was nearly there,' Oona corrected her.

'You'd've seen something.'

'Maybe not.'

'You weren't close enough.'

'That's the truth.'

'Don't talk like that.' A mild reproach.

They went into the living room. Oona stretched out on the long sofa, settling herself among loose cushions. Roz sat on the carpet and leaned back against a heavy armchair, nursing the only glass of Scotch she would have all evening.

'Roz.'

> *My banes are buried in yon kirkyard*
> *Sae far ayont the sea,*
> *And it is but my blithesome ghaist*
> *That's speaking now to thee.*

'Yes, love?'

'Next time . . .'

'Don't ask that.'

'Please. Roz . . .'

Why is it so easy to beg for what you know you'll never get? The sheer perverse pleasure of being refused. You're always safe in choosing the pain you know.

'Don't ever ask that of me.' Roz swirled her drink. 'Your talent is special. Exceptional.'

'It's not a talent.' A shout, but plaintive, and the fight was gone by now. 'I don't want it any more.' A whimper.

Roz let it pass and they were silent for a while.

– Her throat, tightening –

'I felt him,' Oona said suddenly. 'A man's hands around my neck. He was strangling me. I don't know who he is. That was the only thing I did feel out there in the water, and it happened again, just now.'

Roz stirred with interest. 'He was strangling you?'

'I believe so, yes.' Oona shrugged. 'Someone.'

'You're making it all up,' Roz decided impatiently. 'I wish you wouldn't do this to me, Oona. It's so distressing.'

'Sorry. But it's real enough to me.'

'This whole thing, it's what you think you'd *like* to happen, because you didn't make it today.'

'True.'

'Honestly, you can be so hurtful.'

'I don't mean to be.'

'Little sister . . .'

Roz didn't sound bitter or angry, but stoical, pained. Oona was sorry she was doing this to her. The vodka helped her feel a lot better, quieting her mind, but it also made it easier for her to say certain things she otherwise wouldn't.

'I don't mean to be anything.'

'Don't talk like that.'

Oona sipped her vodka and lit another cigarette, loving the way they made her feel – and not feel. It must be said, you do have this talent. Not for living, not for dying – just a horrid little talent. So be it. But the time will come when . . .

> The glow-worm o'er grave and stone
> Shall light thee steady;
> The owl from the steeple sing,
> 'Welcome, proud lady.'

PART I

1

The show was a bit of a disappointment, but Oliver always enjoyed being back in London. There were no real beauties to be had and he couldn't find much that he felt utterly compelled to get. No surprise: he knew that the best stamps always went to auction, and three or four times a year he had his dealer in New York buy or sell a truly special item for him.

Stamps were only a sideline with Oliver. But they had an aura of beauty and serenity, and to be surrounded by them in a place as large as Olympia was soothing indeed. The show just happened to coincide with a visit on other business, and he couldn't pass it up. Besides, the pleasure of the hunt was rich in itself, and did not always have to culminate in a rare find or a spectacular catch.

Oliver checked his watch and made his way to the bar, which was starting to fill up. He had a large Dewar's. He felt edgy in a good way. He was back in his city again. After Cambridge, he had come to London, managed a band that became a fair success for a year or two (he still received modest royalty cheques), invested in a label that continued to prosper, imported American jeans and selected lots of clothing that sold well, and in time he got into several other business ventures. Some were a little less profitable than others, but none lost money. He had a good nose for a fair risk.

Oliver was still, essentially, a maverick, an inspired dabbler who got by on his instincts, but by now he could not conceive of giving up his freedom for a more predictable and secure business career. Besides, he didn't need a regular paycheque.

Now he wanted to do something. There was a party for the Limehouse Knights, a fairly new non-retro neo-post-ska ska band, currently on a roll in the UK, which should be fun – but that was later in the evening.

Oliver finished his drink and left Olympia. It was only a short walk back to the house. He let himself in. Nick and Jonna were off somewhere in the Camargue, supposedly scouting out locations for television ads. Which they were undoubtedly doing now and then, in the odd moments when they weren't busy eating, drinking and screwing their creative brains out. Lucky old Nick and Jonna – well, Nick anyway.

It was a shame to miss them this time around. He liked them both very much. They were long-time friends who ran a successful little film production company. Oliver had the use of their home in Kensington while he was in London. It was on a short terrace, set back from the High Street, overlooking Edwardes Square at the rear. It was actually the kind of house Oliver had wanted to own years ago, when he lived in London.

Now that he could afford to, of course, he didn't. He lived in Manhattan on the Upper West Side, nice enough, admittedly, and New York was a useful base for his many activities. But whenever he was at home for any length of time Oliver found himself trying to come up with reasons to be somewhere else.

Life on the road, no doubt a throwback to those crazy eleven months he'd spent driving the Bombsite Boys around Britain in the van, a different venue every night, dance halls, raucous pubs and grungy rock bars from Glasgow to Portsmouth. Rotten food, empty sex, endless drink, constant bitching, ego wars, troublesome cops and stroppy club owners who invariably refused to pay in full the agreed amount. Crewe, Derby, Slough, Blackburn, Cheadle, Poole, Brighton, Wolverhampton, Cardiff and too many others – oh, yes, Oliver could still remember every wretched stop on that hideous, never-ending tour.

Best year of his life, really.

He called Carrie, but she was out of the office. Lunchtime in New York, and so to be expected.

Oliver took off his shoes, sat in the large leather armchair

and watched the lines of traffic down on the High Street. Should he get another Scotch? Nick had an excellent selection of single malts. Later. He shut his eyes and slept for exactly forty-five minutes, an old trick he had mastered on the road trip.

He took a hot shower, dressed and then tried Carrie again. Now it appeared that she would be out of the office on business for the rest of the afternoon. No matter. He should try to get on better terms with the receptionists there, but they stayed for only a month or two and then left. Hopeless.

Tomorrow he had a late-morning flight to Munich, to keep the vastly talented and desperately insecure Marthe Frenssen in line. They had so much to accomplish before someone else discovered the amazing things she could do with raw flax and linen weaves.

So this was his night on the town. Oliver had a vindaloo at a nearly empty Indian place on Abingdon Road, and then took a cab to Piccadilly. The Esquire was a bit drearier than it had seemed on his last visit. He downed a short and left.

Things were much livelier at the Miranda, on Kingly Street. The doorman recognized him, or at least pretended he did. Inside, downstairs, the late-night crowd was beginning to gather. Here was the old London Oliver knew and, in a way, almost adored. There was something vaguely seedy about it, and yet it had a kind of low glamour. The décor was out of date by a couple of decades but the place was so dark and smoky you didn't notice. The food was hardly memorable, but the floor-show made up for it.

The women were young, pretty and well shaped, and when they weren't busy dancing they mingled without being pushy. They came from places like Southampton and Reading and Peterborough. They wanted to enjoy the fast life in London, have torrid affairs with exciting young men on the make, make some money, catch a break, and, eventually, when they grew tired of it all, land a reasonably reliable gent who had a job in the City and a deposit on a lovely mock-Tudor in one of the better parts of Surrey. If he owned the house and already had a wife installed, that was acceptable too, as long as he could afford to dislodge the incumbent and not lose everything in the process. Hardly any of these women had the bad luck of falling in love to the tune of a net financial loss.

The men were mid-range business types, entrepreneurs, hearty marketeers treating their out-of-town customers, has-beens with a modicum of buoyancy left, villains with their docile flunkeys and dangerous apprentices, and a few deep-pocketed old geezers in for some genteel slap and tickle. It was a crowd that could be merry and loud or strangely tense, but was seldom merely dull.

Oliver fancied himself somewhat apart from the others. They were regulars, and he was an outsider who dropped in from time to time. The club was part of their normal routine, whereas for him it was an occasional rest-stop. He chatted with some of the women, but he didn't buy them a drink from the gilt-edged suckers' menu. He usually ended up discussing markets and trade with one or two businessmen, and he often got a useful indication of how the trends were going before it appeared as an official fact in the *FT* indexes. Most of these men had had their hopes broken more than once, and would again, keeping at it until the day they fell down for good. He knew that what separated him from them was largely a matter of luck.

Oliver stayed a little over an hour. A waste of time, perhaps, and yet it didn't bother him. On the contrary, visiting this club always seemed to make him feel better, in some way he couldn't quite understand. The Miranda was a lingering pocket of myth, the London of the fifties and sixties, the London of Ruth Ellis, the Krays, Christine Keeler and Mandy Rice-Davies, of Rachman and his thuggish winklers, a London that stretched from John Christie to the Beatles and the Stones. By the time Oliver had begun to hear of it late in his childhood it had been fading into dubious legend, and he'd always had the feeling that he'd missed something.

He gave the taxi driver a card with the address in Limehouse and sat back for the ride. He still had good connections in the music industry, and on most trips to London he could expect to be invited to at least one party. The musić business was ever hard and merciless. Denmark Street rules still applied. A kid could write a string of hit singles and still have to scrounge for the cost of a pint. You lived on beans on toast, a squirt of sauce, and by the time you got your hands on money real enough to put in a bank account, you were ancient history. Make way for the new. Oliver was happy to be out of it on a day-to-day basis, and the only thing he missed was the fun of watching unvarnished kids make new music before the grind wore them out.

The party was in a converted warehouse, although what it had been converted to was hard to tell. The crowd was large and many more people were streaming in. The stereo system was cranked up high. There were long tables of food and barrels of quality beer. Say what you want about record companies, but they still knew how to throw a proper piss-up. Oliver wandered around aimlessly for a while, spotting old hands like Marianne Faithfull, Dave Davies, Brian Ferry and a bespangled Gary Glitter.

Eventually he caught up with Ian. Ian was his contact, the name to give at the door. Years ago, he had been a scruffy kid from Woking who couldn't quite master rhythm guitar. But he was bright and eager, and Oliver had given him a useful nudge at the right time. Now Ian was a highly regarded studio soundman, about due for his first major production job. He would probably have found his way there anyhow, but he was eternally grateful to Oliver. People with memory were rare in the business.

They swapped bits of personal news and work talk, and got up to date with each other. It had been three months since Oliver's last visit. As usual they vowed to have lunch or dinner the next time, definitely, schedules permitting.

Oliver didn't mind being left on his own. He picked at the mounds of shrimp and smoked salmon, he sipped Greene King beer and wandered around idly, nodding to some of the same magazine hacks he used to court in an effort to win column inches for his band. They still scoffed free nosh and booze frantically.

He skimmed the surface of the party. After a while, he sat down in an overstuffed old armchair, one of several that were scattered around the perimeter of the huge room. Within a minute or two a young woman came along and perched on its fat arm. She leaned back and sighed. 'I hope you don't mind.'

'Not at all,' he said.

'Only my feet are killing me.'

'Do you want to take the seat and I'll take the arm?'

'Oh, you are sweet.'

They traded places, and she promptly rested her head against his body, just above the hip. She fanned herself with the press booklet that told you more than you would ever want to know about the Limehouse Knights. She was on the tall side, a little skinny and angular. She had short hair and a short skirt, long legs and small breasts. Her name was Becky Something-Something. She was an assistant features editor at a glossy women's magazine. Music was part of her turf. She loved London, loved the scene, got ten invites a week and went to every one of them. Oliver smiled. He knew what it was like to be in your early twenties in London, to connect, to plug into the action. You really *live* and your life is electric, even if you're only one of the minor players on the fringe – as this girl was.

Why tell her how soon it jades and fades? Perhaps she'll be one of the lucky few and for her it won't. She wouldn't believe him, anyway.

Oliver got her a fresh drink. Becky seemed mildly impressed when she heard that he was part-owner of a record label, and she promised to see that future Redbird releases were reviewed in her magazine.

She was even more impressed when he told her he lived in New York and did a little import-export in the rag trade. Exotic shirts and jeans were acceptable. Becky's father, it turned out, had made a fortune on plastic macs, and they were definitely not.

Becky didn't like her father, it seemed, but then she said that

24

he chipped in on her rent – otherwise she'd have to share a flat and she'd tried that and it was bloody awful. So she had her own place, and when she asked Oliver where he was staying in town he knew that he could fuck her if he wanted.

'With some friends,' he said. 'It's handy, I come and go as I please. But . . .' And that was enough to imply in some way that he couldn't take her there.

No problem. They shared a taxi back into the West End, and along the way Becky asked him if he wanted to come in for coffee or a nightcap. Well, yes, that would be nice. She wasn't pretty in the obvious ways but there was something attractive about her. How she moved, her height, the angular gawkiness that she fought mightily to overcome – as if she still didn't know quite what to do with her body. Oliver did.

So he found himself in a small but tidy flat at the back end of Maida Vale, sipping plonk. One sip was enough. And they were stretched out together on a rather hard sofa, Becky with her head resting on Oliver's chest. When he found her breasts, he stroked them lightly. 'So, what's the trouble with your dad?'

'What do you mean?'

'Why do you hate him?'

'What makes you think I do?'

'I don't know. Do you?'

'I don't much care for him, put it that way.'

'What did he do to you?'

'What didn't he? I mean, it wasn't sexual, but . . .'

'He beat you, then.'

'Not exactly, no.'

'What else is there?'

'He – oh God, never mind. It's embarrassing.'

'That's all right. You can tell me.'

'I don't want to . . .'

But she did, and the drink in her helped.

'It's not your fault, love.'

'I used to think it was.'

'Never. It's never a child's fault.'

'He used to give me enemas,' she blurted out, with rather

too much high drama in her voice. 'All the time, and not just when I was little. When I got older, he still kept at it.'

Oliver willed himself to be still, otherwise he'd erupt in laughter. Enemas! 'You think that wasn't sexual?'

'It was a health thing with him.'

'Sugar coating, with a little kink inside.'

'Could be. But at least he didn't make me wear one of those bloody macs. That would've been flat-out perv.'

'When did it stop?'

'When I turned thirteen. I stopped it.'

'Thirteen.'

'He was serious about health, a real fanatic. And still is. Like, you should chew everything fifty times.'

'Fletcherism.'

'And posture. That was another thing. It used to drive me crazy, trying to stand and sit and walk what he called the right way. Which was impossible.'

'The Alexander technique.' Small wonder Becky still had a hard time carrying her body around.

'Did you go through all this rubbish too?'

'No, but I've heard of it.'

'Bastard. Don't know why I still love him.'

He couldn't see her face, but he touched her cheek just near the eye and felt a bit of moisture.

'Tell him how you feel about it. Let him have it full bore. It'd do you a world of good. Clear the air.'

'Very American, I suppose.'

'Charterhouse, actually. I learned the hard way too.'

She shook her head. 'He'd never speak to me again.'

'You'd feel a lot better.'

'I feel better now,' she said, squirming happily beneath his touch. 'You're very nice. And comfy.'

They thrashed around on the sofa for a while, staggered into her small bedroom and fell together onto the bed. They lost some of their clothes in the process, made love quickly and furiously, and then they cuddled and kissed gently, resting.

A little later, Oliver explored her body at a more leisurely pace, administering nip-and-peck kisses to her nipples, belly and thighs. Such long legs, such a long flat tummy. She had rather small breasts, but they were high and firm, still girlish.

Oliver licked her. She didn't know what to do with him, and her awkwardness was beginning to tell. Never mind, darling, some women never learn head – even long after they've become addicted to getting it. English women especially, or so it seemed. Maybe that was why Oliver had married a Yank. Becky began to cry. She held him there, wouldn't let him move. Or stop.

Eventually her hands slipped away and she seemed to sag into herself, dazed. Oliver rolled her over and took her from behind. Slow, gentle, sweet. He wet his fingertip and rimmed her with it tentatively. A long deep moan. A little more, and he could feel the moan in her body now, as strong and resonant as a cello chord from Bach. Yes, Daddy. Becky seemed to fly straight from orgasm into sleep.

One thing: Oliver could never sleep in situations like that. He would lie there afterwards, eyes open or shut, awake. Thinking it was all kind of stupid, though he didn't know why or how, just that it felt that way. Wondering if she would fall in love with him – but, then, they all did. They wanted him to stay for ever or they wanted to follow him back to America. Stay, and stay as tender and frank and understanding and loving as you were, as you really really are. And eat me eat me eat me every night.

Oliver turned his head and stared at her in the grey light. Hair mussed, she did look pretty. Yes, darling, you have a right to some kind of a life, something approximating happiness, all of the usual milestones and millstones. A career, marriage, a house and kids. Click the menu, and make sure you get your full share. Some day, soon perhaps, you'll even get to bury the old bastard in some dreary Midlands plot. Sell his house and all his things, and never visit his grave.

He wanted to wake her and tell her. Becky, Rebecca, my dear child, Something-Something. It will be all right. You *are* good, you *are* pretty. You *see*? It *is* worthwhile. In a way. Somehow. I believe. I do. And so . . . And so . . .

Enemas, for God's sake. How on earth had he managed to keep a straight face? A triumph, really.

She had such a lovely long neck. Such an exquisite throat. Slender, elegant. There was some kind of powerful erotic magic in it, irresistible. Don't forget the people at the party, don't forget the taxi driver. There are a million important factors to consider in the tiniest of moves.

Oliver slipped his fingers around her throat and he squeezed with great gentleness, so as not to wake her.

Such a feeling. Something to think about. Again.

Because, Christ – it would be so easy.

2

The movie did nothing for her, but it was probably her own fault. Carrie had been distracted all day. Taking in the film had been a sudden impulse, and action thrillers could usually be relied on to erase two hours painlessly from your life. But it didn't work this time.

Distracted – and vaguely unsettled. That was the problem. A loss of concentration in the middle of her discussion with the Wellers about redesigning their kitchen. That blank spot while she examined an assortment of Italian tile samples. But it had been a busy day, so a brief lapse was perhaps understandable, and it was not as if anyone else had noticed.

But there had also been that moment yesterday evening when Carrie had been sorting through her underwear to make up a load of laundry, when a tremendous sense of sadness welled up within her. She had no idea how long she'd stood at the hamper, close to tears. Over nothing. Why had it happened to her?

As soon as she got back to the apartment, Carrie called her mother in Pensacola. Nothing much new there. A ziti dinner for the church, a book and bake sale for the local library.

'Are you all right, dear?'

'Yeah, just kind of – I don't know.'

'That would be the blahs.'

Carrie smiled. 'I guess so. Oliver's away.'

A cluck. 'Where now?'

'London and Munich.'

'He's going to turn into Willy Loman on you.'

Carrie laughed. She felt a little better after she hung up, but the mood didn't last. She took a long hot bath, had a glass of

Cointreau with a single cube of ice in it, and skimmed a couple of articles in *Vanity Fair* without noticing what they were about. Later, she sat for a while on the edge of the empty tub, her naked body still moist, strands of wet hair dangling in front of her face, thinking, The blahs?

She put on a white terrycloth robe and went into the living room, bare feet slapping on the parquet in the hallway. She put some quiet jazz on the stereo. Carrie loved their apartment, a co-op in the Dalmas Building on West 73rd, just far enough away from the noise where Broadway crossed Amsterdam.

She and Oliver had put a lot of time, money and labour into the place. They had stripped and completely redecorated it, but it was worth the effort. Decorating was her talent, her career. The apartment her home. New York her city.

Was it Oliver, some uncertainty about her husband? True, he had seemed a little out of sorts before leaving on this trip, but he was always moody, she was used to that and knew how to handle it. He spent too much time fretting over his numerous business involvements, none of which he really cared about that much. She often thought he would be better off to settle on a single area of activity, something that totally absorbed him and brought out the best in him. He was a man of talent and keen business sense, an intelligent man.

Their marriage was sound. Oliver was attentive, he actually listened, and Carrie knew that a man who listened was a gem to be treasured. They made love regularly, and the sex was still good. They talked. They cared for each other. And ... *And what more can you ask?* But enumerating the pluses didn't help.

Carrie poured more Cointreau and added another ice cube. She went upstairs to the master suite and sat on the edge of the bed, trying to think what she was there for, what she should do. Put on a nightgown? Pyjamas? Just panties? Instead, she chose grey jeans, white socks, sneakers and a purple Lakers sweatshirt.

Oliver was gone five or six times a year, a week or two each trip, and that was not great. But when he was around, which was most of the time, he was around all day and at home every night. They would meet for lunch, or in the evening for dinner out. He used the second bedroom as an office. So times like this, times when she was alone, were usually not a problem for her.

Something in the bedroom behind her, she thought. A sound of movement. Holding the sturdy glass like a rock to throw, she went slowly to the open door. The light was still on. The room was the same, bathrobe draped over a chair. Empty. Windows shut and locked. Nothing. The closet – just clothes. Dressing area and bathroom, both fine. Nothing. See? Carrie turned the light off and closed the door as she left the bedroom.

She went downstairs again. Now the quiet mellow jazz was no longer enough for her. Kiri singing Legrand? Ute doing Dietrich and Piaf? But she was not in the mood for any music. She put on the AM and scanned until she came across a late ballgame from the west coast. The subdued drone of the crowd in the background was somehow comforting, while the play-by-play didn't even register. She left it there for a while, until she realized that she might not be able to hear anything else *within* the apartment. Not that there *was* anything else to hear. But Carrie turned off the tuner and sat in silence.

The kitchen. She didn't think she'd heard a sound. Coming from there. The brush of one pant leg against the other? Rustle of fabric in the air? Sometimes the only thing worse than being alone is not being alone. But the kitchen was empty. She took the bowl of tapioca ambrosia from the fridge and ate it – there wasn't much left – standing by the breakfast nook.

She heard Tommy, the resident Irish handyman, bounding down the stairs on the other side of the kitchen wall, his trademark heavy-footed thump trailing away. Probably just solved one more minor mechanical problem for another helpless soul.

Carrie sat down and slid across to the darkened back corner of the nook. It was funny, in a way. They had often joked about it. Her father had waited decades for a plum posting, London or Paris or Rome, and when it came it only lasted one year and three months. A case of cold politics reaching down below the rank of ambassador. Poor man. Australia next.

But that year and a bit happened to come along shortly after Carrie had graduated from Bard. She had nothing definite planned and wasn't even sure what she wanted to do with her modest BA, so she flew off to London with her parents. Took one course at the North London Poly. Met people, both the diplomatic crowd and others. Fell in love with European styles and fashions – a huge new development in her life, since she'd never paid any attention to that kind of thing before. Much too frivolous. Carrie still read books, of course, but the old Eng. Lit. outlook was starting to give way to different and more practical interests.

She blossomed in London. Or at least she liked to think she did. Girl to woman. Finding a sense of direction. Carrie began to look at rooms, to see how they were put together and arranged, and what people did with them. She learned how to see a room, as it could be not merely as it was. Towards the end of that year Xavier Rocher took her on as an unpaid assistant. It was a great opportunity to learn, and she did. After two months, he gave her a small wage. She was in the business.

By then it was known that Daddy was on the way out of town. By then Carrie had met Oliver at a do at the Groucho. His band had recently broken up so he was not in the best of form. They clicked, however. He was irresistible, tremendously attractive, witty, polished, considerate, fun – dear God, how she had fallen for him. She was never quite sure why he wanted her, out of all the women who were available to him, but he did. Daddy and her mother both liked Oliver, and when they left Carrie stayed on in London. Worked with Xavier, lived with Oliver. London was their playground, and it was great. Everything.

She stopped breathing for a moment as she looked through the kitchen and saw a shadow slide along the wall in the hallway. No sound, just a shadow that quickly vanished. Nothing, Carrie told herself. The Dalmas was a good building, there was hardly ever a break-in. On top of which, their apartment was protected by the best locks and security system available. She knew all about it, from work. So. There.

She got up and went through the dining area into the living room. No one, nothing. No more shadow in the hall. She didn't want another drink, but she added a large splash to what was left at the bottom of her glass. She wasn't tired enough to go to bed and fall asleep, so the drink might help. Ought to be a gin, or something equally lethal; the Cointreau was having no discernible effect on her.

There was a sense of displacement, as if Carrie were waiting to resume feeling like herself again. It was absurd, but there you are. More or less.

Oliver would be sleeping now. Must be about four or five in the morning in London, she wasn't sure which. Carrie would admit to a little envy. It had been a year plus since her last visit to London, and she missed it. New York had been Oliver's idea, not hers. By the time they left, she was just beginning to feel more English than American. It hurt. And it took her a while to get established in Manhattan. She had plenty of useful contacts, and that helped enormously. Now she had all the work she wanted, too much at times. But New York was not London.

Practically the last thing Carrie and Oliver did before they left London was to stop in at the Kensington Register Office, and make it official. Carrie's family would have preferred a lavish wedding in the old style (Oliver's parents were both dead, and he was an only child), but everybody was happy for the young couple. Oliver and Carrie, Carrie and Oliver. Happy together.

When she put her drink down on the coffee table and looked up, she saw her father sitting on the hassock on the far side of the room. He was naked, and his body was turned to one side so that his genitals could not be seen. Carrie's breath stopped in her throat. He was there for the longest moment. She tried to speak but the sound barely reached her lips.

'Daddy?'

His flesh looked soft and flabby, his skin wrinkled, though

33

his cheeks showed a little red. He looked tired and drawn, with circles beneath his eyes. His hands moved in tight gestures, as if he were trying to explain something. He spoke to her, but she heard no sound. She thought she saw sadness or sorrow in his expression. Maybe even pain. Carrie was pinned in place with fear and anguish until the apparition of her father suddenly vanished.

Five – no, it was six years ago now.

Carrie sagged back into the leather sofa. Her breath came in short vacant gasps that seemed to originate in her mouth. Her throat was dry, her vision blurred. She had nothing to hold onto because she didn't believe in God or an afterlife or ghosts. She hadn't seen her father since the day of his burial in Vermont six years ago. Carrie had never experienced anything like this and she would never expect to because – but this frantic attempt at reason crumbled. She began to shiver, swamped with fear. She had to get out of there. Immediately.

The telephone rang but she didn't stop.

She took the stairs two at a time, unable to stand and wait for the elevator. On to the street, up Broadway, walking quickly, almost running. But where to? Carrie realized that she had left her keys and wallet behind. Never mind.

She kept walking, sometimes breaking into a trot, because at the same time she felt calmer and yet more frightened and she had to get *somewhere*. Jeffrey and Mark. It came to her when she was at their door on 85th near Riverside Drive, ringing the bell. Oh, please be home.

The next thing Carrie knew, she was swallowing vodka, trying to explain what she was doing there and apologize for it to keep from bursting into tears – all at the same time and not doing a very good job at any of it. Jeffrey raised a napkin and dabbed a drop of vodka from her chin. Oliver didn't like them, but Carrie regarded Jeffrey and Mark as good friends. Wall-covering wizards by day, they worked with everything from antique paper to pressed reed and filmy leather. She had steered some business their way, and they hers.

'Your father?' Jeffrey echoed.

34

'Yes.'

Mark frowned. 'Didn't you tell us—'

'Yes. Six years ago. Heart attack.'

'What did he do, when you saw him there?'

'He was just sitting there, speaking to me,' Carrie replied. 'But he had no voice. There was no sound at all.'

'How long did it last?'

'It seemed like for ever, but probably a minute or so.'

'How many drinks did you have?' Mark enquired with a faintly mischievous smile.

'Not enough.'

Jeffrey patted her hand. 'Well, it's over. You're all right now, just try to relax.'

'Do you think I'm acting crazy?'

'No, of course not.'

'I mean, could I be having a nervous breakdown? Is this how it starts? Seeing things?'

'No, of course not.'

'I did see him,' Carrie insisted.

'Well, yes, of course you did,' Mark agreed.

'I mean, he *was* there. My father.'

'Carrie, nobody doubts you.'

'Do you believe in things like that? Ghosts. Apparitions. Whatever it was.'

'Why not?' Jeffrey said. 'Too many people have experiences like that – it has to be real, somehow.'

'Any problems on the home front?'

'No.'

'You sure?'

'Yes, we're fine. Really.'

'Where is Oliver, anyway?'

'London. Munich later today, or maybe tomorrow. He's been away since last weekend. That was probably him calling,' Carrie added, an afterthought addressed to herself.

'What?'

'The phone rang as I was leaving and I didn't stop to answer it. But it must have been Oliver.'

'What was your father wearing?' Jeffrey asked suddenly.

'I was afraid you'd ask me that,' Carrie replied sheepishly. 'He didn't have anything on.'

'Calling Dr Freud,' Mark said, with a grin.

'No, not really.' Jeffrey ran his hand over his short hair and adjusted his wire-rimmed glasses. 'It's a good sign. You didn't just imagine the whole thing.'

'What do you mean?'

'Remember that party, in Montauk?'

This was directed to Mark, who nodded. 'Yes, but what does that have to do with anything?'

To Carrie, 'Scott, he's a friend of ours. Well, sort of a friend. Anyway, at this party I was in a small group of people, sitting around, talking over drinks, and somebody mentioned these old stories of dead sailors who were sometimes seen in that area. Ghosts, right? Supposedly they'd been lost at sea off the coast of Long Island. Now, Scott is very into this kind of thing, and he said real ghosts always appear naked.'

'If you can believe Scott,' Mark said dismissively.

'Maybe he was right about that.'

'But why?' Carrie asked, trying not to sound anxious.

'Well, think about it,' Jeffrey said. 'When people die they don't take their clothes with them. If it was a ghost, a genuine visitor from the other side, why would it be dressed? You don't really think they're issued with robes and harps, do you?'

'No,' Carrie had to admit.

'It's all in the mind,' Mark said, with a shrug. 'There are no ghosts, there is no other side. It's just your mind trying to send you a message.'

Carrie was inclined to agree. She didn't have much faith in otherworldly things. People may have some spiritual dimension in their nature, a part of them that wanted to link up with a cosmic force, God, whatever, but that didn't make it real. 'I'm just as sceptical,' she said, then added, faintly, 'Or was.'

They talked about it a while longer, inconclusively, and had more to drink. Tiredness finally overtook her. Jeffrey and Mark got her a pillow and blanket, and Carrie dozed off on their sofa. She felt bad about it as she faded away, as if she were being as foolish and self-indulgent as a child. But they were so kind and sympathetic, and she simply couldn't move.

She awoke a few hours later, shortly after six. Grey light filtered into the room from outside. The apartment was perfectly quiet. Carrie sat up and blinked. She couldn't remember having any dreams. Her head ached a bit, and her mouth was gummy with the stale residue of all that drink. She noticed the sound of light traffic drifting up from the street below – Manhattan is never perfectly quiet, least of all at the break of day – and found it rather comforting.

She got up and tiptoed to the seat by the corner window, felt a bit shaky and sat down. Put it in perspective, she told herself. But how? She had no base of experience to draw on, and she knew next to nothing about such matters.

But one thing did seem clear. If the apparition was real on any level, if it had meaning for her in any way, then the answer must be in the words. The missing words. Because her father had been speaking to her. Speaking anxiously.

What had he been trying to say?

3

As always, Charley was the first one out the classroom door. He might never be invited back to Yale but, by God, he would keep the kids busy to the last day. Quite a few had probably thought a visiting lecturer would be soft and easy, the course a relaxer for three credits, but they had learned otherwise by now, these over-privileged boomer-spawn darlings, and he wasn't through with them yet.

He crossed the Old Campus and headed up Chapel Street. Next stop, Gene's Tap, a plain and unpretentious bar out on the fringe of the college neighbourhood. He was a bit early, though that was technically impossible – the only way you could arrive early at a bar was if you got there before it opened.

'Good evening, Professor,' George, the barman, said with his usual exaggerated obsequiousness.

'Associate without portfolio,' Charley corrected.

'Your usual, sir?'

'If by that you mean a pint of piss, the answer is yes.'

Charley downed the beer at the bar, got a refill and took a seat at a rickety booth on the opposite wall. He lit a panatella. Better. Life was definitely better than it had been half an hour ago. Not that life was ever good; it was problematic at best, he would say (and had, too often). However, it also offered a handy array of worthwhile alleviations, foremost among them alcohol and tobacco, a bit of gash.

Forty and one, still young. Enough. Perhaps it was time to think of settling in one place. Trouble was, it might have to be some interior backwater, like Nebraska or Louisiana. God forbid. Charley was an academic nomad. Over the last ten years he'd done time at Leeds, Norwich, Cherbourg, Emory,

Texas, Bucknell, Berlin and Iowa, not in that order. Not to forget Galway.

It was a matter of choice, still. Life on the academic road had its advantages. At about the time you got sick of one place you were toddling off to another. You also avoided for the most part the whole savage sub-strata of departmental politics, the career wars and back-stabbing that took place on every campus.

It was tougher on Jan, no doubt about that. No fixtures, so to speak, no permanent home. But she was used to it. She mucked in, and was often excited about their next destination.

The journals were littered with Charley's papers, every one of which investigated some aspect of the plays, poems and stories of Edward John Moreton Drax Plunkett, a.k.a. Lord Dunsany, literary oddball, neglected master, sublime eccentric. Charley had a part of a corner on Dunsany, his claim staked years ago. If there was ever to be a massive, official biography of the man, Charley knew he would have a fair crack at landing the contract. Trouble was, such a commission would probably never happen. Dunsany remained a minor talent to most, a second-rater in the rankings. And then there was the matter of his personal life, which was dull, to say the least. He rode horses, shot animals and pottered about the family estate somewhat in the manner of a character who had just failed the audition for a role in a novel by Smollett. The geezer hardly even drank. But nobody was perfect, and by now Dunsany was Charley's academic niche. He had a genuine fondness for the old boy, read and reread his pellucid prose with enormous pleasure, and sometimes thought of him as a kind of dead uncle he had never had the good fortune to know in life.

'You're almost too late to be early,' Charley observed, when Malcolm arrived.

'Ready for another?'

'Is that a question?'

Malcolm smiled and went for a round of drinks. A friend for twenty years or so, this Malcolm Browne. Charley and Malcolm had met as students at University College, Dublin. It was around the time the pound was being decimalized, and Charley had come from a distant corner of Wisconsin in search of – what the hell was it, anyway? Joyce, the Ginger Man, Flann O'Brien, Kavanagh, Dunsany, all the usual suspects. Found them all, too.

It was through Malcolm that Charley had landed the Yale gig. Malcolm was a fixture at Yale. Sound critic, excellent teacher, and a bloody genius at the obscure art of departmental diplomacy, with the self-effacing charm and smoothness of Anglo-Irish genes in his blood. Of course, there was a price to pay for this grand success. Malcolm wasn't half the pub-going drinker he had been a while back. All the same, a dear man.

Come to think of it, it had been Malcolm who had suggested this particular get-together. Charley wondered what might be in the offing. Perhaps a week with the Brownes at their cottage on the Cape. Sudden space in a journal for a paper on the influence of Dunsany on Sam Beckett – Malcolm was in tight with several fine scholarly publications. Maybe he just felt the irresistible need for an old-fashioned gargle in a moderately bleak saloon, a valid and perfectly honourable motive in itself.

'Cheers.'

'Your good health.'

'So, have you decided what you're going to do this summer?'

'Staying on a while, I think. It looks as if that Hamilton job might be put back to the spring semester.'

'How are you getting on in the department?'

That was interesting. 'No bother at all,' Charley replied. 'You have a dreadful infestation of multiculturalists, but I try to keep a civil tone with them.'

Malcolm smiled. 'I might have a summer course available, if you want it.'

'That'd be great.' Indeed.

'It's just your basic English comp.'

'A breeze. Consider my ankle chained to the galley.'

'How's Jan?'

'Oh, fine. She quite likes New Haven.'

'Good. You must come up to Wellfleet this summer. Stay for

a weekend. We'll have piles of fresh seafood, kegs of cold beer, and we'll play the Pogues all night long.'

'Sounds great. We'd love it,' Charley said, with enthusiasm. To be fair, a whole week had been a bit much to hope for. 'How's Maggie these days?'

'Very well, thanks. In fact, that's a part of what I wanted to talk to you about.'

'Oh?'

Malcolm looked about as close to embarrassment as he could ever get. 'I think I mentioned to you once or twice before that Maggie has this – special interest.'

'Yes.' Tentative. He seldom thought of Maggie. Wife of a good friend, full stop. Ideal mate for a professor at a place like Yale: good-looking, charming, bright and social. Charley always felt vaguely scruffy around her. Jan and Maggie got along with a functional neutrality, as many wives do when they have no great interest in each other but are occasionally thrown together because of their husbands. Maggie was quite pleasant to Charley, no complaints on that score. 'Folklore, wasn't it?'

'That was her field of study at UCD,' Malcolm said, 'Gaelic folklore. And, in a way, I guess that was what led to this other thing. Psychic phenomena, the paranormal.'

'Oh, Lord, yes,' Charley exclaimed, suppressing a chuckle. 'That's right. Mind-readers and fork-benders.'

Malcolm smiled ruefully. 'Yes. It seems a bit silly, but she's serious about it, and I must say she approaches the subject with a healthy scepticism.'

'Good.'

'And, in all fairness, there are a great many incidents that appear to defy reasonable explanation. People do witness strange things, some very strange things.'

'Yes, no doubt about that.'

Poor Malcolm. Maggie must be going overboard on this hooey, and it could get awkward if word leaked out. New Haven was small enough as cities go, Yale a bloody hothouse of jockeying egos. A typical Parnassus, slippery when wet or dry.

41

'I don't even know if I should be talking to you about this. It's so preposterous and – painful.'

'Come on, mate. Out with it.'

'Maggie insisted that she needed another body, someone to be at the table with them. I had no interest in it, but she dragged me along to see this woman who's supposed to be psychic.'

'A medium, a channel.'

'Sort of. Have you ever been to anything like that?'

'Not really,' Charley said. 'A few years ago, at the Yeats Summer School in Sligo, I sat in with a group of people who were fooling around with a ouija board, but all they did was use it to make lewd suggestions to each other. That was the year Ned Brady lost his thumb in the rope-pull at the farewell party.'

'Oh, yes. Well, anyhow.'

'Your woman.'

'Yes. So I went along, and it was quite a show. There were none of the things you might expect. No table-rapping, no Indian warriors, no eerie lights or bits of cheesecloth. This woman sat there, and these voices seemed to come from – inside her.'

'An actress, yes.'

'Different voices.' Malcolm was so caught up in it now that he appeared to be looking directly into his own memory. 'And the thing is, you could hear two or three different voices coming out of her *at the same time*. I mean, you really could.'

'That wouldn't be hard to do.'

'Possibly, but it looked and sounded real,' he said. 'But it doesn't matter how she did it or where the voice came from. It's what the voice said that concerns me. And you.'

'Oh? What was it?'

Malcolm's eyes dodged around nervously. 'One of the voices sounded very small, very young,' he went on. 'And several times it said *Fiona*.'

A small hole opened in Charley's stomach. 'Yes?'

'And, *Ravenswood*. The two words alternated, *Fiona* and then *Ravenswood*. I heard them both several times, very clearly.'

The hole got much larger. The panatella stub slipped in his fingers, and without looking at it Charley put it in the ashtray beside his hand.

'That can't be.'

'It happened,' Malcolm insisted. 'I was there.'

Charley felt a flash of anger, which dissolved at once. He never thought about this, never. He had put it away long ago, in a precious box at the bottom of a trunk at the back of his brain, locked away for ever. Because it could only hurt.

'It must have been Maggie,' he said.

'No.'

'She must have let on.' Malcolm shook his head. 'She might not even know she did,' Charley persisted. 'These people have a way of getting things out of you. They can take the fillings out of your mouth and you don't even notice until you get home.'

'Maggie doesn't know.'

'Of course she knows.'

'Charley, listen to me. Maggie and I barely knew each other at the time it happened. We didn't start going out seriously for another year or more, and it was a full year after that before we got married. Remember?'

'But she knows.'

'She knows that you and Jan lost your only child, of course. But she doesn't know her name was Fiona. I never had occasion to mention that. It's not a happy subject, and I've never gone into it in any detail with anyone, not even Maggie.'

'But still, it must have slipped out. Sometime.'

'What about Ravenswood?'

It was the name of the house outside Galway where they had been living when it happened. 'Same thing,' Charley said. 'You mentioned it to Maggie somewhere along the line.'

'I know I never did. Later, when we were back home, I asked Maggie what the names Fiona and Ravenswood meant to her, and she had no idea. Nothing. She says the woman picks up all kinds of things, and you have to tune in to the ones that seem to relate to you. Maggie never thought twice about the references to Fiona and Ravenswood because they had no meaning for her. Do you see what I'm saying?'

'It's got to be a con of some sort,' Charley said.

'But why? This woman doesn't know you. She doesn't even know you're living in New Haven, or living at all, or that you're a friend of ours. None of that.'

'I don't go for this sort of thing,' Charley muttered.

'I just thought I should tell you. At first I wasn't going to, but then I realized it wasn't for me to decide. If there was one chance in a million that it was real, then you had a right to know about it and make your own decisions.'

'Real? Real *what*?'

'A real message, I suppose.'

'She was three months old, Mal.'

'I know that.'

'Am I supposed to think that when she got to the other side she grew up and learned English, and now, after all these years, she decides to drop by and have a chat? Fuck it.'

'I'm sorry. I knew it would distress you but . . .'

'You did what you had to. It's all right.'

'We both could use another.'

While Malcolm went for the drinks, Charley sat and stared at the nicks in the tabletop. Fiona. Ravenswood. She never had a chance to grow up. Never learned to speak. When death came, her age was only three months.

It always would be.

He was not wearing well but, then, who does? Life catches up with you. So? If he made it to sixty-five and then dropped dead from the booze and smokes, so be it. Amen, thanks for the crack, it was fun while it lasted.

Chapel Street, he noticed.

Some little time had passed, no doubt. Malcolm went home, after being assured that Charley was okay and could safely manoeuvre the walk to his apartment off Orange. Where Jan

44

was waiting. Bugger that, he wasn't in the mood to face her yet. Poor fragile Jan, a decent woman. Not exactly a brick, though, more like a piece of very thin glass. Always ready to break. It was Charley's job in life to see her through it. Occasionally to reach for the bottle of glue and put the pieces back together.

Howe Street. God put it there so Heather would have a place to live and fuck. Charley made his way up one flight and knocked on her door. She looked lovely, short skirt and elegant blouse, ready for action. She was not, however, happy to see him. Never mind. He swept past her, into the living room.

Oh dear, she already had company. More of her young college friends. Dreadful. Some hideous sounds emanated from the stereo system. Bloody musicologists with their wretched atonal rubbish. They were drinking some foul-smelling brew, as well.

'I suppose that's herbal tea,' he snarled at one of the twee guests, who clutched his stoneware mug protectively.

'What are you doing here?' Heather was fuming.

'I'm not doing anything at the moment.'

'Then please leave. Immediately.'

He turned to face her. 'I told you, a minute of Arnold Bax is worth a year of Stockhausen. A minute of Stockhausen is like a year, and that's a kind of immortality in itself, but—'

'I told you not to come around here like this,' Heather said, in tones of cold fury. 'Unannounced, as if you own the place and can come and go as you please.' To her guests, 'I'm sorry about this. He'll be gone in a minute.'

'Don't count on it,' Charley told them. 'Believe it or not, this is foreplay.'

'Charley.' Heather grabbed his arm. 'Get out, now!'

'I need a place to throw up.'

He looked around the room, and that scattered them. Then, a lot of movement seemed to be taking place. He found himself with his face in the toilet bowl, the water tinted Yale blue. Or near enough. His body heaved. A little liquid came up, nothing

else. A good pisser carries no baggage. The shame of it –
Charley was not even drunk. Not quite, not yet.

He washed his face, rinsed his mouth, put the toilet lid down
and sat on it. Began to cry, couldn't stop. Heather edged into
the bathroom and stood in front of him. She was still sore at
him but had realized by now that something was wrong, and
that it was not just the usual foolish carry-on. Took long
enough for the penny to drop, darling. She brushed his hair
from his face, and with her thumbs wiped tears from his
cheeks.

'What is it, Charley?'

Subdued, still resentful, but concerned. Put-upon once more
and resigned to it. Poor Heather, God love her. Charley didn't.
But Heather and women like her offered consolation to all of
the bruised boys who would never grow up. Like me.

'I don't know,' Charley said, amazed at how puny his voice
sounded. 'I don't know.'

'You'll be all right.'

'Think so?'

A wan smile. 'Yes, I do.'

'That's the first good news I've had today.'

Heather laughed. He held her tightly. He breathed deeply,
exhaled. Steady again, close enough anyway. Shut the door,
make today yesterday and try to forget all about it.

A message from the dead cannot be real.

Must not be answered.

4

Marthe was tied to the hard wooden chair, her wrists to the flat arms and her ankles to the spindly legs. She was naked but for the torn stockings and the leather band that held her neck to the high slats. She kept her eyes down. There were spatter marks of vegetable dye on her face and breasts and arms.

Pick-up at the other end. About time.

A breath of hesitation. 'Hello?'

He noticed at once that she sounded almost afraid to speak. And it had rung a long time before she answered.

'Carrie, it's me.'

'Oliver.' Relieved – too much so? 'Hi.'

'Where the hell have you been?' The more annoyed Oliver was, the blander his voice sounded.

'Oh . . . In and out.'

'I was getting worried about you. I've been calling you for the last couple of days and all I get is the damn machine.'

'I picked up once, but it was too late.'

'Are you all right, love?'

'Well . . . yes.'

'Well, what? What does that mean? What happened?'

'No, really. I'm fine.'

'Carrie, I can tell something's bothering you.'

'I just miss you, is all.'

'I'll be home tomorrow. Late afternoon.'

'Great. How's your trip going? Business good?'

He glanced at Marthe. Her eyes were down but her head gave a slight twitch that meant she'd been sneaking a peek at him. He would remember it.

'Yes, fine. Now tell me what's the matter.'

'Nothing, not really.'

Carrie couldn't lie to save her life, bless her.

'Something upset you,' he said, forcing a calm tone. 'Just tell me what it is, and we can talk about it. Otherwise I'll be worrying about you until I get home.'

They had a very clear line. She sounded as if she were in the next room, and Oliver could almost hear the silent heave of her chest as she took a deep breath. He could see her frowning, and rubbing her forehead – as if that would put her brain back on track and make it easier to talk.

'I saw Daddy.'

She said it so quickly that he wasn't sure what he'd heard.

'You saw what?'

'Daddy.'

'Your – father?'

'Uh, yeah.'

That made no sense. 'Where?'

'Right here. In the living room.'

'What do you mean you saw him?'

'He was sitting there and I saw him. You know, like seeing a ghost, kind of thing.' A squiggle of a laugh. 'But it wasn't just my imagination, Oliver. I did see him. He was right there, like a real, living person. It really happened.'

'Just – sitting there? Then what happened?'

'He was gone. I don't know how to explain it. I mean, it wasn't like I saw him disappear or fade away, and I didn't blink. But he was there, and then he wasn't.'

'That's it, is it?'

'Well, pretty much.'

'Are you okay?'

'Yes.'

'You don't sound it.'

'It scared me at the time. I'm better now, though.'

'You just imagined it, love.'

'No . . .'

Oliver could tell that she didn't want to argue, but neither

48

was she willing to concede the point, and he didn't want to upset her any more than she already was.

'You should have had somebody come and stay with you.'

'I went out, I had to get out of here for a while,' she told him, almost breathlessly – now that she had started, she wanted to talk about it. 'I went over to Jeffrey and Mark's. They were the nearest. They gave me a drink and calmed me down, and later I fell asleep on the couch. They were very kind to me.'

Those two. Of course they'd take care of her. Oliver would be surprised if they didn't tell her she was right, she *had* seen a genuine ghost, encourage her all the way.

'Ah, well. Good.'

'They really are very sweet, Oliver.'

'I know, I know. Well, you're home now.'

'Yes.'

'And everything's back to normal?'

'More or less. There is one other thing.'

'What is it, love?'

'Daddy was trying to say something to me.'

'He spoke to you?'

'He was speaking, yes. But I couldn't hear anything. I saw him moving his hands and mouth so seriously. You know, like when you're in the middle of explaining something to someone.'

'Yes.'

'But there was no sound at all.'

'Don't worry about it,' he said. 'If—'

'But I do know one thing.'

'What?'

'It was about you.'

That was a bit of a facer. 'Me?'

'Yes,' Carrie said firmly. 'He mentioned you.'

'How do you know that?'

'I've been going over it in my mind ever since, the way his mouth was moving, and the one thing I can make out is your name. It's very clear. I even checked myself saying your name

49

in a mirror to make sure. The movement is distinctive. It's the one word I know I saw him say.'

He had no idea what to think. A phone call, a matter of simple consideration, really, to let her know where he was and to make sure she was okay – something a lot of husbands wouldn't bother to do – and now it was becoming a distraction.

'What did he say about me?'

'I don't know. All I got was your name.'

'Well, that seems a little odd but—'

'You're all right, aren't you?'

'Of course. Fine. And, as far as I know, I haven't been in any danger so he couldn't have been trying to alert you or warn you about any – I don't know, an accident. Whatever.'

'That's good. Oliver, I'm so glad you believe me.'

That was annoying, but it was his own fault. The way he was talking to her could be taken as tacit acceptance of the entire incident, as if he were automatically confirming her belief in it as an actual ghostly visitation. He meant no such thing.

'I believe you *think* you saw him,' he said carefully. 'And that it seemed real enough at the time. But was it your father, appearing from beyond the veil? I rather doubt that. I'm sure there's some more mundane reason for what happened.'

He could tell that she was disappointed. She didn't say anything for a few moments.

'It doesn't matter how we account for it or how we describe it,' Carrie told him finally. She sounded quite sure of herself by now. 'The important thing is what it means.'

Oliver had had enough. It was not the kind of thing he would have expected from Carrie, normally a sensible and pragmatic woman. He promised her that he would discuss it with her when he returned to New York, and managed to get her off the subject.

Her father. Talking about Oliver? Meaningless. Which was why he was annoyed that it bothered him so.

He hung up a minute later, and stood there feeling deflated. It was a huge room, a loft, with skylights painted a translucent white. There was a stark, harsh quality to everything in it. An industrial stench from the chemicals. Racks of material drying. Looms and spinners. Vats and baths, carboys and flasks, tubes and condensers. Gas burners. Ovens.

He went to Myra. Marthe. Whatever.

Her nipples were hard with anticipation.

He took her by the hair, turning up her face slightly so that her hair fell back to one side. Veronica Lake. Brilliant cheekbones and a good jawline. Cold fire in the eyes. You could do almost anything with a woman like this.

'Wo ist dein Vater?'

'Tot.'

'You looked at me.' Nothing. 'You looked at me while I was on the phone.' Still nothing. 'Didn't you, *Hündin?*'

A tiny nod. He slapped her once. He allowed her to savour the sting for a few seconds. Then he held the back of his hand close to her face. Marthe rubbed her cheek against it. She kissed and licked it, sucked his knuckles. Never taking her eyes from his now.

'*Und wer ist der Sklave hier?*' he said softly.

She smiled, and then began to laugh.

It had been a mistake to shut everything up. Carrie opened the curtains and pulled up the blinds. That's better. Sunlight on a gorgeous Saturday morning in May, things to do, an apartment to clean. Oliver would be home later.

Carrie put on some music, loud, and went to work. It wasn't as if the place were a mess. Conchita had been in on Tuesday, as usual, and all that was required now was a light dusting. A trip to Zabar's. Then a bath and shampoo, fresh sheets, pillowcases. Stop – before the list gets any longer.

Oliver had been quite concerned on the phone yesterday. He didn't entirely believe her, but that was to be expected. He was one of the last people in the world who'd believe in such a thing happening. He had picked up on it right away and made her tell him about it. Carrie had intended to wait until after he got home, after sex, after dinner and after a few drinks, when they were both lazy and utterly relaxed.

But now she was glad that he had pushed her. It was out in the open, her spooky little incident, and by the time he got home the Big Deal would be no big deal at all. Oliver took things in his stride, he was quick to adjust. Calm, cool, sensible. He would try to convince her that it had just been her imagination. She wasn't buying that, and she hoped they wouldn't argue about it.

Carrie came to the shelf where her opal sat. Her father had found it on one of his excursions into the Australian interior. It was a stunning piece, the size of a dinner dish and roughly the same shape. A thin layer of dazzling blue opal in the middle of barren brown rock. She called it the Lake on the Moon.

A good man. Once in a great while, when he was pleased about something and feeling mellow, he might have a cigar with a glass of fine brandy. Otherwise, he didn't drink or smoke. But his heart had given out when he was a spry fifty-five. God, it still hurt to remember. Michael Brewster, her father.

Growing up, Carrie had glimpsed snatches of Kuala Lumpur, New Delhi, Karachi, Dublin and (smelling of another low political move) Lagos. And then Harare, Zimbabwe. And finally, London. But by then Carrie was an adult. And along came Oliver.

It amazed her how quickly she had adjusted to that ghostly incident. When Carrie had walked through the door the next morning, she felt a tremor of fearful anticipation, but she was determined not to surrender to it. She was back home. It was her home, and everything would be all right. Somehow.

And it wasn't a minute later when she suddenly found herself visualizing the image of her father again, and she could see in her mind one of the words he had spoken. Oliver.

Carrie dusted the opal carefully, Lake on the Moon. She did the rest of the living room, threw some clothes in the hamper and neatened up the kitchen. She put on the kettle to make a cup of tea, and scanned the *Times* while waiting for the water to boil. Nothing grabbed her attention.

It was so tantalizing, to think of communicating with

someone who was dead. Reason told her it was so unlikely. Where *was* the other side, anyway? Even as a child Carrie had found unconvincing the idea of heaven and hell. It was equally difficult to believe in limbo where certain unhappy spirits were trapped after death, appearing at times to the living. Was she supposed to think that her father had been languishing somewhere out there, for the last six years, before suddenly visiting her?

She made a small pot of Palm Court tea and placed it on the table in the nook, letting it steep. Carrie had been brought up nominally as a Catholic, but her parents had never been diligent practitioners. She had been taught the basics, received all the childhood sacraments, and had absorbed a little Church lore. It was something of a hit-or-miss education; she had never had the faith crammed into her head. And that was perhaps unfortunate. Carrie might now have a much clearer understanding of the – mythology concerning death and an afterlife.

In her widowhood, Carrie's mother had become more involved with the Church. She was a regular attender for the first time in ages. No doubt there was comfort in it, for those in need, along with social contact. But Carrie would never discuss it with her mother. Religion, death, Daddy. It wouldn't be comfortable, and it probably wouldn't do either of them any good. Carrie did have a brother, Jim, a few years younger, but he was a Marine, away on embassy duty in Buenos Aires. They weren't that close.

The music finished, but she couldn't be bothered to get up and put something else on. The tea was ready. She sipped it and set the cup back in the saucer. As Carrie looked up, and sat back against the bench-seat, she saw her father sitting directly across the table from her, three feet away.

She clapped a hand over her mouth, smothering a ragged noise that was partly a scream and partly a cry of anguish. She shrank back as far as she could, as if she wanted to sink right into the woodwork and the wall. Her whole body trembled violently.

The look of pain and sadness in his face was unbearable. He

opened his mouth, starting to speak, but then faltered – seeming to lack the strength. One hand reached towards her. The cup fell over with a thin clatter.

'No,' Carrie wailed. It was wrong, somehow. She slid along the seat into the corner of the nook. It was a bad decision, she realized dimly, and now she had nowhere to go. This was her own father, he wouldn't hurt her, and yet it seemed all wrong for him to be there. She didn't want to feel his hand on hers.

He couldn't, anyway. His arm stretched across the table and covered the thin ribbon of spilled tea, but fell short. And then it disappeared. He was gone. A gasp of relief. But Carrie felt bewildered with shame and guilt, as if in some way she had failed him. Tears ran freely down her face.

It was real, it actually happened. Her father was trying to communicate with her. The second time now, in a matter of just a few days. And she couldn't handle it. Carrie had reacted to him with fear and abject weakness. She felt pathetic, so inadequate, and she couldn't stop crying.

The spilled tea was smeared along the table.

Daddy.

5

It wasn't the greatest apartment in the world but, God knows, he'd lived in far worse. It occupied the upper floor of an older building just off Orange Street, barely within reasonable walking distance of Yale.

The second bedroom served as his office/study, but his books spilled over and took up space throughout the apartment. He had accumulated thousands of volumes, including many valuable firsts of Anglo-Irish pedigree. The hardest part of this tinker's life was packing and transporting books. But they were indispensable. They couldn't be locked away in storage somewhere. The secret of mental balance for Charley was to be found in a houseful of good books – and a decent drink now and then.

Jan looked in at him, gave a nod of no apparent meaning, and wandered off. Well, she was like that. Quiet, you might say. A woman who kept to herself but could socialize if it was required. The girl next door *manquée*. They first met while undergraduates at Northwestern. They had an affair of the heart, if not of the groin, and then were apart during the first year of his post-graduate work in Dublin. With his MA in hand, Charley returned to the States long enough to marry Jan, pack up their things and bring her back to Ireland. He got a part-time lecturer's post at University College Galway, and spent the rest of his time working on the Dunsany thesis for his Ph.D. Rented a lovely little house outside the city. Ravenswood, by name.

Jan had never done anything with her BA in English. Liked to read those windy historical novels but never wanted to teach. She had picked up some basic computer skills along the way, and usually managed to land a clerical job wherever they were living, like the one she currently had at a mail-order firm dealing in computer parts. It offered a middling wage, always handy, and where there was no challenge there was no stress.

Just as well. Jan was a different person after Fiona's death, and she never quite came all the way back from it. He had recovered, in time, gathered himself and carried on – still essentially the same Charley O'Donnell. But Jan, not quite. Something in her was permanently lost, a sense of confidence, perhaps, her faith in life itself. She became less a participant, and more a passenger seeing out the ride.

It didn't help that they couldn't have any more children. A final twist of the knife. Perhaps they could, but simply didn't manage the trick. The biology of it was inconclusive: either her eggs grew more resistant or his sperm had lost some of its vigour. Arcana like that, with hints of psychological causes.

In recent years sex had become largely symbolic. They made love once or twice a month and there was nothing much to it. In all fairness, he'd always been a little too quick and inattentive at it. But it could also be fairly said that Jan had never shown any interest in becoming a skilled, exciting lover. She'd always preferred the affectionate aftermath to the mechanics of the main event. And that's what they had come to, skipping the sex most of the time, and cuddling each other for the soothing warmth and comfort as they fell asleep.

Jan must know that he satisfied his sexual needs elsewhere, but if she did she didn't let on, much less make an issue of it. Charley tried to be careful and discreet. The age of Aids and an increasing awareness of women's rights forced new considerations but didn't significantly reduce the range of opportunity. People were people, and college campuses would always be highly charged with sexual intensity.

And so, this marriage. There was still something good in it, he believed. He could have given up and left her long ago, and she could have done the same, but they clung together. It was far from a model marriage, but a thread of purpose and devotion ran through it. There were moments of genuine affection, fondness.

He longed to tell Jan about Malcolm's strange story. But how could he? She had been there when Fiona died, and the merest mention of the subject might be enough to unravel her. She never brought it up.

Maybe they should have sought more psychological counselling, although it seemed like they had had plenty at the time. Everybody from the parish priest to the county social worker offered their well-intentioned advice, and there had been sympathy and support from family and friends. Charley and Jan had had a hard time absorbing half of it, the rest washed on by. But there are some things you can never talk away.

Now this terrible story. Had it come from anybody else who knew him, Charley would have regarded it as a cruel joke. But Malcolm would never have considered doing such a thing, and his discomfort when he had mentioned it to Charley had been plain to see. There was no doubt that the psychic incident, or whatever it had been, had struck Malcolm as very near the real thing. Improbable as that seemed.

But was it? Charley was aware of a certain irony. He had devoted a good portion of his adult life to the work of Dunsany, whose books were saturated with the fantastic, the improbable and the supernatural. Charley had no doubt that if this had happened to Dunsany, the old boy wouldn't have batted an eyelash. He would have seen it as a glimpse of secret truth, as an intrusion of the higher reality into our drab everyday world.

Could Charley simply dismiss it, chuck it all aside as sheer nonsense? He wanted to, but it wasn't that easy. If, as Malcolm had said, there was one chance in a million that the incident was real, not a contrivance, then he couldn't ignore it.

At the moment, a more likely explanation suggested itself to him. This woman, the putative psychic, had most likely picked up on the residual accent in Malcolm's voice and tossed off a random bunch of names and phrases associated with Ireland. Fiona was a common Irish name. Even Ravenswood was not so remarkable; there were Ravens-this and Ravens-that throughout Ireland. The country had entirely too many ravens by far, alas.

That was how they worked, he thought. They threw out dozens of verbal titbits, hoping that at least one would trigger an association in the mind of the gullible customer. They watched carefully, and when something scored a hit they added a bit more to it, feeling their way, building on whatever the poor hapless soul unwittingly provided.

But. Charley had futzed about this for a couple of days and still didn't know quite what to do. Finally, he reached for the telephone and punched in Malcolm's number.

'Listen, mate, any chance you and your good lady wife could spare me a few minutes at short notice?'

Bethany, where the hills begin. Malcolm and Maggie owned an old farmhouse that had been fully renovated and redecorated. The kids, two or three, could be seen and heard from time to time out in the yard or thundering on the stairs inside. He really ought to make a point of learning their number and names one of these days. But he'd gone off other people's children long ago.

They sat outside the kitchen, on a patio made of old brick. There were pots and planters full of herbs and spring blossoms, a trellis half covered with a new growth of ivy. Malcolm brought wine glasses and two open bottles of Margaux to the wrought-iron table. Maggie looked altogether too good for a repeat mother, in snug jeans that showed off a fine backside and a man's shirt that was not so loose it didn't hint at certain delightful motions and features occurring on the inside.

Heaney's latest collection was moved reverently to one side as Malcolm poured the wine. Heaney was right on track for Oslo, and Malcolm was just about the top Heaney man in the world. Look at him, will you? Maggie, Heaney, Yale – when had Malcolm ever made a bad choice? The likely lad.

'All right, now,' Charley said, after they had touched their glasses. 'About your woman. I want to know more.'

'I've met a lot of these people and attended a lot of their

sessions,' Maggie said promptly, as if she had been waiting for a chance to discuss it with him. 'And she's as close as they come to the real thing. In fact, I'd say there's no comparison at all. I've never seen anyone as good as she is.'

'So you believe it, then?'

Maggie hesitated. 'I believe there's something going on but nobody has a clear idea what it is. For all the studies and investigations that have been done, going back to the turn of the century, our understanding of psychic phenomena is limited. The history is largely anecdotal.'

'You don't think it's just a case of fraud?'

'It is in most cases,' Maggie agreed, with a nod. 'But then you find the one case in a thousand, and it's so convincing that the only explanation seems to be you've witnessed a real paranormal event.'

'So you think these folks, the few real ones, are tuning in to actual messages from the dead?'

'No, not necessarily,' Maggie said. 'It may be that certain individuals have a vastly greater sensitivity to other people and situations. And their subconscious minds can pick up and process information that's there all along but which the rest of us fail to notice.'

Uh-huh. 'The grape squash is very tasty, squire.'

'Help yourself to more,' Malcolm said, with a smile.

Charley refilled his glass. Maggie had lovely teeth, small and pearly and very slightly uneven. Bless her for never having had them straightened. They were desperately sexy.

'That all sounds very reasonable,' Charley said. 'But what if she noticed your hubby's lingering Irish accent and decided to drop some names and phrases with Irish associations, thinking one might ring a bell in his mind?'

'That's possible,' Maggie said. 'It's a common technique. What you have to do then is follow it and see where it goes. If you're careful not to give out any solid information, it usually leads nowhere because the psychic quickly runs out of material to recycle.'

'They're the fakes.'

'Some, yes,' Maggie conceded reluctantly. 'But, even then, I think that most of the ones with no real ability are still trying to help people. They're sincere in their efforts. But there are those who are simply out to make money.'

'You think this woman is real?'

'Oona. Yes, she may well be.'

'Oona?'

'That's her name, yes.'

'Is she Irish?'

'Scottish.'

'Aha.' Close enough, Charley thought. 'Did she ever happen to live in Ireland?'

'I have no idea.'

'You don't think she might have heard about your daughter,' Malcolm said. 'Surely that's a stretch.'

'Why not? It was big news in a small country.'

'That's possible too, I guess.' But Maggie seemed doubtful. 'Though I still don't see why she would bring it up.'

'Because she noticed that Mal's Irish.'

'But she wasn't aware of any connection.'

Charley didn't want to argue; that wasn't the point of the exercise. 'How did you hear about her in the first place? Does she advertise, or what?'

Maggie smiled. 'No. Some do, but they're not the ones worth seeing. It was word-of-mouth. I get a newsletter from a group that studies psychic phenomena, and it mentioned rumours of a woman in the New Haven area who was said to hold remarkable sittings. It took a while for me to find her, and then persuade her to let me take part in one.'

'You had to persuade her?'

'Oh, yes,' Maggie said. 'The first time we met, she told me she didn't think she could help me because I had come to her out of curiosity, not need, and that was true enough. She's rather exclusive. She will only agree to work with certain people, and she won't have anything to do with those who want help or advice in business and financial matters, for instance.'

'No media,' Malcolm added.

'Oh, yes,' Maggie said. 'We had to promise we'd never say anything about her to the media. She has a terrible fear of being hounded and sensationalized.'

Charley smiled thinly. 'Pardon me, but it all sounds as if she just plays hard to get. The exclusive clientele, the refusal to lend her so-called talents to money-making and a ban on media contact – which probably means she's dying for the TV cameras to turn up at the front door. I don't know. Sounds like she really wants to build a mystique.'

'But that really is the way she does things,' Maggie said. 'She has some rich and powerful clients, and they compensate her generously. But she could make a lot more money if she wanted to, and she doesn't.'

Charley topped up his glass. 'What does she use? A crystal ball? A ouija board? Cards?'

Maggie shook her head. 'She talks, and at times it seems as if different voices come from her.'

'Do you believe it?' Charley asked her, with sudden emotion. 'Do you believe that the spirit of a dead child could be hanging around somewhere out there in the ether? That she picked up some English, a language she never lived long enough to learn, and now decides after all these years have gone by that she wants to send a message? Do you believe that, Maggie?'

'If we're to believe in any of this,' Maggie explained, 'the role of the medium is crucial. It's not that your daughter has learned English – the English comes from the medium, who has the ability to receive or sense a presence, a message. Which is also why your daughter didn't communicate directly with you, because you're not a medium, you're not sensitive in that way and so she can't get through to you directly.'

'Ah, the medium again.'

'As for the time difference, the people who study this field will tell you that maybe the message was out there all along and either didn't get picked up until now or was received by someone to whom it meant nothing, and so was ignored. And they will also tell you that time might not mean the same for those on the other side as it does for us.'

'The other side,' Charley echoed. 'Is there an *other side*, Maggie? Do you believe that?'

She laughed. 'Who knows? Not me.'

'But you've looked into this subject at length. What's your feeling about it? What's your best guess?'

Maggie shrugged. 'If you're going to investigate the paranormal, you have to proceed on the basis of certain assumptions. It's not that you assume they're true, but that they're at least possible. And then you follow them, hoping that they'll lead you somewhere. To some truth you can know.'

'You do believe it, then?'

'Like I said, I believe there's something to it, but I don't know what that is. It may be a matter of certain things that the human brain can do but which we still don't recognize.'

'All right.' Charley sighed heavily. 'If you were me, what would you do?' he asked them both.

'Talk to her,' Maggie said immediately.

'Try not to volunteer anything,' Malcolm advised.

'But do talk to her.'

As expected, Charley thought unhappily. Dig up the horrible past – so you can bury it all again.

6

'I've got a difficult situation with Marthe.' Oliver picked at the remains of his salad, then moved the dish aside. 'I'm not sure what to do.'

Carrie dipped a spoon into her *caldo verde*. She fished up a small chunk of *chorizo* and a few shreds of kale.

'What's the problem?'

'It's this process of hers,' he said. 'The results are very good so far. Fantastic, really. It needs a lot more testing but the next big step is bringing it to production. We need to work out an agreement with someone who can do the job properly.'

Carrie gave a slight shrug. 'There must be plenty to choose from. Clothing manufacturers – right?'

'Oh, yes, plenty. But I want to be in a position to exercise some control over this. It's beautiful. It's like discovering a whole new cloth and having the chance to be the first person to introduce it to the world.'

Carrie smiled at him. 'It's not the money, is it?'

'The money will be great,' Oliver told her. 'But to have a hand in something new . . . That would be sweet.'

'Like you did with the band.'

'Yes.'

'What about Marthe?' Carrie asked. 'What's she like?'

'Brilliant. Neurotic as hell.'

'Is she – pretty?'

Aha. 'If you like that Teutonic look. Strong features, but a little too strong, if you ask me.'

Carrie smiled. 'Can you trust her?'

'I hope so. But I don't know.'

'How did she discover this process of hers?'

'Pure luck, I think. I guess no one ever bathed and poached linen in the same acids she uses. And the rinse is important as well. I have no idea what's in it, but it finishes the job. And then there are the weaves – she's developed a new set. It's incredible, the whole thing.' He poured more *vinho verde* for both of them. 'Anyhow. I probably ought to stick to what I do best, which is buying and selling. Find a big producer, sell the rights and let them take it from there. Right?'

'No. You're very good at buying and selling,' Carrie told him, 'but what you do best, and you're really very, very good at, is discovery. Finding people and things, seeing their potential and knowing what to do to fulfil it.'

Oliver liked hearing that. In fact, it was what he tended to believe about himself. Some people make, others find.

After they left the restaurant they walked around aimlessly for a while. It was a balmy Sunday afternoon, and it was pleasant to be out on the streets of Manhattan. He put his arm around her shoulder as they strolled along.

The way Carrie's body nestled lightly against him reminded Oliver of the first time he met Marthe – at the textile fair in Frankfurt. They had bumped into each other as they leaned closer to peer at some fabric samples on a display stand. It was really nothing, an accidental bump of no significance. But a few seconds later, she had definitely nudged him aside. Maybe it was the crowd in Halle 5, the stale air and the sweaty heat, or the lousy German food he had eaten. Oliver was annoyed, and he elbowed her immediately in return. Most untypical of him.

Then he saw the look on her face, the fire and hunger in her eyes, and he realized that none of it had been an accident. Then she astonished him. She took a pale scrap of wrinkled cloth from her pocket, rubbed it slowly across his cheek and said, 'Have you ever felt anything like *this* before?' No, on all counts. Oliver brought her straight from the Messegeland to his room at the Park Hotel. The feel of that cloth on his cock made flannel seem like barnyard denim. She was a scrapper, a rough-and-tumble lover who liked to be pushed around and handled. Marthe. An event waiting to happen. Now in progress.

Remembering that day and the next few days that had followed it, Oliver realized he was getting an erection. Not a good idea, at the moment. He steered Carrie to an outdoor café, where they had a liqueur. He lit a Senior Service, tapped the box lightly on the table, and wondered what Ian Brady and Myra Hindley might be doing just then. The Moors murders. Must be getting close on thirty years ago now. O England, my England.

Carrie was in good form, he thought. Considering how she'd sounded on the phone the day before, Oliver had half expected her to be in a wobbly state of mind. But when he arrived back at the apartment yesterday she had been fine. Very calm, settled, as if she had already worked out the whole thing for herself. That was the Carrie he knew and respected. Loved, yes; loved.

They'd barely even mentioned that business about her father. A drink, a cuddle, great sex, and then the jet lag caught up with him and he slept right through the evening, the night, late into Sunday morning. It was always like that when he returned from a business trip overseas. Being away, if only for a week, made you quite horny for the one at home.

'So,' he said, 'you're all right now?'

'Yes.'

'Good. And what did you finally conclude about that curious incident you had the other day? Whatever it was.'

'I saw my father,' she said flatly.

'Oh.' So it wasn't a dead issue yet.

'Can we talk about it now?'

'By all means.'

'I had my doubts. Even when I told you on the phone that it was real, I still had doubts about it. But then ...' Hesitation as Carrie's eyes locked on the glass of Cointreau she held. 'Then I saw him again yesterday morning.'

'Yesterday?' Mildly surprised. 'A second time?'

She nodded. 'It was late morning. The apartment was full of

sunshine, all lovely and bright. I was having a cup of tea, and I looked up and he was sitting there, across the table from me in the nook. As close as you are now.'

'Your father. You're sure about that?'

'Oliver, of course I'm sure. It was Daddy.'

'How clear and – solid – was it?'

'As clear and solid as you are.' Her throat tightened. 'It was just for a few seconds, but he was so vivid and real. I even noticed the grey hair on his chest, and his skin was so loose and saggy. And grey. Oliver, it was . . . awful.'

'God, you must have been absolutely shattered.'

'I was, for a while.'

'But you seemed fine when I got home, and that must've been, what, just a few hours later?'

Carrie nodded. 'It took me a while to get over it, but then I accepted it.' She looked so earnest now. 'I *had to* – it was so . . . undeniable. I had no choice.'

Oliver didn't know what to think. It all seemed so foolish, and yet at the same time it was worrying. Carrie had no history of anything remotely like this nonsense.

'Was he talking about me again?'

'No. I think he tried to speak, but couldn't. He stared at me. Oliver, he looked so sad and anguished. It was awful to see in somebody you loved. I felt so helpless, so useless to him.'

'Carrie, you have nothing to blame yourself for.'

'I know, but that doesn't make it any easier.'

'What did you do?'

A sheepish smile. 'I went to Zabar's and bought some food. And by the time I got back to the apartment I felt better. I was okay about it. Not exactly great, but okay.'

He patted her hand and smiled with affection. 'Funny how a spot of shopping will put a person right.'

'Oliver, what do you think?'

'I don't know,' he replied. 'I just don't know what to say or think. I mean, you hear of things like that happening, but it all seems so – unlikely.'

'I know.'

He shrugged. 'Besides, what can you do about it?'

'I have to do something. It isn't over.'

Suddenly Oliver felt weary. He said nothing, but he frowned dismissively. He wanted to leave the café. He was tired of sitting out on the sidewalk. The people passing by were vaguely menacing in their breezy cheerfulness.

'You'll be all right,' he said perfunctorily.

'Does it bother you?'

'It's all right, love.' Gently, patiently.

'And when it happens again?'

'*If* it happens again, I shall have a word with your dear old dad, man to man sort of thing. Set him straight. He's not behaving like a proper gentleman.'

Carrie laughed and squeezed his hand. 'I love you.'

'Then take me home and pamper me.'

'You got it.'

Nothing happened. It was a relief, in a way, but she had to fight off an odd feeling of anticlimax. Work kept her busy every day, and Oliver was with her at home every evening. Her life was back to normal, more or less. At any moment Carrie expected to see her father again, but for the next week there were no shadows, glimpses or full-blown visitations. She had Saturday brunch with Jeffrey and Mark at a brasserie near the Lincoln Center.

'Maybe that's the end of it,' Jeffrey said.

'But why?' Carrie asked, puzzled.

'To see you,' Jeffrey went on. 'And the second time did the job. Finished it.'

'Just to see me?'

'And to have you see him. The second time was to make sure you knew that it was real, and that closed out the episode.'

'The psychotic episode,' Mark said, with a grin. 'Don't worry, darling, we all have them from time to time. Life just wouldn't be worth living without them.'

Carrie gazed at her rocket salad, wondering why she had

ordered it. She didn't much like rocket and there seemed to be about five pounds of it on her plate.

'But even if that's true,' she said, 'I still don't know why it happened. I mean, why now? I don't understand.'

Jeffrey shrugged helplessly.

'You missed your man,' Mark said. 'That's all it is. Since Oliver got home and started sleeping in his own bed again – I mean your bed, of course – everything's been fine. Right?'

But Carrie knew there had to be some other reason behind it. Oliver was away on business regularly, and she had got used to that long ago. Nothing strange had ever happened before while he was gone. Until now. What did it mean? Carrie had been given a definite message, and had to decode it.

Jeffrey gave her Scott Crawford's telephone number. He was the editor of a line of books on the paranormal and other New Age topics – they'd mentioned him to her that night Carrie had crashed out at their place after the first visitation.

A few days later, working up her nerve, she called him and tried to explain briefly what had happened. She wanted to learn more about these things, and wasn't sure how to go about it. She wondered if he could give her some advice. At first Crawford sounded wary, but as soon as he understood that she was a friend of friends and not looking for a quick book contract, he agreed to see her. They met after work at the bar in the Royalton.

'Mrs Spence?'

Carrie turned towards the reedy voice. 'Yes?'

'Scott Crawford.'

'Thanks for meeting with me.'

They shook hands, sat at a small table and ordered a couple of white wine spritzers. Crawford was fortyish, with thick curly hair that was expensively styled, a suntan and a custom-tailored linen suit. He was a bit short and didn't look at all bookish or editorial. A prosperous travel agent, perhaps.

'Well, then,' he said. 'Tell me about yourself. Background and so on, and then exactly what happened.'

Carrie gave a brief recital – growing up in various embassy

enclaves, college, London, Oliver, New York, her father's death, and then the recent visitations she had experienced. 'You know,' she finished, 'I never believed in anything like this. I believe in it now, but I don't know *what* to believe *about* it. And that's what's really bothering me. I want to know what it meant and why it happened. I want to understand it.'

Crawford nodded, fingers steepled at his chin. 'You have no idea how many people go through something like that. Millions of them, and it changes their lives for ever.'

'Yes.'

'Now, the obvious explanations. You probably won't like to hear it, but they're often true. You *could* have imagined seeing your father. You *could* have had a kind of waking daydream. It's a very common occurrence and sometimes we don't even notice it or remember any of the details. So, it *could* be a random event that replayed itself once in your mind, and is over. In which case it has no real meaning or importance, and the best thing to do is to forget about it.'

Carrie nodded. 'I understand, but it was far more real than a daydream. I remember all of the details so vividly.'

'Right, yes,' Crawford agreed. 'The next thing you'll have to consider is that these incidents were merely the symptoms of a personal crisis. Some trouble at work or at home, and the stress builds up inside of you, and you may not even realize how much it's beginning to affect you.'

'I've thought of that,' Carrie said. 'I really have. But I just don't see how that could be it. My work is going fine, I've got plenty of it and I enjoy doing it.'

'Good, good.'

'And at home, Oliver and I have no problems. Nothing of any consequence. I mean, we seldom even disagree about anything, let alone quarrel.'

'Is there anything that the two of you avoid discussing? An unpleasant subject you both find easier not to mention?'

'No.' Carrie shook her head. 'Honestly.'

'Could your husband be having an affair?'

'No.'

'Could he be having sex with somebody else?'

Carrie faltered slightly. 'I have no reason to think he is. None at all,' she added, regaining some confidence. Crawford had mentioned the one thing she hadn't yet seriously considered, but she was not afraid to face it. 'Certainly not here in New York. Oliver does travel a lot on business, and what he does when he's away, I have no idea. But if something did happen then I think it would most likely be a one-night stand, and frankly I wouldn't feel terribly threatened by that kind of thing.'

'Well, good.'

'I'd be hurt, of course,' Carrie said quickly, thinking that she might have sounded too reasonable, 'but I don't think I have any reason to worry about it. Honestly.'

'I'm glad to hear it,' Crawford said, smiling. 'I'm sorry to hit you with such personal questions but it often turns out to be a marital problem and not a genuine paranormal event. So, you do have to explore that possibility.'

'I understand.'

'Telekinesis, poltergeists, demonic possession, hauntings – in many of these cases, when you look carefully at them, you will find a teenager at the centre of it, usually a girl, and usually going through puberty. They're often disturbed or abused in some way. Most of the time it's personal and psychological.'

'But you do believe that sometimes . . .'

'Oh, yes, of course,' he said. 'But before we get to that, I must ask you if you take any drugs or medication.'

'No, I don't.'

'What about alcohol?'

'I'm a light social drinker,' she told him. 'I did have a bit of liqueur that night, the first time, but not much, and the second time was mid-morning and I was drinking tea.'

'Sounds fine,' he said. 'All right, Mrs Spence. Now, let's assume that what happened to you was genuine.'

'Yes.'

'What do you want to ask me about it?'

That threw her. 'What was it?'

'I don't know. A ghost? That's an old worn-out term, loaded

with dubious connotations. I think it's more helpful to consider these things as a form of communication.'

'He was naked,' Carrie said suddenly. 'Jeffrey told me that you had said that made it more likely to be genuine, because the dead don't take their clothes with them when they die.'

Crawford seemed to find that rather amusing. 'Jeffrey *would* misunderstand that, now, wouldn't he? But it doesn't necessarily prove anything. Stop and think. Dead people don't take their clothes with them, true, but they don't take their skin and bones either, do they?'

'Well . . . no.'

'So, what you saw was a kind of projection. It was the form and language of a particular communication.'

'From my father.'

'That seems likely.'

'In the afterlife.'

Crawford frowned. 'That's another weak term, *afterlife*. As if death is an end. But maybe it's just the continuation of this life, in another form, here but unseen and unheard – most of the time. Maybe *here* is all there is, and it's for ever.'

'But . . .' Carrie had the feeling that she wasn't making any progress, that Crawford might continue to offer nothing more than nebulous ambiguities. 'What would be the point of it?'

'Simply to communicate.'

'To communicate what?' she persisted.

'That he survives, that there is continuation. To remind you of him, and his love for you.'

'And that's the end of it?'

'Quite possibly.' Crawford signalled for another round. 'I know that most mediums and channels profess to carry on endless conversations with the spirits of the departed, but you shouldn't put much stock in that. The best and most likely cases of real contact are the briefest glancing hits, like the ones you seem to have experienced.'

'There has to be more to it.'

'You want more. That's understandable. We all do.'

'No,' Carrie insisted, surprised at the surge of conviction in

71

her own voice. 'He was in such pain, or sadness, and he was trying to tell me something.'

'If there is more, something will happen.'

'Could it be a warning? An omen?'

'Could be. There are lots of possibilities.'

It was maddening. 'This doesn't help me at all,' she said in exasperation. 'I want to do something, I want to understand. I don't want to sit around waiting and hoping, I want to take the next step myself.'

Crawford stared at her, then sighed.

'Mrs Spence, if you want to invest your time and money in this, you can. But I want you to understand that the chances are really very, very slim that it will lead anywhere. It's a rarity when genuine contact is made at all, far rarer still for it to be continued or revived. You can spend months and even years at it, and end up knowing nothing more than you do now.'

'How can I try?'

Crawford sighed again. 'A medium. I think channel is a terrible word. Anyhow, most of them are either deluded fools or outright frauds, but there are a few – very few – individuals who appear to have remarkable abilities.'

'Can you put me in touch with one of them?'

'She might not even see you,' Crawford warned. 'But there's a very interesting young woman in Connecticut . . .'

7

Charley poured a generous amount of gin into a glass pitcher and then added Sauterne. He stirred, tasted the chopstick, added more Sauterne and tasted again. Too sweet: another splash of gin. The object was neutrality. Ah, yes.

'Here, try this.' He handed Heather the drink.

She made a face. 'It tastes strange.'

Charley gave a wicked low laugh. 'It's called Dog and Duck, and it was cooked up by the obscure Welsh spook writer and genial essayist, Arthur Machen. I suppose that you've never even heard of him, poor ignorant child of the times that you are.'

'Never. What's it supposed to be?'

'The martini from hell.'

'You can't taste the gin.'

'Point. And when you wake up, it'll be September.'

'Did you mix it right?' Heather could be so uncooperative. 'It has a horrible stink and it looks like pee.'

'Keep drinking, my sweet.'

He changed the music, putting on the Hamilton Harty disc to which he regularly subjected Heather, in the admittedly faint hope that it might eventually leach into her brain. But she was a graduate assistant in musicology, and you couldn't tell her anything. He plopped down into a heavy armchair.

'Charley, you didn't tell me there already is a biography of Dunsany. I was in Sterling yesterday, and I looked him up in the subject index, since you're always mumbling about him, and I saw this biography listed. Is that why you've never followed through and written one yourself?'

'I don't mumble,' he said. 'That's a shoddy piece of work,

that one is. An anecdotal account of the life, zero analytical content. Magic realism is never mentioned, but the Latins adore the little git. They'll tell you straight up.'

'So why don't you do it properly?'

'I may yet.' A change of subject was called for: he was in no mood to be lectured on career moves. Heather was a darling, and she certainly meant well, but she was still young and hopeful and she knew nothing about the subtle compensations of decline. 'Heather, let me ask you something. Do you believe in ESP, ghosts, the spirit world, messages from the dead? Do you think there's anything to it?'

She blinked. Thought. 'Well, maybe. Why not?' She sat up a little straighter in her chair. 'Well, yes. I do.'

Not quite a monument to Aristotelian logic, Charley thought, but every generation must find its own humble way.

'Why?' he dared to ask.

'I know a few people who have experienced it,' Heather told him. 'My mother, for one. Years ago, before I was born, she got all shivery and trembling. It was in the middle of a warm summer afternoon and she suddenly felt cold and frightened, and couldn't do anything for an hour or so until it passed. It turned out it was at about that time that her cousin died in Vietnam.'

'A cousin?' Didn't seem quite right to Charley. That sort of supernatural carry-on ought to be restricted to members of the immediate family.

'They were very close,' Heather explained.

'So, what would you say it was, exactly?' he asked. 'How do you account for something like that?'

'I don't know,' she admitted cheerfully. 'But it happens to people often enough, so there must be something to it.'

Ah, yes. There must be something to it. Charley had heard that before, and found it unsatisfactory. All the same, it was a tricky point to get around. Reasonable people, like Maggie, felt there had to be something to it. Sensible and highly intelligent people, like Mal, were open to the possibility. And, give Heather her due, she was a bright lass and a solid academic.

So why did he resist?

The original incident itself was reason enough. No one in their right mind would want to recall the sheer godless horror of it. Then there was the idiocy of the claim. It was an insult to the intelligence to suggest that some potty old woman could pull down a message out of thin air from the dead. Long dead. If you needed more, there was the pointlessness of it all. You proceed on the basis of certain assumptions, Maggie had told him. Okay, but where does it all lead? Assume it was a real message and that it came from Fiona. What could she say? *How I dearly wish I wasn't here. It's cold and dark and lonely.* Like that.

People had been fooling around in this line for ages, gazing at tea-leaves, shuffling Tarot cards, peering into crystals and rattling tables – and yet, what was there to show for it? No clear, consistent understanding, not even a slim foothold of solid ground. Nothing at all.

'Why did you ask?'

'Funny thing happened to a friend of mine.'

'What was it?'

Charley frowned. 'He was at a seance, I guess, some kind of psychic gathering, and right out of the blue he heard the name of somebody he'd known years ago.'

'Did anyone else there know the name?'

'Apparently not. That's what's spooky about it.'

'A dead person?'

'Oh, yes, yes . . .'

'Wow. What did he do about it?'

'Not much you *can* do, is there?'

Charley got up and poured himself some more of Mr Machen's inspired punch. He topped up Heather's glass too. It seemed to be giving her an attractive smutty glow.

'Maybe he could help.'

'Help how?' Charley asked warily.

'If a spirit is troubled, not at peace.'

'Oh?' Charley didn't want to hear any more about it, but he had to eventually. It was the one niggling thought that wouldn't go away. Maggie and Malcolm hadn't even mentioned it, no doubt thinking it would be too painful for him, and they had probably known that he would find his own way to it sooner or later. 'Just what is that supposed to mean? Not at peace?'

Heather shrugged. 'A restless spirit that's trapped between this world and the next?'

'Why would it be trapped?'

'Perhaps it can't let go and needs help. Perhaps it has to make peace with the living before it can move on.'

'Unfinished business, sort of thing?'

'Yes. Well, when you hear about a place that's supposed to be haunted, it's usually something like that. Some dead people can't cut their ties to this world. They're not ready to depart, so their spirit lingers on. You know?'

God, it was ludicrous, Charley thought. As if the dead were jet planes lined up on some cosmic runway and had to have their wings de-iced before they could take off. Crazy.

Or was he being too sceptical? Maybe he was so addicted to rationalism that he could no longer cope with true uncertainty. How were you supposed to deal with it or respond to it? Charley had no skills in this area.

'So what would you do in that situation?' he asked. 'How would you help a restless spirit?'

'Gosh, I have no idea,' Heather said, with a laugh.

Fair enough. Look at me, will you? Asking questions like that and expecting a sensible answer from a person who listens to some of the worst racket in the history of human sound.

'Maybe it was his angel,' she offered.

'His angel?' Wild disbelief. 'Guardian angel?'

'Yes, they're very popular these days. Nice idea, I guess. I saw the author of a book about them on TV not long ago.'

'Bullshit is what it is,' Charley said bitterly. Where had Fiona's guardian angel been *that* day? Down at the pub, having a quick pint? Away on an errand for the Boss? 'Complete bullshit. Fuck that shit. Angels.'

Heather's eyes widened. 'Charley. What is it? Was it you? Did that happen to you?'

'No, it really was a friend of mine. Honest.' Technically true. Heather knew nothing about Fiona, and Charley didn't care to unveil that grim megalith of history to her.

'Only you seem so intense about it.'

'I'm sorry. Bad mood.' Charley rallied himself. 'Maybe if you were to hitch the hem of that skirt a bit north of your knee. I'll fetch another pail of the right stuff.'

Heather could be wonderfully teasing and seductive when she was given a hint, bless her. Jan would give you a blank look if you said something like that to her. Fifteen years ago she would have given you a blank look. Alas and alack, a lass with a lack. And so – an occasional drink, a book, music, a secret dalliance, whatever it takes to get your mind off morbid thoughts.

Because the thought that something of Fiona might linger on to this day, restless and unhappy, that was unbearable. Where does it end? Does it ever end? Or is there some torment beyond death, a bleak and barren limbo of infinite misery to which even innocent wee babes are consigned? And, if that were true, surely no living person could do anything to help. You can't storm the kingdom of the dead and perform heroic Dunsanian rescues. It's just not on. You can't help the dead, old son.

And yet. And yet. And yet.

How could you not try?

The best part of a week passed before Charley arrived at Lea Crescent. Time enough to feel foolish, and guilty. He had called up and spoken to some woman but had found himself suddenly so tattered with emotion that he was barely coherent, and afterwards he could hardly remember a thing she'd said to him.

Late afternoon was the best time – she had said that, or so he seemed to recall. Westville was a small neighbourhood of quiet streets and older homes, duplexes and triple-deckers. It took a few minutes of cruising around before Charley found Lea Crescent. He pulled his aged green Volvo to the kerb and checked the house numbers. Third one along, near enough. He cut the engine, which died with its usual clatter and wheeze.

The house was set back from the street and on a knoll. The yard was narrow, bordered with tall but stringy hedges of hemlock and shaded by a couple of huge sugar maples. There was a flight of cement stairs from the street, and then a stone pathway rising more gradually across a spotty lawn to the front porch.

The house itself was not unattractive. It looked large and roomy, but it needed a bit of scrape and paint in places. At a guess, it was fifty to sixty years old. Charley climbed the four steps to the porch. He felt nervous, and that annoyed him. They were auditioning, he reminded himself, he wasn't.

The woman who answered the door was a good deal younger than he had expected, young enough to pass for an undergraduate. Her jeans and sweatshirt were from an expensive mail-order catalogue, and she wore thick white socks with no shoes. She was tall, with fair skin and long auburn hair. A bit of all right.

'I called a few days ago? Charley O'Donnell.'

'Oh, yes. I'm Rosalind Rodgers. Do come in.'

Charley followed her into a front room just off the entrance hall. She shut the door behind them and they sat down on either side of a large glass coffee table.

'How can I help you?'

Charley perched on the edge of the armchair and cleared his throat. 'Well, somebody suggested that I get in touch with you. I need some advice. I lost someone. A dear friend,' he added, on an impulse. 'He may be trying to reach me or he may need my help in some way. I'm not sure, and I don't know about these things, but if there's a chance that you – or Oona, is it? If she can help me I'd be very grateful.'

'Yes, Oona.' Rosalind nodded once. 'When you say that you've lost someone, I take it you mean he died.'

'Yes.'

'Because we get both kinds of cases. Runaways, abductions and others presumed still living, as well as the dead.'

'I see. No, this person is dead.'

'All right.' Another brief nod. 'I'd better explain a few things so there's no misunderstanding. Oona doesn't claim to conduct conversations with the dead. She isn't a channel, in the sense that most people understand the term.'

Charley nodded. Her eyes were flat blue, almost slate, and she had three jet studs in one earlobe.

'Oona has a very special talent,' Rosalind went on. 'In the right circumstances she can open new lines of understanding, and that can make a profound difference to the people involved. It's often a difficult process that takes time, but it can also be as brief and inexact as looking through the window of a train as it speeds by. And that may be all you ever get.'

'That would be something.'

She was studying him carefully. 'But you may come away with less than you thought, or in some way be the worse for it.'

'How could that happen?' Aside from losing money.

'You may think you know what you'll find on the other side, but you're never sure until you actually do it.'

'Yes, well, I'm quite prepared to come away empty-handed, if that's the way it is. But I have to try.'

'It can be painful.'

'A little pain's good for the soul.'

'I mean, very painful. I mean, deeply disturbing – in ways that could change you and stay with you permanently.'

'What's the worst that can happen?' he asked. 'That I learn my friend has been sent to hell for eternity?'

'No,' she said. 'That's not the worst—'

The door opened at that moment, and a younger woman stepped into the room. Young enough to pass for a high school senior, Charley noted. A cut-off Morrissey T-shirt, Spandex racing shorts, knee socks that were bunched up around the high tops of her sneakers, and an astounding flame of thick black hair that shot out and down and away from her head. Slimmer, not as tall, and yet there was a facial resemblance. The kid sister, most likely, and an eyeful at that.

'There you are,' she said to Rosalind. But then she noticed Charley. 'Oh, sorry.'

She started to back out of the room but stopped, looking at him intently. She came closer and Charley felt unnerved suddenly by the ferocious hunger in her eyes. It was a peculiar look that made him think she might be marginally deranged, and all the more disconcerting on such a lovely face. The closer she came to him, the more she seemed to fill the room and crowd him. His thoughts appeared to be fraying visibly around the inner circumference of his eyeballs. Now he could see that her eyes were a very intense blue, deep enough to approach dark purple. Charley could imagine a pinhole of light burning through his forehead, then out through the back of his skull. Himself leaking away.

'You've come to see me, haven't you?' she said.

'No, I—' But he stopped. Surely not.

'Oona,' Rosalind said. 'Mr O'Donnell.'

'Ah.' Oona smiled. 'At last.'

'Mr O'Donnell has lost a friend.'

Rosalind's words sounded flat and faintly silly, as if only last week he'd misplaced a body around the house.

'I've been expecting you,' Oona continued. She seemed to be speaking to a hitherto unknown part of his brain.

'We were discussing a possible appointment.'

'Of course he's coming,' Oona said, without turning her eyes from Charley. 'But it's not his friend.'

'It's not?' Rosalind didn't sound surprised.

'No. It's his daughter.'

He was aware of his mouth opening, but it took ages for any words to emerge. 'How do you—'

'It happened long ago and far away.'

His chest heaved, and the inrush of oxygen brought with it fear and anger. Fear that this was real, too real; anger because it had to be a clever trick, somehow.

'How could you know that?'

'She *let* me know—'

'Oona, please,' Rosalind cut in. 'Now's not the time.'

80

'It's all right, love,' Oona told her.

'I just finished hearing that you don't deliver messages to or from the dead,' Charley said.

Oona perched on the arm of the loveseat, away from Rosalind. 'People expect too much,' she said. 'So we have to let them know that they will probably never find what they want. But there are times when it seems to work, and I receive knowledge that's clear and direct. It's not an everyday thing, but it does happen.'

'Who told you about my daughter?'

'You said it was a *he*.' Rosalind, mildly reproachful.

'That's all right,' Oona told her again. She fixed Charley with a look of understanding and sympathy. 'As I just told you, it was your daughter who made herself known to me.'

'When was this supposed to be?'

'A while back. Not long ago.'

'Why didn't you call me and tell me about it?'

'I had no idea who you were.'

'She didn't give you my name?'

'No.'

'What about her own name?'

'Fiona.'

Dear God. Even if he told himself that Maggie or Mal had to have revealed it to her, somehow it didn't help at all. His daughter's name hit him like a jab in the throat.

'Do you know how old she was?'

'Just a baby. I'm sure that she's trying to reach you. She has knowledge she wants to share with you.'

'Knowledge from an infant,' he said.

'Our notions of time and age don't count for much when we get into this area.'

'Where is she?'

'There. Here. It's all the same. You can think of her as somewhere out in the reaches of heaven, if you want. Or here in this room with us. Both may be equally true. But it's best not to think in terms of a particular location. You'll never get to the bottom of it and it doesn't matter anyway.'

'And you can get in touch with her whenever you want?'

'No, no, nothing like that,' Oona replied, with a short laugh and a shake of the head. 'It's a difficult process to describe. Sometimes it works and sometimes it doesn't. But your Fiona is trying to help from her side, and now that we've found you it may be a good deal easier.'

Charley still wanted to feel angry, but it had seeped out of him. He felt bewildered. He had expected some pudgy, middle-aged pudding of a woman, not this tasty little nymph all decked out to wow the boys at the mall and give dirty old men like himself warm and liquid dreams.

'How much does it cost?'

Oona instantly looked disappointed in him.

'If you want to make a gift, you may,' Rosalind said. 'But it's not expected or required. This is not a business.'

'You have to invest *yourself* in it,' Oona added. 'Money is of no consequence in these matters.' She came around the coffee table, and stood closer to him. She smiled forgivingly. 'I know what you're thinking about me, and I have a fair idea what you're going through over your daughter. You're not ready, but you will be soon. Come back and see me then.'

'Maybe,' Charley said, his voice dry.

'You must,' Oona told him, as she turned and started to leave the room. 'I'm the only one who can help you.'

8

The interval didn't last. After Carrie met Scott Crawford, she decided to wait a day or two before doing anything, to think about it some more. She wasn't sure quite what to make of him. Crawford believed in parapsychology and the paranormal, he took Carrie seriously, and he had been helpful. But he'd also tried to discourage her.

He was probably right. You could get your hopes up too high and spend a lot of money for nothing. It could turn into an unhealthy obsession, an endless quest that never pans out. Scott wanted her to understand that. Fair enough.

The suggestion that these experiences could have their roots in a personal matter, that it could all be in her head, still bothered Carrie. It had to mean some sexual problem between her and Oliver or, even less likely, something between her and Daddy dating back to childhood.

Carrie could understand why Crawford considered this angle, but it was wrong. It had no basis in fact, so it could not be an explanation for the apparitions she'd witnessed. Her father was a fine and honourable man who had never done anything improper in his diplomatic career, let alone with Carrie. And as far as her marriage was concerned, she decided to confront Oliver about it. Just to make sure.

'What was that?' He was reading *And England's Dreaming*. He peered at her over the top of the book.

'Is there anything bothering you?' she repeated.

'No, not at all.'

'Are you sure?'

'Positive. Why do you ask?'

'Is there anything you're not telling me?'

'Oh, lots. My other wife in Cleveland, the secret jobs I do for the CIA. But nothing important, no.'

Carrie smiled. 'And you're happy with our marriage?'

'Yes, of course I am.'

'Our relationship? The sex is still good for you?'

'You're terrific, love, you really are.' He placed the open book flat on his chest. 'What's this all about anyway?'

'I just needed to hear it.'

'Something's bothering *you*.'

'Not really. It's just that thing with my father, you know, and it got me wondering about me, and you, and I wanted to be sure there wasn't some problem we need to face.'

'It says here there isn't.'

She felt a little better. 'Same here.'

Maybe Scott Crawford was right. Maybe it was just a one-off thing that had happened to her. Two-off, to be exact. It had lasted less than ten seconds, combined. Maybe that was all there was to it, over and done with. One of those things, odd and mysterious, but ultimately meaningless.

So Carrie decided to hold off on consulting that woman up in Connecticut. A day. Two. The interval went on. Oliver seemed more attentive and considerate but without making her feel as if she were some kind of a mental patient who required special care. They had a wonderful Indian meal at the Ooti, went to see Albee's *Three Tall Women*, and had some cherished evenings staying in – watching movies, playing cribbage, listening to music and making love.

Carrie continued to have breakfast coffee and evening tea in the nook, and to use the living room as always. If she came home and found that Oliver was out, she felt no great rush of anxiety. She was home. Her home, where she belonged.

Carrie also thought that she had learned something from the two incidents. What had frightened her most about them was the unnaturalness – they were freakish and wrong, and they didn't belong in the order of everyday things. So when they had happened, she was shocked and deeply disturbed.

So much so that perhaps she had been unable to take in fully what had really been happening. What had she missed? If it happened again Carrie wanted to control herself, to study it closely, as calmly as possible. She wanted to learn from it, rather than just react instinctively against it. She would have that chance.

Annemarie Clement, who was now the Contessa di Lamborghini (as they liked to joke), and who was also an old college friend, recommended Carrie to a cherubic Belgian gentleman with an empty apartment in Yorkville and heaps of money to spend fixing it up. Annemarie and Carrie still talked regularly on the phone, though they no longer moved in the same circles. Annemarie was married to some phoney Italian count, charming Euro-trash who dabbled in Formula One racing, and her picture could often be found in the social columns. Carrie was quite fond of her.

Monsieur Chauvet had a certain dubious charm of his own. He kept apartments in Ghent and London, and now had acquired the place just off York Avenue. It was large and had potential, but it had been left in bad shape. Carrie would have to start from scratch. Which was ideal.

She saw the place once with him, and they agreed to terms. He was in a state of exhaustion, he explained to Carrie, although he seemed to her to be as relaxed as a sandbag, and he was about to spend a month resting in Menton – poor man. He gave her the keys to the apartment. She went back to it after lunch one day to see how the rooms handled sunlight, take some measurements and photographs and sketch the existing layout.

The doorman admitted her and checked her ID carefully, which was good to see. It was obviously an expensive and secure building. She took the elevator to the fourth floor and entered the apartment, making sure to lock the door behind her. She went through all the rooms once, a quick tour to confirm that she had the place to herself. It was empty, stripped, the air stale and sticky-warm. Carrie put her things down on the bare floorboards and went to work.

She was there for nearly an hour and a half, clicking off photographs, jotting down numbers and scribbling several pages of notes. Good, it was all good. She had a crowd of ideas. It was a great place and it was begging to be reborn. One wall could be removed in the long corridor that ran the length of the apartment. Carrie picked up her things and glanced again down that corridor before leaving. It was dark and tunnel-like, a dreadful design job.

She didn't even notice him there at first, but then she did – a man standing at the far end of the corridor. A silhouette, with the late-afternoon western sun falling aslant in geometric lines through the window behind him.

Think, don't panic.

It must be an intruder who had somehow got in through a window without making any noise. Carrie could try to unlock the door and get away, but she calculated that he would probably be on top of her before she managed to stick her head outside and scream for help.

Her hand was shaking, but she reached into her bag and found the canister of pepper spray. She had never used it before but she knew that the police did – so it must work. She held it up, moving her eyes quickly to make sure the nozzle pointed in the right direction. Now, if she could only remember, were you supposed to shake it? Were you supposed to fire it when your assailant was six feet away or ten?

He just stood there, apparently staring at her for what felt like a very long time. Carrie didn't bother attempting to speak to him. Her free hand started for the lock.

He came running. One instant he was still, the next he was flying at her silently. She remembered that. There should have been a lot of noise from the bare floorboards, even if he'd been wearing sneakers. But there was no sound at all. She let go of her bags, stiffened her stance, snatched her free hand away from the door and used it to brace the arm with the pepper spray. The man swept down the corridor towards her. She fired once. It had no effect on him.

He emerged in the brighter light of the entry foyer, and she could see him clearly for the first time. She fired, and clamped her finger to the button now for continuous spray. It seemed to pass right through him. He was greyish-brown from head to foot, a sepia figure with remotely humanoid features that seemed to be twisted and smeared into themselves so that his face was hardly recognizable as human. A grotesque echo of a man. He was going to crash into her, Carrie realized dimly. There was nothing she could do about it, she was frozen to the spot.

His body flew into hers, his face into hers, a glimpse of an unbearably elongated eye rushing directly into hers. It felt as if she had been hit by a wave of frigid moisture, so shocking to her system that it nearly knocked her out, and at the same moment she could hear *him* shriek in agony – from within her body, the awful noise filling her, seeming to swell her brain and resound in the chambers of her heart, devastating her with shared pain.

She tottered, then something smashed her knee and the back of her hand banged against the floor. Carrie slid down onto her side. She was stunned but still conscious. She saw the floor and the walls. She felt incredibly weak, her arms and legs as useless as string. She wondered if she were dying, and already half-way out of her body. There was a lingering clamour in her ears – but no, not just her ears. It was fading away on the inside of her flesh and bones. Beneath her clothes she felt damp and chilled. Her knuckles were scraped, a headache began to drum at the temples, and she saw the canister of pepper spray on the floor several feet away. Carrie turned to look around. No one. Nothing. She was alone, the apartment still locked.

I'm not going crazy, she told herself, because it doesn't happen like this. Does it? Carrie struggled to her feet. She reeled precariously, as a sudden wave of nausea and dizziness hit her, and groped for the wall to steady herself. It took a few moments for her vision to clear and her breathing to settle down somewhat. Her heart was still pounding fearfully.

Okay, she thought, okay.

You have my attention.

*

Oliver listened patiently to her story. He had no idea what was going on any more. Carrie still seemed to be herself, steady and sensible, but what she was saying was the stuff of fantasy or mental illness. He had written off the first two incidents as transient aberrations. Now this. It wasn't her father this time. It was something else, an escalation.

The supernatural cut no ice with Oliver. Other people could believe in it, of course, and he would never consider that reason enough to doubt their sanity. Unless it went too far, and became irrational, obsessive.

'What do you think it was?' he asked her.

'I don't know,' she replied, matter-of-factly. 'I honestly have no idea at all.'

He couldn't get over how composed and self-possessed Carrie was as she spoke. She appeared to have digested the experience and come to certain conclusions about what she intended to do in response to it. The rest of the story dribbled out, and Oliver was less than pleased. The gay guys had passed her along to some enthusiast in such matters, who in turn had redirected Carrie to a medium in Connecticut.

Now Carrie wanted to go to Westville and discuss it with the woman. He voiced no objection. What was the point? She was the one who was undergoing this experience, whatever it was, and she was the one who would have to work her way through it. He could offer sensible advice, but he knew that Carrie wouldn't listen to it until she was good and ready.

If it began to get out of hand and Carrie showed any sign of becoming erratic in her behaviour – well, then, Oliver would have to step in and find her some professional help. He couldn't let this become a threat to his marriage. He was comfortable in it and he had a strong aversion to any upheaval.

'Will you drive me on Saturday?'

'Are you sure—'

'It's okay if you don't want to. I can drive myself, or get the train and a taxi.'

'No, I don't mind,' he said reluctantly.

*

'Nice car.'

Oliver looked up from the book and turned his head slightly. He was sitting back against a cushion wedged in the corner on the passenger side, his legs stretched across the front seat. He had the roof down because it was such a glorious day, quite warm for the first week of June, with low humidity and a caressing breeze. It was a kid, a teenage girl, apparently on rollerblades.

'Thanks.'

Her dark hair was braided and pinned up in coils. She had a sweatband around her forehead, two more on her wrists, and a thin silver chain that hung close to her throat. She wore opaque blue sunglasses and an oversized Yale T-shirt. Pretty. She hovered, edging closer to his jade Saab.

'So, what're you doing here?'

'I'm waiting for someone,' he said.

'Your wife?'

'Yes.'

'You from England, or something?'

'Yes, I am.'

'Thought so. You have an accent.'

'So do you. Where are you from?'

She pursed her lips and crossed her arms over her chest, and he figured that she had been trying hard to lose her accent.

'Canada. Very boring.'

'Do you live around here now?' She nodded twice. 'Do you know the woman who lives up there?' He gestured back towards the house on the knoll. She glanced at it briefly.

'A little.'

'What's she like?'

'There's two of them.'

'What are they like?'

'Kind of weird. They keep to themselves.'

'What do they do?'

'Not much that you see.'

'One of them is supposed to be a psychic.'

'Is that where your wife is?'

'Yes.'

'Having her fortune told?'

'Who knows?' he said, with a frown. 'Does she seem to have a lot of visitors calling?'

'You see cars here.'

'Every day?'

The girl shook her head. 'Three or four times a week.'

'What do the neighbours think of her?'

A bored shrug. 'They don't care, long as she doesn't bother them or create a nuisance with the traffic.'

'What's your name?'

'What's yours?'

'Oliver.'

'Hmmn. You don't look like an Oliver.'

'What do I look like?'

'I don't know. A Michael, maybe.'

He raised an eyebrow. 'My middle name.'

She grinned. 'Wow. Lucky guess.' She parked her hip along the side of the car, as if she were thinking about hopping up to sit on the fender. 'Oliver's okay too, you know. It's got kind of a roll to it.'

'Well, I'm used to it.'

'You ever been to India?'

That caught him up short. 'No. Why do you ask?'

'Just curious. I want to go there some day.'

'Why India?'

'I don't know, just to see it,' she said. 'I saw some movie on TV that took place in India and it looked kind of interesting. I mean, you hear the name of a city like Bombay, and you think it must be incredibly different. Exciting, exotic, dangerous. Know what I mean?'

'I suppose.' Bombay. 'Are you in school?'

'Not any more.'

'So what do you do now?'

A shrug. 'Not much.'

'Got a boyfriend?'

'No.' One slow shake of the head, looking away.

'I find that hard to believe.'

'Me too.'

'You didn't tell me your name.'

She had her hands on the fender, as if she were about to hop up on the car, but then she pushed off and skated in a tight loop that took her behind him and quickly back again. She braked next to him and leaned very close.

'Gotta go. Nice talking to you, Oliver Michael.'

She had lovely teeth and lips. He thought he caught a whiff of spearmint in her breath, and something else – *Muguet de bois*? He couldn't make out her eyes. She was smiling.

His face tingled. 'You too.'

She spun around. 'Later,' she called back, as she sped away down the sidewalk. He watched her in the side mirror. She went into a low crouch as she approached a sharp bend, and then rose as she sailed into it. The last he saw of her was a slender leg sticking straight out behind her as she whipped around the curve and out of sight.

Carrie didn't say much about her meeting, but she seemed satisfied. She had been in there a little over an hour. They stopped for something to eat before driving back to New York.

'How much did she charge you?' he asked.

'Nothing.'

'Do you really think you'll get anything out of this?'

'Yes.'

Just that. 'Well, good.' She was upbeat, positive. It was as good a time as any. 'Carrie.'

'Yes?'

'I've got to pop back to Europe.'

'When?' The usual hint of resignation and disappointment in her voice.

'Towards the end of the month.'

'How long will you be gone?'

'Ten days or so.'

'What for?'

'There are two auctions I'd love to attend, one right after the other. Kohler in Wiesbaden, they've got some Prussian covers and multiples that are staggering. And Craveri in Lugano, a Saar Occupation collection that sounds quite impressive.'

'Have Ivy & Mader bid for you, like they usually do.'

'I'd really like to see these items,' he explained. 'There won't be any more major events until the summer's over. Besides, I have to stop in Munich and finalize things with Marthe.'

'Oh.'

'Listen, love. Wiesbaden's boring but Lugano is lovely, and I'll be there on a Thursday and Friday. Why don't you come over and we'll have a dirty weekend in the Italian Alps?'

'Oh.' Much brighter. 'That would be great.'

'Good.' If it meant putting Marthe off for a few more days, so be it. The bitch would wait for him. 'Let's do that.'

Carrie nodded, but was quiet for a few moments.

'Oliver.'

'Yes?'

'I'm going to see this woman again and I'll have to schedule it for when you're here.'

'Why? Just take the car,' he said. 'Or—'

'Well, no,' Carrie interrupted gently. 'The thing of it is, she says that you have to be there too.'

9

He'd read it a hundred times, give or take a few. It was so important to him, had been for years. But exactly how many years was it? Ten, certainly. Fifteen, most likely. Twenty? No, not that far back. Well, maybe. That was about the time when he was just beginning to discover Dunsany, and the enchantment took firm root in Charley's soul.

It was a short story called 'Where the Tides Ebb and Flow'. In it, a man has done something so terrible he is denied a proper burial on land or sea. He doesn't know what his offence was, but he knows that he did it. His friends slay him and carry his body to the banks of the Thames in London. They put him in a shallow grave, so that the mud covers everything but his face.

He must lie there and observe the desolate houses along that stretch of the river. The tides come and go. The County Council discovers him and tries to give him a Christian burial, but his friends dig him up again and return him to the shallow grave along the Thames, his face exposed to the world.

Time after time, over the years, people attempt to bury him in the proper fashion, but his friends always dig him up and take him back to the edge of the river. Finally, he seems to achieve peace when a savage storm comes along, and scatters his bones far and wide among the isles down the estuary. But the tide gathers him up and returns him to his place in the mud.

Centuries pass this way, and the city of London itself dies. The buildings around him crumble, and there's nothing left to see but a few birds that sing to him. *He only sinned against*

Man, it is not our quarrel, they say of him. He thinks he can see one of the gates of Paradise, and he weeps.

So did Charley on more than one occasion when he reread the story, though always with the help of a suitable libation. The poor bastard never did find out what terrible thing he had done. And why were those men who punished him called his friends? But these were just the sort of little mysteries that Dunsany loved to create, and never explained.

When *was* the first time he read it? Was it before Fiona died or after? The question seemed important, although Charley couldn't say why. Couldn't answer the chronological question either. He had certainly read Dunsany's work before Fiona was born, but that story? Impossible to say.

Was he supposed to dig up Fiona now? Unbury his only child for the purposes of some impossible dialogue? That woman, Oona, had been a startler. Not really a fully grown woman yet, more of an idiot-child. Either that or a bloody clever schemer. It was enough to make you want to lash out and strike back at any person who trifled with your heart like this.

Let the dead lie sleeping in their graves.

He pushed the book aside on his desk and heard Jan pottering about somewhere in the apartment. Literature ultimately lets you down. Life, too. Everything fails you, and that is probably why you ultimately fail yourself. Was *that* the sin?

Oona. He wanted to think that she'd rigged the whole thing. Perhaps she had hired a detective to dig up the sorry details of his life. But why? It couldn't be the money, he had very little of that – and what else was there?

Afterwards he'd discussed it with Malcolm and Maggie, sopping up large quantities of Moselle as he related his meeting with the two young ladies of Westville. Maggie was all the more convinced that he was on to something and that Oona was authentic. Malcolm was intrigued, though still cautious and noncommittal.

It was time for decisions, Charley knew. This was about his

94

daughter, who was dead and buried in a mossy old churchyard in a small town in the far west of Ireland.

When he considered it later, what had unsettled him so much was that Oona could only have been a small child herself at the time of Fiona's death, two or three years old, and Rosalind not much older, not enough to make a difference. They could have been in Scotland or Ireland and perhaps even have heard the news. But would it mean anything to them? Could they have retained the story and kept it in mind ever since? It was so unlikely.

And their paths cross all these years later in Connecticut, where they somehow notice that Charley happens to be a visiting lecturer at Yale, and that he's the father of the child who died long ago and far away? No, surely not.

Charley picked up the telephone and hit the numbers. A ring and an immediate pick-up. At her desk.

'Hello.'

'Is that Rosalind, or—'

'Yes.'

'Ah. Charley O'Donnell.'

'Oh, good,' she said blandly. 'I'm glad you called.'

No doubt. He put his hand over the mouthpiece and exhaled, a sigh of distaste. To be doing this.

'I'd like to fix a time.'

'Of course. I was going to call you.'

'Why?' As if he didn't know.

'Two things. Oona wants you to know that when you come next time you must bring your wife with you.'

Out of the question. 'That's not on,' he told her.

'Please think about it,' Rosalind said. 'I know it might be difficult and painful, but without your wife's presence the whole thing would probably be pointless.'

'*Might* be difficult and painful for her?'

'Please think about it carefully.'

'What was the other thing?'

'Oona has received another image.'

Oh, yes, as expected. They hadn't heard from him, they were afraid he hadn't taken the bait. Set the hook again, deeper.

'What do you mean, an image?'

'She's sure it has to do with your daughter.'

'What is it?'

'Everglo.' A slight pause. 'Everglo,' Roz said again, as Charley's vision skittered wildly out of focus. 'Does that word mean anything to you?'

Let him be drunk for this, let him be good and stocious. It was the only sensible policy. It would blunt the force of Jan's inevitable reaction, and it might also distract her an important little bit from the full force of his message.

Well, it was a theory. Charley went to work on it, and when he was happily buzzed and no longer felt terrified at the idea of talking to Jan, he went looking for her.

She was in the bedroom, propped up, watching the usual late-night talk-show rubbish. The paperback in her hand was as thick as a brick, and on the cover it showed one of your Spaniard-type chaps out of the Middle Ages. He was leering down the admirable cleavage of a dark-haired sloe-eyed buxom wench. Nice position to be in, Charley thought wistfully.

'Jan.' She looked at him. No expression. Good. 'We have to talk, love.'

She tapped the remote, turning off the television. A little too quick at it for it to be a good sign. Never mind. He eased himself down on the edge of the bed and took her hand. He rubbed it gently. Poor woman. Long-suffering. Norwegian stock. From the flat heartland of the country, like himself, but very much in the dolorous Irish tradition of womanhood.

'I hate to even bring it up,' he said.

'What is it?'

'Something's happened. I think.'

'Tell me.'

Concerned, a hint of anxiety, but still so eager to hear the worst. Women couldn't wait to get to the weeping and wailing and gnashing of teeth part. He stroked her hand lovingly.

'It's about – first, let me explain something.'

'It's about Fiona.'

'How do you know that?'

'Because I heard from her.'

Oona? Rosalind? If they went behind his back and spoke to his poor wife, by God he'd murder the pair of them.

'Heard from who?'

'Fiona,' Jan said flatly. 'I've heard from Fiona.'

Sentenced

'I want the four of them together.'

'Why?' Roz asked absently.

'Not the first time but at least once,' Oona said. 'Maybe the second session.'

'Why bother doing them as a group at all, then?'

'To see what it sparks. These four people are special, they seem to be connected in some way. I don't know how or why yet, but they are. Put them all together, and it should stir up a lot of psychic motion. I want to try it.'

Oona slid down in the tub until all of her was submerged in the hot water beneath a layer of fragrant bubbles, except for her face. The room was full of steam, and moisture trickled down the mirror. Roz sat on the floor beside her, back to her, with her head resting on a thick towel that cushioned the lip of the large old bathtub.

The water felt so good, you could lose all awareness of your body in it and drift like a spirit. Almost. Water was, somehow, her destiny. Sooner or later. A foot of it in a bathtub was all she was allowed, after what had nearly happened last summer.

How on earth had she lived so long? Lack of trying. If she really meant it, if she made a serious effort, the results would be different. But something kept her alive, and only part of it was herself. People. The people who drove her to despair also kept her tied to life.

You don't mean it, you know you don't. You think you want to get away, but you'll never let go. You have it too cushy, for one thing. Dying is hard, that's another. If you need more, try this: the pain can be sweet. Enough said.

'He's going to get me.'

'Who?'

'One of those two,' Oona said. 'I'm not sure which yet, but one of them will do it.'

'Must we discuss this?' Roz asked with weariness. 'You want every man who comes along to murder you.'

'I'll be right one of these days.'

'You won't because it's not about them, it's all about you. You may see things hidden or buried in other people's lives, but you have a blind spot about yourself.'

'You could be right.' It was a thought.

'I know I am.'

'Maybe.'

'About me, as well. Thank God.'

'Oh, I know things about you.'

A laugh. 'Such as?'

'Wouldn't you like to know.'

'If there was anything.'

'You're not my real sister.'

'Oona. Look at my face some time, and then go take a peek in the mirror. Let me know the results.'

'That might not mean anything.'

'Where do you get such foolish ideas?'

'The telly.' They both laughed. Then: 'He asked me, did I have a boyfriend.'

'Who?'

'The man. Spence.'

'What did you tell him?'

'I always tell the truth, you know that.'

'So?'

'Nothing. Just so you know.'

'It's not as if you ever wanted one.'

'No . . .'

'Did you?'

'Not a boy, no.'

They both laughed again, and Roz sat up to turn round. She used a fingertip to splash a couple of drops of water onto Oona's face. Oona smiled but said nothing. Her eyes were shut, and her face was like an island floating in the suds and blue water.

'So pretty,' Roz said softly.

'Just pretty?'

Another splash, another smile. 'You're starting to get all waterlogged and rubbery. Time to get out.'

'In a minute.'

'It's bad for your skin, love.'

'Everything is. Light. Water. Heat. Cold.'

'Not everything.'

'Yes, it is.'

Roz slid a hand into the water and ran it lightly along the inside of Oona's thigh. 'Not everything.'

'Mmmm.'

'Come again?'

Oona could tell Roz was grinning. 'Mmm-hmm.'

'First, the shaver.'

'Again, already?'

'Just a touch.'

Oona got up and stepped out of the tub. While the water was draining, she turned on the tap and quickly washed her hair. Roz towelled her down and applied a few smears of shaving cream. Oona sat on the edge of the tub with her legs wide apart and worked on her hair with a brush and dryer.

'So pretty.'

'Just pretty?'

'Beautiful . . .'

Oona smiled. 'Which part of me do you mean?'

'All of you.'

Roz gave her a teasing lick. They went into the bedroom and Oona stretched out face down. Her hair was fluffy, though still moist in places, and it reached nearly to the base of her spine. Roz carefully moved it aside and rubbed Oona's back and legs and arse with witch hazel. It evaporated quickly, but it had a very pleasant tingle and it cooled her skin. Roz followed it with a woodruff-scented herbal cream. Followed that with her tongue, in deeper but still-teasing exploration.

Oona rolled over, hair across her face and tumbling over the edge of the bed. She let Roz make love to her. This is how the angels make love. It is pure and beautiful and should never end. If only it could be the two of them – far away from anywhere and anyone. A cottage in the Highlands, the distant north, and close to the sea. There would be a coastal village, very small, where they could get food and supplies, but they wouldn't be a part of village life. People would be polite and friendly when they went to town but otherwise would leave them alone. Surely they could afford that now. A lot of money had come their way over the last couple of years, and all thanks to her.

If they lived that far away from people, there could be no intrusions. Her mind and heart free of it all. It was a little like trying to imagine heaven. Why not? Why was she here in the crowded north-eastern corner of America? It was all wrong, it did her no good, never would.

Because you can't go back.

She wasn't sure she believed that any more. Besides, it must be better to die at home than in some foreign place.

Roz worked her with tongue and lips and teeth, and Oona gave herself to it. Thought dissolved, a kind of release, and it was good, very good. But, as always, sex was a kind of parole that in due course would be revoked. The hazy glow faded and you found yourself back in the same old prison, body and soul. What was my sin? Where did I go wrong? But she knew, she knew.

As always, Oona cried. She showered Roz with kisses of pure affection, feeling as if her heart was laced through with rivers of happiness and sorrow, bewildered.

A drink, a smoke, Chrissie Hynde singing – Roz's choice, and Oona would follow it later with the Battlefield Band, the blessed sound of crazy Scotsmen wailing.

The Highlands were so empty. They had to find a place there some day. Let me live in the heather and peat and misty rain, and one day let me fall down and die there. Let the kelpie take me, and God forgive me for my sin.

A cloud of spices hit her nostrils, strange, unfamiliar and burning. Her eyesight was jarred, her mind swam in a fog of dark colours. The glass slipped out of Oona's hand, thumping distantly on the carpet. She tried to hold onto her cigarette, shovelled it blindly towards the ashtray when it burned her skin. She tried to stand but everything was aswirl and she dimly felt Roz taking her naked body in her arms, trying to lead her down and onto the bed, to settle her. It was the same old thing.

'*Ah – ah – ah – agghhh—*'

Struggling just to gasp, because the air wouldn't flow into her and her body wouldn't draw it. Teeth chattering, and just as quick as that she was drowning on air, sucking it in like a river or an ocean. It tasted silvery, ran like mercury in her throat. Oona's fingers fluttered uselessly, she wanted to hold Roz close to her but her hands wouldn't work.

'*When the Laird – when the Laird—*'

Roz had her on the bed now, but Oona's body shook and jumped uncontrollably and Roz had to lie on her, containing her to some extent with the naked warmth and strength of her own body.

'Okay, it's okay, love,' Roz crooned comfortingly. 'Here I am, right here, right with you, love. Can you feel me?'

'*Went to – went to – wentto wentto—*'

'I know, I know.' Stroking Oona's face and hair.

Bam bam bam, a man's face poking into hers, her eyes and brain, like shards of glass lancing into her, the taste of blood on her tongue and the heat of it on her lips, Roz clamping a hand between her teeth to keep her from biting.

The man's hands around her throat—

His head seems to be inside hers, crowding her brain to the corners of her skull, crushing the awareness out of her until it is reduced to a dark, reptilian glimmering. It goes on this way, and he hammers her into a dull, sensate residue, a thing consigned to the mud, barely alive. He leaves her there, as if she were an abandoned house in some remote glen of the Highlands, leaves her to crumble and collapse in on herself.

Then he is gone and she is not. Her body hums down to a

low vibration, quivering. Her skin itches and she feels as if things were growing all over her, invading her – moss, lichen, spider's web, snail's slime. Skin flaking like rust. She can breathe but the air is like fine dust, all dust in her.

'*Aaaahhhhrrrrggggghhhh—*'

Blood bubbles in her nostrils, life bitterly storming back from the inside. Such a disappointment. Oona gasps now, getting hold of her breath again, cycling down. A gentle voice drifts into her awareness. Roz.

'All right now. It's all right now.'

'Unh . . . unh . . . unh . . .'

'You're all right, love.'

Oona tried to force a smile but had no idea whether her face complied. The usual calamity, nothing special. Roz had a bit of a smile, the signal to her. They had been through this a million times, they knew the drill.

Long ago and far away some men had put her brain under a big microscope and taken a peek. Had given her all these tests. Told her it was nothing. That is, it was something, to judge by all these events – but nothing they could find. No temporal lobe thingy. No organic fruit-bruises. Electrical system, check. Blood, same thing. Chemical, spot-on.

Even the shrink said she was a sweet lass, an angel, weally. It was all dweadfully stwange. Perhaps she would outgwow it. If not in this lifetime, maybe in the next.

Oona still missed Dr MacLeod, thought of him every now and then. She had told him one day that he gave her a metallic feeling, most peculiar. He laughed. Died in a motor crash a month later. All these years since, and never a glimmer from him. Which, by now, was a pretty bad sign.

It wasn't Oona's fault, and she didn't blame herself for it. That one wasn't her doing. The damage had been done long before then, but it was the first time Oona noticed – all of the things she noticed.

Someone would have to end her life to right the wrong she'd done. That much was certain. She couldn't do it herself, or she would have long ago. A man would have to come and do it. And it would involve water.

Roz led her slowly into the bathroom. Oona saw herself in the mirror, her face covered with freckles of blood, her skin streaked and blotchy with shades of pale. Eyes lost, but coming round again. Too bad. Roz ran warm water and washed her with a face cloth. Oona felt like putty.

'Better?'

'Oh, sure,' Oona replied. She gave a bitter laugh. 'It was just a light brush, that time.'

PART II

10

'You have to hand it to the Germans,' Oliver said, stopping long enough to glance at the CD case. 'Even when they sing love songs it sounds like they're putting the boot in.'

'It does not,' Carrie said, smiling.

'I'm going to shower and change now.' He started up the stairs to the master suite. 'You're not ready, are you?'

'Yes.'

'What, already?'

'Yes.'

He checked his watch. 'You're not in any great hurry,' he said, with good-natured sarcasm. 'I'll be down in about twenty minutes.'

'Fine.'

She thought Oliver was taking it fairly well. He had agreed to drive Carrie to New Haven and participate in the first session with her. He didn't like the idea very much, but he was trying to be a good sport about it.

Carrie had taken an immediate liking to Rosalind – which had soon become Roz as the two of them talked at the first meeting. It might be a bit of an act but Roz came across as concerned and eager to help. She seemed familiar with some of what Carrie had been experiencing. No question, it was all part of Oona's territory.

That meeting with Roz was a help in itself. Carrie felt as if she had someone on her side now, someone who knew about these matters. Something unique had intruded into her life. It was frightening, disturbing, threatening, disorienting – and more. It had the potential to unravel the whole fabric of her everyday life, but Carrie was not about to let that happen. She would do whatever it took to resist, and understand.

The session was scheduled for four in the afternoon, and Roz had told her that it could be as brief as half an hour or that it might run on into the evening. Carrie had no idea what to expect but the edginess and anticipation she felt was good. If she were to do nothing else, at least she was going on the offensive for once, and there was a measure of satisfaction in that.

It was madness, but hopefully of a trivial and passing kind. Oliver believed that all of life, to some extent, was a matter of consenting to the illusions of others while still inhabiting and preserving your own. Carrie saw herself as a designer whose work was useful and, in some way, important to people. Oliver regarded himself as a discoverer and developer, whose work had some social or cultural role, clothes being a small but important element in human behaviour. Even the psychic Oona probably believed that her trade was a vital service to needy people, quite apart from any cosmic significance she undoubtedly attributed to it.

None of it really matters in the long run, but ... These are the kind of illusions we all carry around with us, so that we can continue to do what we do and somehow make it from one day to the next. People need a rationale.

But Oliver didn't want to see this nonsense become the focal point of Carrie's life, the central illusion. He couldn't put up with that. It would be the same as losing her.

He and Carrie didn't talk much on the way. Traffic was light and they made good time along the Connecticut coast. They were early enough to stop for a snack. They sat out in the car with the roof down. Carrie had a large cup of ice cream, Oliver iced tea and a cigarette.

'Oliver, you're not going to say anything, are you? I mean, if you see something that's obviously wrong or kind of—'

'Faked?'

'Staged. Yes.'

'Cheesecloth dangling from a bent coat hanger, a skip in the tape-recording of eerie sounds and mystic voices?'

'You won't point it out and make a fuss, will you?'

'That would be bad form.'

'We'll talk about it later, when we're alone.'

'Of course.'

'I'm not saying don't look for that, because I will. If it turns out to be hokum, you know I'll drop it.'

'That's the attitude, ducks.'

He had the right attitude as well, Oliver thought. Tolerant and sympathetic, but occasionally amused or embarrassed by it, he would show no hint of belief. The more Carrie persisted in this, the more awkward she would feel. Sooner or later, she would snap out of it.

'Oliver, isn't it?'

'Y-yes.'

He was seldom caught that unawares. Hard to believe, but he could see that it was true. The rollerblading dolly who'd spent ten minutes chatting with him the last time was Oona, the medium. Oliver had to smile, and she returned it. She didn't let on that they'd already met so he didn't say anything either.

Clever, amusing, but a bit too much. If he had been on his guard when he entered the house, he was doubly so now. People who play little games like that need to be watched.

So did the other one, Roz. She was in on the joke, he could see that at a glance. Sisters, and Roz the older by two or three years, he would guess.

Oona wore a long, loose-skirted dress, mossy green. She was barefoot and had a thin piece of braided black leather wound tightly two or three times around one wrist. Another strip, like rawhide or a bootlace, circled her throat. No jewellery, though he couldn't see her ears for all of the hair – unpinned now, it was a wide black river flowing from her head.

Roz, in contrast, wore industrially faded blue jeans, plain

loafers and a white oxford shirt. An opal ring, a clutch of very small hoops in each ear. Fiery auburn hair.

He hadn't expected anything like these two. But he was fast at adjusting, and now he felt alert with curiosity and suspicion. They might be a visual treat but that was all the more reason to be wary and watchful. He wouldn't trust them for a minute.

The women were chatting earnestly but about nothing of any importance. Oliver followed them into a large L-shaped room with the short foot along the back of the house. Glass doors opened onto a small patio. The ceiling and bare walls were matte white, the floor glossy oak with a few expensive oriental rugs scattered about. There was very little furniture, a couple of torchères, some floor mats and a lot of plants in stands and urns, artfully arranged.

The main portion looked like a chapel or meditation room. There was no altar or shrine as such, but a shallow stone basin of clear water placed in a large bed of black sand apparently served as the visual focus.

The windows faced south and west, and at present were shaded with thin curtains that admitted soft light. Roz was talking about people who blocked out any light and took all kinds of odd steps to avoid so-called interference with psychic vibrations, which she and Oona seemed to find amusing as well as unnecessary.

Oliver scanned the room carefully, but there was hardly anywhere to hide props or electronic devices. They might have tiny mikes or camera lenses planted where he wouldn't spot them. They could have speakers mounted flush to the floor, under the rugs, or behind painted-over paper spots in the walls. If so, he was confident he'd notice when they were used.

They went to the smaller side area at the back of the house. It was separated by a half-wall topped with a full-length planter overflowing with graceful arcing ferns and vines that trailed to the floor. Inside, there was a raised platform along three sides of the walls, covered with thick mats. Oona's place was in the corner, diagonally opposite the narrow entrance: it was a couple of inches higher. There were two more stone basins, though much smaller, built into the platform in the other two corners; each one contained fine white sand that had squiggles or lines drawn in it but no water. The open floor in the centre of the area was covered with deep green carpet.

Oh, yes, it was all very California. Not quite what he had been expecting, but in its own way certainly no surprise.

Roz drew the curtains across the large glass doors. They were of the same thin material as on the other windows, and the afternoon sun showered the secluded area with a diffuse golden light. Must be a bit drab and grey on rainy days, Oliver thought, but then he noticed some short fat candles strategically placed.

'Would either of you care for something to drink?' Roz asked, as they sat down on the platform.

'No, thank you,' Carrie answered.

Oliver shook his head. 'Can I smoke?'

'Sure you can,' Roz answered. 'Move one of the candles, and use the glass dish as an ashtray.'

'I smoke,' Oona said. 'Some people will tell you that drink or tobacco will get in the way of a successful hearing like this, but I don't find that to be the case. Anything that helps people to relax helps the process.'

'What about disbelief?' Oliver asked. He saw a sudden flash of alarm on Carrie's face. Good God, she's probably thinking, We haven't even started yet and he's at it. 'I just thought I ought to let you know ahead of time that I'm pretty sceptical about all of this, and if that's going to jeopardize—'

'It's no problem,' Oona said, smiling. 'That's another of those silly things you might hear. You'd think we were using a delicate little radio set that has to be tuned just right. But if a person or spirit wants to communicate with us from another level of existence, it won't be blocked all that easily.' Oona glanced at Carrie. 'You've learned that already.'

'Yes.'

'Well, good,' Oliver said drily. He offered Oona a Senior Service, and she took it with a grateful nod. She reached out to touch his hand lightly as he lit it for her. Oliver was seated to her left and Carrie to her right, while Roz had taken a place somewhat removed from them, near the entrance. She had a notepad and pen, ready to jot down vital messages from Beyond.

'I like to start by telling people that I really don't have a clue about this,' Oona went on. 'We use terms like *spirits* and *communication* and *levels of existence*, but we honestly don't know what they mean – or if they mean anything at all. I don't have an answer to the question of life after death. I could claim that I do and make one up for you, but you would never know for sure if it was true or not. I don't want to mislead anybody.'

She sat cross-legged, and she rocked forward and back again very slightly as she spoke. Her hands moved in small, restrained gestures that demolished the thin plume of smoke rising from her cigarette. She puffed quickly, didn't inhale, and soon tapped it out in a glass dish. Her voice was clear and well defined, with the echo of an accent that Oliver remembered.

'Now let me tell you what little I do know,' Oona continued. 'I seem to have an ability to *sense* or to *receive* and *relay* bits of *information*.' One hand opening and closing tightly, accenting the words. 'Some of it may mean something to you, but most of it probably won't. You have to watch and listen carefully, because figuring it out later is the tricky part. It usually seems to be about some person who is dead, but again you'll have to make what you can of it. I won't sit here and tell you it's a real message from a departed soul, because I just don't know whether it is. I don't know why or how this happens, or what it is. I can't turn it on or off, it happens or it doesn't, but it usually works best in situations like this. I need to be close to certain people. The women are more sensitive to it, and that helps, but it's also passive. The men seem to be the enablers. That's why I like to work with couples. It's even better with two couples, but this is your first time.' Then Oona stopped, and appeared to smile at herself. 'I should tell you that this part is still guesswork, based on my experiences with a lot of people. I've been this way a while now.'

That last was an odd throwaway that didn't sound like part

of her regular patter. Oliver was struck by the offhand note of regret in it.

'Now, I also have to warn you that you might see some things that disturb you. Don't worry about me, I'll be fine. You won't cause any harm if you interfere, but it isn't necessary. If you have any concern, look at Roz. She's been through it all before. Of course, that doesn't mean you're stuck here. If you choose to leave, you're free to do so at any time. Okay?'

They nodded. The look on Carrie's face was a bit worrying. She appeared to be buying into it in blocks of shares. He didn't like that.

'Any questions?' None. 'Now the embarrassing part.' Oona took Oliver's hand, held it in both of hers, and began rubbing it lightly, the way a blind person would explore something without seeing it. 'I need to feel and touch you. Just a little, not in a naughty way,' she was quick to add, grinning. 'Something about the contact, and the feel of your pulse – ooh, there's yours, so strong – somehow it seems to help.'

The warm-up was over and she was getting into it now. There was more liveliness in her eyes – Oliver took notice of them, as if for the first time. A beautiful shade of deep blue, they were of ordinary size and shape, with fine lashes and no make-up. She had a way of letting the eyelids droop partially closed as if she were about to doze off, then swiftly opening them very wide – at which point her eyes appeared to flare with light and hunger. Oliver knew that look, and began to feel intrigued.

'So much, very fast,' she said, still rubbing his hand. Her eyes moving about, fixed on nothing. Her delicate touch moved up his wrist, under the cuff of his jacket. 'Very strong.' Now her eyes locked on his. 'So many rich moments.'

Oliver wondered how to take that. Oona slid closer to him and began to feel his face, again very much like a blind person. She seemed to be looking into herself, or some invisible point in the air. His forehead, eyebrows, eyes, cheeks, lips – she roved down his face. Oliver gave a tiny wink to Carrie, who seemed to find all this perfectly valid and even fascinating. It was much too fashionable for Oliver, touchy-feely nonsense. But he could enjoy the softness of her touch, the texture of her skin on his. Another time, another place . . .

'None of it's clear,' Oona said, somewhat like a tour guide describing things the passengers couldn't see. 'But there is so much and it has such density.'

Yes, yes, Oliver thought impatiently.

'Immense, immense.' It was almost a gasp.

Oona suddenly swung round, and repeated the entire process with Carrie. There was something approaching a smile on her face now, as if she found Carrie a more agreeable subject, easier to read. She took Carrie's hand and rubbed it against her face. The incipient smile vanished, a look of uncertainty taking hold in her features.

'Yes, yes, yes, yes. Women are so sensitive, they carry all of it around with them all the time.' Oona was talking rapidly, without focusing on anyone in particular. 'Sometimes I can get a little carried away at this, so if it starts to bother you, just push me off like you would a puppy who's too friendly. It won't bother me or ruin anything. But saying something to me might not work, the noise is starting to come into me and I probably won't hear you soon.'

Oona's hands were exploring Carrie's neck and throat, and it was as if she had never encountered that portion of human anatomy before. Very small, tentative touches, slowly moving over every inch from the collarbone up to and along the jaw. Carrie blinked a couple of times and held herself rather stiffly, but she didn't appear uncomfortable.

'So much noise,' Oona said plaintively. There were signs of distress emerging on her face. 'It's like a wave, and you tumble into it. The sea.'

Oona nearly pulled Carrie over, placing her hand on her own chest. Carrie's eyes widened at this more intimate move, but she didn't resist. Almost immediately Oona let go, and turned again to Oliver. She did the same thing, grabbing his hand and holding it flat to her chest. He couldn't feel much of her breast but he knew at once why Carrie had looked so startled. Oona's heart was banging at a gallop. It actually worried Oliver. The girl had a thin sheen of sweat on her forehead now. Her eyes were wide open and as brilliantly vacant as polished gemstones. She rocked back and forth, more energetically now. Oh, there – his hand slipped in her grasp as she moved and he had a brief sense of her breast, petite and girlish. Oona pulled his hand to her side and held it very tightly; she did the same with Carrie on the other side, the three of them linked now with Oona in the middle.

'The sea, the sea, the sea . . .'

Over and over again, like a mantra, but uttered with a voice that was low and urgent, as if she were repeating instructions to herself. Her hands might be small and delicate, but there was tremendous strength in her grip – and even as Oona squeezed, her thumb moved about in a tight circle and stroked his skin as if it were a lucky penny.

'The sea, the sea . . . Coming, coming . . .'

Well, if it's good for you. Oliver's mood was switching off and on now. He was alternately engrossed and indifferent. Oona certainly put herself into the performance, say that for her, but he still couldn't help thinking that that's all it was. A clever performance.

She let go of their hands and slid back against the cushions as if she wanted to sink into them. She squirmed to one side and then the other, as if to shrink away from something. Her eyes fluttered in bursts, and fell shut more often than not. What she said now was an indistinct blur of words, a garbled drone with a harsh edge. Her hands lay at her sides, shaking helplessly. The fingers moved slowly, numbly, in empty gestures.

Then she let out a frightening yelp and her hands shot down between her legs, buried in the folds of her loose dress. Oliver noticed her toes, stretched rigidly and twisted. Her body quaked and the rough drone had become a prolonged whimper. Her mouth hung open and her chin was wet with flowing saliva. The cords in her neck stood out sharply, her jaw shuddered. The words came, a rapid staccato, heavily accented, yet disjointed.

'*Hie to moorish gills and rocks prowling wolf and wily fox hie you fast he wants nor turn your view he wants he wants though the lamb bleats you you you to the ewe he wants oh couch oh couch your trains he wants he wants your flight your safety parts with parting night on distant echo borne the pilgrim on his way comes the hunter's early horn he wants you wants you wants you the the the the torch the torch that cheats benighted imp and fay is done is done is done—*'

It was cut off violently. Oona recoiled as if she had just been slapped hard. Her mouth was open, jaw rigid. Her nostrils pulsed and her breath was loud and ugly. She seemed to be in the throes of hyperventilation. Oliver's eyes glanced briefly toward Roz but she was writing a note, unconcerned.

A roaring gasp, and then Oona rolled over and threw her arms around Carrie's waist. She pressed her face to Carrie's hip, her eyes moving frantically.

'The sea, the sea, the sea . . .'

Her hands patted Carrie's arms, and she began to pull away. She slid across the cushion until the top of her head bumped into Oliver's leg. She was on her back, fists held together over her breasts. Her legs were somewhat apart, and her body rocked from the waist down. The bottom of her dress had risen to her knees, and her slender calves and small feet looked oddly vulnerable as the muscles in them strained and contracted. Her hair fell over most of her face now. The voice that came through it was deeper, huskier, almost masculine.

'*The torch the torch the finger flames flames fingers he has to kill me kill me kill me come to kill me come come come hie now to moorish kills hie now to empty spaces FATHER come to kill come come come close to me now now father what father what father what he wills kills fingers flames neck—*'

She stopped suddenly, eyes bulging open. She resumed almost immediately, but her voice was completely different.

'*No no no you don't want Chik Pavan sir that is not for you*

dear sir that is singing and dancing and wasting all of your time
sir you want Ballapul dear sir that is the very place—'

Oliver pressed a hand to the back of his neck.

Oona seemed to collapse into herself, gasping, trembling and murmuring. A little-girl voice that said nothing and trailed off in tiny sobs. Tears filled her eyes and she curled up weakly in a foetal position.

No one moved. Everybody was silent for perhaps a couple of minutes, sensing that it wasn't over yet.

Oona slowly raised her head. She was chalk-white, her eyes still staring into space. Without using her hands, she sat up in a slow but fluid motion. She didn't seem to be breathing at all. Her hands open, palms up, as if in a question. Oliver saw blood, tiny red crescents where her nails had cut into the flesh. Then he saw a trickle of blood appear in one nostril. It ran down to her lip and into her open mouth. She didn't move her mouth, lips or throat, and yet more words came, like breath, and they bubbled the blood. The bubbles burst and then reappeared. The voice was male, rich and resonant. Familiar.

'He turns back rushes back to you wants you watch out watch
out child he turns bad rushes bad to you in the compound bad the
compound he turns bad runs watch out – CHILD—'

Oona lifted one hand to her mouth, as if in shock and fear at the sight of something unseen. There was blood all over the lower portion of her face when she began to gag. Her tongue came out a little, her throat stretched tight and choking sounds barked out of her heaving body. Oliver felt a drop of blood land on his hand, but he didn't move or take his eyes from Oona. She reached for a cushion, as if to steady herself, and then lowered herself to it. Curled up. Eyes closing.

Carrie looked utterly stricken.

Roz gestured for them to follow her.

Yes, Oona would be fine, Roz assured them when they were in the front room. Oliver accepted a glass of Scotch and knocked it off quickly. He smoked a cigarette and stood close to Carrie and Roz. They were talking about words like *father* and *child*. Maybe they were important, maybe others were important. But these were just Roz's impressions. Carrie should think about everything she had heard. Words didn't always mean what they appeared to mean, and it usually took repeated sessions for their true significance to emerge clearly.

'I've never seen her go into it so quickly,' Roz was saying to Carrie. 'She usually meanders all over the place for a while before she finds her way into it. But today she got on track in no time at all. I can't get over it.'

Oliver walked in short circles, impatient. He wanted to get out of there, and return home. Call Joe Barone on the telephone. There were things he needed to know, and do.

How did she get the blood in her nose? Was it something she did when her face was down, out of sight for a second?

How did she speak without moving her lips or mouth or any of the muscles in her throat? A speaker in the rug beneath her? He could swear the words came from her but . . .

There were tricks, there were ways to do all kinds of things that looked amazing at first. But . . .

What about her heartbeat? Oliver wished he could have taken her pulse towards the end, when she was really flying. But there were even ways to do that too. And yet . . .

None of those things mattered.

Because at certain moments Oona had found the correct voice. The exact voice of . . .

'My father,' Carrie was saying. Her eyes shiny. 'He called me *child* like that when I was very young. I know it sounds stiff and impersonal but it wasn't, not the way he said it . . .'

Carrie wiped her eyes and looked away. Roz rubbed her back comfortingly. No doubt Roz had seen this many times before. She would be experienced in pushing all the right buttons. The touch of sympathy, the look of concern, the assurances—

'That was *his* voice,' Carrie repeated, almost as if she were arguing with herself. But as happy as she was stunned.

Yes, it was the old boy's voice. Uncanny, but somehow true. Now it was too late to nitpick their techniques. Oliver went to the window. Grey dusk outside. A cigarette.

It wasn't that Oona might be genuine – he could see that in some way or sense that had to be the case.

So it didn't matter.

It wasn't that she had somehow conjured up the very voice of Carrie's long-dead father, astounding as that was.

He didn't care much about that.

It was the other voice that had risen from Oona's throat. A voice from Bombay. It was another lifetime. No one in the world knew that voice, except Oliver. That was what mattered.

That was what had terrified him.

11

'What do you mean you heard from Fiona?'

'It was in a dream.'

Charley stared at her. Jan didn't handle it very well. She appeared visibly to be losing confidence in her own words as soon as she spoke them. She blinked a couple of times and looked like she wanted to say more but couldn't find anything.

'You saw her in a dream,' Charley prompted.

'Not exactly.'

'What then? Just tell me the whole thing.'

'I saw her pram,' Jan said falteringly. 'I know it was hers from the rattles and plastic doodads that hung across it, for the baby to look at and touch – remember?'

'Yes.'

'The sea was in the background, like at the house. You know how you just know some things in a dream?'

She was looking hopefully at him for confirmation of almost every sentence. 'Yes.'

'Well, I knew it was our house, even though I didn't see it. The pram and the view of the sea were exactly the same. And the sky turned very black.' That was enough to summon tears to her eyes, but Jan blinked them back and continued. 'And I heard her voice. She said it was all right.'

'She didn't have a voice,' Charley said calmly. 'She was an infant. She didn't have a human speaking voice.'

'But it was Fiona.'

'How do you know?'

'I just know.'

Jesus, why argue? 'Did you actually see her?'

'No.'

'But she said it was all right.'

'Y-yes.'

'What was all right?' Say it aloud, woman.

Jan was close to tears again. 'What happened. She doesn't blame us. You weren't there, but I was. Charley, Fiona doesn't blame me for it.'

Jan put a hand over her mouth, then held onto her jaw. Her entire head was shaking with nervous emotion.

'Ah, Jesus.' Charley put his arms around her and pulled her to his chest. Now she let go, sobbing and trembling freely. 'Of course she doesn't blame you or me, love. How could she? There, there now, come on. It's bad enough it happened, but there's no point in guilt or blame. It happened, that's all. It was a long time ago. It's over and done with. Remember what everybody told us then? We have to let her go. Let her rest in peace.'

'She told me.'

'Well, good. There you are.'

Oh, yes, the poor woman was still haunted by it. Charley had known that all along, but Jan seldom allowed it to break through to the surface like this.

'When did you have this dream?' he asked.

'A few nights ago.'

'Have you ever had it before?' A nod against his chest, but Jan wouldn't face him. 'Many times?'

'Yes.' A tiny voice.

'Over the years?'

'Yes.'

'Why didn't you ever tell me?'

'I couldn't.' Now Jan pulled back her head and looked up at him. 'It was always just the pram and the sea, nothing else. No voice. I didn't want you to feel any worse than you already did. But it was different this time. She spoke to me. Charley, it was like Fiona's soul communicating directly with mine and she told me it was all right. It was not our fault.'

He nodded. There had never been any forgiveness, until now. Sixteen years of suffering and secret penance for imaginary sins that were never committed, and now, at last, she lets you off the hook. And me, by extension. Well, how nice.

But it wasn't Fiona, of course. It was Jan, his poor broken lady wife, Jan. Her mind, in its self-torture, had finally found a way out of the anguish. A dream. If it actually worked, fine, but Charley had no faith in it. The dream and Fiona's voice were just another delusion. Somehow, it wouldn't last. It would lose its potency, and the curse would come back to haunt Jan again. A month, two months from now, some time soon – and she'd find a way to start blaming herself once more.

The strange workings of the human mind. Just to think about it was enough to deflate any anger, and leave him feeling merely sad. Another sad eejit in the toils of a remorseless fate. What to do. Have a drink. It occurred to Charley that it might be an extremely good idea to get Jan a bit sozzled, take her to bed and send her to sleep on clouds of erotic bliss. He could do it, if he really put his mind to it – among other things.

'What were you going to tell me?'

Oh dear. Forgot about that part. 'Nothing, really.' He no longer wanted to mention Oona. If Jan thinks she has found peace or absolution, good; let her be.

'It was about Fiona.'

'No, not really.'

'Charley.' Suddenly, alarmingly firm. 'Tell me.'

She could get bloody-minded like that, and he knew there was no way he could avoid giving her at least a partial explanation. So get it out, all of it, and hopefully be done with it. Charley hated these moments.

'I met this woman. A spiritualist, I guess . . .'

He tried to put a negative spin on it, downplayed the entire business and gave the impression that he was only going to bring it up in the first place because it was so odd and silly.

But Jan wasn't having any of that. She listened to him with obvious fascination and seemed to find it all perfectly credible. She nodded constantly, until he suggested that Oona must have learned about the O'Donnells somewhere and was trying to use that to take money from them. He probably didn't even believe it himself any more. Jan frowned at the unlikeliness of it and shook her head. Before he was done, Charley knew he was done.

'It can't be coincidence. Fiona speaks to me in a dream and then reaches out to you through this other woman. She must have more to tell us. It's not over yet.'

'What more can she have to say?' Charley asked in a tone of feeble protest. 'Her message to you ended it, surely.'

'No, I don't think so.'

'Jan, we—'

'We have to find out. We can't just ignore her.'

Ignore her? Listen to yourself, will you? How bizarre. It was never going to end. That was the truth of it. Jan had found a way to forgive herself, but that wasn't good enough. There had to be more. There would always have to be more. Fiona was never going to be truly dead, as long as either of them lived.

God, when it came to life and death people would grab at any crumb of immortality. He despised himself, not least for giving any credence to this. Yes, he had gone to Westville, thinking he had an obligation to do so if there was half a grain of truth in it. And yes, he had half convinced himself that there *was*, and he was going to drag his wife along to a seance.

But now, hearing Jan's dream and seeing her reaction to what he had told her about Oona, he couldn't stand it. Charley felt as if he and Jan were entering a shared madness, a sad, desperate folly that would do neither of them any good at all.

He hated it.

By the time they went for their first session with Oona, his anger had burned down to a low-grade heat, a residual smouldering of resentment. Charley no longer had any control over the events in progress. Very well. He would go along because there was no easy way out. Besides, he was largely responsible for this state of affairs.

Charley paid little attention to the palaver at the outset, the explanations that were not explanations, the playing down of mystical expectations in order to build them up. It was a clever routine, what he took in of it, but he had no use for it. He had one thing in mind, and that was to keep an eye on Jan. If it got to be too much for her, he would take her away. By force, should it come to that.

The next step was an unexpected touch. Literally. He liked the way Oona started crawling all over them. Himself, anyway. A pleasing bit of contact. Oona was a bit young for Charley's play group – he liked to graze the graduate pastures – but she was a toothsome little lass. For her part, Jan endured it with a stoic expression. Not the physical-contact type, Jan. No doubt there was a rationale for this business: you have to get in touch with your body before you can get in touch with the spirits, some such ethereal New Age folderol. He could think of another one: if you rub the punters the right way, they'll be in a better mood to buy the rest of the performance.

'The flow, the flow, the flow . . .'

Quite right too, Charley thought. We must go with the flow. Whatever the flow was supposed to be.

Oona seemed to be going into a mild trance state. If you're willing to credit that sort of thing. Charley glanced at Roz, by herself in the corner. All business. Roz was closer to his play group, and a woman with more of a body on her. He looked back to Oona, who was writhing impressively.

'Wenda, wenda, wenda, wenda . . .'

She could wriggle all over him, as far as he was concerned. Oona's hand patted the air in front of her face, and she had the look of the blind in her eyes. She'd broken out in a sweat and fetching little tendrils of black hair clung to her face – then Charley noticed the way her cheeks changed colour so quickly. Red as a virgin's blush, then chalk white and streaky. As far as he could tell she didn't have any lipstick on but there was a bluish shading in the skin about Oona's mouth. Was she asthmatic?

'Wenda – wenda – wenda—'

Oona's body froze. Her eyes fluttered and her voice changed sharply, became a halting child-like singsong.

'When the last laird of Ravenswood to Ravenswood did ride to

124

woo to woo a dead maiden to be his bride beyond a beyond take
me beyond a kelpie's flow to Ravenswood take me beyond a I am
beyond a kelpie's flow flow flow the laird the laird to woo beyond
to be a dead maiden stable his steed in the kelpie's flow a dead
maiden beyond his name lost for ever glow ever more lost lost—'

So this is the start of it, Charley thought. All the same, he
couldn't help but feel a prickle of disquiet as the nerves in the
skin on his arms and face reacted to Oona's recitation. This
was the kind of thing that had caught the Brownes' attention,
for certain. Charley filed a couple of quick mental notes for
future consideration. It seemed so convenient, the way she
made mention of Ravenswood right off the bat. More important was the way Oona pronounced the words 'beyond a'. Run
together, with a marginally lengthened 'o' in there, it could be
mistaken for 'Fiona'.

Oona had gone limp, but the rigidity came back into her
body again just a few seconds later. Her vacant eyes widened,
her jaw extended itself unnaturally, and the spate of words
resumed in a shuddering rhythm.

'Hie to moorish gills and rocks wily wolf and prowling fox O
birds of omen dark and foul night-crow raven bat and owl oh no
oh no oh no leave the sick man to his dream all night all night all
night he hears your screams as the laird comes down to Ravens-
wood to who to who to who is dead the dead maiden beyond the
kelpie's flow oh no oh no birds of omen night-crow raven bat and
owl leave him leave him ghaist-like she fades she fades O kelpie
quench in bog and fen beyond a bog and fen the laird the laird is
lost for ever more for ever glow his name lost for ever more—'

The girl subsided for the time being. She looked empty and
weak, and her breath came in shallow gasps. Charley had to
admit that there was a kind of raw power to the performance.
There was no doubting Oona's effort. She put herself into it
and flat-out raved. It could work like a spell on you, if you
let it.

But years of labouring over words had taught Charley a
thing or two. Oh, he caught the reference to Everglo all right,
and it was understandably disturbing. And yet, it could just as

easily have been 'ever glow', and have no relevance to them at all. Ravenswood was the only unambiguous term but it was a place name, probably a common one throughout Britain and Ireland; it might sound like a strong link, but it was actually the weakest. And if Fiona was a misreading of 'beyond a', which was quite possible in the fervid excesses of Oona's delivery, then the whole thing was meaningless to them and collapsed like a house of straw.

There were other parts that had sounded fascinating, but he would have to consider them later. Oona was stirring again. Her voice was shrill now, an accusatory cry. Her fingers, stiff and claw-like, pulled the skin on her face back and raked through her wild mane of hair.

'You don't want a baby I don't want a baby you don't want a child I don't want a child – a CHILD – watch out CHILD the bird of omen night-crow raven bat and owl the laird comes for you who woo the dead maiden ever more you don't you don't you don't want a baby I don't want a baby will kill you wax wax wax—'

Charley's eyes were on Jan. At the eruption of those first words, she flinched visibly. Her hands were twisted in a fierce grip of each other on her lap. Don't you see, love? It's all a fog of suggestion and similarities, designed to let you associate freely and fill in the gaps. It was so hurtful and untrue.

' – wax wax wax wax wax—'

Another temporary subsidence. But the yapping repetition of the word *wax* got through to Charley. Paraffin was a form of wax. A derivative, wasn't it? Refined, distilled, whatever. It had been an Everglo paraffin space heater that had taken the life of their daughter. First the fumes, the smoke, and then the flames. Nearly took Jan as well.

Charley looked from Jan back to Oona – her face was cherry red now, the sudden sight of it making him catch his breath. She had wedged herself hard against the cushions, close to Jan, with her legs extended towards Charley. Little bare feet and red welts on her calves – appearing, it seemed, even while he watched. It must have been a momentary illusion, and they had been there all along. Oona's voice turned flatter and broader.

'*Font – Font – Font – Fontane – Fontayna – dead maiden stable your steed by the edge of the lake where the kelpie waits the laird the laird of Fontane Fontayna Fon Tay—*'

Abruptly back to a previous Scots snarl.

'*The corbies wait the corbies keep the corbies come when you fall asleep oh no don't oh please don't do that to me the corbies wait please don't FATHER the corbies keep MOTHER the corbies come when you're asleep Font Font Fontane Fontayna—*'

Oona kicked the air several times, while pressing her face into Jan's arm as if to hide. Hesitant at first, Jan cautiously put an arm around Oona's shoulder and gently stroked her cheek to comfort her.

Charley heard his wife say: 'I know. It's all right.'

What was this? Damned if he knew. Oona had pulled another rabbit out of the hat. Jan had been born and raised in the small southern Wisconsin town of Fontana, which did happen to be on a lake. But, in itself, that fact meant nothing.

Oona tore loose from Jan, sat up and screamed. Her face was racked, and blood oozed over her lips. Her fingers clutched at her forearms compulsively, then picked at the skin on her cheeks. The scream drained her, and when it finally ended in a dying moan she toppled forward across Charley's legs. He caught her, easing her down onto the cushions beside him.

She felt cold, too cold. He looked at Roz, who returned his gaze evenly but said nothing. Jan was weeping. Charley reached for Oona's hand and checked her pulse. Nothing. Somewhere, it's there somewhere. But he couldn't find it. Cold as marble. This was wrong. He tried to find the artery in her neck, but again he failed. Charley put his ear to her chest and forced his mind to concentrate. Surely he would hear a heartbeat, especially coming right after all that exertion. But he heard nothing.

'Leave her be,' Roz told him.

'There's no pulse,' he said. 'She has no heartbeat.'

'It's just that you can't hear it.'

'I'm damn sure I'd hear a heartbeat,' he said angrily.

'It's all right,' Roz insisted. 'This happens. She'll come out of it later, if we leave her be.'

Jan was still crying softly to herself, eyes locked on Oona. The show was over, apparently. Oona was all right? Well, fine. Let her lie where she fell. Blood and screams. It had unnerved him, and now that he was beginning to think again he felt annoyed and put-upon. Words and associations, blood and screams. It was eerie at moments, yes, and finally disturbing, in a way – but if there was a point to all of that, it escaped him.

Charley would have preferred the voice of a ten-thousand-year-old Indian chief, telling them that mankind was despoiling the planet and that they had to change course before it was too late. Well, yes, Chief, now that you put it like that, we have to agree, and we'll get on to it right away. Next time call collect if it's that kind of Big Picture message.

He put his arm around Jan as they left the enclosed area and went to the front room. He noticed that she seemed to be keeping a significant inch or two of space between them.

'Are you all right?'

She merely glanced at him, then away. Apparently not. But at least the tears had stopped. Charley had the uneasy sensation of failure to do the right thing. Somehow. But he hadn't a clue what it was or how to correct the fault. That gave him a feeling of peevish inadequacy and a desire to leave. And a desire to get some serious drink inside him.

But first, the folly-up. Charley made an effort to appear interested as Roz talked to them about meanings, how they should reflect on what they'd heard, and more like that. Jan listened. Said nothing. Jan was sad. Too sad, even for Jan.

A curious shift had taken place. He could see it in the way Roz talked to Jan. This had started out as Charley's problem but now Jan had moved to the centre of it. Jan was the focal point. Jan would want to come back for another session, with or without him. It was obvious from the look on her hungry face, as well as the way Roz concerned herself with Jan.

That bothered him, but only a little. He knew that he would

be expected to tag along in future, to be there for Jan. Had it ever been any different?

'Your wife has a very strong influence,' Roz said to him, by way of casual explanation. Of something, no doubt.

'Really?'

'Yes. Her presence was an enormous help to Oona.'

'How so?' he dared ask.

'In all of it, the entire experience,' Roz answered. 'Women are more sensitive than men, somehow, and that helps.'

Oh, yes. Women are more sensitive. He'd heard that before. Funny how it was always some woman telling you.

'I see.'

Jan was quiet in the car. Too quiet. Charley said nothing until they were back at the apartment. He got himself a towering highball, rye and sweetness. He fired up a large Dominican. He went to Jan, who was pottering about mechanically in the kitchen, rearranging cups and glasses with runic obscurity.

'She never mentioned Fiona at all,' he said.

'Believe me, that doesn't matter.'

'Jan, what we heard tonight was a jumble of words,' Charley said, trying to keep a civil tone. 'Some of them might seem to mean something to you or me, but they don't add up to a single coherent thought or message. They were tossed out there for us to play with, and turn them into something.'

'You saw her,' Jan said sharply. 'You saw what happened to her. The changes she went through.'

'Fainted, I suppose. Overdid the hyper bit.'

'Her body.'

'What about it?'

'The marks on her,' Jan said fiercely. 'She didn't just see something, like in a vision. She experienced it all over again, in her own flesh.'

'No, no, I don't buy that one.'

Jan shook her head. 'You missed it.'

'What?' Charley demanded. 'What did I miss?'

'Fiona is here. Fiona has come for us.'

12

Some of the offerings were so beautiful that Oliver felt close to tears. It was hard to explain, even to himself. He had tried on a few occasions to share his love of stamps with Carrie, but the words always seemed to elude him. She understood the collecting bug and she knew that some stamps were valuable while others were not, and of course she could see the pleasure Oliver got from it. But the passion? Carrie didn't get that at all.

To Oliver stamps were a dazzling universe of miniature art, intricate, layered in arcane history, utterly pure and beautiful. Real stamps, not the modern rubbish with its hideous colours and revolting graphics. Oliver wouldn't touch anything that had been issued since 1945, and most of his collection dated from the nineteenth century. He had been bitten early, and devoted to it ever since. Thanks to his father. The hours the two of them spent together poring over stamps had been the best in Oliver's boyhood.

The Kohler preview left him shaky with delight. He wandered away from it and settled himself in a narrow *bierstube* a short distance from Wilhelmstrasse. Lately, he had been drawn to old German and Swiss cantonal covers: whole envelopes adorned with frankings and cancellations, multiple stamps and other postal markings that were added *en route*, as well as a handwritten name and address. A good cover was an artifact that combined history, geography and a personal human element – an echo from someone's long-forgotten and inconsequential life. A kind of beautiful ghost.

He had Carrie and Lugano coming up at the weekend. He was looking forward to it. It almost hadn't been going to happen at all. Carrie had wanted to come but felt she couldn't take the time off. She had too much work to do now, including the job for her Belgian, and a list of other people who couldn't be kept waiting long. Oliver persuaded her that she could spare two work days. Carrie would fly out Thursday night and arrive in Lugano Friday morning. They would have three days and nights together. She could catch a Monday morning return flight and be back home at the apartment late that afternoon.

A curious peace had taken hold since that shattering first session with Oona. Carrie was in contact with her father. She believed it, and that was all that mattered. Communication wasn't easy – in fact, it was pretty damned hard to figure out just what the old boy might be trying to say to her. But the contact was a reality to her. It gave Carrie a rationale to continue with the psychic process.

It was a bit different for Oliver. Panic. Fear. His life was ending, and not the way he wanted. Oona appeared to know him much too well. That could be a problem. Was a problem. A major problem. Had to be addressed. Solved.

He bought another beer and flipped through the pages of the Kohler catalogue again. No doubt about it, he could spend thirty thousand dollars in Wiesbaden without giving it a second thought. But that would be extravagant for one auction.

At least there was no immediate rush to deal with Oona. She only did two or three sessions a week. Took too much out of her, and she had to recharge her emotional batteries. Something like that. She had other clients, and couldn't take Carrie – and him – again until the end of the month. Time enough for Carrie to reflect, and to prepare herself for the next message from Daddy. Time enough for Oliver to plan, and act.

Question. How much did Oona understand of what she appeared to know? Maybe none of it. That would be great, but he couldn't take a chance. The girl had already made a point of establishing a small zone of secrecy with him by not letting Carrie know that she had met him the week before. A small point, perhaps, but one worth bearing in mind.

Question. How did Oona know about him? Several years ago, Oliver had made an unplanned stopover in Bombay, while *en route* from Bangkok back to London, his suitcases crammed with samples of lush Thai silk. He had never been to India. It was an impulse, a whim. Why not? He could afford to indulge himself like that. A couple of days in Bombay. He might even take a train down the coast and investigate the fabled hippie haven of Goa. Check the scene, meet a few stone burn-outs, drink some beer on the beach. There might be a semi-exotic female waiting for him . . .

But it had been in Bombay, not Goa. And at Ballapul, not Chik Pavan. The little man whose voice Oona had rendered so well that the hair on Oliver's neck had bristled at the first sound of it. The very words. Oona could never know that, not unless the unfortunate little man had come to America and had told her. But he hadn't. He was dead. Oliver had killed him. You have to, if you want somebody dead.

It had been unnecessary and unfortunate, but there you are. His attitude was fairly simple. If the situation comes down to your life or mine, you go first. Oliver hadn't asked for it to happen the way that it did.

Answer. Oona was genuine. On some level, in some way, Oona had an ability to know dead and buried parts of your life. Parts no one else knew, and that you never even thought about any more. Oliver had no idea how she did it, how she arrived at or received this information, but the precise mechanism was beside the point. Oona was genuine. No other explanation would hold.

But her ability was clearly limited. If you thought of it as a powerful searchlight, capable of penetrating the dark nights of the past, then it was also huge and unwieldy. Apparently Oona had little control over it. Moreover, she didn't understand the half of what she revealed. By herself Oona was dangerous, like a tin of explosive chemicals that required proper handling.

But when you added Roz to the mix, all bets were off. There was something very worrying about the efficient note-taker on the edge of events. Calm, cool, capable. Cunning. Calculating. He had to assume the worst about her. Roz was the one who would fit the pieces together. Oona could supply the knowledge. Roz would understand it and use it. Roz was a cunt.

Oliver's eyes went back to the photo of a German cover that broke his heart. A letter envelope sent from Munich to Leicester in 1861. There were five Bayern stamps on it, two 18 Kreuzers in orange-red, and three coat-of-arms lower values in a vertically cut franking strip. Besides the original München cancellation it had acquired a couple of thimble postmarks in England, along with a triangular handstamp that was either a mistake or a display of excessive zeal and self-importance on the part of some provincial clerk. A beautiful specimen, right down to the elegantly looping penmanship in the name and address.

Too expensive, certainly.

Oliver had some ideas. There were any number of things that he could do, but the first step was knowledge. The more he knew about those two women, the better able he would be to handle them appropriately. He didn't want to hurt them, far from it. Oliver found Oona almost irresistibly attractive, with her gorgeous hair and slender neck. He would love to gain one-to-one access to her, so to speak. New Haven was a bit close to home, though, and he still had Roz to consider.

Anyhow. They must be rendered harmless to him.

He finished his beer and checked his watch. Fuck. He went to the bar and got another beer. Ten minutes later, he glanced up from the Kohler catalogue.

'Where the hell have you been?'

'Shopping,' Marthe replied breezily, as she put her bags down on the floor. 'You know how they say, darling. So much leather, so little time.'

Oliver blinked. Perhaps it was witty in German.

'Come here and stand in front of me.'

Marthe did so, her back to the bar. The place was quiet, an unemployed type working the pinball machine and a couple of soggy drinkers trying to stay on their bar-stools. The barman, a Turk, had his nose in the newspaper. Oliver put his hand up

Marthe's skirt and eased a finger into her. She was always ready.

'I like that,' she said.

'You do?'

'Oh, yes.'

'In that case.' Oliver took his hand away from her.

'Oh,' she said, with a pout.

'Let's go back to the Schwarzer.'

'Buy me a drink first.'

'You can have one there.'

'But my feet are in pain here.'

'You must be very happy, then.'

She smiled. 'If you don't buy me a drink, you won't get to see what I bought, and that would be to miss something.'

An empty threat, but Oliver bought her a drink. When he and Marthe got back to the hotel he found a message waiting for him. A note from Carrie, sent by fax.

> *Oliver, can we make it Paris in September instead?*
> *Too much is happening here & I'll hate myself & be*
> *lousy company if I take time off now. Buy something*
> *beautiful and TAKE CARE OF YOURSELF PLEASE!*
> *XXX – C.*

'Fuck.'

Oliver tossed aside the fax. Marthe picked it up and began to read it. Oliver went to his bottle of duty-free and poured a large measure of single malt. She could stay at home. That was all right. He didn't mind that. But he disliked surprises.

'So, what's the problem?' Marthe said, dropping the fax on a side table. 'Now we have the weekend. It's better.'

Oliver lit a cigarette. Think. 'No.'

'No what?'

'I'll see you in Munich on Monday, as scheduled.'

'But why?'

'There's something else I have to do.'

*

134

'You may be in danger,' Oona said.

'Danger?' The word didn't sound quite real to Carrie. She put down the cup of tea and switched the phone to her other hand and ear. 'What do you mean?'

'I was thinking of you a little while ago, and the sense of things began to come back to me,' Oona explained. 'And it's more a sense of danger now than it was at our session. It was then as well, but not nearly as much. It feels stronger and closer now, and I wanted to let you know.'

'Danger – but from whom, or what?'

'I don't know.'

'Surely not my husband,' Carrie said flatly.

'No, I don't think so.' A pause. 'But the sense of danger is all around both of you.'

'You mean he could be in danger too?'

'Yes, or instead of you.'

'Oh, God.'

'Carrie, all it means is that you should pay more attention to things. Be aware. Think about where you're going, how you'll get there, who you'll be with. Things like that.'

'Yes.'

'It doesn't mean that anything is going to happen. It's not a direct indicator. It may only mean that your emotional balance could be thrown off by something. It may only mean that your job or personal life may be disrupted by argument or confrontation, a disagreement. Things like that.'

'I see.' It sounded a little better.

'The sense of danger can mean physical harm, but that's only one part of it. Most of the time it means some kind of a threat or hazard in your mental and emotional life. You shouldn't take it lightly, but you don't have to panic about it.'

'Okay. I understand.'

'But whenever I get this sense, I have to tell the person as soon as I can because it wouldn't be fair to wait until the next time we meet.'

'No, of course not. I'm very grateful.'

'Talk about it with your husband, and—'

'He's in Europe. On business.' There was a silence lasting long enough to make Carrie wonder if they'd been cut off. 'Oona? Are you still there?'

'Sorry, I was just trying to figure that in. How long is he going to be away?'

'Until the middle or the end of next week,' Carrie answered. 'But I'll see him this weekend. I'm flying – whoa! Hey. I was going to meet him in Switzerland for the weekend. Do you think I ought to risk flying?'

Not long ago such a consideration would have seemed utterly absurd to Carrie, but now it felt natural and important.

'See, I've got a problem here,' Oona said, sounding girlish and embarrassed. 'I don't know what to say because I don't know the answer. Most of what I get is non-specific so I can't start telling people what to do or not to do.'

'I didn't mean to put you on the spot like that.'

'I don't want to ruin your—'

'No, of course not. It's not your decision.'

'A weekend in Switzerland. I mean, wow.'

Carrie laughed. 'Well, I'll see.'

'You could have a great time,' Oona went on. 'Or you could have a bit of trouble. But the same goes if you stay home.'

'I understand.'

'Carrie.'

'Yes?'

'Did Roz tell you it was okay to ring me?'

'Yes. She said if I had to, I could.'

'Right. Well, I just want you to understand. It's usually better if I don't see any of the people I'm working with between their regular appointments.'

'I know. Roz explained.'

'I just want to make sure you know that you can ring me up if you need to, any time. If I'm busy with someone I'll get back to you as soon as I'm able. If you have another incident, or if you decide to stay home this weekend and you feel uncomfortable on your own, give me a call. It'll be okay.'

'Thanks. Maybe I will, if I'm here.'

'Good.'

The tea was cold. Carrie threw it down the drain. She had to have something with a little more bite to it now. She nursed a vodka cooler. She had to think. Danger. But it was hard to know exactly what Oona meant by danger.

If Carrie had an argument with Lorraine at work and Lorraine stormed out, would that be it – the moment of danger? And if it was, then once it happened would that be the end of it? Or would the danger linger on, like a stalled weather system?

A plane crash was easier to reckon. It would seem cowardly to cancel Lugano just because of a vague warning, especially when Oona had said that Carrie could be equally in danger by remaining in Manhattan. But an aeroplane flight was an obvious risk, in the circumstances. Oliver would be a little upset about it. But why tempt fate? Carrie would not let this thing beat her.

How far she had come in such a short period of time – a few weeks, barely a month. But what a month. It was hard to take in all of it, and understand. Hard to believe. Still, it would now be far more difficult for Carrie *not* to believe.

Her life was changed. She had seen enough. It was as if a new dimension of existence had been revealed to her. But Carrie instinctively felt that it was a dubious privilege at best, more likely to bode ill than good. There was no sense of the divine in what she had experienced, no feeling of heavenly presence. It was wrong. It threatened her in some way.

Her only hope was to learn how to fight it and survive. It was not something to be ignored – once you see it, you can never turn away.

Oona was the confirmation. It made perfect sense to Carrie that certain individuals would have the ability to gain partial access and serve as conduits. There had always been prophets and seers, people with a special gift.

She had expected all kinds of arguments from Oliver, but he

had fallen into a quiet, subdued mood. He didn't argue, he knew. As Carrie did. There was nothing remotely vague about the sound of her father's voice. The rest of the session was powerful and persuasive, but the voice was sufficient in itself. There was no way to doubt it or explain it away.

It was the scariest thing. To see and hear it – you could never be the same person again.

Carrie put on Grover Washington, Jr, and let the silky music settle around her. Poor Oona. She was like a child possessed by something monumental. A great gift, but a terrible one as well. It simply devastated her when she tapped into it, like a furious storm raging within her. So important, so terrible.

She was a young woman, of course. Eighteen, nineteen, maybe even twenty. But it was hard not to think of Oona as a child who needed comforting and loving care. Your heart went out to her, you wanted to shield and protect her. Imagine what her life must be like. Had she endured this since early childhood?

It occurred to Carrie that Oona's telephone call might have been about more than warning her of possible danger. There was a sense of loneliness in Oona's voice. Thinking back on it again, especially the end of the conversation, it seemed to Carrie to be the voice of a girl rather than a woman, a little girl – a child in need.

Rain so light it was almost a mist, but thick in the air. A familiar crowd – it seemed as if he knew them all. Silly thing to think, but he often felt that way. It was the anonymity. The miraculous way a city throng could feel like family.

Oliver stepped on his cigarette butt, moved further down the walk and lit another one. He'd been there a while already but he didn't mind the wait. Sometimes it helped.

Talk about going to great lengths, foolish errands. But why not? If you don't do these things in life you diminish yourself, you regret it. There are occasions when failure itself is a kind of prize, and success – oh, success can be too sweet for words. Either way, you're better for it.

Hanover Square.

Well past an hour. She finally emerged, same clunky walk and father-rigged posture. Still looking for her own body. She headed towards the Oxford Street tube station. He caught up, and fell in step beside her.

'Becky.'

Turn. Look. Stop. 'Oliver . . .'

'Hi.' Said that just right.

'Hello.'

Very cool. Weeks had passed and he had never called her on the phone or even sent a postcard. He'd warned her that it might be like that, and Becky hadn't been surprised when it was but she had nursed a tiny hope. Now she didn't want to show him how she felt inside, at least not so soon. But he knew. Becky was grateful, deeply grateful.

They always were.

13

Charley sloshed around the last of the Jameson's in the glass. Malcolm topped it up with another healthy dollop.

'Thank you, squire. I seem to be soaking up rather a lot of your booze lately.' He turned again to Maggie. 'The thing of it is, Jan seems to mean it literally. Fiona has come to get us for what happened to her. To avenge her death.'

'Oh, that's taking it too far,' Maggie replied.

'Of course it is,' Malcolm agreed.

'Crazed ghost-child seeks revenge,' Charley muttered. 'It's Hollywood tabloid gothic.'

'It doesn't worry you, does it?'

'What, the revenge part? No, of course not. But I have to live with Jan, and she's good and hooked on it now. I'm worried about her. I'd just as soon stop this whole business and forget about it. But that might hurt Jan, too.'

'That's right,' Maggie said. 'It sounds as if she needs to have this contact, to get whatever she can from it.'

'So, no matter what I do I'm stuck.'

'But there are signs that you're making progress.'

A believer, Maggie. However much she may couch it in terms of sceptical, rational study, she was a believer at heart.

'Progress. Your woman put on quite a show, but it doesn't mean anything as far as I can tell.'

'You've only been to one session.'

Charley sighed with exasperation. It was raining outside. They were in Malcolm's library. Other people may have a study or a den, but Malcolm had a library. Oak shelves, floor to ceiling, and french windows to a secluded side garden. More books than Charley, many more. Lovely. The trees and lawn were very green, and with the drizzle coming down the whole place had the lovely feeling of an Irish country house and idle days of the landed gentry.

'It doesn't hold up.' Charley had already explained to them his thoughts about how certain words could be easily mistaken and invested with false significance. The Brownes agreed there might be something in that, although Maggie didn't believe it important enough to change the overriding significance of Oona's abilities. 'The text is faulty,' Charley continued. 'The more I think about it, the more I'm sure there's something wrong with it.'

'Don't try to force conclusions before you have enough to go on,' Maggie told him.

'Can either of you remember anything else Oona said when you first heard the words Fiona and Ravenswood?'

Maggie shook her head, looking regretful. 'Those two words didn't mean anything to me at the time, and it's hard to pick any one area out of the whole flood of words and images.'

Malcolm nodded. 'I was struck by the words immediately, but my impression is that they popped out by themselves, unrelated to anything else being said. It was like a voice on the outer edge, trying to get into – the rest of it.'

'Yes,' Maggie said. 'I got the distinct feeling that there were several – presences – struggling to get through. That's a fairly common phenomenon, by the way.'

'Well, she only spoke with one voice at a time when I was there,' Charley said. 'Some of it sounded distinctly old-fashioned and almost literary. It bothers me.'

'Can you remember any examples?'

'Oh, sure. I've been fiddling around with it for days now, but it makes less sense than an Ashberry poem.'

Charley reached into his jacket pocket and took out a couple of folded sheets of paper. After he had given up trying to talk reasonably with Jan the night of their session with Oona, he had retreated to his desk in the hope of finding something useful to do. Instead of classwork, he ended up jotting down anything he could remember Oona saying. It didn't amount to much, but Charley had been studying it in his spare moments ever since.

'Here,' he said. 'Try this. Moorish gills. Bird of omen. Bats and crows and owls. Bogs and fens, the kelpie's flow.'

'Sounds like Scottish folklore,' Maggie said. 'But you need more. You can't isolate a few simple words and phrases, you have to find the larger pattern of meaning. By the way, you know what a kelpie is, don't you?'

'Rings a bell.' Charley shrugged.

'It's a spirit or demon that haunts rivers or lakes,' Maggie explained. 'They would try to drown any person that comes along. The bog and fen are appropriate.'

'All right, let's see. Next, the last laird of Ravenswood.' Charley glanced up. 'I thought Oona was referring to me when she said that. The last laird of Ravenswood went down to Ravenswood to marry a dead maiden. It sounded almost like part of a ballad or a poem. The dead maiden – was that supposed to be Fiona? But then the marrying part is hard to figure.'

Malcolm sat forward. '"The laird of Ravenswood to Ravenswood did ride. To woo a dead maiden for his bride."'

'That's exactly right,' Charley said. 'That's the very same cadence and rhyme as well – hey, how did you know that?'

'Because I bloody well know it from somewhere,' Malcolm said distractedly, as he tried to recall the source. 'Scott.'

'Scott?' Charley echoed.

'Scott.' Malcolm got up and went quickly to one section of the bookcases that lined the room. 'Sir Walter Scott.' He found the volume he was looking for, and took it down. He began to flip the pages as he returned to his chair. He glanced up at Charley and asked, with a smile, 'How's your Donizetti?'

'Still functioning, thanks.' Malcolm loved opera. Charley didn't. 'How's yours?'

'Donizetti's *Lucia di Lammermoor* is based on the novel *The Bride of Lammermoor* by Sir Walter Scott.'

'Yes,' Charley said. 'And?'

'Okay, listen now,' Malcolm went on. 'I knew I knew this.' He began to read from the open book.

'"When the last Laird of Ravenswood to Ravenswood shall ride,
And woo a dead maiden to be his bride,
He shall stable his steed in the Kelpie's flow,
And his name shall be lost for ever more!"'

'That's it,' Charley said promptly. 'That's exactly what I heard Oona say. She cribbed it. We've found the little darling out, is what we've done. Here, give us a peek.'

Charley took the volume from Malcolm and gazed at the quoted passage. By God, they had her. No question. Oona had taken the four-line lyric from Scott, played around with it a bit, adding a few other words to break it up, and then fed it out as if it were some oracular vision or message from beyond.

He held out the book to Maggie. 'Here you are.'

She leaned forward to look at the quatrain, but didn't take the book from him. She nodded. 'Yes. So?'

'So?'

'So what does that mean to you?'

'It means she cobbled together her little *recitativo*, using Scott and who knows what else. She did it, obviously, to create something that would sound suitably strange and disturbing. So a poor fool like me would think there was some hidden significance in it. That's what it means.'

Maggie shook her head. 'Charley, remember one of the first things that puzzled you? How could Fiona know English?'

'Yes.'

'Well, this poem from Scott is the same sort of thing. It's the language of the medium. Oona must have read this and it has remained in her memory. So it's a part of her mental vocabulary. If it came out in a session, it was because the words were useful to her as a way to convey some other meaning or message.'

'I hear what you're saying, Maggie,' Charley allowed. 'But it could just be part of her technique.'

143

'Perhaps, but I still think you're trying to take the easy way out. You ought to focus on what's relevant to you in these words, not where they came from.'

Charley nodded politely, but it didn't matter. Now he had something tangible that he could show to Jan. If he could just discredit Oona, then Jan might stop chasing and being chased by the dead. It was worth a try.

A cup of tea at the kitchen table. Bewley's own, which he hoarded for special moments; its use now would not escape Jan's notice. How many wonderful mornings had he spent in that café on Grafton Street, poring over the *Irish Times* or some obscure Irish literary journal? Endless pots of tea, lashings of warm buttered toast. Glorious. He could suffer that life again.

'Jan.'

'Yes?'

'About – here, your tea's ready,' he said, pouring. 'About Oona. I've been thinking about it. Reflecting.'

The right word. Jan nodded approvingly as she took her seat at the table. 'Good.'

He lit a small mild cigar.

'The thing I don't understand is, before we went there you were convinced that Fiona had spoken to you in a dream, and that she said she forgives you – us. Everything was all right.'

'Yes, I know.'

'It was nobody's fault.' Jan nodded at that, but with less conviction. 'Then we go to see Oona and she does her thing, and I saw and heard the same things you did. I didn't get any clear sense or meaning from it, but you apparently did. You now appear to have changed your mind around, one-eighty, to where you think Fiona has returned to punish us in some way.'

'Yes,' Jan said simply. She sipped her tea and gazed at him with calm, very sad eyes. 'In a way.'

'Why?' Charley asked. 'I don't see where you get that from. What did Oona say to give you that idea?'

'It was – everything.'

'Everything in general?'

'The overall sense of it, yes,' Jan replied. 'But also in a few of the specific words she used.'

She was trying to be reasonable, bless her.

'Do you mean things like the laird of Ravenswood?'

'Yes.'

'And the dead maiden?'

'Yes.'

'I can see why you might think those words apply to us, but I don't see the threat in them.'

'It isn't a threat.'

'What else could it be, then?'

'Resolution. Completion.'

'But where did you hear that?' Charley pressed, trying not to sound angry – though it did anger him.

'It's hard to say,' Jan told him. 'But it's there.'

'Don't you think that maybe you could be reading a bit much into it? You don't know for sure how it was meant.'

'I do.'

'Fiona has come back for us. We have no choice, and that's all there is to it.'

'That's right.' Almost cheerful.

'And what does she intend to do with us?'

Jan suddenly couldn't speak. Tears welled in her eyes. She turned away from him. Charley was miserable. All of this murky nonsense, Oona and the paranormal, was so useless. You could bat it around for ever but never get anywhere, and the worst part was that you could convince yourself that you did understand it – which state Jan seemed to have achieved.

He took the two sheets of paper from his jacket pocket and unfolded them on the table. He pushed them across to her.

'I wrote down some of what Oona said. You probably remember parts of it better than I do.'

Jan looked at the paper, and nodded. 'Yes.'

'You remember those words?'

'Yes, of course.'

'Good.' Charley opened the volume of Scott that Malcolm had loaned him. He turned it round so that Jan could read the open page. 'Now, look at this,' he said quietly, as if sharing a cute secret with her. 'I found the same words, exactly. She got them from *The Bride of Lammermoor* by Sir Walter Scott. She broke them up a little bit, but they're the same. As you can see.'

Jan studied the page, glanced again at Charley's notes and then looked back at the book.

'So?'

That again.

'So? So the use of Ravenswood doesn't have to have anything to do with us. It comes from a novel written more than a hundred and sixty years ago, set in Scotland. I don't know why Oona used it, but she did, and there it is.'

'Oona didn't choose it, Fiona did.'

'Jan, really. Think about what you're saying. I've put the evidence right in front of you and you're trying to rationalize it away. But you can't.'

'Think what you want, Charley.'

'Jan, please. This is not about us. It's bogus.'

'I'm sorry you think that,' Jan said, in the same maddeningly calm flat-line voice. 'It is about us. It's all about us.'

Charley controlled himself, just. He left the notes and the book on the table and went into his study. He had a study, not a library. It could be a small library, if he ever got round to organizing it properly. But when you know you're going to be on the road again next year, what's the point?

There was nothing he could say to her, nothing he could do. He felt useless, and he wasn't sure he cared any more. What's the point, Charles? He could let her go to Oona alone while he kept out of the whole unfortunate business. But that would be petty, and it was probably not a good idea to leave Jan to a fate she so fervently wanted. Someone had to protect her, and that was his job. He went back into the kitchen to let her know that he would be there with her, however foolish he thought it was.

Jan was standing in the middle of the room, holding the large bread knife. She appeared lost, gazing down at her hands.

Then she gave a startled glance in his direction. Charley forgot what he was going to say. He tried to hide the alarm he felt.

'What're you doing with that?'

'Putting it away.'

The heel of yesterday's loaf was buried in the trash where he'd thrown it that morning. Neither of them had bought a fresh loaf since. Had the knife been left out? He wasn't sure.

'See that you do.'

14

'Oliver.'

'Hmm?'

'I know I shouldn't bother you about things like this, but I do think we ought to . . . think about them.'

'What is it, pet?'

They were sitting next to each other on the bed, against the veneered headboard, both naked. Becky had the sheet pulled up to her neck. Oliver was drinking her white plonk and smoking. Her garden flat in Maida Vale. For all of the neat furnishings from Heal's and Harrods, no doubt bought by Daddy, the place had a glum and grey feeling about it. He had so many flats like this in his past, so many of these women with lousy plonk . . .

'I was so happy to see you yesterday,' Becky said. 'It was a wonderful surprise. I wasn't sure I'd hear from you again.'

'I told you I'd be in touch.'

'I know, but people say things.'

'I meant it.'

'I know, and it's great to have some time with you,' Becky said. 'I just wish we had more of it.'

'I know.' What the hell? Say it. 'So do I.'

'That's what bothers me.' Hesitant, anxious. 'I guess I'd like to know how I should think about – us.'

'Fondly, I hope.'

A brief smile. 'You know what I mean.'

'I do what I can, love.'

'Oliver. I know you're married and all that.'

'Rather.'

'And you have a lot of business interests that take up your

time. I do want to see you – don't get me wrong. But I don't want to be . . . just . . . the one in London.'

A mild show of principle. He liked that. Of course, it was totally meaningless. Fuck me all you want, but please don't take me for granted.

'I understand.'

'I mean, when you're not here—' But Becky didn't seem to know the rest of her thought.

'You have your own life to live,' he said helpfully. 'And I hope you're getting on with it. I don't want you sitting around and waiting by the phone, or anything like that.'

'No, well . . . I don't. But I'll be thinking of you, and that does affect what I do and who I see. You know?'

'You just carry on as you see fit, love,' he told her. 'The fact is, I have no hold over you.' The reverse of that obviously could go without saying. 'And the next time I'm in London, if I ring you up and you tell me you can't see me again because you've fallen in love with this smashing bloke from the City, well, then, I shall adjourn to a pub and have a quiet drink, and feel rather sad about it. But I'll be happy for you as well, and I'll think about the very splendid moments we spent together.'

Dear God, what utter rubbish. It must have worked, though. Becky didn't seem to know what to say, poor inarticulate child. She was gazing down at her hands, looking a bit wistfully pleased with herself.

'Well . . .'

'Look, Becky,' he said amiably, 'why don't we give ourselves a little time, and see how things work out?'

'Yes, I think we should.' No hesitation now, a quick lunge for the status quo.

'Good, so do I.'

Oliver got out of bed and crossed the room. He scanned her paperbacks and compact discs, but was not really interested. He put on Des'ree, just to hear something besides Becky.

Oliver was aware of her eyes on him. Evidently Becky didn't have many naked men walking around her flat. Too bad, you should get laid more.

'Come here.'

'What?'

'Come over here,' he said firmly. She started to reach for her dressing gown. 'No. Just bring yourself.' Slow, stiff and uncomfortable. When she was still several feet away from him he held up a hand to stop her. 'Becky, love. You're gorgeous. But I want you to put your shoulders back and stand straighter.' She did so. 'That's better. Now let your arms hang naturally, don't hold them by your side like that. Better. And lift your head up a bit. Chin out. That's it, that's it. Now stay like that when you walk, and come here.'

'Yes?' Shy, compliant. Expectant.

'Great,' he told her. 'Now you're walking and standing like a *woman*. Don't you read that magazine of yours? Doesn't it give you tips like this?'

'I guess.' A nervous giggle, and then she started to slouch and fold up into herself again.

'No, no,' Oliver said. He put the palm of one hand over her chest, the other in the small of her back. 'Pay attention, don't collapse into that slouch again.'

Becky was responding to the closeness, and his hands on her. He was beginning to enjoy it as well. Oliver's hand slid up her throat and adjusted the line of her jaw. He started to kiss and nuzzle her neck.

'You know,' he said, 'I'll be in Germany a lot this summer and autumn. I have a major project in the works. I was thinking we could meet there some time. You know, for a long weekend, hire a car, see some of the Bavarian countryside.'

'That'd be great.'

'If you want.'

'Oh, yes.'

'If you can get a few days off work.'

'I'm sure I could.'

'Do you like my mouth on your body?'

'Yes . . .'

'My tongue?'

' . . . Yes . . .'

The muscles in her rump and thighs were taut, and her hands lightly touched his shoulders.

'Nobody talks to you like this, do they?'

'No . . .'

'Nobody does this to you, do they?'

' . . . No . . .'

'Do you want me to?'

Fingers pressing on his shoulders. Tentative at first, as if she would hardly dare to convey a natural desire. But then a little stronger. The body always wins out.

'Tell me.'

'Yes – *yes*—'

With pleasure. He loved women, he loved the way their minds worked, which was unpredictable; and he loved their bodies, which were delightfully different.

Afterwards, he had to carry Becky back to bed, and they fell together in a tangle of arms and legs, drifting along in a lovely post-sex fog, blitzed with pleasure and half asleep. Even so, he remembered that he had to ring Carrie.

Oliver put his head between Becky's smallish breasts and she flopped a weak arm over his shoulder. She was in a light sleep, stirring a little whenever he moved but unable to open her eyes. She had such fine, pale skin.

The thought of ringing Carrie depressed him. Oliver had to, he wouldn't be able to get through another day without knowing if she was all right and what she was doing. It was a silly control thing, he supposed, but he couldn't avoid it.

His eyes were wet. He wanted to cry for the sheer relief he knew it would bring. Silly. Oliver rubbed his eyes and breathed deeply, then he brushed the moisture from his finger onto the downy skin between Becky's breasts. He turned his cheek, and he blinked until his eyelashes tickled her. Becky moved and gave a sleepy murmur of happiness.

Later, he told her a few things.

'It's very important that you don't mention me to anyone. Not my name, not what I do. Nothing.'

'I know. Don't worry, I won't.'

'It's just that a lot of people in London know me, and if it got back to Carrie – well, there could be problems.'

'Yeah. Your wife might be upset.'

'It's more than that,' he explained patiently. 'It involves money and business. Everything. If I gave her an excuse and she decided to use it, I could lose a lot. American laws can be very tough on the husband.'

'Are you thinking it might come to that?'

Divorce. No doubt a giddy thought – for Becky. Oliver had to suppress a laugh. Divorce? In your dreams, girl.

'Who knows? The point is not to give her anything she might be able to use against me. London's a big village.'

'I understand. Mum's the word.'

'Exactly.'

'You're safe with me. Always,' she added, with a meaningful romance-novel gaze, her fingers stroking his chest.

'Good.' Oliver smiled at her.

Carrie had dinner on Friday evening with Jeffrey and Mark at their place. Nothing fancy, just good chilli, a light green salad and plenty of icy Mexican beer. They were very sweet to her and insisted on escorting her home, checking out the apartment to make sure that every room was okay.

'Safe and secure upstairs,' Jeffrey announced, as he returned to the living room.

'Same down here,' Mark confirmed.

'Do you want us to stay and protect you?'

'No, don't be silly. Thank you both very much for a lovely evening. I'm really grateful. It was just what I needed. And I want your chilli recipe. It's *primo*.'

She had a nice buzz from the beer and she was too tired to do anything except take off her clothes and crawl between the sheets. She fell asleep almost immediately.

Some time later she was awakened by the sound of the moving men. Such a nuisance. No consideration. Grunting and heaving, their heavy shoes clomping on the parquet. Still mostly asleep, Carrie got out of bed to tell them to be quieter. The apartment was dark and silent, and there were no removal men.

Of course not. It was the middle of the night and, besides, they weren't moving anywhere. Ever. What had she been thinking? Nothing. She was in a daze, still asleep on her feet. Must have been a dream. Carrie returned to bed.

Much later, or so it seemed, the noise was back. She became aware of it as a distant thumping at first, but then it seemed closer. Within the apartment. Moving – for the life of her it sounded like men moving things. Carrie didn't move. Her eyes opened. It was still dark and the bedside clock showed that only a few minutes had passed.

She tried to think. Her head ached faintly. Perhaps it was Oliver. He had changed his plans and come home a few days early, but he didn't want to wake her. He was bringing in his suitcases and some gift packages. That would be nice. Carrie waited, her mind drifting in and out of sleep. She waited for Oliver to slip into bed and wrap himself around her. She thought of his body, and how she missed it beside her.

But he didn't come to bed. The noises continued, clumsy and disturbing. The people downstairs would be annoyed. Then Carrie remembered that flights from Europe usually landed in New York in the late morning or afternoon. Not at night.

She sat up again and looked at a spot in the darkness where she knew the bedroom door stood ajar. There was no light coming from out there, the rest of the apartment. But the noise had not stopped. Carrie was more awake now and she still heard it. She was sure it came from the living room.

She swung her legs around, out of bed. The noise continued. She was wearing only bikini briefs so she fumbled around in the dark, found the T-shirt she'd worn the previous afternoon and pulled it on. Her eyes were slowly adjusting. She went to the door and found it with her hand. The lumbering sounds still came from below.

Carrie touched the railing at the top of the staircase. The living room was dark, though some light filtered in from outside. Within a few moments she was able to make out certain large and familiar shapes – the Roche-Bobois, the home entertainment unit. No one there. Nothing happening. Just those sounds, louder now, as if she were closer to the source.

Carrie started slowly down the stairs. There was nothing to see when she reached the living room, but those sounds continued all around her – as if she'd now stepped into the middle of some invisible activity. Heavy lifting. Deep grunting. More of that leaden pacing back and forth, nowhere. Wordless voices, somehow distorted – a low rumble of simmering agitation.

Carrie hit the wall switch and the table lamp went on. The living room was suddenly cast in the warm, familiar glow of muted light. No one there, of course, nothing happening. But the same noise persisted. Incredible. Carrie was still struggling out of her beer-hazed sleep, but she was at last beginning to understand that she was in the middle of another event.

She took a few steps into the room, and felt something passing by just inches from her. She turned and looked around, but saw nothing. It happened again, a blurry movement in the air that she glimpsed briefly and dimly out of the corner of her eye. It made her think of leathery wings rustling and unseen birds sweeping past her.

The noise was constant. Carrie hadn't heard anything on the three previous occasions so this was a new turn. And already it had lasted longer than the other incidents. Someone was running. Carrie picked out the sound of running footsteps from the jumble of noise. It seemed to be coming from the kitchen. Carrie went to the hallway and looked in that direction. Suddenly the noise was a tremendous clatter and the grotesque sepia creature flew out of the darkened kitchen. He ran right past her, and Carrie felt the rush of air in his wake. She rocked back a step. She caught her balance and edged into the hallway.

The door at the far end was wide open. She knew that it had been closed: it always was, when that room wasn't in use. It was the second bedroom, Oliver's office. The lights were off but the room was faintly illuminated. Carrie approached the door.

It didn't look anything like Oliver's office. A chipped and faded linoleum floor. Walls made of cheap wood, painted a garish blue. Tinny, alien-sounding music floated like smoke in the air. Carrie noticed the heat. Sweat broke out across her forehead and face. There was a metal bed with a thin mattress on it. A woman flat on her back. The man knelt over her body. She was between his legs, and he was sitting on her belly. Strangling her. The woman's legs kicked and jumped uselessly. Carrie gasped.

He turned and stared at her. When she saw him run by on the way from the kitchen, she hadn't been quite sure. But now Carrie knew that it was the same figure, the one she had encountered at Monsieur Chauvet's apartment. Those warped and smeared features.

His whole face was twisted, and his eyes were out of kilter. But he seemed to focus on Carrie now, and immediately those eyes struck her as undeniably human. This was no demon or fiend from any hellish otherworld. It was – or had been – a man. And the recognition of that was somehow far worse than anything else she might have imagined. Carrie stumbled back a step or two and reached for the door to steady herself. Instead, she knocked it loudly against the wall.

He leapt off the bed and was on her in an instant, his hands at her throat. Carrie sagged dizzily. The stifling stench of an unbearable odour. The force of his eyes, which seemed to push her own eyeballs back into her brain. His grip like a metallic cable winding around her neck, cutting off her breath.

The sense that she was dying.

Carrie pressed her hands against his face and tried to shove him away. His skin felt like rippled glass coated with a thin layer of slime. The tinny music was louder, a shrill pain in her ears. She realized that she was in the room, on that bed, and he was sitting on her belly as he choked her. Carrie was the other woman. Her hands slid off him, and it was impossible to resist or push him away. Futile. She was dying. But then there was a mangled shout from the doorway, a sudden flurry of activity nearby, and a few moments later she was alone.

Carrie saw nothing now but knew he was gone. She was on her knees, one hand gripping the corner of the desk for support. She followed the light and made it into the living room. I am still alive, she told herself, though she hardly believed it.

She sat down on the sofa, fell onto her side, curled her legs up close to her, and began to shiver. She was cold, and reached up to pull the afghan over her body. Her face felt damp, and she touched it. Blood, from her nose or mouth. She tried to wipe it away, and her face felt sticky with it. She remained on the sofa until daylight filled the room. Then she got up and tottered into the kitchen. She knew the number.

'Hello?' Sleepy.

'Oona.'

'This is Roz.'

'Roz, this is Carrie Spence.'

'What's the matter?' Suddenly alert, anxious.

'It happened again, only worse. Much worse.'

'Are you all right?'

'No.'

15

'What's the point?' Charley asked. 'If you know what Fiona wants with us, why do we have to do this again?'

'Because it's part of it,' Jan replied.

It's part of it. As if that made any sense. But they were on their way to see Oona again and there was no way out. Charley was perplexed, and a little worried. Jan was increasingly silent around their apartment. She sat and stared a lot.

She still went to work, and presumably she still functioned adequately there since she hadn't been fired. But at home she showed signs of being in retreat. She had started leaving her clothes draped over chairs or lying in a heap on the floor beside the bed, and she'd never been sloppy like that. Or she would do a pile of laundry but then leave the wet clothes in the washer. By the time Charley found them, they had more wrinkles than the late Mr Auden's face.

Charley felt as if he were caught in a zone of futility. He had a powerful desire to do something, to act in a way that would be useful and decisive and would protect Jan. But Jan believed in Oona, and that Fiona's ghost had come for them.

Charley was convinced that, before too long, this terribly sad delusion would crumble. Oona's ambiguous and suggestive arias couldn't work indefinitely. They would lose their power to hold Jan. Fiona had to appear. Fiona had to speak, and say something important. But she wouldn't. Fiona was dead, and the dead stay dead. No matter how hard Oona tried, she would never be able to conjure up Fiona's spirit or voice. Sooner or later Jan was sure to accept this unavoidable fact.

It hurt, it really hurt to disbelieve. Half of the battle, Charley realized, was with himself. Even he wanted to think that his daughter survived in some way, and was trying to get in touch with them. It was such an attractive, seductive idea. The ghost of a life that had barely begun. Speaking to her parents across the great divide. Oh, yes, it was appealing. It seemed so right. It had a sense of fairness and justice to it.

'You know, Jan . . .'

'What?'

'I'm not trying to start an argument or anything. And I do think Oona is remarkable in some ways. But I can't help thinking that she must be . . . disturbed. Somehow.'

'You mean, mentally ill?'

'Well . . . disturbed,' Charley said. This seemed a safer line to take than claiming Oona was an outright fraud. 'I mean, it's not natural, is it? People aren't born that way. She must have been through something in her life to make her like that.'

'Does it matter?'

'Of course it does. She—'

'Did Yeats have a special talent? Cézanne? Mahler?'

'All great artists have talent and vision,' Charley replied. 'But please don't try to tell me your woman is in the same league with the likes of—'

'Your woman,' Jan repeated, with a laugh of contempt.

'Pardon?'

'Your woman this, your man that. It's the way you insist on talking, Charley. Those Irish phrases and idioms, as if you were born on the banks of the Liffey instead of a crossroads farm town in Wisconsin. As if you were a hard-drinking native Dubliner. I used to find it charming. Years ago.'

'I'm Irish through and through,' Charley muttered.

'And you can tell who's disturbed.'

Jan laughed to herself. Charley held his tongue. He would not let it degenerate into another slanging match. The cow. He concentrated on the traffic. The usual bottleneck inching along into Westville, otherwise not too bad.

The fact that Jan could needle him that way was in itself an encouraging sign. It showed that she had some fight left in her. That business with the bread knife had bothered him for a couple of days, but he'd watched her carefully and seen no repetition of it. Jan wouldn't hurt herself or him – not if she expected some act of ghostly retribution from Fiona.

What he feared much more was that Jan might suffer a mental breakdown. Driven over the edge by a poisonous mixture of Oona's antics and lingering guilt. Then what? Treatment and care. Was his own future role to be that of a nurse? Charley found it an appalling prospect. But he couldn't leave her just as things got really bad. He might have a peculiar notion of marital fidelity, but he had remained with Jan all this time and he'd never desert her merely for the sake of convenience.

That was faithfulness, the genuine item, and it made Charley feel a little better to affirm it once again.

'Is it all right to speak?' Charley asked. 'I mean when you're in the middle of your – thing. I wouldn't want to interrupt anything important.'

'That's not a problem,' Oona said. 'If something occurs to you, just say it. You won't do any harm.'

'Ah, good.'

So agreeable, this Oona. He still didn't know quite what to make of her. She seemed perfectly innocent, a sunny and cheerful young lady who was out to help. Pleasant, attractive. She imposed no special rules or conditions, which was the opposite of what you would expect for events like this. And while they took place in the little snuggery at the back of her living room, Oona gave the impression that she could stage them anywhere, almost at the drop of a tweed hat.

This session began as the first one had, with Oona jabbering on while she rubbed their hands and touched their faces. It was easy enough to endure, but still seemed rather silly.

'You're so sensitive,' Oona was telling Jan.

Oh, yes, he'd had occasion to observe that – once or twice a year, perhaps. Since when was being guilt-haunted the same thing as being sensitive? Jan, of course, was eating it up. Her eyes tearful already, her head nodding in agreement. Yes, yes, I'm so sensitive, please tell me more.

It was so disheartening. With Maggie, at least, it could be described as a kind of research. She might believe in it but she was also investigating something that could be traced back to her studies of old Celtic folklore. The crazy women with the gift of vision. Witches or seers, whatever. Charley and Jan had no such rationale. Just an old tragedy, and nothing Oona said would ever change it in any way.

'*Wenda wenda wenda*—'

She was on track. They had explained this. Oona often had to cover old ground to find the way. Every time out she advanced a little further along. So they said.

'*Wenda wenda when the when the*—'

'Laird,' Charley prompted.

'*When the laird the laird the laird*—'

'When the last Laird of Ravenswood to Ravenswood shall ride, and woo a dead maiden to be his bride,' Charley quoted, 'he shall stable his steed in the Kelpie's flow, and his name shall be lost for ever more.'

Oona's mouth continued to move but she had gone silent, her eyes blank and her fingers making empty gestures in the air. Roz gave him a puzzled look but said nothing. Jan's expression was one of tight-lipped, hard-eyed annoyance.

'Sir Walter Scott,' he told Roz. '*The Bride of Lammermoor*. It rang a bell the last time, and I tracked it down. It may not be exactly word for word, but that's more or less it.'

'How interesting,' Roz said.

'Yes, it is.' A cool one, that girl. 'What do you suppose it means?'

'I don't know.' A hushed tone, telling him to shut up.

'Well, she's quoting Sir Walter Scott,' Charley persisted. 'I find that rather curious, and I'd—'

Jan and Roz waved him silent. They were gazing at Oona, who was flat on her back, her limbs straight and her body shuddering tightly. Sweat was pouring off her face, which had turned bright red and now was shading into a ghastly purple.

Her breathing was somewhat quickened but still close to normal. Her lips were pulled back from her teeth in a painful grimace. Her jaw jumped, and the words came out in tortured clots of sound.

'*Youdontwanna bay bee Idontwanna bay bee—*'

'That's not true,' Charley said softly, but angrily.

'*Wickedwickwickedwickwickedwick—*'

Oona's hands flapped uselessly. She looked half dead. The colour had drained from her face, and her skin was streaked with grey and white. Her eyes were shut, but tears flowed freely from them. As before, Charley found these physical changes impressive and weirdly fascinating, but he also resented them.

And there hadn't been anything wrong with the bloody wick in that ancient Everglo paraffin heater. That wasn't it at all. It shouldn't have been used in the nursery, that was the unfortunate truth of the matter. Nothing more, nothing less.

'*Adare–Adare–Adare–Adare–Adare—*'

Jan clamped a hand over her mouth and Charley could feel the skin tighten on his face. The bitch. The anger he felt undercut the creeping sense of fear on the edge of his mind. It had never been in any newspaper or media report, as far as he knew. It had never been made public because it was irrelevant. Everybody knew about that cursed jerrycan of fuel, but not that it had the name Adare on the side of it in chipped letters. Adare being the name of the local shopkeeper who had supplied it to Charley. There was no way Oona could know – Christ, he was tired of thinking that each time Oona said something she wasn't supposed to know.

'*A daring bird of omen bird of doom daring to daring to dare to come come come oh no oh no oh no don't come—*'

Charley exhaled. *Dare. Daring.* So it wasn't necessarily a mention of Adare at all. Just another case of the words sounding alike, being virtually the same, and thus triggering a connection in his mind and Jan's. He would tell her that later, not that it would do any good. But you have to put things on record.

'Dunsany had a bird of doom,' he pointed out affably. 'It's

in *The Gods of Pegana*, his very first book. Every writer worth his salt has at least one bird of omen or bird of doom in their work – it's required. Symbolism 101.'

But Jan and Roz ignored him. Fair enough. He was playing the spoilsport and they had no use for it. But it seemed to him that someone had to take on that role, however thankless it might be, and he was the only person present with the detachment to see through the veil of dubious links and associations.

'Dontdontdontdontdont – don't lettem come don't lettem come don't wanna – don't wanna – baybee – the corbies come the bird of doom the corbies shadow in the room – oh no oh no—'

'Fiona,' Jan wailed helplessly.

Oona writhed and twisted, pinching her arms and body. Her skin turned white then red where she picked at it. There was a look of strange pleasure on her face, a kind of fierce smile that seemed to defy her obvious discomfort.

Her light cotton dress was drenched in places with sweat and stuck to her. The sleeves were bunched up above the elbows, the loose skirt crushed in a clump between her knees. Her hair hung in damp, tangled strands. Oona's eyes opened and closed, rolling about aimlessly, seeing only within.

A trance. Okay, so she goes into a trance state, as much as anybody ever can. Charley would give her that. But there was no special benefit or magic to it. It was a form of escape. People push themselves into a trance and think they've made a mystical connection. But it was imaginary, illusory, the product of their own subconscious minds off on a toot. You could reach the cosmos and the past just as well by meditating serenely, or having a few pints in Mooney's on a quiet afternoon.

'Don't go don't go don't go now—'

'I'm sorry,' Jan sobbed.

'Don't leave the laird the bird the shadow the smoke the lie in the lie of the light – the glow—'

'Fiona, I'm so sorry . . .'

It was possible, just possible, to look at Oona in such an

extraordinary state, to hear the words flowing and jumping out of her, and to believe it. You almost had to work harder to reject it. But you had to reject it, because otherwise everything else in your life spun out of control. And fell away, empty and drab and meaningless.

If you could communicate with the dead, how could you spend your time doing anything else? If you could cross the barrier to the afterlife, or another dimension of being – whatever it might be – how could you go back to teaching, writing, cleaning house, watching a ballgame or dulling your mind with drink? Surely you would feel compelled to spend every waking moment of your life on it, trying to perfect it and understand it. To do anything else would be an outrageous waste of time and opportunity. You would have to devote your whole life to it.

To the dead.

Oona had fallen still. She looked wrung out and limp, like a floppy doll that had seen too much careless use. Charley hoped the show was over. He wanted to take Jan home.

Oona sat up and looked around. Her eyes were clear and wide open now, but she still gave the impression of being blind, or of seeing something other than her immediate surroundings. Her eyes were a brilliant blue, but were lost.

'Don't leave me, Mam. Please don't leave me here like this. Mam, please don't. Stay with me, Mam. Take me with you. Don't leave me here like this. Please don't.'

The voice of a child, small and pleading. The words didn't come in synch with Oona's occasional lip movements. They seemed to float out of her mouth unaided. But what was most disturbing about it, shocking even, was how frail and human that tiny voice sounded. And yet it had a crushing sense of reality, after, of the incantatory outbursts that had come earlier.

'Don't leave that there, Dad. Please don't do that. Not in the corner, not in this room. Mr Adare told you, Dad. Leave it loose, not tight. Leave it in the shed. Dad, don't—'

'God.'

'Don't forget it there like that. Don't leave me here, Mam. Take

me with you. See the corbies in the tree. See them on the wall at the back of the garden. Take me with you, Mam, stay with me this time. Please—'

Jan was sobbing violently, but no sound came from her. She leaned forward, hands clasped at her mouth, and put her forehead to the cushion at Oona's knees.

'*Mam? Dad? Where are you?*'

Oona began to gasp, her cheeks coruscating with fear in the blood. Her voice rose, and yet seemed to lose strength, or hope. Her fingers trembled at her breast.

'*Mam? Dad? Don't leave me this time. Stay with me. Take me with you this time. Mam? Dad? Please! PLEASE!!*' ·

Her voice became a scream, and Oona repeated those same few monosyllables over and over again. Her face was twisted, racked with terror, and the veins in her neck stood out like cables.

'*Mam! Dad! Where are you? Don't go!*'

Jan: 'I'm – so – sorry—'

Charley felt as if his chest was full of knots. He couldn't move, couldn't take his eyes from Oona. He wasn't breathing, and he seemed to be strangling inside.

'*PLEASE! PLEASE! OH PLEASE!*'

A shriek in the teeth of death, and then Oona's voice reeled off into wordless, skirling yelps, raging hysteria. Charley felt as if steel bands were snapping inside him, and he took her in his arms suddenly. Stroked her hair and face. Contained her, as she collapsed in his embrace.

'It's all right.' His voice congested. 'I'm here.'

16

'This is not a good idea,' Roz said with a look of reproach. 'If it were up to me . . . But she does want to see you.'

'I'm sorry.' Carrie didn't know what else to say. When she had phoned earlier that morning, she had suspected that Roz and Oona were not quite in agreement. But even if she only got to see Oona for five or ten minutes, it was necessary. What had happened was so terrible, and Oona was the only person who could help.

'Well, anyway. She wants to see you alone. As long as the two of you just talk, that's okay. But if she shows any sign of going into a spell again, I want you to leave the room and let me know at once. I'll be down here.'

Carrie nodded. She followed Roz up the front hall stairs to the second floor. Oona was in the master bedroom at the back of the house, propped up against a bank of pillows. She had a stack of women's magazines beside her, and the television was showing a music video. She was wearing light summer pyjamas. She had a cigarette in one hand, and there was a tall glass of tomato juice on the night table next to her. Her face lit up with a big smile when she saw Carrie.

'Hi, come on in.'

'Hello.'

'Are you all right, love?' Roz asked.

'Yes, thanks. Fine,' Oona answered dismissively. She patted the bed, and said to Carrie, 'Here, come sit with me.'

Roz left the room, leaving the door open an inch, as Carrie sat down on the edge of the bed, facing Oona.

'I'm sorry to trouble you like this.'

'Oh, that's all right,' Oona told her. 'I'm really glad to see you. But I guess you had a rough night.'

'Yes, I did.'

'I'm still glad you didn't fly to Europe.' Oona tapped out her cigarette. 'Do you want a Bloody Mary or something?'

'Oh, no, thanks.'

'Come on, have one with me. Please.'

'Well, maybe a weak one.'

'Good.'

Oona reached down to the floor beside her and came up with a clean glass and a bottle of vodka. She poured a large measure, then topped it off with tomato juice from another bottle. That was it, a far cry from the Bloody Marys at the Carlyle. Carrie took one sip and held the drink.

'You probably think I'm terrible, drinking at eleven o'clock in the morning,' Oona said, with a brief giggle.

'No, of course not. Oliver and I often have a Bloody Mary or a Screwdriver on Sunday morning, with the papers.'

'Well, I probably do drink too much,' Oona said, without any hint of regret. 'But I don't like sleeping pills, and a couple of drinks makes it easier to sleep without dreaming. During the day it helps hold off the voices and visions.'

'They happen that often?'

'They would, yes. Unless I'm too weak from the last time or if I'm feeling mellow enough with drink.'

'And you have no control over it?'

'Not a lot. Not much at all, in fact.' Oona grinned. 'But never mind about that. What happened last night?'

Carrie told her how the incident had developed, from the odd noises and the sight of the figure running down the hall and into Oliver's office, to the way the room was changed, the strangling, and how Carrie then found herself in the victim's place.

'You didn't recognize anything about him?'

'No. The eyes were human, but the rest of his features were so distorted and freakish.' Carrie shook her head. 'But I could actually feel his hands on my throat. I could feel his body as I

166

tried to push him away. His skin was hard and smooth but slimy. It felt awful, and it was totally real.'

'Can you remember anything else?'

'There was an awful smell.' Carrie thought about it for a moment. 'A smell like dirt, like wet soil.'

'Right.'

'And there must have been some other person present because I heard a garbled voice from the door. That was when he stopped choking me, and he turned and looked towards the door, and then it all ended. When I came out of it, I was alone in Oliver's office and the room was back to normal again.'

Oona nodded. 'When I sensed danger around you, I guess this was what it was about. It may or may not be meant literally. It might only be a representation of something else. The experience of smell and touch are very important because they both suggest immediacy, proximity.'

'You mean something's going to happen to me, and it's closer now? It could be very soon?'

'I think so,' Oona said. 'It's much more developed than the previous episodes.'

'What should I do?' Carrie asked.

'Try to be ready for it, whatever it is.'

'But how do you get ready for something like this?'

'By thinking and expecting, and being sure of yourself.'

'Am I in real danger?'

'Yes, but as I told you the other day it may not be physical danger only. It could be emotional, psychological or spiritual. Everything is connected.'

'But it could be physical.'

'Yes,' Oona said, with a look of regret.

'What I saw and experienced, being strangled,' Carrie went on. 'That could really happen to me.'

'Well, yes,' Oona admitted. 'But, as I said, it seldom turns out to be that specific and literal. It's a warning.'

'So I have good reason to be scared.' Carrie felt as if her life were tilting on its axis and that she faced a new alignment of unseen forces and factors. The threat of physical danger had not seemed real to her until now.

'Is it about my father?'

'He's probably part of it.'

'My husband?'

'He seems to be a part of it as well.' Oona sat forward and took Carrie's hand. 'But it's all about you, really. That's why it's happening to you. It's about you.'

Carrie felt frustrated and resentful. There seemed to be no clear answers. She found some reassurance in the way Oona spoke, so calmly and matter-of-factly.

'You're not afraid for me.'

'No, I'm not.' Oona squeezed Carrie's hand. 'I feel you're going to be all right. One of the reasons this is even happening to you is that you're a sensitive. So it *can* happen to you. And that means you're probably equipped to handle it.'

'I'm glad to hear that,' Carrie said with a nervous laugh in her voice. 'At least, I think I am.'

'It also means you're a bit like me.'

'Does my being here bother you?'

'No, at least not yet. I feel very good, in fact, clear and wonderfully empty. For me, empty is the best.'

'Roz didn't want me to come. Of course, I can understand it from her point of view. She's just looking out for you.'

'Well, Roz and I have a history,' Oona said. 'She does take very good care of me and she loves me, and I love her, but when I don't do as she wants she gets a bit grumpy.'

'You're sisters, right?'

'You'd think so, wouldn't you?'

'Well, yes.'

'So do I. Most of the time.' Carrie must have looked quite puzzled, for Oona laughed and patted her hand. 'That must sound funny. You see, Roz and I were together when we were very young, but then we were apart for a while. So neither of us is – well, leave it at that.'

'I'm sorry,' Carrie said. 'I didn't mean to pry.'

'That's all right. I know you're not being nosy in a nasty way, like some people, and I don't mind if you want to ask me any questions. But I may not answer them all.'

'Have you always had this ability or . . .?'

'I think so, in a way,' Oona replied. 'But it only became obvious in the last couple of years. That's when I first started trying to use it to help other people.'

'How old are you?'

'How old do you think?'

'Eighteen?'

Oona grinned with delight. 'It's been three years since I saw the last of eighteen.'

'You look younger than twenty-one.' Carrie remembered Scott Crawford telling her that many cases of strange paranormal events centred around teenage girls going through puberty. The time frame would almost fit in Oona's case as well. 'Why is this happening to me now? I'm thirty-two years old,' Carrie said. 'Nothing like this ever happened to me before. There were no signs, no—'

'Until now. And bang, it hits you.'

'Yes.'

Oona gave her a sympathetic look. 'People grow and change. You're not the same person you were five or ten years ago, that's one part of it. Also, you might not have noticed some very small signs that did occur in the past. They can be easy to overlook. And then there's the matter of other people and events that touch on your life. All of these things shift and develop in their own way over time, until you're in a position where you see things in a new focus – and you can see whole new dimensions of existence, starting with your own.'

'It scares me, and I don't know whether to run away from it or to try and fight it.'

'You can't run away,' Oona told her. 'But you can fight it. Fight *to understand*. That's the only way. You'll be all right. I have that feeling about you. You'll probably live a long life and end up a very wise old lady.'

Carrie smiled. 'I feel better just hearing you talk about these things so calmly. Thank you for letting me come and spend a few minutes with you.'

'It's nice to have a visitor.'

'Well, I should let you get some rest and—'

'Oh, don't go.' Oona was suddenly upset. 'Are you on your way somewhere? Do you have to go do something?'

'Well, no, but—'

'Then stay a while.' Oona had a begging, little-girl smile on her face. 'Please.'

'If you're sure I'm not bothering you.'

'No, I'm fine. Maybe you're helping me in some way because I'm not getting any intrusion at all. It feels great.'

'But you will tell me to leave if it starts?'

'Sure.'

'Okay, fair enough.' Carrie took another sip of her drink, trying not to wince. 'Oona, how about if I show you how to make a real Bloody Mary?'

They made some proper Bloody Marys and watched old movies on cable, laughing at Laurel and Hardy, chuckling at *The Saint*, and finally nestling tight against each other through a bleak little *noir* thriller called *Roadblock*. By the time the doomed anti-hero had been gunned down by the police in the dry riverbed in Los Angeles, Oona was asleep, her face resting on Carrie's bosom. Carrie had one arm across Oona's shoulder and she stroked her hair and cheek gently. She drifted in and out of sleep herself, holding Oona protectively. At some point Roz looked in on them.

'You'll be Mother, if you don't watch out.'

'I don't mind,' Carrie answered truthfully.

'You can say that now.'

'What do you mean?'

'Ah, never mind.'

'Oona asked me to stay and she seems fine. But I don't want to cause any trouble or hard feelings with you.'

'I know,' Roz told her. 'You mean well enough. But there's more to it than you know. You've no idea, really.'

They spoke in subdued tones, but it still felt uncomfortable to Carrie to be discussing something that involved Oona while the girl was right there in her arms. She checked, and Oona was deep asleep. Her breathing was rhythmic and a very faint whistle came from her slightly parted lips.

'No idea of what?'

Roz stepped closer to the bed. She looked almost apologetic as she spoke. 'It's very easy to fall in love with her. There's plenty who did before you, and you surely won't be the last. The next thing is, you'll want to help her.'

'I wouldn't presume to know how—'

'Not yet, you wouldn't.'

'I still don't understand what you're getting at.'

'Don't expect her to love you in return. She can't. And it won't be long before she disappoints you. So don't set yourself up for a let-down, that's all I'm saying.'

Carrie could hardly believe what she was hearing. It was so bizarre. She made an effort to keep her voice from rising.

'I don't know why you talk about love. I respect and admire her, and I'm very, very grateful to her for the help she's giving me. If that's what you mean by love, fine. Otherwise, I have no idea what you're talking about.'

'Just don't jump to the wrong conclusion. Oona is Oona, and that won't ever change. You can't help her. You can't save her. And she's the one won't let you.'

'I had a dream.'

'A good one, I hope,' Carrie said.

'I don't know.' Oona sat up and rubbed her eyes, looking so much like a child. 'It's really weird.'

'Why?'

'First of all, I don't remember very many dreams. The drink is supposed to keep you from dreaming – or at least remembering what you dreamed.'

'Otherwise you have nightmares?' Carrie asked.

Oona nodded. 'Not exactly nightmares. But for me dreaming is usually like having a spell. More of the same. It crowds my brain. I don't know if that makes any sense, but it's a bit like being suffocated – only inside your head.'

Carrie nodded sympathetically. 'What was this dream about? Do you remember much of it?'

'Just a fragment.' Oona sat back and lit a cigarette. 'It was by a river, but it was in a city not the countryside. There were mechanical things around and it just felt like a city. And there were a lot of children running and yelling. But I couldn't hear anything clearly. What I remember most was a terrible sense of something being wrong. That's why the kids were running about and screaming – they were screaming.'

'Anything else?'

Oona shook her head. 'Just panic. That's what I felt. It was pure panic, as if my head was going to explode.'

'Were you one of the children?'

'No. I was just, like, observing it all.'

'Was it because I'm here?' Carrie asked.

'No, oh, no.' Oona was alarmed. 'I think it would have been worse if you weren't here. I woke up and I was in your arms, and suddenly I felt very safe. It was the nicest feeling.'

'Good, I'm glad,' Carrie said, smiling.

'Will you stay on?'

'W-when, now?'

'Sure.'

'Oh, no. I should—'

'Look, it's getting dark out,' Oona said, pointing to the window. 'You don't want to drive all the way back to New York at night. By yourself.'

'It's still—'

'To an empty apartment? Why bother, if it's not necessary? Why not stay on here with me? That'd be better for you, and I'd enjoy it so much.'

'I'd hate myself if you had another spell because I'm here. It's bad enough that it happens in a scheduled session.'

'I'll be okay, I promise.'

'Oona, you can't promise that,' Carrie said. 'You told me

172

you don't have any control over it and other people bring it on. We shouldn't push our luck and maybe ruin a good day.'

'But I just know it'll be okay,' Oona insisted. 'Your being here seems to help in some way, I think.'

'It's nice to hear that, but—'

'Please?' Oona didn't wait for an answer. 'You're staying overnight,' she went on. It was both an order and a plea. 'Just say yes, okay? Just say yes.'

'Yes.'

Roz didn't seem upset or surprised by the news, and she took Carrie into her own bedroom to get her a nightgown and robe.

'I tried to talk her out of it,' Carrie said weakly.

'Not to worry. It'll be like a night off for me. I may go into town and see a film. Haven't done that in ages.'

'Roz, if you do go out...'

'If it comes on her, don't try to force her out of it. That just makes it worse. Let her come out of it by herself, she will soon enough. Then you have to clean her up and be there for her. She'll need you.' Roz smiled mirthlessly. 'But you might be lucky, and nothing happens.'

They ordered in Chinese food and ate it on the bed, as they watched more movies on television. Oona seemed perfectly content to spend all day and night in her bedroom. After the meal, they switched vodka mixers and made Black Russians. Carrie drank hers slowly. Oona got rather merry but she never lost control of her speech.

They were like a couple of high-school girls, chatting about food and fashions and music, whatever came to mind. There was no weight to it, but Carrie soon realized that this was exactly what Oona wanted and needed, the chance to relax with a *friend* and to act like a girl who didn't have a care in the world.

'What's it like being married?'

It was probably inevitable that the talk would get around to the subject of men, sooner or later.

Carrie smiled. 'It's good most of the time,' she answered. 'You can't take it for granted, you have to work at it.'

Oona nodded, but she wasn't satisfied. 'I mean, I hope you don't mind my asking, but what is it like when a man enters your body? Is it awful? Is it great?'

Somehow Carrie was not surprised to learn that Oona was still a virgin. Sex could be difficult enough at times, without the unique complicating factors that Oona would have to consider. The prospect of suddenly being seized by a psychic episode in the middle of making love must terrify her.

'It can be awful or great,' Carrie replied. 'If the man is concerned about giving you pleasure and not just getting his own, it can be wonderful. And if he knows what he's doing,' she added, with a laugh. 'Otherwise, it can be a drag.'

'Does it hurt?'

'It can, if he's rough or in a hurry. The main thing is to be with someone who cares about you as much as you do about him. Then the rest of it usually works out.'

'I don't know,' Oona said doubtfully. 'I can't imagine it. I'm *invaded* enough as it is, if you know what I mean.'

Oona fell asleep first, some time around midnight. She dozed off with her head against Carrie's arm. Carrie managed to switch off the table lamp without waking her. She watched TV for a few more minutes, then clicked it off with the remote.

The house was silent. They hadn't seen any more of Roz, and Carrie didn't even know if she was home. But everything had gone well. Oona seemed to have enjoyed herself, and Carrie was happy enough to believe that her being there had done some good. Oona deserved more than just scattered moments of respite.

It did feel a little strange to go to sleep in an unfamiliar house, in someone else's bed – and with that someone also in it. But Carrie didn't mind, and the vodka had left her drowsy enough. Oona clung to her, and Carrie soon drifted off.

She was dimly aware of Oona tossing and turning a lot during the night. Part of Carrie's brain remained alert to the possible occurrence of a psychic episode. But it was never enough to wake her, as Oona always settled again quickly, hugging her.

When Carrie finally woke up and opened her eyes, she could see a hint of grey in the light outside. It took her a couple of moments to realize where she was.

Oona was crying. In her sleep. Softly, whimpering. Carrie realized that the front of her nightgown was quite damp. She sat up, trying to think. She was supposed to be there for Oona, but not to try to force her out of it. Let her come out of it on her own, that was what Roz had told Carrie. Anyhow, it might only be another dream, not a serious episode. She held Oona, she brushed the hair from Oona's face and lightly rubbed her back.

'Franny . . . Franny . . .'

Oona's voice was tiny, between sobs. Carrie's eyes widened in the dark. Her skin felt charged, as if a dry static wind had just swept across it.

'Franny . . .'

God, how many years ago had it been? Seventeen? Eighteen? Something like that. Franny Hagstrom, blonde, sunny, bright and precocious, had been Carrie's best friend. Like her, Franny was a daughter of the diplomatic corps. Carrie had spent a summer at the Hagstrom cottage on Big Moose Lake in the Adirondacks. She would later wish she'd paid more attention to the place because it was at Big Moose Lake, one summer day in 1906, that Chester Gillette had taken Grace Brown out in a rowboat and, in a secluded cove, clubbed her with a tennis racket and drowned her. It was the murder case on which Theodore Dreiser had based his novel *An American Tragedy*, a huge clumsy masterpiece of which Carrie later grew rather fond, if only for the association with Big Moose Lake.

Where, one summer night, Franny slipped into Carrie's bed or Carrie slipped into Franny's – to this very day she was not sure which way it had been, not that it mattered. And there had been some nervous, tentative kisses, some delicate, thrilling touches, exploration, and flashes of pleasure that had more to

175

do with the *new* and the *forbidden* than with actual physical sex, since neither of them knew exactly what to do.

Dear God, to be that innocent.

It was the first time since puberty that Carrie had been in bed, naked, with another naked person, and the delight, the shock of it was still the most vivid part of her recollection. There had been no repeat encounter, just the one experiment. They were able to smile and giggle about it later, perhaps because they had learned that they were really more interested in male bodies than in each other's. Something like that. Who knows? For Carrie it was still a sweet memory of lost innocence, alive and safe in her heart. Another time, another life.

The following year, the Hagstroms were posted to some other corner of the globe. Carrie and Franny wrote letters for a while but eventually they tapered off and then stopped. It was sad but not unusual. Everyone has youthful friendships that fall away in the course of time. Carrie had no idea where Franny might be now or what kind of life she had made for herself.

'Franny . . .'

Or if she was even alive.

Oona rolled over, moaning like a child in distress. Carrie felt the warm soft smoothness of Oona's belly beneath her hand as the pyjama top had either come unbuttoned or ridden up across her chest while she was tossing about. She could feel the firm bone at the bottom of Oona's ribcage.

Carrie's mind flashed back again to Big Moose Lake. A brief glimpse of Franny in the early-morning light. The two of them so slender and self-conscious, teenagers awkward in their bodies but by then daring enough to be able to look at each other to satisfy their curiosity.

She had no idea why, but the recollection of those moments brought tears to her eyes. I'm too young to feel old, she tried to tell herself, too young still to look back on my youth and cry with joy and sadness. Not yet. And yet . . .

Carrie noticed that the shoulder straps on the nightgown she wore had slipped down when she felt Oona's face on her bare skin. Oona settled her head in Carrie's cleavage, her mouth pressed to the curving side of one breast, her hand resting lightly on the other. Carrie felt confused, and her throat had gone dry. Her own hand stroked the small of Oona's back.

'Mammmmm . . .' Oona purred happily in her sleep.

17

'Her name isn't Rosalind Rodgers.'

'What a surprise,' Oliver deadpanned, although he then
allowed a brief smile at the corners of his mouth.

They were in Kelleher's on Third Avenue. It was starting to
fill with the after-work crowd, mostly middle-aged business
types who preferred an older bar that hadn't been tarted up
the way so many other joints on the street had.

Oliver and Joe Barone had already secured a booth towards
the rear of the bar. Joe was an old acquaintance from the times
when they were both actively involved with rock groups. A roadie
with a New York punk band the first time he went to London,
Joe later became a much-sought-after security expert for arena
and stadium gigs. He had his own crew and he dealt only with
headliners. He had also developed a sideline business in
personnel fact-checking and corporate intelligence-gathering.
Oliver had called on Joe's services in the past and had avoided
one unsound business deal.

'Well, she's Rosalind Rodgers now,' Joe amended. 'She went
to civil court and had her name legally changed.'

'Where?'

'Right here in New York. Queens, two years ago.' Joe had a
slim folder on the table in front of him, but he didn't bother to
check it. He stroked the carefully cultivated two-day stubble on
his chin as if it gave him real pleasure. He had steel-grey hair
that clung to his head in tight curls, longer at the back. 'Her
real name is Mary Rosalind Brodie.'

'Aha.'

'She's twenty-three years old.' Joe sipped his beer. 'She was born in Glasgow, Scotland, and her last known address on your side was Newcastle. Nobody says upon-Tyne, do they?'

'No,' Oliver replied, with a laugh.

'Didn't think so. Newcastle. By the way, wasn't that where the Animals came from?'

'Yes.'

'Thought so. Anyhow, Newcastle was only three years ago, so she's been a busy lady. Her point of entry was Niagara Falls, so she came through Canada. I'm not sure about the exact dates, but she wasn't in Canada for very long.'

'Lovely. Please go on.'

'She has a visitor's visa, and it's been regularly renewed. She has her own money, so the visa is no problem. Shortly after she changed her name, she bought the house in New Haven and paid in full, one hundred and ninety-five thousand dollars.'

'Christ.'

'No fear of the IRS, but I'll get to that in a minute.' Joe lit a thin miniature cigar. 'To go back a step, when you want to change your name here you have to give a reason. You can't just do it to hide a criminal record or escape debt, obviously. Okay. The reason she gave was business purposes.'

'Business purposes?'

Joe nodded. 'Which is funny, because she's not in business. But it's a commonly given, and accepted, reason. The interesting part of this is, she didn't change her name back in your dear old England. You have a different system there, apparently.'

'Deed poll.'

'I guess. It may only mean that she intends to stay on here and eventually become an American citizen. That she doesn't care about England and just couldn't be bothered.'

'She's still Mary Brodie there.'

'Correct.' Joe tapped his cigar on a flimsy ashtray. 'Now, the money thing. I couldn't find any wire transfers from England or Canada, or anywhere else for that matter. So she's gained all her wealth since she came here. Not that it's an enormous amount of money. A hundred-odd thousand in bank accounts, and the house in New Haven. That's about it, but it's a lot for the short time-span involved, and when you're unemployed.'

'Yes, it is.'

'I can tell you that she pays her taxes. She's legal and in the clear with the IRS. I couldn't get to see the actual returns but she has no problems in that direction.'

'She's legal,' Oliver repeated. 'Does that cover England as well? Or did she leave a situation behind?'

'Maybe, but it's definitely not a criminal matter. Both the court and the immigration people would check on that. She wouldn't be here and she wouldn't have been able to change her name if she had any criminal record. Anywhere.'

'Okay.' Oliver was disappointed to hear that.

'About the money, I really don't know yet. I found a lot of deposits, all for amounts ranging from a few hundred dollars to a couple of thousand. Lots and lots of them.'

'People give it to her,' Oliver told him.

'Oh, that's nice. Is she a whore?'

'More like a pimp. Her sister's a psychic and people give them money for spiritual advice.'

'That makes sense now. Must be a good act.'

'Yes,' Oliver said. 'It is.'

'Her sister is the Oona you asked about?'

'That's right. Tell me about her.'

'Wish I could.'

'What do you mean?'

'I drew a blank on that one.'

'But what little did you find?' Oliver asked.

'Nothing. *Nada*. Zip.'

'How is that possible?'

'Easy,' Joe said. 'It means that she didn't come into this country under the name of Brodie, and she didn't later change her name to Rodgers. If you can give me her last name, whatever she goes by now, I can probably get a line on her in a day.'

'Does this mean they're not sisters?'

'It doesn't mean yes and it doesn't mean no. All it means is that she is and has been using another name. And I guess you don't happen to know what it is.'

'No.'

Oliver absently tapped one end of a Senior Service on the table, then lit it. He had learned a little, but not nearly as much as he had hoped. Nothing at all about Oona. Nothing of a criminal nature. But what Joe had found was at least enough to suggest that further investigation was warranted. Their behaviour was unusual, and it hinted at something in the past. Oliver was eager to pursue the matter.

'As far as Roz is concerned,' he said, 'did you check back into her history in England or Scotland at all?'

Joe shook his head. 'Not yet. If you want me to, I can do that. But it'll cost more and it'll take longer. What I did so far was fairly routine, the things I'd do to check out anybody on this side, and there's still more I can do here. But if you want me to work the other side, I'll have to get some help over there. It's no problem, it just takes a little more effort.'

Oliver nodded. He thought about it while Joe went to get a fresh round of drinks. His first instinct was to have him follow up on whatever else he could on the American end and also set things in motion in England. But no, Oliver immediately saw the potential downside in that course of action. It might be better to keep Joe out of it from now on. To this point it was a simple enquiry, nothing remarkable. But the more Joe was involved in it the less scope for potential action Oliver might have later. And the situation could turn drastic.

'Psychic, huh?' Joe sat down with the drinks.

'Yes, of a sort. Carrie's rather taken with her, but so far very little money has actually changed hands.'

'Good.'

'They don't ask for any. In fact, they give the impression that they really couldn't care less about it.'

'The spiritual angle,' Joe said. 'The more you tell people that money isn't important, the more they want to give it to you. That's basic. If your wife doesn't start donating, they'll begin to drop some hints. Count on it.'

'I'm sure.' He wasn't at all sure, but that was the correct response. 'I had hoped they might have a bit of a history, which I could use as a counter-balance, but what you've found is pretty slight. Unusual, but hardly damaging. Oh, well.'

Joe nodded. 'They've been careful.'

'I'm surprised that they've been able to make so much money in such a relatively short period of time.'

'They probably got lucky as soon as they hit New York,' Joe said. 'If they met the right kind of person, somebody with money and status, the word-of-mouth would do the rest. They can make a lot of money fast, if they're regarded as hot.'

'I suppose you're right.'

'What do you want to do about it now?'

'I don't see much point in further action,' Oliver replied. 'Do you?'

'Frankly, no. It's your money, and if you want me to I'll keep on digging. But it doesn't look very promising.'

'I appreciate what you've done.'

'No problem.'

'There is one thing,' Oliver said.

'What?'

'I'm going to be in England again next month. I might just check first-hand to see if there's anything obvious on the record there. If I have the time.'

'Want me to find you a local guy to help out?'

'Well, don't set anything up because I may not even bother with it. But if you can give me the name of someone reliable, it might come in handy.'

'Will do. Give me a day or two.'

'No hurry.'

It was a couple of days after Oliver's return before Carrie consciously thought about it and realized that they had not made love since he got back. It was usually one of the first things they did after being apart for any length of time. It disturbed her that Oliver had not arrived home hot and hungry for her. It disturbed Carrie even more that she had taken so long to notice. She had not been waiting for him with her usual urgent sense of need and desire. It seemed as if they were both, separately, different now in some way, and when she realized this she didn't know quite what to make of it.

Was it because of the latest incident in the apartment? She had been afraid to mention it to him. It was so graphic and terrible, he might begin to think that she really was in the process of a breakdown. But Carrie couldn't keep it secret, and when she did tell him about it Oliver reacted calmly. Almost too calmly. He made sympathetic noises and raised his eyebrows, but said very little. It was as if he were preoccupied, and had been from the moment he had walked through the door.

He had bought one cover at Lugano, but when he showed it to her he didn't seem very enthusiastic, and then he locked it away with the rest of his collection. That, too, was a change in the pattern of normal life since Oliver usually left a new purchase on display for a while, to be adored and savoured.

He told her that his business had gone well and that he had sorted things out with Marthe, but he didn't really explain it to her and she sensed that perhaps the important decisions had been deferred. Oliver was quite capable of brooding about things like that for days on end before snapping out of it and knowing just what he intended to do.

But Carrie hadn't pressed him about anything. It scarcely occurred to her. The interest was missing. She had her own set of concerns to deal with and they were more vital to her than the tedious details of fabric production and commerce. It did worry her a little that she felt this way.

When she told Oliver that she had stayed overnight with Oona he tried to mask his disdain. She knew he didn't care for Oona. Oliver had acknowledged the voice of Carrie's father, but in the days afterwards he began to suggest that it had been a similarity at best, and that they had both been overly influenced by Oona's theatrics. Oliver didn't want to believe.

Carrie didn't have the luxury of choice. She knew what she had experienced on four separate occasions and what she'd heard emanate from Oona's throat. As if all that were not enough, she had also heard Oona, in her sleep, summon up the memory of an old friend of hers, Franny Hagstrom. And it had taken Carrie a while to understand just how eerie *that* was.

None of these things could be explained away or ignored. It was evidence, it was real, and what it all amounted to was a form of unknown truth that had to be faced. The alternative, Oliver's attitude, seemed to be wilful ignorance.

Carrie tried to be alert to everything around her, while not giving in to paranoia. She drove back to Manhattan on the Sunday afternoon and went to work as usual on Monday morning. She took care, but went about her business. Nothing happened. Oliver got back from Europe on Thursday, was out for a while on Friday evening but otherwise busied himself at home. All fairly normal, and yet somehow different. Both of them were different.

She didn't call Oona during the week. There was no need to consult her, and Carrie felt somewhat confused about her personal relationship with the girl. That Sunday morning Oona had woken up slowly, clinging to her. She was groggy, her limbs loose and floppy, almost like a narcoleptic. At times she would put her hands on Carrie's breasts or around her hips, and would plant tiny kisses on her throat. There was something undeniably sexual about this, and there were a few brief moments when, against her wishes, Carrie felt aroused by it. But it had happened largely in Oona's sleep, and it also seemed in some way to be essentially babyish, innocent in nature. Oona clung to her and touched her as an infant does its mother, seeking the protection of her embrace and the deep warmth of her body. Whatever sexual dimension there was to it seemed incidental and beside the point.

Mam. Oona had murmured and mumbled it again many times that night. It took a while for Carrie to understand it, but when she finally grasped its true significance it explained a lot. She'd thought that Oona was saying *Ma'am*, which seemed oddly formal and unnecessary, but then it dawned on Carrie: the word was *Mam.*

She knew from her years in England that it was common usage in the north and in Scotland for Mom or Mum – for Mother. Then she realized that Oona was clinging to her only as an infant did to its mother. Carrie felt relieved at first, but also troubled and deeply saddened for Oona.

Hadn't Roz warned her?

It was difficult to know what to do. Carrie admired Oona as a person with miraculous abilities, and looked to her for crucial help and guidance. How could she, at the same time, treat her as a forlorn child in need of love and mothering? In any event, she simply couldn't play the mother. It wasn't possible. She had a life in New York, a husband and a career.

Fortunately, Oona appeared to know that there was a natural limit to the situation. When she finally had awakened that morning she was friendly and as girlish as she'd been the night before, but ever so slightly distant. She was re-establishing the proper balance and space between them.

Carrie felt relieved, but also freer to show her affection. She gave Oona a big hug and a kiss on the cheek as she was about to return to New York. The good feeling stayed with her through the week.

Until Oliver arrived home, at which point a sense of nervous anticipation began to take hold. By Saturday the mounting unease had reached the point where Carrie felt she had to do something. Tomorrow was Sunday, and she still wasn't sure if Oliver intended to accompany her to New Haven for the second session. He'd only promised to go once.

Things unspoken, things still undone – Carrie realized that they hadn't made love since before his trip, and suddenly she had a rush of desire, a need for her husband. She wanted to put her arms around him, to feel safe within his embrace, and to have him fill her with his strength. She wanted to know that there was no distance between them, that everything was all right.

Carrie put on her navy-blue Wakefield pyjama top. It was a size too large, loose and rather boxy, but it hung beautifully on her and she knew that Oliver liked it (if the number of times she had to resew buttons on it was any indication). They settled in on the couch with drinks and a movie – *La Femme Nikita*. It held no surprises any more, since it was one of Oliver's old favourites, but Carrie didn't really mind seeing it yet again.

By the time the film ended they were into some heavy petting and deep kissing, but it didn't last long. Oliver wriggled out of his pants as he rolled her onto her back, slid between her legs and then into her, and it was all over a minute later. She felt disappointed, not so much because the sex was unsatisfying but because she had wanted the intimacy to be prolonged, to form a cosy cocoon around the two of them that would last for the rest of the night.

But Oliver had a cigarette lit and was channel-hopping with the remote while she was still catching her breath and struggling to sit up. Face it, you just got fucked. To be fair, it seldom happened like that.

'Oliver.'

'Mmn?'

'Are you going to New Haven with me tomorrow?'

'Oh, shit.' Annoyed, but not angry.

'You don't have to if—'

'Never mind. I'll go.'

'I don't want you to if you're going to resent it.'

'I don't resent it,' Oliver said, unconvincingly. 'But I do think it's a waste of time.'

'After what we heard the last time?'

'*Thought* we heard,' he corrected.

'I know what I heard,' Carrie insisted quietly.

'Well, we differ on that point.'

Carrie frowned. Nothing would be resolved, they would argue politely and then just set it aside. She hated that. But Carrie hated even more the thought of going to sleep with unhappiness or anger lingering actively between them.

'If you don't believe any of it, why bother?'

'For you,' he said. 'Because I love you.'

But then Oliver stayed up, drinking single malt and smoking, flicking aimlessly from one channel to another, while Carrie went to bed. She felt cold. She got up to put on the pyjama bottoms, but they didn't help. She felt cold and empty and alone.

18

Dunsany was right, the world was a very queer place. But it was no comfort to think that there were other levels or realms of existence beyond the one we currently inhabit. It filled Charley with dread. The idea of life after death troubled him.

'I mean,' he said aloud, 'what's the point?'

'What?' Heather asked. 'The point of what?'

'Going through all this, day after day, night after night, weeks, months, great bloody years of it. What's the point if, at the end of it all, you have to start mucking about all over again on some other plane of being? Act Two, life goes on, but without the humble pleasures of your poor old body.'

'Ah, Charley.'

'It's enough to give you the willies.'

He slammed his empty glass down on the table, and then went to the bar. They were in Gene's Tap, and had been for two hours now. Never mind, there was still light in the sky outside, which meant it was still quite early. Charley felt all right, whatever dark considerations nagged at him, but the drink was beginning to show in Heather, who had consumed three absurdly pastel daiquiris that had no place in a place like Gene's. Charley glowered at George, the barman, who smirked as he served a fresh round.

'I don't think I want another one,' Heather said foggily, as he parked the vile concoction in front of her.

'Just nibble at it around the edges, then.'

'Charley, I don't like sitting around and drinking like this in the middle of the day.'

'It's almost night,' he pointed out.

'I mean it. You don't take me seriously.'

'I certainly do, love. I depend on you.'

'What's that supposed to mean?'

'It means that my life is in your hands,' he told her. 'You keep me sane. I live on the edge, and—'

'What's that mean?' she cut in. 'You live on the edge. You told me that the first time we met, and I still don't understand what it means. The edge of what?'

Everybody was so damned literal these days. 'Heather, it's just an expression. The emotion is what counts.'

'I don't feel happy. I ought to be happy when I'm with you. But I'm not happy.'

Oh dear, this was serious. He had another six months in New Haven and it would be a shame to lose Heather this soon. Perhaps he ought to take her out to dinner – for a change.

'Darling, I—'

'I want to go home.'

'Well, of course.' Even better: home to bed.

But back at Heather's apartment, she wasn't having anything of the sort. Charley was affectionate and attentive, to the best of his ability in that direction. He listened dutifully to some of her favourite racket, which he could not quite bring himself to consider music. He spoke fondly of Heather's many virtues and qualities, while taking care not to mention her breasts. She was in no mood to be reminded that naughty sex was at the centre of their relationship.

But Heather ignored his soothing words. She sat planted in an old armchair, knees locked together tellingly and feet splayed apart. Charley recognized that pose from his high-school years. It was a position adopted by good young ladies at a certain time of life. It meant: access denied.

'Charley, I just want to go to bed. Alone.'

'Ah, Heather . . .'

'I mean it. I'm tired and I want to be alone.'

'After I send you wafting off happily to dreamland on clouds of bliss and tingly little wavelets of joy.'

Heather screamed.

'What is it, love?' he asked, with concern.

'Alone.' She gave him a hard stare.

Apparently Heather wasn't having any. Perhaps the time had come to pull out all the stops and tell her about Fiona. That would surely dampen her eyes – those wayward orbs currently frosted with a rosy shade of pink that somehow suggested certain laboratory animals. If necessary, he could even mention Oona and all that recent misery – though Charley was trying hard not to think about Oona.

'Heather, I never told you this but—'

'*Alone. Now.*'

Sex isn't everything, Charley thought morosely as he re-entered Gene's Tap and made his way to the bar. George soon caught sight of him, and sauntered along with an excessive look of sympathy on his face – but amusement in his eyes.

'Back already, Professor?'

'I forgot something.'

'And what would that be?'

'A pint of plain.'

'And for the young lady?'

'Fuck off.'

The Saturday-evening crowd had claimed all the tables so he had to perch himself on a stool at the end of the bar, next to an ancient jar of pickled eggs and a hanging piece of cardboard that held brown strips of dead fish embalmed in Cellophane.

Charley puffed on a Connecticut Valley cigar that suited the lugubrious drift of his present mood. The trouble with drinking alone is that you end up thinking about what you want to forget. The worst part is, it begins to feel good.

Charley believed in Oona now. *What* he believed was far from clear, however. That she was one of those crazy women out of old folklore, women who could see and hear and know things that other human beings couldn't? Women possessed of a touch of madness and magic – at one time they were regarded as more or less the same. That much, yes; Charley would have to concede that. There was no other explanation for the fact that Oona had uttered a few things known only to himself.

Such as the exchange with the shopkeeper, the warning he had consciously discounted later.

A little packet of woe you have to carry around with you for the rest of your foolish life.

Well, guilt was a fine thing in its own nasty way. There's nothing you can do about it, either. Once the little bugger moves into your house, it's there to stay.

But Fiona? Charley still resisted the notion that his dead child was somehow back in the everyday world. Oona might be able to read the deepest recesses of his mind, or she might see events that had happened long ago and far away – but that didn't mean a dead soul was on the loose and out for blood.

The idea somehow offended him. What was he supposed to make of it? That his daughter was a free-floating spirit currently in the vicinity, hovering over New Haven? Where was she at this very minute? How did she occupy herself when she wasn't speaking through Oona or appearing in Jan's dreams?

Charley resented the way that he had reacted. Oona had been in great distress, no doubt about it. Her act was real, and when he had finally grasped that, he had responded instinctively, reaching out and taking the poor girl into his arms, trying to comfort her until the terrible moment passed.

He didn't regret what he had done for her, but he did resent the way he had been manipulated into such an emotional state of mind. You silly eejit! If you ever read Dickens you'd probably break down and cry buckets when you got to the part where Little Nell died. Theatrics, is what it was.

Oddly enough, that he had come to accept Oona as a legitimate medium had had a kind of liberating effect on him. There was no longer any need to argue with himself about *that* point, so he could focus on the larger question: what did all of it mean? What did it say to him about his life? And Jan's.

But here, as before, Charley ran into a blank wall. He had not learned anything new. He saw no lesson. There was no dazzling revelation. The message from Fiona – if, indeed, you believed that Fiona had been there – amounted to nothing more than a suggestion of her presence. No doubt there were some people who would find spiritual comfort in that kind of message, but Charley wasn't one of them.

If there was an afterlife, a higher plane of being, then why would anyone who crossed over to it ever bother returning to this earthly realm and fretting about their past life?

Bugger the spiritual. Whether it was there or not, Charley couldn't deal with it. He found it easier and much more sensible to put his trust in science. Oona was genuine? Okay, fine. The human brain was a marvellous and mysterious organ, one that still defied anything like full understanding. So, let us say that the brain is capable of rare and remarkable feats, such as those Oona had apparently demonstrated. We don't understand how or why, but the answer must lie in the brain, still waiting to be discovered. It could have something to do with the electro-chemical nature of messages within the brain, low-frequency radio waves, or the way that matter and energy could be interchanged. Stuff like that. And it might have something to do with the nature of information itself: who was to say that the entire history of human life wasn't floating around permanently in the ether, tiny packets of data that could be accessed by human brains that had developed or been malformed in some peculiar way?

That made sense. The only trouble was, Charley couldn't be entirely sure about any one part of this business, and that was what so distressed him. He couldn't bear the thought that Fiona really might be in some state of unrest, in need of their help, or trying simply to communicate with them. If the spiritualists were right, what then? What could he do?

Play out the game with Oona, see where it led. But that was a depressing thought. Lonely, desperate people sitting around in a room in Westville, depending on every obscure word that emerged from the mouth of a bizarre prodigy. Deciphering whatever seemed to relate and discarding the rest.

Sir Walter Scott, for Chrissake.

It was hopeless, all hopeless.

*

Charley walked home, navigating Chapel, the Old Campus and the Green. He hadn't noticed how humid it was that night until he arrived back at the apartment and started to peel off his outer clothing. It was wet. He was drenched with sweat. It was far worse inside. They didn't own an air-conditioner and the windows were all closed so the sticky heat and humidity had simply accumulated, hour by hour, within the walls.

Couldn't count on Jan for anything any more. Charley opened all the windows. The night air was getting cooler, and it would clear out the apartment by morning.

He leaned close to Jan in the bedroom – she was asleep, and a low-grade snore emanated from her. Typical. She'd wake up in the morning with a headache and clogged sinuses if he didn't let in the air, and you couldn't tell her it was her own fault.

Charley padded around in his bare feet and underwear, going into the kitchen to grab a cold beer for a nightcap and then into his study to drink it within the protective shield of literature. His sacred womb-tomb of books. *Yes, and so what?* There are some people who can't even get to sleep unless they have a gun handy. Books were infinitely superior, the best refuge, and you couldn't accidentally blow your wife's head off with, say, the poetry of Derek Mahon. Though it might be interesting to try.

The beer was sufficient to ease him over the edge. Charley felt his body begin to swim as he finished it. He would find his way to sleep in no time, if he could find his way to bed – or even if he couldn't. Intoxication was too glorified a term. The grog had merely hammered his fraying consciousness into submission for a few hours. That was the point.

When he awoke, Charley realized a couple of things before he opened his eyes. He was in his own bed, with his body nestled in well-worn pockets and moulded around landmark bulges. At least he hadn't passed out on the narrow couch in his study or the sofa in the living room. And it was light outside, for light penetrated his eyelids – which felt as if they were bonded shut.

He knew it was still early because there were no sounds of

traffic outside. So it was much too early to wake up on a Sunday morning. He didn't move, hoping to drift off again. But then he became aware of a small, persistent noise.

Human. Sobbing. Nearby. It was so muted that it was worse than wrong – it sounded like somebody half paralysed, or being strangled to death. It had to be Jan, he realized at last. She must be having a nightmare. Bloody nuisance. Charley pushed his hip against hers – or where hers would normally be but wasn't. He muttered something vaguely comforting, still trying not to let himself awaken completely. But the noise continued, accompanied now by a fretful rustling of the sheets.

Fuck me. He was waking up now, there seemed to be no way to avoid it. Charley pushed himself up on one elbow and forced open his sticky eyes. Jan was huddled against the headboard, her body as tight as a baseball. Tears were streaming from her eyes, and her fists were pressed so hard to her mouth that she looked as if she were trying to eat them.

Jaysus, now what? Charley was about to sit up and snap her out of it when he heard another rustle from below. He turned his face and saw a crow perched on the footboard of the bed – a huge crow, feathers greasy and iridescent, like gasoline on asphalt, a pair of amber eyes, stark and baleful.

'What the—'

There was another one on Jan's dressing table, one on his bureau, a pair on top of the television set – there must have been a dozen in the room. In some useless corner of his brain Charley realized that he had not only opened most of the windows last night but the outer screens as well, enabling these hideous crows or ravens – *corbies* – to enter the apartment. But it did him no good to know that now. He began to scream at them.

He grabbed his pillow and swung at the nearest bird, yelling in fear and anger. That kicked a prop loose within Jan, and she began to wail loudly as her fingers fanned across her face. The crow spread its wings, rose from the footboard and the others began to stir.

'Get out! Get out of here!'

Charley continued to scream as he swung the pillow at them. He reached down beside the bed, got hold of a shoe and flung it at one. He hit a small lamp and knocked it off the dressing table. That set all of the birds in motion. Suddenly the room was full of crows, hovering almost lazily. Their wings seemed enormous, unfolding, flapping, filling the air with black slashes, and the movements created a terrible leathery clamour of increasing noise. They cawed and squawked as they circled about like sadistic harpies.

Charley felt like a madman, screaming, swinging the pillow, grabbing the clock, a book, slippers – whatever he could get his hands on – and flinging them at the ugly beasts. He had a definite sense of losing his mind and not caring.

He felt incredibly vulnerable, naked but for a pair of boxer shorts. But the crows stayed away from him, and they found their way out of the window at a sneeringly indifferent pace. He tried to smash the last one with the pillow, thinking wildly that he would tear it apart with his bare hands. But the evil bird slipped out of reach and disappeared, braying loudly as it wheeled off towards Orange Street.

There were splotches of crow shit everywhere, he discovered, as he moved through the apartment, slamming down the screens. He was stepping in it in his bare feet, but he didn't care. As soon as the windows were secure, Charley went straight to the study to get a drink. His hands shook as he poured a large Powers, downed it in two gulps and splashed another measure into the glass. It hit his stomach like liquid fire and he nearly heaved. His whole body trembled and his breath came in ripping gasps.

'What do you want? What do you want?'

19

Oliver seemed to be in a good mood on Sunday afternoon when they drove up to New Haven. He smiled a lot at her, although it was that quick and easy business smile of his. He hummed to the music he put on the CD player (Thin Lizzy) and tapped his fingers on the steering wheel. Perhaps he really was in a better state of mind, but Carrie had her doubts. The day had turned black and rainy and traffic was slow on the Interstate, which usually made him fume with impatience.

'I told you about the others,' she said.

'What others?'

'Oh. Sorry, I thought I did. Oona has asked another couple to sit in with us today. I don't know who they are.'

'Why are they going to be there?'

'She thinks it might help,' Carrie told him. 'They've been going through something similar, I guess.'

She thought Oliver would be annoyed, but he merely gave it a few moments' consideration, and then chuckled.

'Maybe she wants increased psychic vibrations,' he said, with a sidelong glance at her. 'The more the merrier.'

'Oona hopes that our presence might help make a breakthrough on their side, and vice versa.'

'What exactly is a breakthrough?'

'I – well, I'm not sure.'

'I suppose we'll know it if it happens.'

Carrie felt grateful – Oliver was being so reasonable, not at all negative. The traffic began to improve once they got east of Bridgeport, but the leaden sky turned blacker and the rainfall rapidly increased.

'It's a tremendous strain on her.'

'Yes,' he said. 'It must be.'

Another couple. It was a new wrinkle, but why should Oliver care? Safety in numbers. Maybe it was Oona's way of multiplying the ambiguities, thereby making it easier for the punters to find associations in the outpouring of her words and images.

Play along. Oliver had already convinced Carrie that he was sceptical of the whole thing. It seemed necessary, if he were to preserve his freedom of action. If Carrie knew that he believed in Oona's powers as much as she did, he would inevitably be drawn into the process to a much greater degree. Now he could act like a concerned husband, but an agnostic. He maintained a slight but significant distance. Carrie knew that he would be there for her but that ultimately it was her problem, not his.

And later, whatever might happen, she would be less inclined to think that it could involve him.

Besides, he believed in Oona's powers – but not in Oona. At least not the way Carrie did. Whatever the explanation, Oona knew something about him, and that created a sense of threat that Oliver could not tolerate. He wasn't afraid of being hauled back to India to face trial – that was absurd, impossible.

But where would Oona stop? He could not let the process go on indefinitely, if it meant that, among other things, he was going to be peeled like an onion in front of Carrie. Fortunately, Oona didn't seem to have much control over what she was doing. Oliver had convinced himself – and he knew he might be wrong – that he could monitor the situation and somehow intervene in time to head off any new problems before they arose. Before Oona or Roz fully understood. Before Carrie began to wonder about him. Before he started to feel the pressure and had to take more serious action. It was a dodgy game. That was the only good thing about it.

He smiled to himself when they were introduced to the other couple. The woman seemed to be in a trance, but jumpy as a bird. The husband was obviously a drinker, with a washed-out face and a bleak, tired look about the eyes. Somehow they struck Oliver as exactly the kind of people who would seek out Oona – people who went through life already half haunted by their own neuroses and inadequacies and were looking for spiritual rescue.

'Charley O'Donnell,' the man muttered.

'Oliver Spence.'

O'Donnell had a clammy handshake. He knocked back a Scotch and steered Oliver to the sideboard where the drinks were set out on a silver tray. He helped himself to another, and didn't offer one to Oliver.

'Have you been to these sessions before?'

'Yes, but just one,' Oliver replied. 'And you?'

'Twice. What do you think?'

They spoke in a low tone, but Roz and the two wives were busy chatting on the other side of the room while Oona had yet to put in an appearance.

'It's all a bit strange, really.'

'Are you English?'

'Yes.'

O'Donnell nodded approvingly. 'Strange is right. You know what I noticed the first time?'

'What?'

'You won't believe this. Some of what Oona was saying came straight out of a novel by Sir Walter Scott.'

'You're joking.'

'No, really. *The Bride of Lammermoor.*'

'You're sure of that?'

'No doubt about it. I looked it up.'

O'Donnell seemed quite pleased with himself. It could be an interesting piece of information, if true, although Oliver didn't see any special significance in it at first glance.

'Well, well. Did it mean anything to you?'

'I thought it did,' O'Donnell replied. 'But when I realized that it was Scott, I knew it had nothing to do with us.'

Not very convincing. Probably what he wanted to think, but couldn't quite accept. Otherwise, why come back?

'Do you think she's – all there?' Oliver prompted, knowing that O'Donnell was only too eager to talk.

'No.'

'Ah. You may be right.'

'But I also think she's genuine. In some peculiar way.' He finished his drink and gazed longingly at the sideboard.

'It's still early days for us.'

'I see.' O'Donnell glanced at the women and decided that it was safe to snag one more drink. 'I told her, you know,' he said, as he took another quick splash of Scotch. 'Oona started to come out with more of the same thing during our second session, so I jumped right in and finished it for her.'

'What, the passage from Scott?'

'Yes. I recited it out loud. The whole thing. The sister gave me a dirty look but it stopped Oona dead in her tracks for a minute. Then she went off in another direction. Still, it makes you think.'

'It certainly does.' The bold fellow. 'Well done.'

O'Donnell managed a grim smile. The poor sot, all he wanted was a bit of approval now and then.

Jan O'Donnell was in bad shape. From the moment they met Carrie could see that. The woman tried to smile, and nodded as Carrie and Roz chatted, but she barely spoke. There was a hollow look in her eyes. She was so timorous that Carrie was sure she'd been hurt repeatedly, beaten down, either by her husband or some element in the paranormal process. And the husband didn't make a very good impression when they were introduced, merely grunting at Carrie and then lurching off for another drink.

Carrie had sympathy for the woman, but also felt relieved in some way – and then, immediately, guilty about *that*. It was a little like being in a doctor's waiting room and noticing that the other patients were worse off than you were. She wondered if, after several visits to Oona, she was going to end up looking like Jan. What if the incidents became more graphic and unbearable but Oona was unable to provide any real help?

She didn't want to think about it. Fortunately, Roz was in a talkative mood, friendly and upbeat, so Carrie could drift along with the small-talk and avoid her worries.

A short while later Oona entered the room, providing further distraction. She looked nearly angelic, a Pre-Raphaelite vision of girlish beauty, with long, flowing black hair, alabaster skin, and deep, piercing eyes. She wore a light summer dress of slate blue and ivory, with a fine floral print, a shirred empire waist, and front buttons from the scooped-out neckline to the middle of the calf. The top button was undone, as were the rest from just over the knee down to the hem. Oona also had on espadrilles with long ties cross-wound several inches up past the ankle.

She appeared to be brimming with confidence and excitement. She went straight to Jan, took the woman's hands in hers and spoke a few quiet words to her. Jan smiled faintly. Then Oona turned to Carrie, put her hands on her shoulders and hugged her, giving her a light kiss on the cheek.

'My friend.'

'Hi,' Carrie said. 'It's great to see you again.'

She meant it. Oona's presence had boosted her spirits in an instant. She was amazing. How did she get herself up for the ordeal and actually seem eager for it? Once again, Carrie felt a rush of respect and affection for her.

Oona went to the seedy Mr O'Donnell next, pausing just long enough to say something and rub his forearm – he was wearing an old cotton shirt that was a bit frayed at the collar, with the sleeves rolled up.

Then she turned to face Oliver, and did the same thing with him. Just a few words that Carrie didn't catch. Rubbing his arm below the short sleeve of his Madras shirt. Oona started to turn back toward the women, but then stopped and took Oliver a few steps away. She spoke to him again. The exchange lasted for one or two minutes. Oliver gave a short laugh, but his jaw clenched and his eyes were cold and narrow as Oona turned away from him.

Carrie wondered what that had been all about.

*

The smarmy English bastard. They think they own the bloody world. And what does he do? He peddles clothes. Typical. Just another ragman. Clever, of course; bazaar-smart. He had spotted Charley for an academic quickly enough, and no doubt regarded him with similar contempt. Spence would think that he dealt with the real world, whereas Charley hid out in an ivory tower. The usual stereotype. Well, chum, I can tell you I've had a little contact with your so-called real world, and literature has it beat hands down. Money-grubbing, no-taste git. Wouldn't know a work of art if it ran up and bit him on the ankle.

Jeans, for Chrissake. Denim. Ugh. Charley, who stuck with his faithful corduroys right through the summer, was not impressed with Mr Spence. Charley had made an effort, had tried to talk to the man and even tell him a few things about Oona, but it was like poking rubber. Spence had nothing to say. He nodded and murmured without moving his lips, and stood there with an air of bland certainty.

Never mind. Charley was in a good mood, surprisingly so. A few hours ago, all was hell. Jan catatonic. Himself scared down to the crap-smeared soles of his feet. He'd been in a sorry way, no doubt about it. Fretted and stewed for some little while, and Jan mewing forlornly by herself like a crazed kitten.

Crows. Or ravens. Charley couldn't have told the difference if his life depended on it. It was frightening, of course, kind of like waking up and finding yourself in an out-take from the movie by Hitchcock. But that wasn't Tippi Hedren in bed with you. And the damn birds hadn't actually menaced them – they merely seemed menacing by the simple fact of being there. It had to be a very bizarre coincidence. Unusual behaviour for animals, yes, but city birds were known to be rather bold.

When Jan finally began to speak again, she had been convinced it was a message from Fiona. Ravens from Ravenswood. Predictable, and apparently logical in a highly irrational situation. But Jan had no answer to his simple question: what if he had not opened the screens in his tipsy state the night before? Obviously, the birds could not have got in and the incident would never have happened.

Charley knew how eerie it was, but he refused to jump to the most extreme conclusion about it. That was unnecessary.

Still, at the time he'd felt fairly shattered.

But the whisky had steadied him in due course – and had held off any hangover that might have chimed in for good measure. He had regrouped himself and scraped up a little more strength. The usual miracle. That was the key to life. Evil doesn't last. It goes away. It will come back and have another go at you, you can be sure of that. But in between the evil times, you can recover. You can convince yourself it's all still worthwhile.

Sure it is.

You'd think it was a party they were throwing this time, the booze out in a help-yourself mode and ersatz music playing on the stereo. Some mind-dulling New Age rubbish.

Oona came in, sparing Charley any further duty on the social front with the Englishman. She was quite the darling today, with her skin polished and buffed, her hair magnificent and a lovely dress that clung lovingly to the parts of her tender body that it didn't leave exposed.

'Thank you for coming today,' Oona said, when she got to him. She stroked his forearm pleasantly.

'I wouldn't miss it for the world, my dear.'

'You're teasing me.'

'I'm trying.'

'I think it's going to be very special today.'

'Be gentle with me. And yourself as well.'

She laughed at that, patted his arm and turned to the Spence character. Charley savoured the last of his drink, in case it was a while before he got another.

The smug Englishman fancied Oona as well, Charley could see that at once. Probably did well with the ladies, him being a man of the world with all that rag-trade money and a veneer of Anglo-Saxon self-assurance.

Charley's eyes moved to Mrs Spence. Did she see any of the

same things he did in her husband? Probably not. Or maybe she was an oh-so-sophisticated type who didn't mind turning a blind eye to the minor human foibles, as long as she was well provided for and the proper public image was maintained. She was rather attractive in her own right, tall and adequately fleshed with the kind of elegant facial features you might see on a delicate cameo. But you married a bounder, gel. Comes from not reading Arnold Bennett early enough in life.

Roz went into her squadron-leader spiel. Charley paid little attention. Let's have another drink, he thought, or let's get on with it. Oona drifted closer to him, close enough for him to notice now that she smelt wonderful. Sort of woodsy, minty. Something abstruse and herbal, no doubt.

Then they began to move to the other room. She stepped in front of Charley, who had taken up the rear. She slowed up, and he had to stop or step around her. He stopped, and she turned to face him. Aha, the vixen had a flirty smile for him.

'Charley.'

Her voice was low and conspiratorial, definitely arousing. She leaned closer, and Charley instinctively bent down as if to kiss her. He felt himself going all soft and fuzzy at the edges, like the first time he'd met her. It was the kind of dizziness you want very much to give in to, because you know the fall is bound to be worth the price. Watch it, mate.

'Yes?'

'You may have to do something for me.'

'Anything. Anytime.'

'Thank you.' Pleased. Her hand on his arm.

'What is it?'

'I don't know yet.'

'Oliver.'

'Hello.'

'I'm glad you came.'

'It's important to Carrie.'

'And to me,' Oona told him.

'Nice of you to say so.'

'No, really, it is.'

'Why?'

'Because I know about you.'

'Oh? And what do you know?'

'You want to kill me,' Oona answered. Her eyes were fierce with excitement, as if she were relishing a reckless dare.

'Is this one of those psychological games?'

'Sort of.'

'Thought as much.'

'But you know I mean it. Don't you?'

'Hardly.'

'And you know it's true.'

'What on earth gives you that idea?'

Oona stepped closer to him and began to rub his arm. Oliver wished he'd left his jacket on. Oona gazed up at him. She had a way of creating a zone of intimacy with someone, as if she had pulled a bell-jar down over them. She was still smiling.

'Becky.'

It had been a long time, years, since Oliver last felt as if his knees had dissolved. His body held up, of course. He didn't flinch, although he thought he felt a bit of colour rushing into his cheeks. Oona was watching him so closely that he felt naked. He felt as awful as he could ever remember feeling.

'Pardon?'

'Becky. The name seems to mean something to me,' Oona said. 'Does it mean something to you?'

''Fraid not, no.'

'Ah, well. It's all right, Oliver.'

'What is?'

'What you want to do,' Oona told him. 'When the time comes, I might even help you get away with it.'

The room had been changed somewhat. They were going to use the main area, not the small alcove at the back. Plant-stands at the four corners of a large Saruq, a wide array of pillows around a low mahogany table, and in the centre of the table a dark stone basin the size of a garden birdbath. It was full of clear water, with a thin layer of fine white sand on the bottom.

Carrie saw that it was still pouring outside, sheets of rain slapping against the windows as the wind gusted. The room lights were off, but two or three dozen short fat red candles had been lit and strategically placed, including some between the planters on each side of the rug.

They took their places, Roz directing. Carrie and Jan were to the right and left of Oona respectively, Charley and Oliver at the bottom arc of the round table, their backs to the window. It was about to start happening fast, Carrie realized, with a feeling of vague concern. Oona lowered herself to the pillows in a very wobbly manner, and her eyes were already beginning to roll around without focus. There was apparently no need this time for her to warm up and ease herself into it. Roz quickly stepped out of the immediate area, sitting by the wall, notebook and pen ready.

'Oh, Jesus, I don't believe it,' Oona said to herself, as she clamped her hands on the edge of the table. 'The river's swollen today and we're at the rapids.' She smiled wanly, and for just a second her eyes caught Carrie's. 'Hold on, folks. This is going to be sort of like putting my head in a blender.'

'Will it be all right?' Roz asked loudly.

That alarmed Carrie. There seemed to be an undercurrent of tension and danger in the air, and for Roz to ask a question like that only made matters worse. The last time, she had acted as if nothing could possibly be a serious problem, even in the moments when Oona had been obviously in extreme pain.

'Oh yeah, oh yeah, oh yeah . . .'

'Oona, are you sure?' Carrie asked.

'Surrrrre . . .' Oona's body swayed. She reached out, bumped Carrie's arm and fumbled at it as if her fingers were useless and beyond control. 'Make love to me like the angels, honey, can you save me save me save me *save me* . . .'

Her hand fell away from Carrie's arm. Oona began to pat and clutch at herself, as if to make sure that her own body was still there. Her hands went up to her face, then down along her throat and finally took hold of her shoulders. She continued to sway, rocking her upper body in a roughly circular motion. Sounds that meant nothing came from her mouth. Suddenly she stopped, leaned forward and threw her arms across the table on either side of the stone basin, her forehead pressed to the wood. She began to talk in a voice that was almost normal, but seemed about to cry.

'Touch me touch me please touch me now . . .'

Carrie didn't hesitate. She put her hand on Oona's arm, and the others followed her example. Some of the urgency went out of Oona's voice, but she continued to repeat the same words. She stayed that way for about a minute, and then slowly sat up. She gently pulled her arms away from them, and smiled. She looked at each of them, nodding as if pleased. For a moment Carrie almost thought it was all over.

'Wild,' Oona said, a dreamy look in her eyes. 'It's so wild today. This is something else.'

'Oona,' Carrie said.

'Mmmn?'

'Are you sure you're okay?' Oona gazed at her. Moistened her lips. Said nothing. 'Oona?'

'She's fine,' Roz noted, a mild scold.

Oona was still moistening her lips with her tongue, and then she began to move her jaw as if trying to speak. But no words or sounds emerged. This seemed to bother her. An anxious look clouded her face, and her eyes were restless, fearful. She worked her throat as if she had a thin fishbone stuck in it. She began to gag, or was trying to cough, but still made no sound. The colour was gone from her face – but soon came back as a ghastly creeping blueness. Her eyes widened in panic.

The incident disappeared. Oona gave Carrie a startled look, and then began to cry. The sounds of weeping were normal, though babyish, and she appeared to have no more difficulty breathing. There were no tears, and she stopped crying a few seconds later. She looked lost and forlorn, like a child left alone suddenly for a few minutes in some unfamiliar place.

'*Save me save me save me aaaahhhh save me love me love me oh love me like the angels honey...*'

Her voice low, as if trying to remind herself of something, and also seeking an elusive rhythm. Oona shook her head, unhappy about something. She's still only on the edge of it, Carrie told herself. Oona pulled her knees up close to her body and wrapped her arms around them, still rocking herself tightly. The words gave way to unformed grunts and abortive shouts. Her eyes locked onto some invisible point in the air.

'*Don't leave me don't leave me Daddy Daddy Daddy Mam Mam Mam Muh-muh-muh-muh oh shit oh shit oh shit hey you hey hey you there come here then come here yeah you hey fuck me too lick me love me love me love me like the angels—*'

Oona's voice deepened and speeded up sharply.

'*He stops he turns he runs to you runs runs runs to you runs to you to kill you he kills you kills you kills his hands on your throat squeezes the life out of you into his eyes eyes eyes I I I I can't save you save you save me save me oh save me please don't go don't leave me again oh no oh no oh no oh mother father sister daughter save me oh no he says child he says child I can only try to tell you child he says this man will kill you too too too two times then oh yes he says oh yes oh yes oh yes I can I can only try to save you save me save me don't go again—*'

Oona stopped abruptly, her eyes fluttering, her mouth open as she gasped for air. Then she tilted her head to one side, and her eyes narrowed. She looked as if she were trying to overhear something, but was having difficulty. A moment later, she began to speak in a normal voice – but it was amazingly like the voice of Carrie's father.

'*You only have to look at him.*'

Oona started rocking again. The man's voice trailed off in a prolonged whine. Carrie sat back against a pillow. She didn't turn her head, but her eyes glanced towards Oliver. He caught her look, and smiled reassuringly at her. He nodded, as if to say he had recognized her father's voice too, but he raised his eyebrows to indicate that he had no idea what it meant.

'*He used to be a sweet boy.*'

Oona's head hung forward, as if she were drowsy and couldn't keep her eyes open, but her face was hidden behind her hair. The voice continued after another pause.

'*But that was a long time ago. You only have to look at him now to see. Something went—*'

Hesitation. Carrie looked down. Everyone was still and the room was silent except for the sound of the rain on the windows. Carrie had the profound sense of being in her father's invisible presence, and of being close to understanding what he wanted to say to her. Very close, but still not there.

'*Used to be a sweet boy, but something went wrong. You only have to look at him to see. Sweet boy, something went . . .*'

Carrie started to glance towards Oliver, but stopped herself. She looked up, deliberately turning to Oona again.

Oona was motionless and silent for what seemed like a very long time. Then she raised her head, and some of her hair fell off to the sides of her face. She was trembling, her eyes tight and her fists pressed together at her throat. Suddenly, a scream exploded from her, so loud and violent that everyone else at the table recoiled.

'*Mr Oliver! What are you doing?*'

The voice was perfect. The bitch had it word for word. She was something else. Oliver felt as if his body had turned to sand and was blowing away grain by grain in a rising breeze. As if he were beginning to disappear. But he wasn't, couldn't.

The voice changed, low and racing.

'*He stops he turns he looks back he starts to run run runs back to the bed where he has fucked you he takes you rolls you on your back takes you takes your throat he is between your between your legs again his hands take the breath from you sucks you into his eyes eyes eyes I I I oh you can save me save me save me oh no oh no in Ballapul it is in Ballapul I die I die I die—*'

The voice trailed off briefly, but then returned once again as the miserable little man Oliver knew too well.

'*Mr Oliver! What are—*'

Oona stopped abruptly, as if frozen. She made a sharp noise with her tongue that sounded like a stick breaking. She repeated it several times, at regular intervals. Oliver nearly smiled, it was so incredibly accurate. The neck snapping. He felt bemused, and oddly distant from himself. He sighed impatiently, a gesture of false indifference, but no one was paying any attention to him. They all stared at Oona.

To this day, he didn't know why he had stopped and returned to the room. Flipped the whore, knelt on her and killed her. It was the heat, the place, the cheapness of life, the sheer vacancy and meaninglessness – but these were retrofit elaborations, spun from the missing core of the act itself. All he knew for certain was that he had done it, and that he had killed again a moment later when his little guide blundered into the room.

He had wanted to see Chik Pavan, one of the places where the young prostitutes were kept in cages. Supposedly notorious. He thought it was probably designed that way to appeal to foreigners on the prowl. But he never got there. The man persuaded Oliver to go to Ballapul instead.

Ballapul was a crumbling tenement complex that had gradually been taken over by the sex business. There were four buildings around a ratty central courtyard, where people cooked over charcoal fires and kiosks sold murky potions in unmarked bottles. Music blared from every apartment, all of it different but all of it jarringly shrill and loud.

The four cement buildings were connected by internal halls and outdoor balconies and porches. The entire compound was thick with people, some of them Westerners like himself. Oliver paid off the man who had brought him there, agreeing that they'd meet later, and for a while explored the place on his own.

There were three floors to each building, and it looked like each apartment ran into the next so that the total effect was of wandering through a vast maze, a warren of cramped passages and stark little cells that were painted a claustrophobic deep blue, from the scabby floors to the cracked ceilings.

It was frightening, in a way, perhaps because it was so dark and utterly alien. You really felt that you could die there, and no one would notice. Part of that was true.

Some of the young girls were pretty, darkly exotic with eyes of astonishing depth, though many were unattractive, tubby, garishly made-up and with repellent faces. The one Oliver chose had a heart-shaped face and large shimmering eyes. She was short and petite, though her nipples were large, dark and womanly. He paid the fussy madam, who stayed in the front room, and the whore led him to a cubicle at the end of an interior hallway.

The sex was uninteresting and soon done. But, then, it had not cost very much. That should have been the end of it, fifteen minutes from door to door, and it nearly was. But something made Oliver stop while he was in the corridor on his way out, and then he turned and dashed back into the tiny room. No passion, anger, nothing caused it. But he wanted to do it, however reckless and suicidal it seemed – and he truly did have the sense of gambling his own life on a throw of the dice.

Perhaps that was it.

The woman out front was a problem that could be avoided, for a short while anyway. Oliver had already noticed another exit to the landing at the end of the corridor. But he hadn't counted on the guide, the enterprising fellow who'd brought him there in the first place. They were supposed to meet later by the gate at the front of the compound.

But Oliver should have known better. He was the man's 'job' for the evening, his source of income, and he wouldn't let Oliver get away until he'd extracted every rupee that he possibly could. There were other gates, many ways in and out of the compound, and he probably feared missing Oliver later. So he'd tagged along at a discreet distance, keeping a proprietary eye on Oliver, and as soon as enough time had passed for the usual fast fuck, he'd come down the corridor to make sure Oliver didn't choose to leave that particular area by the other exit. The poor devil didn't want to lose a customer, was all.

Said, 'Mr Oliver! What are you doing?'

The only thing Oona got wrong was the scream. In fact, that

exclamation had come in the form of a shocked gasp, not much more than a hoarse whisper. One quick step, and Oliver had him. Then he shoved the bodies behind the bed, where they might not be seen at first – he was sure that every second mattered. The corridor was empty, and Oliver hurried silently out of the other door to the landing. Slipped into the passing crowd. It was night, and that helped, although he still hadn't heard any outcry by the time he got to the gate and left the compound.

He walked a fair distance before flagging down a taxi. That was the worst of it, to be alone in the dark in some unknown part of Bombay, fleeing a crime scene. He was sure that his life was effectively over. He would be caught and sent to prison. Oliver vowed to kill himself as soon as he got there, rather than rot in some Indian pesthole for the next thirty years.

He took the taxi driver's advice on a good nightclub, had a strong drink, and then walked back to his hotel. Sipped his duty-free Scotch, smoked cigarettes until dawn, and waited for a knock on the door. It never came. He checked out later and caught his flight to London. There was no trouble, no suspicious looks, not a single awkward question. And, to Oliver's very great relief and surprise, that was the end of the grisly interlude.

Sort of.

Oona seemed to be in one of her temporary lulls. She rubbed her face, smiled hazily and burbled meaningless sounds. Whatever came of this, the only thing he could do was deny it. Dismiss it with a laugh. Nothing could be proved, after all. Two anonymous natives had died in a Third World slum a long time ago. But even that much could not be shown. Not now. Not by anyone here. The best Oona could do was raise the subject, not the dead.

Oliver smiled again a moment later when he glanced at Carrie and saw that she was looking at him.

'Bird of night bird of prey ravens crows and corbies blacken the sky in the middle of the day it was the day it was the day we

*played oh no oh no don't leave me please don't leave me there oh
no oh no the barn the birds of night the birds of prey the day we
played not the barn—'*

Here we go again, Charley thought. Oona was shaking and
her voice was a useless drone, like an engine idling. He glanced
at Jan, and felt a stab of concern. His wife looked terrified. Her
eyes were wide open and she was frantically wringing her
fingers. Calm down, girl. He tried to get her attention, but Jan
was not to be distracted. She was locked in on Oona now.

'Fon Fon Fon Fon Tayna Fontayna Fontana—'

'Yes,' Jan murmured anxiously.

That's it, Charley thought, write the damned script for her,
why don't you? They must love you.

*'Fontana Fontana the barn the lake the day we played the day
the birds of prey came to say eat you eat you they'll eat you out
past the barn the lake Fontana look out child—'*

'I was three,' Jan said to herself.

What was this? Jan had grown up on a farm in Fontana,
which was just another hick town in southern Wisconsin. Over
the years he had heard stories from Jan of her childhood and
adolescence, a typical chronology of joys and sorrows, milestones and memories, images from Norman Rockwell and
Grant Wood. Nothing remarkable, unless you considered her
move from the Future Farmers of America to English literature
a shocking leap.

*'Don't want don't want don't want the runt don't go not now
not here don't want the runt—'*

'They didn't,' Jan said. 'They didn't want me. They called me
Runt, too. Gail and Sue.'

'Jan, please,' Charley felt compelled to say.

He had thought that Oona was speaking about Fiona, and
meant to suggest that he and Jan hadn't wanted the child.
Which was a lie. But now it appeared that Jan thought it was
about her. She was the youngest of five children, and he knew
that her two sisters had called her Runt. But he had always
understood that it was a trivial family joke, the kind of thing
you may not like when it's happening but tend to remember

fondly later in life. Jan had never given him any indication that
it had been all that painful for her, and still was, until now.

'*Stay stay stay I said please but stay stay stay they said I had to
stay there till they came come back come back the barn the barn
the birds came off the barn the roof oh no oh no—*'

'Only three,' Jan said. 'The clearing beyond the barn. Sue sat
me down there and said don't move.'

'*Come back come back and then you see you see oh no the dead
grey squirrel in the grass oh no—*'

Jan gasped, tears in her eyes. 'It was just a game of hide and
seek, but sometimes they'd play it as a trick on me. One of
them would hide me somewhere and tell me to wait there until
the others found me, but then they wouldn't come. I was too
young to know what was going on, and so I'd sit there and
wait. And wait. And nobody would come.' Jan gave a shuddery
laugh. 'Seems like it took me years to catch on, I was such
a . . .'

'*Ashes in the grass grey and red colour of the dead the dead the
dead squirrel in the grass oh no sister sister brother mother father
sister don't go don't go don't leave me again—*'

Oona was curled up tightly now, lying with her head on
Jan's knee. Oona barely moved. Her eyes were wide open and
her hands covered her chest protectively. She spoke in what
was nearly her normal speaking voice, but the words came in
short, jagged spasms that didn't always match the slower
movements of her mouth.

'*Bird of prey bird of night raven crow and corbie come oh no oh
no blood on the grass grey and red I'm dead I'm dead—*'

'That's right,' Jan said. 'There was a dead squirrel beside me
in the grass. I don't know if the other kids put it there, or if it
just happened to be there, but it was only a few feet away. I
wanted to move, but I couldn't. I don't know why, maybe it
was because I'd been told to stay put, and at that age I did
what the older kids told me, regardless. And I didn't want to
look at it, but I had to, because I'd never seen anything that
bloody before. I was three. The birds had been at it already.'

'*Mother sister father brother help me help oh mother save me save me save me can you save me—*'

'And they came back for more.'

Jan seemed to be in a trance of her own. But she spoke in a soft voice, and the only obvious signs of distress were the occasional tears that trickled down her face. Oona, on the other hand, was rigid with terror and pain, and her voice grew fainter, as if she were speaking from the bottom of a cave.

Charley was vaguely annoyed by all this, but fascinated too. He knew nothing about the story Jan and Oona were jointly exploring, least of all whether there was any truth in it. But he had been paying fairly close attention, and he couldn't honestly say that Jan had been leading Oona, that Oona was simply using clues given to her on a silver platter. Perhaps Jan had already provided the basic outline when she was talking with them in the other room, earlier. But at this stage, Charley would not put anything past Oona. Perhaps she was seeing something that really happened to Jan at the age of three. That only made it worse, of course, and Charley wished again that they had stayed home.

'*Wings around my head around me oh no birds of night birds of prey come sweeping round me in the middle of the day they pick and stab and poke and tear all is blood and flesh—*'

'And the eyes,' Jan continued. 'The whole flock came back, ten, fifteen of them. And they flapped and walked all around me and kept on eating the squirrel, pulling it apart bit by bit, and I remember how they jabbed and pulled the eyes out and ate right through the hole, into the skull.'

'Jesus, Jan. Please.' But she wasn't listening to him.

'They didn't hurt me. They just – touched me.'

'*Mother! can you can you save me save save me please please don't leave me alone here Sister! Brother! Father! Mother!*'

'But nobody came back for me. Until later, much later,' Jan said. Absently, she began to stroke the side of Oona's face. 'Nobody came.'

Oona's voice suddenly changed. She sounded older, less of a

child. She sat up and gazed at Charley, but it was not as if she were seeing him. She was gazing blindly in his direction.

'When the laird the laird the laird when the laird went down to Ravenswood to Ravenswood with his bride his bride—'

'I didn't want to go,' Jan said. Another tear escaped from her eye and coursed across her cheek.

'Oh no oh no oh no don't leave me—'

Charley exhaled and sat back, feeling as empty as a sack of skin and bones. Now he could see where Oona was leading him, and he felt stripped of his intelligence, suddenly stupid and vacant. It was true, Jan had wanted to rent a house or a flat in Galway, to stay in the city. He was the one who had preferred the rustic whitewashed cottage a few miles out in the countryside, where on a good day you could just see the sea.

Ravenswood. His wife had apparently suffered some childhood trauma over crows or ravens, and he'd taken her to a place called Ravenswood. Brilliant. Why hadn't the stupid bitch ever let on? It was his doing, and yet he couldn't help feeling angry that Jan had silently agreed, had gone along with his wishes. Charley was the Laird of Ravenswood. He'd taken his young bride there. This was all still Scott, of course, but at last he could see how Oona had mangled it into a kind of rough truth.

'Don't leave me don't leave me don't leave me—'

Which was exactly what he'd done – left her out there when he went into the college every day. He had lectures, tutorials, notes to take in the library, bookshops to browse. And all those merry hours spent in pubs with his colleagues, his students.

Oona screamed: *'Mother don't leave me!'*

'Just for a minute,' Jan answered, tears running freely down her face now. 'It was just for a minute.'

'Oh no oh no oh no Mother!'

'To get a cup of tea.'

Oona thrashed wildly on the cushions, but her arms were held tightly to her sides. She struggled as if she were trying to get out of a strait-jacket. Or, Charley realized, as if she were all wrapped up in blankets. Her voice raced, frantic, trapped.

'Bird of night bird of prey come to get me in the middle of the day raven crow and corbie come oh no oh no oh no dark of day black in the sky raven crow and corbie come to circle in and take my – oh no oh no oh no – Muh–muh–muh–Mother!'

'It was such a lovely day,' Jan said, her voice dull. 'Too nice to stay indoors. You were in the pram. I was reading Flann O'Brien, *The Dalkey Archive*. In the backyard – the garden, they call it there. I didn't care for the book, so I went to get some magazines. And I put the kettle on for a cup of tea.'

'Black black black black black – Mother! don't leave me Mam don't leave me oh no oh no Muh–muh–muh–Mother! Mam!'

'I waited for the water to boil. I was reading an article about the hostages in Iran. I waited for the tea to steep. When I got to the door to the backyard, they were on the pram. Black, like a collar round you.'

'No,' Charley struggled to say, his throat clogged, his face burning with blood in the skin. 'No.'

'Save me save me save me save me save me save me Mother can you save me save me save me—'

'Fiona . . .'

'Muh–muh–muh–muh—'

Rain spattered the windows. Oona writhed furiously and then let out one long savage scream that lingered in the room even after her voice had collapsed.

'Couldn't,' Jan continued vacantly. 'I couldn't move, I saw the blood on their beaks. I didn't hear you. There were five or six of them. I didn't hear you at all.'

'This didn't happen,' Charley stated.

'I threw something. It was too late. I threw something and yelled, and they flew off a little ways. I got you then, but it was too late. And I wanted to go with you, I didn't want to stay there any more. You must take me with you. I didn't want to let you go, I didn't, I didn't. But I couldn't move.'

'This is not true,' Charley said bitterly, staring down at Oona. She was lying still, as if dead. If only you were. 'Yes, there were ravens in the area, but this is – fantasy.'

Jan turned to him. 'So I took her into the new nursery, and

I started the fire under the crib. I put the heater and fuel can by it and I got down on the chaise and waited.' Jan started to cry again. 'Whoosh . . . it would have been all right, too. If only the van man didn't come and save me.'

The man driving by, who'd seen the smoke and flames from the road. He had managed to pull Jan out, not badly burned but half-dead from the heavy fumes. Mr Hurley, by name. Mr Hurley, who had not been able to get back inside for Fiona.

The things you remember. Days later, surveying the charred remains of the cottage, Charley had come across a coffee mug from the Kilkenny Workshop in the trampled garden grass near the place where the pram had been, and wondered. *I threw something.*

'Don't,' Jan said piteously. 'Don't save me . . .'

'Jan.'

Oona's mouth was open, slack. She still didn't move, but a voice emanated from her. A child again.

'Mother don't leave me Father don't leave us don't go don't go don't leave me again no more no more no more I want you I want you Mother Father you left me left me left us – you.'

Oona seemed to crumble into herself.

Charley had to move, to do something.

Carrie wondered if it was over. Oona was still and silent, curled up between Jan and Carrie. Her eyes were open, gazing off at the window. Tiny beads of saliva had gathered at the corners of her mouth.

Charley O'Donnell got up and lit a thin cigar. He paced by himself, away from the rest of the group. His wife didn't move. She had stopped crying and was sitting passively now, staring at Oona and stroking her hair.

Carrie wondered absently if the O'Donnells had just had the kind of breakthrough that they wanted – or needed. Their story sounded too terrible to be true, like a nightmare that becomes a confused part of everyday life.

But her mind was too full of her own frightful and uncertain thoughts to worry about anybody else's problems for long. Oliver looked patient and imperturbable. He let out a small sigh every now and then, but otherwise hardly stirred.

'Love me like the angels honey . . .'

Oona rose and sat back on her heels, legs apart. She rocked very slightly, rolling her head around on her shoulders as if to loosen stiff muscles in her neck. Carrie saw that her eyes were nearly closed, and then Oona's hair swung across her face. After a moment or two of unintelligible moaning, Oona began to speak in a female voice with an English accent.

'I don't want don't want don't want to want to want you just to be the one the one the one in London no no Becky darling Becky no no not like that be careful of your teeth gently with the lips and tongue not the teeth that's it that's better bye bye let's go bye bye Bayern Bayern München Bayern bye bye Becky—'

Oona put her hands between her legs, up under the skirt of her dress. Rocked slightly for a few moments.

'Bye bye bye bye Bayern Becky by my my my Marty Marty Marta Marta Martha Martha my my my Myra! Myra! my Myra! be my Myra and eee–eee–eat-uh eat a eat a eat a Ian Ian Ian eee–and–oh oh my my muh-muh-muh Myra—'

She froze for a second.

'The knife. Here. Beautiful.'

Charley O'Donnell came closer, apparently curious now. He stood near the edge of the group and watched.

Oona stuck out her tongue, bit down hard on it, and let the blood ooze over her chin. She made rasping, gurgling sounds, and the blood flew from her mouth in a fine mist. Carrie saw some of it dapple the water in the stone basin, and tiny pink plumes were visible against the white sand as the blood diffused.

Oona's head was slung forward, on her chest. A moment later she began to speak in the voice of a young man.

'Look at her. Beautiful. Now my heart is full.'

Oona threw back her head, and her long hair whipped through the air. Her face was smeared red, her eyes were quite bloodshot now, and she began to tremble violently. The palms of her hands, scratched and cut, were held open on her thighs. She seemed to spit out the words in tortured clots. Blood flew from her, and she spoke in several voices, each one tumbling out of the last, careening into the next, so that it often seemed as if two, three or even four of them were struggling to be heard at the very same instant.

'Bye bye Mummy bye bye bye bye Daddy bye bye – oh no oh no don't go don't leave me again – you don't want a baby you don't want a bay uh bee – love me like the angels honey – Franny love me love me love me please – first it was Mummy then Daddy then a then a then a then a – what are you doing! – eat my Ian Myra my Myra eat my Ian Myra eat it – muh muh muh Mother Father Sister Brother come back – to me to me meet me in the kelpie's flow and your name shall be lost for ever more ever more ever more lost lost lost in the kelpie's flow meet me in the kelpie's flow your name shall be lost for ever more ever Moher Moher Moher muh muh Mother Mother don't go – corbies cliffs sea me in the sea—'

Oona came to a sudden halt for a few seconds, although her body continued to rocket within itself. Carrie realized that she felt cold, and she glanced up briefly. The room was murky, full of what she first thought had to be smoke – either from the many candles, or a fire somewhere in the house. But then she noticed that it felt cool and damp on her skin, as if a raincloud or fog had drifted in through an open window. It was dark outside, rain still pouring down, driven by the wind. She saw that the windows were steamed up, covered with a fog of condensation.

Carrie felt as if she were drowning.

Charley relit his cigar.

'See me by the sea me in the sea the little bastard get hers now oh no oh no see them run they run they run catch her push her down oh no oh no oh yes oh yes when you slam down the rock do you feel it in your heart do you feel it feel it feel it oh yes catch her push her pick a rock a chunk of brick cement concrete stone a rock in the back of the head oh no the angels love me now

like oh yes oh God the sea by the sea by the see me love me now
don't go don't leave me now don't go don't go muh muh muh
Mary Rose Mam by the sea the kelpie strikes take me take me
with you this time see them run they run they run take me don't
go don't—'

The words died abruptly. Oona seemed to be tottering as she sat there on her heels. A terrible whine came from her, and her face was contorted with pain. So much blood. It was terrible to watch something like this, Charley thought, terrible too that you can hardly bring yourself to look away from it. Whatever she may be saying about any of us, she is killing herself by inches. She writes these mad moments in her own blood. Oona had something of the deranged poet about her, slowly eviscerating herself to find an impossible truth.

But was there such truth? Was there anything?

He was still wondering what Oona had meant when she told him that he might have to do something for her. What?

Charley had no idea. About any of it. All he knew for sure was that he wanted another drink. Then he noticed that his hands and face were damp. There was a mist in the room. Now the other three looked from Oona to the heavy stone basin in the centre of the table. The surface of the water seemed to glitter and flash, as if it were glowing with pale green fire. The mist was thicker over the basin, like a small cloud gathering to itself.

Then everything broke up madly.

Oona's whine grew harsher and louder, turned into a fearful wail. She clawed at the bloodstained front of her dress, popped a button and clawed at her skin. The others turned back to her, and Charley stepped closer. He caught a glimpse of Roz, her body tense, looking as if she were about to stand up from her seat on the far side of the room.

Jan and the Spence woman both had tears in their eyes again, but neither moved or attempted to touch Oona, who seemed to be losing herself in an unravelling frenzy – about to explode. The Englishman, Charley noticed, had a fine speckling of blood on his face – he'd caught some spray, and didn't know it yet.

Oona's keening soon became physically unbearable. It rasped your skin, lanced into your ears, your brain, and raced like acid down the inside of your spine.

Oona pushed herself up, so that she was kneeling straight as a schoolgirl at prayer. Roz was on her feet, moving. But before she could get there, Oona gave a paralysing scream. Charley felt stunned by the depth and force of it. She sounded as if she were trying to find certain words, but couldn't – and that only made it so much worse, somehow.

A second later, chaos and panic.

'Oona? Are you—'

'Honey, don't—'

Oona dived forward and slammed her forehead against the thick rim of the stone basin with a splintering crunch. Blood flew off to the sides and blossomed like red ink in the water. The basin was so solid and heavy that it barely moved. The water did slosh around in it a little, sparkling coldly.

'Oh, God!'

'Oona!'

'Jesus,' Charley muttered.

Roz got there just as the Spence woman was trying to put her arms around Oona, and the two of them grappled with her. Jan sat still, with a dazed look on her face.

'Help me with her.'

'Have you got her? Easy there.'

Oona slid off the table and onto the floor, face up. Blood gushed from the torn flesh, drenching her face and flooding over her lips. There was an ugly sucking noise, as Oona drew it in with each gasping breath, but then the blood came right back out of her in a choking foam.

Charley stepped back out of the way. He discovered that he was shaking and shivering uncontrollably.

Oliver backed away and stood near O'Donnell, but not so close that he had to speak to him. He lit a cigarette and watched the women trying to help Oona. You do know me, he thought. You know what I learned from the incident at Ballapul.

That I like it.

So don't cheat me now.

20

Carrie insisted that they wait for news about Oona in the emergency room at St Raphael's Hospital. Oliver had driven them there, and then wanted to leave for New York, but Carrie refused to go until she heard something. The O'Donnells had decided not to trail along to the hospital, and went home.

Oona was still unconscious when they arrived, her skin pale and cool. Carrie was terrified for her. But at least the heavy bleeding was under control. Roz had quickly wrapped ice cubes in a towel, and she pressed it firmly to Oona's forehead in the back seat of the car.

'I'm going to tell them that she slipped on the wet path and hit her head on the stone step,' Roz said, as they pulled into the entrance. 'You can imagine what it'd be like if I told them what she was really doing.'

Carrie nodded. It was a small lie but it didn't change the nature of the injury, so she would have no problem going along with it if anyone questioned her. The ER was not too frantic and they soon took Oona in for treatment. Carrie and Oliver remained in the lounge while Roz was busy with the paperwork.

'Do you know what she was saying during the session?' Oliver asked her, his tone almost too casual. 'Oona.'

'What?'

'There were some lines from Morrissey songs, twisted around and broken up,' he told her. 'The Sex Pistols, I'm pretty sure. O'Donnell heard parts that were apparently lifted whole from some book by Sir Walter Scott.'

Carrie couldn't be bothered to respond to that, and a little while later Oliver stepped outside to have a cigarette. As if it would make any serious difference where certain words and phrases might have originated – they essentially came from Oona, and she would use whatever language she required to convey the meaning of the visions and voices she received.

This terrible incident showed how unbearable the process was for her. Carrie could only imagine how awful it must have been for her to be driven to such violence against herself. For a while further sessions were obviously out of the question.

Before Oliver came back inside, Carrie scribbled off a cheque for a thousand dollars. She didn't know if that was too much or too little, but it was something. She slipped it to Roz, who appeared a few minutes later with a preliminary report. Oona was conscious, but still groggy. She had a bone contusion but no fracture in her skull. It was probably not a serious concussion, but she might have to stay overnight.

'You're not going to be able to visit her, regardless,' Roz said. 'The fewer people she sees now, the better. I'll take her home in a taxi as soon as they let me and I'll try to give you a ring tomorrow. You might as well go along now, you still have a fair drive ahead of you.'

It was not a pleasant one. Carrie still didn't know what to think. Oliver occasionally cursed the storm and road conditions, but otherwise he said nothing. Carrie was riding with a man she no longer knew as well as she thought she had. Eight years was a long time, in many ways. But it was not enough. A veil of doubt hung between them now.

Carrie wasn't entirely ready to believe that her husband had murdered anybody, assuming that to be a correct understanding of what she'd heard. Oona had warned her about taking things too literally. Oliver wasn't a violent person: he had never lifted a finger against her and she had seen him walk away from potential bar fights.

But the killings with which Oliver had been associated in today's session matched in several ways the scene she had experienced in his office. Carrie had discussed it in some detail with Oona but that didn't disqualify it – Oona had mentioned Ballapul in their first session.

Carrie had heard her father's voice again, saying something about how he used to be a sweet boy. The words were Oona's, but the voice was authentic, and Carrie felt certain that it referred to Oliver. *Something went wrong.* That was a message of warning, surely. But was it to Oliver, or about him?

It could relate to the future, or the past. It could refer to danger on one of his trips abroad. That danger might not even be physical: it could be a business setback. There had been an obvious reference to Marthe Frenssen and Munich. Oliver had high hopes for their project.

There was another reason that the mention of Marthe bothered Carrie. When your husband is thousands of miles from home with a young single woman, you're inevitably going to wonder. Perhaps that was what her father was warning her about. Oliver spoke to Marthe on the phone every week – to save him more trips to Germany, he explained. Marthe was some kind of a genius, brilliant yet temperamental, ambitious and driven, but an insecure person inside. He had to treat her like a hothouse plant. So he said.

Carrie had no control over what Oliver might do while he was in Munich with Marthe. She knew that it was pointless to torture herself with speculation. If her marriage was going to collapse, she would find out in due course.

And how did that relate to the foreign voice, the killings, which also seemed to involve Oliver? There had to be more to the complete message, much more. It was so frustrating. Carrie felt she had learned much in two sessions, but the essence of it still eluded her. One more session might be enough – but for the time being that was not possible.

When they got back to the apartment, Oliver had a couple of sandwiches and Carrie made a pot of tea for herself. She should have been hungry but wasn't. After he had eaten, Oliver poked around upstairs and in his office for a few minutes, then joined her again in the nook. He had a tumbler of Scotch with a single ice cube floating in it, and he lit a cigarette.

'Well?'

'Well what?'

'Did you have the breakthrough you were hoping for?'

'I don't know,' she said. 'There's so much to think about. I haven't really begun to sort it all out. I was still thinking about poor Oona.'

'That's understandable.'

'What do you make of it?' she asked.

'I don't know,' Oliver told her. 'It's all a bit beyond me, frankly. I mean, you hear Oona say things that seem to relate to you or me or the O'Donnells, but how are we supposed to make any sense of it? It's not as if she's saying, Beware of the tall man who wants you to invest in Malayan tin mines, or something.'

'No, it isn't.'

A moment later, Oliver hesitantly said, 'Carrie.'

'Yes?'

'There is one thing that I feel I should mention, coming out of today's session.'

'What?' Carrie felt a twinge of anxiety.

'Shortly before we met, when I was starting to bring clothes into Britain, I spent rather a lot of money to fly out to Bangkok and investigate Thai silk. It was a mistake. The silk is lovely but expensive, and the marketing is tricky. Anyhow. On the way back to London my flight stopped in Bombay, and I decided to take advantage of that and see a bit of the city. It was one of those spur-of-the-moment things. I stayed for two days and then flew on to London. But while I was there I got into a minor argument with my guide, the chap I hired to drive me around. He wanted to take me to Chik Pavan or Ballapul, which were a couple of famous, or I should say infamous, red-light compounds in Bombay. As far as I'm concerned, that's an easy way to lose your wallet or catch something nasty, and I'd already passed on the same sort of thing in Bangkok. But we did exchange sharp words about it – you see, they would pay him a commission and he didn't want to do without it. Anyhow, I thought it might help if you knew.'

'That's it?' Carrie said, after a long pause.

'That's it,' Oliver confirmed. 'God only knows how Oona

was able to conjure up Ballapul and Chik Pavan, with my name, but she did, and she even caught some of the anger in our argument. What it all means, I don't know. It was a trivial matter.'

'You just had an argument.'

'Yes, that's all it was.'

'Well. Thanks for telling me.'

'Perhaps you can make something of it.'

'No, I have no idea,' Carrie said. 'I did wonder about it, when she mentioned you, but the other names meant nothing to me. At least you've cleared up that part of it.'

'Only a little, I'm afraid.'

Oliver smiled and shrugged. He went off to stare at the TV or his stamps, something. Carrie felt a headache coming on. She felt as if her brain were being flooded with fear and sadness, as if everything was now in grave doubt. You have just gone through the worst minute of your life since the day you learned that your father was dead.

Because Oliver was only pretending that he didn't know what to make of today's session. Because Oliver had not mentioned the obvious references to Marthe and Munich. Because his explanation about India was worse than nothing, it was a lie.

She was certain of that much.

'Oona's home now,' Roz said, when she called Carrie early the following afternoon. 'She should be all right.'

'I'm so glad to hear that. How serious is her injury?'

'She did get a nasty concussion, but there doesn't appear to be any permanent organic damage.'

'Thank God for that.'

'She just needs to rest and heal,' Roz continued. 'Lots of sleep, no moving about, and time'll do the rest. She's young and healthy. They think she won't even have a scar.'

'Good. Do you have any idea when I might talk to her? Just for a minute on the phone, to say hello and wish her well.'

'Perhaps tomorrow. She's on a painkiller right now and kind

of drifts in and out of sleep, which is good for her. I'll give you a ring tomorrow if she's up to a brief chat.'

'Okay, please do.'

'I hope you don't mind if I cut this short, but I have a lot more calls to make and appointments to cancel. This is terrible. It's going to hurt some people who depend on her.'

'I can imagine.'

Only too well, Carrie realized, after she hung up. She was one of those people suddenly cut off from Oona. She was on her own for the present.

The rest of the week was uneventful, aside from the demands of her work. In a way, it was a relief to be able to concentrate on her current commissions. They absorbed her and sent her home each evening both physically and mentally tired, so that she had no trouble falling asleep. Carrie soon stopped wondering if the next moment was going to bring another sudden, dreadful invasion. Nothing happened.

By the following weekend she allowed herself to consider it in a new light. Perhaps it was over. Perhaps there had been a breakthrough for her at the last session, and she simply didn't understand the full extent of it yet. She felt good. She would like to discuss it with Oona, but Roz hadn't called her again and Carrie was reluctant to bother them if it wasn't a matter of real urgency. Unless you hear otherwise, assume that Oona is making a steady recovery. Let the days keep going by like this.

They spent a quiet weekend around the apartment. Oliver was not very talkative, but he appeared preoccupied rather than in a bad mood. He carried a thick file of papers around with him everywhere and he would study it and jot down notes, even when he was watching a movie on television.

The doubt – and even anger – that Carrie had felt in the immediate aftermath of the last session remained within her, but there was little she could do about it. She watched her husband and wondered about him, but no answers came to her. Carrie knew she ought to discuss it openly with him and push him to speak more honestly – but she was afraid of what she might hear.

On Sunday evening, Oliver came out of his office with that file in his hand. He went straight to the drinks cabinet and poured a glass of Scotch, to which he added a splash of bottled water. As he headed back to his office he stopped suddenly and made a face, like someone who has just remembered an unpleasant chore. Carrie sat frozen, her pen poised over the *Sunday Times* acrostic puzzle. She knew that something was coming.

'I have to fly out next Sunday night,' he said, almost as if it were an afterthought. 'England, then Germany. Just for a few days, I think. A week at most.'

'But why?' Carrie felt a cramp in her side. 'The last time you went you said that was it for the summer.'

'For stamp auctions, yes,' Oliver replied blandly. 'But the linen project is moving ahead all the time. I've got to see some chemical processors in Manchester, and then a bunch of lawyers in Munich about the licensing and patent arrangements.'

He had a look of weary resignation on his face, almost as if he were inviting Carrie to do him a favour and find a way for him to avoid all this tedious running around.

'Is it really necessary?'

'Absolutely unavoidable.'

It was true to form, in a way. When Oliver had a problem or a major decision in his business he usually spent a while mulling it over, as he had the last couple of weeks. Then he would come up with a plan of action, and there would be a burst of frenetic activity.

And yet the news left her queasy and fearful. This time *was* different. Nothing in Carrie's life was the same as it had been, since the ghostly incidents started and she had first consulted Oona. Everything in her life was blurred with uncertainty now.

'Oliver.'

'Yes?'

'Is there anything going on between you and Marthe?'

He seemed to find that amusing. 'Just business, love, nothing else,' he replied, with a lingering smile.

'Oona mentioned her.'

'Did she? When?'

'Last week, when we were there.'

'Oh, yes, so she did,' Oliver said. 'Don't make the mistake of thinking that every word she speaks has special significance, because it doesn't. A lot of it is just plain raving. Whatever pops up in her mind, rock lyrics, passages from books she's read, and who knows what else? If you attach importance to every scrap of it, you'll be in thrall to her for the rest of your life.'

'I suppose that's possible.'

'Look,' Oliver said, trying to sound reasonable, 'it's only natural for you to wonder about Marthe, but there's nothing in it at all. If there were, I certainly wouldn't throw away a hundred and fifty dollars a night for a room at the Regina Hotel. If you want to see my receipts, you're welcome to them.'

'No, no.' Carrie shrugged helplessly. 'I'm sorry, Oliver. I don't mean to sound like I'm questioning you.'

'Well, it does a bit.'

He turned away, went down the hall to his office, and closed the door behind him. It was not exactly the kind of warm, loving reassurance you might hope for from a spouse who understands that you're having a difficult time with things at the moment. It was more like a corporate policy statement.

But thank you all the same, Carrie thought. And for leaving when you did. Because if Oliver had stayed longer and continued in the same vein, she would have apologized to him again. However many times it took to end an exchange that probably could not be resolved anyway. And then she would have hated herself for it.

Two days later the telephone rang shortly after Carrie got home from work. Oliver had just gone out to pick up some liquor from the store around the corner.

'Hello.'

'Guess who?'

'Oona?'

'Hi.'

'Oh, I'm so glad to hear you,' Carrie said, quickly putting the phone to her other ear. 'How are you?'

'Fine, I think. Guess what?'

'I can come up and visit you.'

'Ah, well, soon, I hope. But that's not it.'

Carrie's heart sank, but then she tried to sound bright and cheerful for Oona's sake. 'I don't know, what?'

'My head's empty.'

'You mean—?'

'No voices, no visions, nothing.'

'My God.'

'Maybe it worked, eh? What do you think?'

'I don't know, I mean—' Mild panic was what Carrie felt. What if she continued to experience those dreadful incidents but Oona no longer had the ability to help? 'It sounds like the best thing that could happen to you . . .'

'Could be, but it's too early to tell,' Oona said. She was moderating her enthusiasm, no doubt because she could sense the concern on Carrie's part. 'Probably won't last, but for the past week it's been great. I feel like I've slept for the first time in ages.'

'That's wonderful.'

'You're all right, aren't you?'

'Yes,' Carrie answered. 'So far I haven't had any problems. Nothing at all.'

'Good. I'll have to think about it when I'm in the proper frame of mind again. I haven't been able to give much thought to what happened, and what it meant for you and the others.'

'Well, don't,' Carrie said. 'At least not until you really want to. I've been fine since that session and I'm okay now, so there's no need for you to do anything.'

'Great.'

'Maybe it's over for me, too. I've been wondering if there was a breakthrough and I just haven't grasped it yet.'

'Well . . .' Oona sounded doubtful. 'Let's hope so. Anyhow, I wanted to say hi, and tell you that I miss you.'

'Well – I – I miss you too, Oona. I wish I could come and visit you for a little while.'

'Soon. Next week.'

'That'd be fine,' Carrie said. 'Whenever.'

'We'll both need it by then.'

'What do you mean?'

'I'll be desperate for company. I already am, in fact, and you're the only person I'd really like to see,' Oona said. 'And you'll be—' But she didn't finish it.

'What?'

'I don't know, it's just a feeling I get. That you'll need some company as well.'

'Oliver's going away next weekend.'

'See, that's it. Where's he off to this time?'

'England and Germany.'

'Some people have all the luck.'

'It's work, not pleasure.' At least Carrie hoped that. 'In the last session you mentioned Munich and Germany, as well as the person Oliver's doing business with there. Marthe.'

'Is that right?'

'Do you have any idea why they came up?'

'I don't remember anything from that session.'

'Oh.'

'But don't worry, it'll probably start to come back to me in a few days. That's the way it goes. Do you see how I've already had a few inklings just since we've been talking now? That shows it's on the way back.'

'It's because of me,' Carrie said. 'Oona, maybe I shouldn't come up to New Haven. I should stay away.'

'No, don't say that. If it's going to happen, it'll happen. It's not you, love. It's me, it's always been me.'

'Oona . . .'

'I hear the Warden coming. Talk to you later.'

21

'Charley.'

'Yes, my dear?'

'You have funny knees.'

'What's so funny about them?'

'They're bumpy.'

Nuala Browne dashed off, no doubt to tell her brother Gerry how bold she'd been. Nuala was three. Or four. Something like that. In addition to the younger pair, the Brownes had a couple of almost-teens who were out at present on an errand of mischief with the girls from the cottage down the road. Good kids.

Charley leaned forward to check his knees; they didn't look very funny to him. But he did feel a bit odd in Bermuda shorts. He didn't own much in the way of beachwear, but you can't lounge about on the Cape in cords and a sweater in the middle of July. So there he was, a self-regarded calamity in technicolour shorts, a faded Pogues T-shirt and silly flip-flops that flew off his feet every time he took a step.

Still, Wellfleet was lovely, the cottage great, the beer and food fantastic and the company simply the best. He felt pretty good, all things considered, and even Jan seemed to be responding favourably to the change of scene. Charley had been pleased when, the night before, Malcolm and Maggie had asked them to stay on for an extra couple of days. Oh, aye.

Some cottage. The house had more square feet of floor space than any place in which Charley had ever lived along the dusty academic trail. The Brownes rented it out for most of the summer – a smart idea, the place paid for itself. Quite nice, too. Some people caught all the breaks. Still, not to complain.

'Here we go.'

Malcolm came back out onto the deck with a fresh pitcher of draught ale. He refilled Charley's pint glass and then topped up his own. Before taking his seat again, Malcolm tapped on the CD in the portable stereo on the picnic table, replaying *If I Should Fall From Grace With The Lord*. The boys from County Hell singing songs about the drinkitations.

'You do Bacchus proud, Mal, I must say.'

'It's great to have some time off with you. And I think Jan's enjoying herself. Do you?'

Charley nodded. 'She seems a bit more at ease. It helps to get away for a while. I was afraid she might find it tough to be around your kids, but she's as fond of them as I am.'

'Yes, she really is,' Malcolm agreed. 'I wondered about that as well, but she seems fine.'

'She's coming along, I think.'

'Have you seen any more of the famous Oona?'

Malcolm had waited a couple of days before asking, considerately enough, not wanting to stir up the waters and perhaps spoil their weekend. Maggie hadn't enquired either, though Charley could see that she was anxious to know if there had been any developments. He appreciated their patience and tact. He glanced back towards the cottage for a second, and then to Malcolm.

'Is Jan still in the kitchen with Maggie?'

'She was, but as I was getting the beer just now she went to your bedroom to have a lie-down before dinner.'

'Ah, good. Yes, well, we did visit the famous Oona the week before last,' Charley said. 'It was a joint session, with some other couple. I didn't much care for them, but it sounded as if they also had a mysterious violent death somewhere in their past, so I suppose that's why Oona brought us all together.'

Malcolm sipped his beer. 'How did it go?'

'Quite a performance, really. Oona ranted and raved, tossed and twitched and squirmed. It went on for some time. Our friend Sir Walt put in another cameo appearance, but the highlight came when Oona smashed her head down on a stone basin. She really did a number on herself. There was blood all over the place, and she knocked herself out. They took her to the emergency room.'

'You're joking.'

'No, really. The sister called up the next day and told me that Oona had a concussion. She was going to be out of business for a while. Still is, for all I know.'

'Christ. So, nothing was actually said that—'

'Related to us and Fiona?'

'Yes.'

'Well, quite a bit, in fact,' Charley admitted. 'But it was not Fiona herself, and I have no idea what any of it was supposed to mean. I almost wish that some ectoplasm had come floating out of Oona's nose or a ghostly face had appeared in the air over the table. Something like that, real or fake, but something that you could see or touch and focus on. But it all comes down to words and voices, and some of the words are fascinating and some of the voices are remarkable – but it's not enough, it has no intrinsic meaning. The only way it can work is if you *confer* significance on what you hear.'

Malcolm nodded, smiling. 'Yes, but how does Oona find words and phrases that mean so much to people?'

'It's uncanny at times.' Charley helped himself to more of the beer. He had no desire to go into how explicit Oona had been the last time – much too explicit for his liking. To recall the details was unbearably painful. 'She has a touch of the mad poet about her, if you ask me.'

'You know,' Malcolm said, 'some people think that parapsychology and the paranormal will be the next big developmental area in the field of psychiatry.'

Charley laughed. 'That sounds about right.'

'Have you decided whether Oona is genuine or not?'

He was stuck. Charley didn't want to lie to his friend and say that she wasn't, but he didn't want to concede that she might well be – and then have to explain why. 'I'm not sure I know either way. Part of me wants to believe, while the other

235

part wants to run away. She often comes close to the mark, which makes her interesting. But it's too painful.'

'I can imagine,' Malcolm said sympathetically. 'What about Jan? How does she feel about it now?'

'She's a soul in need, Mal. It says something to her about Fiona. It hurts her but she thinks that's necessary and proper. She's locked into it, and nothing I say makes any difference.'

'Does she still think Fiona has come back for revenge?'

'She hasn't repeated that lately but, to tell you the truth, we don't even talk about it any more. It goes nowhere.'

'Ah, she'll pull out of it, don't worry. As time passes, and now she isn't seeing Oona, she'll get over it.'

They were silent for a few moments, watching the sea as they enjoyed the music. The only trouble with moments of serenity and pleasure like this, Charley thought, is that they're a con. The good food and drink, the wonderful company, the lovely setting, you want to think this is life. It isn't. Life is the nasty little bugger getting ready to hammer you again. Had enough? Too bad, I'm not done with you yet. Moments like this – they're just the sixty seconds between rounds, over too soon, and then you have to haul your sorry ass back out into the middle of the ring. And, as if that isn't bad enough, you're also receiving messages from the dead. You haven't even got to *the other side* yet, and already you're in trouble there as well.

Hit me again, I'm starting to like it.

'Mal, do you believe in an afterlife?'

'Ah.' Malcolm smiled and sat back in his chair. 'That one. The brain says no, the heart says yes. But it's easier to say no and the easy way usually turns out to be wrong.'

'So, you're a believer.' Mild surprise.

'In a way, I suppose I am,' Malcolm said, almost sheepishly. 'I used to feel that all that literary despair and existential *angst* in the face of the meaningless void was pretty much spot-on. But it's just as arbitrary as any other explanation. There might be a spiritual plane. Why not something more?'

'Something . . .'

'You don't think so.'

236

'No,' Charley said, 'I'll stick to the literary void. It's simple and tidy. Besides, I like the idea of being recycled into a clump of moss and catching drops of foggy dew every morning.'

'It's a form of drink,' Malcolm observed, winking.

'I knew there was a reason.'

Later, he went to wake Jan for supper. She was asleep on the bed with just a sheet pulled over her. She seemed too still and quiet – Jan was usually a bit of a noisy breather in the old sack, biology's rebuttal to erotic romance. Charley sat down and gently patted her shoulder.

'Jan . . . Wakey-wakey . . . Time for supper . . . They're going to toss the lobsters in the pot any minute now . . .'

She spun round suddenly to stare at him, pushing herself up on one hand. Her face was puffy with sleep, and she seemed lost. But her eyes were wide open and had the chaotic look of terror in them. She didn't know him. He tried to take her hand in his but she pulled away from him, the fear mounting.

'Hey, it's me. It's all right, love . . .'

He must have awakened her from a dream, and not a very happy one at that. She was still caught up in it, and she made Charley think of a wild animal trapped in some confined space. He wasn't ready for another dream-message from Fiona. Never would be.

'Jan, it's me. Relax. Wake up.'

She exhaled sharply, and then began to breathe more normally as some of the tension left her. But she still regarded him with shock and uncertainty.

'There,' Charley said. 'Are you all right now?'

'You were dead.'

'Was I? Oh dear.' He put on a good-natured smile. 'Well, as you can see, I'm not quite there yet.'

'You fell in the sea and you were gone.'

'Crikey.' Maybe that kelpie got him. 'It was just a dream, love, it doesn't matter. Splash some water on your face and come along for dinner when you're ready.'

*

'You'd think she was looking at a ghost.' Charley turned on the tap and drew a pint of ale. 'Perhaps I *am* a ghost, and she's the only one who realizes it. I like that idea.'

Malcolm smiled; Maggie didn't.

'That would explain a few things,' Charley continued. 'Like why I feel out of it half the time, or why the deconstructionists in the English department look right through me.'

Malcolm laughed; Maggie didn't.

'I know what you're thinking, love,' Charley said, as he put an arm around Maggie's waist – very nice, too. 'You're thinking that dreams are sometimes prophetic. Am I right?'

'It did occur to me.' Maggie was preparing lemon and butter sauce to go with the lobsters, and she smiled at him. 'If I were you I'd stay away from the water.'

'I'll make a point of it.'

'And think about what she said,' Maggie added.

'Oh, I draw the line at that,' Charley said. 'Thinking just gives you headaches. Right, Mal?'

'I hadn't thought about it.'

Maggie groaned. 'Get out of here, the two of you, you're no help at all. And please change the music.'

'Perhaps we ought to oblige the chef,' Malcolm said.

But Jan entered the kitchen then. She didn't seem to notice the others. She didn't appear to know where she was or what she was doing. She hesitated in the doorway for a moment, walked to the counter and looked around as if searching for something.

'Hello, love,' Charley said. 'Care for a drink?'

Jan didn't seem to hear him. She ignored them and wandered out of the back door onto the deck, where she stood uncertainly for a few seconds, and then sat down on one of the chairs facing the sea, her hands folded in her lap.

'Still waking up,' Malcolm murmured politely.

Maggie looked at Charley.

He shrugged. 'Is there a Donizetti in the house?'

*

238

They didn't speak much on the drive back to New Haven. They hadn't spoken much at all lately, so that was nothing new. It was not his fault, Charley thought. He made the effort regularly, but Jan would reply minimally and conversation tended to peter out before it ever got going.

All the same, the long weekend on the Cape with the Brownes had been a success. Charley had enjoyed it, and, for the most part, Jan had held her own. She went shopping at the factory outlets with Maggie one day, pottered about the small towns with the rest of them on their various excursions, sat on the beach and watched the kids when they were swimming, and once even went clam-digging with them at low tide.

But there were those moments when Jan was preoccupied, her mind elsewhere on other business. There's nothing much you can do about that, Charley told himself. Be there if she needs you, that's the length and width of it. For the rest, it's up to her to find her own way out of the prolonged funk.

It was just possible, he knew, just possible that all those terrible things he'd heard from Oona were true. That as a small child Jan had been psychologically scarred by an experience with crows or ravens. That years later she might have found the same kind of birds fluttering about Fiona's pram and been temporarily unhinged by the sight.

But, as far as Charley knew, crows and ravens were scavengers that didn't attack living creatures. Certainly not human babies. Or might they? And could Jan have reacted in that way, setting a fire, hoping to die with Fiona? It was too much. He had a hard time accepting the idea that, for so many years, he might not have had a clue about what really happened that day.

But the story had emerged from both Oona and Jan. Why would they come up with such a horrible version of things if it wasn't essentially true? It was hardly the kind of fantasy you'd expect a medium and her client to dream up together.

But what he thought was secondary. It was what Jan believed that really mattered. She was the one who had carried it around inside her all this time. Besides, Fiona was dead. That part of the nightmare was true, regardless of the other details. What difference did it make if the corbies had—

Stop, damn it.

Charley's mind recoiled again. He simply couldn't deal with such gruesome images in connection with his own daughter. It was unbearable, and his brain went into a spasm of avoidance whenever they floated too close to his consciousness.

He had been partly to blame. He had accepted that ages ago, but now he seemed to understand it more thoroughly. Charley had brought his wife and daughter to that place, and left them there. He had created the scene and set the stage. He'd behaved in less than admirable fashion in town, which no doubt came across to Jan at home; Jan was no fool. So the prevailing emotional atmosphere at Ravenswood had been largely of his own making. It all added up to a fair share of the guilt. When a tragedy like that happens, the way you live your everyday life, with all its selfish assumptions and petty vices, can turn into a damning indictment.

You live with the death because you have no choice. Just as bad was the blindness. Everything had looked fine back then. He had a young wife, a first child – with the idea that more would come – and he was at the start of a promising academic career. Well, it may have looked fine to him, but it had been an incomplete picture.

And if only part of what Oona had revealed was true, Charley had been living blind ever since. It was humbling, and it hurt. When you devote your life to great literature, you're supposed to understand something about the truth of human experience. But he had read much and learned little, it seemed. Do we ever get to see the whole picture for even one second?

When they parked in the small yard behind their apartment building, Charley put his hand on Jan's knee as she was about to get out of the car. She looked at him.

'Thanks for coming to the Cape,' he said. 'And it was nice, wasn't it? Did you have a good time?'

'Yes.'

He leant across the seat and kissed her cheek. 'You know I still love you, Jan. I always have.'

'I know, Charley.'

'I'm always here for you.'

'I know. Thank you.'

'Are you feeling all right?'

'Yes, I am.'

They were both in the kitchen, about an hour later, early in the evening, when it happened. Charley was sitting at the table, looking through the mail, while Jan was at the counter, clearing things away after their light meal of sandwiches.

'Look at this,' Charley said, happily waving a letter in the air. 'Somebody wants to reprint that little essay I did a couple of years ago on Dunsany and Maeterlinck. Isn't that nice?'

Jan glanced over her shoulder at him, but said nothing. She turned back to the cold-cuts she was rewrapping in plastic bags for the refrigerator.

'Of course, there's no money in it,' Charley continued. 'And Maeterlinck was such a bore. Quite apart from being a plagiarist and an all-around gobshite of the first degree. Perhaps they'll let me touch it up a bit.'

Charley flipped through a catalogue from a book dealer. Not much of burning interest, but he would probably find something to order in due course; there was always another book.

He lit a thin cigar. He would have to call Heather tomorrow morning. Things had been decidedly cool on that front, but there had been signs last week that she was beginning to thaw.

At some point Charley noticed that Jan was standing still at the counter. Doing nothing. Her back was to him, her hands flat on the Formica. The platter of cold-cuts and the various plastic bags were still there. Jan was looking up, as if she had spotted a cobweb or a moth by the ceiling. She stood there like that for a minute. Two. Too long.

'Jan?'

She looked down, but again seemed to lapse into vacancy, not responding, not moving. She has got to see someone,

Charley told himself. A psychologist, a counsellor, whatever, some person who was properly qualified and skilled. It probably wouldn't be easy to persuade her, but—

Jan reached along the counter and picked up the small knife they'd used to slice the deli pickle. She held it, and stared at it as if she'd never seen anything quite like it before.

'Hey, Jan.'

The movement was so quick Charley didn't understand it until she tottered around in his direction and blood sheeted across the kitchen, some of it lashing him. His mind went blank, but he saw that she'd opened half of her throat.

'Jan! No! Jesus!'

His foot slipped on the blood as he jumped off the chair but he got a hold of her and tried to clamp the gaping wound shut and somehow save her. But the blood squirted and trickled out of his fingers. Jan's eyes were rigid, fixed on him, and they were like a couple of hard blue stones, cold, unseeing, remorseless.

He pounded on the neighbour's door, shouting. He got on the phone, trying to explain to 911. He was back with Jan, trying to hold her together.

You had this life in your hands.

His voice seemed distant, like heavy balloons bouncing off the walls and ceiling. Charley felt as if he were coming apart, breaking up in random cells and molecules and atoms, that he was scattering, exploding right out of himself and flying away in a million different directions at once.

This life too.

22

Mr Patrick Pond worked from an office above a tea shop on Kilburn High Road, but that was altogether too close to Becky's flat. It was highly unlikely that Oliver would run into her on the street, especially in the middle of a workday, but he didn't want to take any unnecessary chances. He didn't even want Nick and Jonna to know that he was in London, otherwise they'd expect him to stay at their house in Kensington and there would have to be dinner and talk – and none of that would do.

So Oliver checked into the Bonnington Hotel on Southampton Row and arranged to meet Mr Pond in the bar at four o'clock that afternoon. The place was fairly deserted, which perhaps was due in part to the ersatz Polynesian décor. The England–West Indies cricket match was on the television and a few businessmen who had slipped out of the office early were watching it.

Mr Pond was just ordering a drink when Oliver came in. There was no mistaking the man. Tall, thin, cadaverous, he had a face like an old shoe that had never dried out properly. He wore a grey cloth mac, and looked every inch the unglamorous detective who would spend his entire working life in a chilly office over a greasy tea shop in Kilburn. Still, he had Joe Barone's tentative recommendation, and he had sounded competent enough when Oliver spoke to him on the telephone the week before. He had a cool but firm handshake. Oliver paid for the drinks and they settled down in a banquette well away from the Test match.

'Now then.' Mr Pond extracted a slim grey folder from his

briefcase and pushed it along the table to Oliver. 'This is your copy of our report. Shall I summarize it for you now?'

'Thank you.' Oliver picked up the folder and looked at the typed label on the front of it. *Subject: Mary Margaret Rosalind Brodie.* And beneath that, *Client: Oliver Spence.* Oddly enough, the name Pond & Associates was absent. 'Yes, please do,' Oliver said, setting down the folder again. He already felt the makings of another disappointment.

'Right. I understand that Miss Brodie, or Miss Rodgers, as she apparently now calls herself, has been in North America these past three years.'

Oliver nodded. 'I believe so, yes.'

'We were unable to trace any record of her here in that time period, so it sounds about right. Her last known address in this country was Durham city, and she was there for approximately five years altogether.'

'Not Newcastle?'

'No, Newcastle was earlier. But, as you may know, Newcastle and Durham are only about twenty miles apart.'

'Yes.'

'While she was living in Durham she had a number of low-wage jobs. Barmaid, fast-food waitress, that sort of thing. Shared a flat with some other shop girls, but in the last couple of years she had her own bedsitter. She had a modest bank account but no credit, no property, no assets worth mentioning.'

'She was that poor when she left Britain?'

'Not quite.' Mr Pond allowed himself a brief smile. 'Just two months before she left, she deposited a cheque for the sum of twelve thousand pounds.'

'Aha.'

'Yes. I'm sorry that we were unable to determine the source of that money but this kind of information is rather difficult to come by, as I'm sure you can appreciate.'

'Yes, of course.' Oliver was beginning to be annoyed by Mr Pond's somewhat fussy way of speaking.

'In any event, it was apparently all legal and above board.

Within a few days of depositing that cheque, Miss Brodie remitted a portion of it to the Inland Revenue.'

'That's her.' Roz was certainly a stickler about paying her taxes, wherever she might be.

'She closed the account shortly after that,' Mr Pond went on, 'and presumably used the balance to finance her move to North America. But if I may jump back a bit, there are some things you should know that will explain why she was in Durham.'

'Yes, please.' Oliver lit a cigarette, as Mr Pond declined the offer of one. 'Carry on.'

'Miss Brodie was born in Glasgow twenty-four years ago now. Mother, Ellen Rodgers, later Ellen Muir, later Ellen Brodie, and finally Ellen Rodgers again. Now deceased, by the way. Alcohol, drugs and too many of the wrong men, which probably explains why your Miss Brodie's father is listed as unknown.'

'I see.'

'They bounced around a bit. Glasgow, Belfast, Glasgow again for a while, Hull and Doncaster, before they eventually landed in Byker, which was an old slum neighbourhood around the Byker Bridge in east Newcastle.'

'Yes.' Oliver knew vaguely where that was. He and his band had been to Newcastle twice, but the pubs they'd played were in the city centre.

'Now, when they got there the slum-clearance scheme in Byker was fairly well advanced and they didn't qualify for new housing, so they soon drifted further on down to Scotswood, which was the worst of the worst slums in Newcastle. I know what I'm talking about, by the way. I'm a displaced Geordie myself.'

'Is that right?' Oliver took it to mean that he was in for some tedious anecdotes of local history.

'Oh, yes,' Mr Pond continued. 'Of course, it's been a good few years since I've been back, but I know the place quite well. Scotswood was named for the many Scotsmen who moved down for the jobs at Swan Hunter and on the docks, so it's not surprising that Ellen Rodgers should end up there. But by then shipbuilding was well on its way into the grave, and what was already a grim area was rapidly becoming much nastier and more violent. You had hundreds, thousands of men idle, hanging about in the streets and drinking up their dole money in the working-men's clubs, and they were not at all enlightened when it came to the way they treated their women. Abuse, neglect, hunger—'

'How many children did she have?' Oliver interrupted.

'I was just coming to that, but I wanted you to have a clear picture of the place, how bad it was. I do think it's important. It was something terrible, especially for the womenfolk.'

'An urban wasteland.'

'One of the worst,' Mr Pond said. 'Ellen Rodgers had been living in places like that all her life, but Scotswood was really the bottom of it for her. Now, according to the records, she had five children. In each case, the father was listed as unknown. Ellen was a full-time project for the social workers. There were men coming and going at all hours. The last job she held was in Doncaster, a kiosk at the race-track, and she soon lost that over a suspicion of petty thievery. Skimming the take, no doubt.'

'About the children.'

'Yes. In Scotswood she limped along on social security and any cash she could pry loose from the man of the moment. Not all of the children lived with her all of the time, some came and went on a fairly regular basis. They were farmed out to relatives in Glasgow, or removed to temporary foster care. You see, Ellen herself was often away for brief periods, in jail for some minor offence, or in hospital when the drink got out of hand, or else she'd run off for a quick romance with some fellow and the children would be left alone until she turned up again. Now, whenever Ellen was absent your Miss Brodie was the one who acted as substitute parent. There was an older brother, John, but he was in trouble or missing most of the time. There were three other children, two young lads and one girl.'

At last. 'Oona.'

Mr Pond smiled. 'Clare Oona Muir, yes.'

'What is this business with the names?' Oliver asked. 'Why are there so many of them? And yet you said that the fathers were listed as unknown.'

'Right. Apparently Ellen used whichever name she fancied at any given moment,' Mr Pond explained. 'There was a Mr Muir and a Mr Brodie, and she was married to both of them, but neither stayed around for very long, and there were other men on the scene, before, during and after the marriages. So Ellen insisted that she could never be sure which man fathered which child. She gave the children surnames on the basis of proximity of birth to marriage but it was merely a gesture. I did manage to locate and speak to one of the social workers who dealt with the family for a time while they were living in Scotswood.'

'Did you?' Oliver was beginning to warm to Mr Pond.

'Yes, and she remembered them quite well. She said that one of Ellen's many nasty tricks was to use this uncertainty over the identity of the fathers as a weapon against her children, to keep them dependent on her.'

'I'm not sure I follow that.'

'As the children got older, she didn't want any of them to run off looking for Dad, you see. So Mary Margaret—'

'Roz.'

'Rosalind, yes. She was left in no doubt that although she had been given the name Brodie, Mr Brodie was not her father and had no interest in her. Same thing with Clare Oona and Mr Muir. And so on, with the others.'

'Sounds like Ellen was quite a piece of work.'

'Monster, is the word the social worker used.'

'Really.'

'She was the queen bee at home, I gather. She not only kept the children tied to her but, as I said, she was often missing for days and sometimes even weeks. But her absence had the effect of increasing their need and dependency. She was negligent most of the time, tyrannical and demanding, but she knew how to dispense love and attention in spot-doses, just enough to keep everyone in a very tight orbit around her.'

'Like supplying an addict.'

'That's it, exactly,' Mr Pond agreed, with a nod.

'What about physical or sexual abuse?'

'I did ask. The social worker refused to discuss it in any detail, but she did say that in situations like that you can take it for granted that there's some level of violence, whether it be spankings, slappings, whippings or more severe beatings. And she said that psychologically it was an incestuous environment. But the sexual abuse, if there was any, most likely came from the men who passed through, Ellen's boyfriends. Again, it's not all that uncommon in such a disordered home for the boyfriend to have a go at one or more of the children. Behind the mother's back or, sad to say, often with the mother's tacit acceptance. Of course, we don't know for certain that it happened but—'

'It probably did.'

'Exactly,' Mr Pond said. 'Don't forget, in that type of an environment, mean and cramped, with no moral centre, the children grow up very quickly, if you know what I mean.'

'You did well to uncover this much information.'

'I had a bit of luck getting on to the social worker, but it really wasn't that difficult. There's plenty of people up there who remember this particular family. Only too well.'

'Oh?'

'It was just ten years ago this very summer.'

'What was?'

'When Clare—'

'Oona.'

'Yes, Clare Oona Muir. She killed another child.'

Oliver exhaled and sat back. He glanced around the room, a little bit of Tahiti in Bloomsbury, and he caught the eye of the barman. He nodded for another round of drinks. Oh yes, this was better than he had thought, far better than he had dared to hope. Oliver lit another cigarette.

She was like him.

'So. Please go on.'

Mr Pond extracted a second grey folder from his briefcase, and pushed it across the table towards Oliver. It was a good deal thicker than the folder on Roz. 'This is your copy of our report on Clare Oona Muir. Unfortunately, because she was so young, she had no public record in terms of employment or bank accounts and the like. So what we did for you was assemble a set of newspaper clippings about the case. It caused quite a stir at the time, so there's a fair bit of coverage.'

'That's fine,' Oliver said. How odd. Ten years ago he had been living in London, or was just about to make the move, and yet he couldn't recall hearing anything in the news about the murder. But no doubt he'd been wrapped up in his own life and the band's business. And he didn't know himself yet.

'Cases of children killing other children are still rare in this country,' Mr Pond continued. 'There was the recent one in Liverpool, but prior to that I think you might have to go all the way back to this one.'

'How did it happen?'

'Oona was eleven years old at the time. She and the other kids she hung around with used to play on a piece of waste-ground behind their street, near the river. A lot of concrete rubble, a few demolished buildings, an abandoned warehouse, overgrown with weeds – a miserable place, grim and barren. The children played there by day and at night the local teen-agers took over, drinking and partying, a bit of drugs, a bit of sex and so on. I suppose it was the only place they had to go. A certain number of adults also used parts of the place. Derelicts, the meths-drinkers, the homeless – some of them slept rough there.'

'Right.'

'One day, it seems, Oona lured a four-year-old girl away to a secluded corner and bashed her head in with a stone or a piece of brick. The victim was a neighbour's child and there wasn't any feud between them, so there was no rhyme or reason to it, but you wouldn't expect it to make much sense when the murderer is eleven and the victim four.'

'Did she admit to the crime?'

'Oh, I think so. Yes,' Mr Pond replied. 'The one quote I remember had her saying more or less that she wanted to see what somebody looked like when they were dead.'

'Christ.'

'It might make a certain kind of sense to a child that age, but only a child raised as she was.'

'Was her sister there that day? Rosalind.'

'I think the most you could say about any of Ellen Rodgers' children was that they were either half-brothers or half-sisters to each other.'

'Oh, yes, of course.'

'But to answer your question, yes, Rosalind was in the same general area at the time of the murder. But she was with some of the other neighbourhood kids, and they were all at a fair distance from the exact spot where the killing took place. Remember, she was a good three years older than her sister, she was a teenager. Rosalind no doubt had her own, different crowd of pals.'

Oliver nodded. 'So there was never any question—'

Mr Pond shook his head. 'No.' Oliver was glad. 'Rosalind was actually the closest thing to a success story in that family. She held them together when the mother was away or acting up, she finished school and, as I said, she held jobs and gradually moved up a bit, to the point where she could manage to pay the rent for a bedsit of her own.'

'Yes.'

'That twelve-thousand-pound payment is a puzzler but it does suggest some business sense. I think she may have received it as payment for a newspaper interview. We never located one with her featured, but that doesn't mean there wasn't one.'

'That's all right,' Oliver said. 'I'm not really interested in the exact source of that money.'

'Well, then, let me just finish up on Oona now.'

'Please.'

'Considering her age, and the results of the various mental

tests and psychiatric evaluations they did on her, Oona was never brought to trial or convicted of any offence.'

So she had not illegally entered the United States, and she really didn't have a criminal record.

'It's a murky area of English law, or was at that time,' Mr Pond went on. 'I'm not sure about now. But obviously they were not about to turn her loose, as if nothing had happened. She'd have been strung up from the nearest lamp-post overnight. There were a lot of hard feelings in the community and around the rest of the country. There was another odd fact that came into play, however. England has no facilities for the detention of children so young who commit serious crimes.'

'None?'

'None at all.'

'So what did they do with her?'

'She was sent to the remand home for children in Low Newton. It's not a criminal facility but it does house troubled children. It wasn't a popular decision. Some people thought it was a little like putting the fox in the hen-house, but there weren't any good alternatives. Low Newton is located in Durham county.'

'Aha. That's why Roz moved to Durham.'

'Yes, she broke away from the family circle, such as it was, two years later, when she turned sixteen. News reports indicate that she visited Oona as often as regulations allowed.'

'How long did Oona remain at Low Newton?'

'The best part of seven years,' Mr Pond replied. 'She was released when she reached the age of eighteen, as they no longer had any legal grounds for holding her.'

'Why not?'

'Legally she was detained for her own protection,' Mr Pond replied patiently. 'And for psychiatric treatment. But she had not been convicted of any crime because she'd been declared unfit to stand trial, on mental grounds. When Oona turned eighteen she became an adult under the law, and other factors came into play, some of which worked in her favour.'

'But why couldn't they just commit her to an adult facility for further treatment at that point?'

'Obviously they couldn't do that as a punitive measure, and apparently it wasn't justified in view of her progress.'

'You mean they thought she'd been cured?'

'At least to the point where she was no longer regarded as a threat to society. There may also have been other considerations we don't know about. The authorities may have been given a quiet word that Oona would be taken in charge by Rosalind, and that the two intended to leave Britain permanently. It might even be that the twelve thousand pounds Rosalind received was provided by some wealthy do-gooder for just such a purpose.'

'I suppose that is possible.'

'By all accounts, her record at Low Newton was adequate. No major infractions, no trouble-making or violent behaviour. But it showed no special achievements of any kind. She took classes and received passing grades. She saw counsellors, social workers and psychologists, the usual battery of experts. We couldn't see any of their reports, obviously, and we didn't come across any public comments about her by any of the personnel at Low Newton. It was all done very quietly, her release. No doubt they hoped to avoid re-inflaming public opinion about her, and for the most part they succeeded. I assume that Oona slipped out of the country a short while later with Rosalind.'

'She must have done,' Oliver said.

'Yes. Well, I think that's about it, in brief. You'll find more details in the news reports, but do bear in mind they're not always completely accurate.'

'Of course. Thank you very much. You've been very helpful, and at such short notice.'

'Thank you.' Mr Pond handed Oliver a slip of paper. 'This is our bill, if I may.'

'Certainly.' Oliver took out his cheque book on the Coutts account that he still kept open in England.

Mr Pond smiled. 'I would like to ask you something in turn.'

'Yes?' Oliver said warily.

'This is your business and I have no wish to pry, but as I'm from Newcastle, and I do remember this case, I can't help feeling a tiny bit curious about Clare Oona Muir. If you happen to know, would you mind telling me what she's doing now?'

Oliver laughed. 'She's a fortune-teller.'

Mr Pond blinked, and then realized that, in fact, Oliver was perfectly serious. Now he looked somewhat disappointed, but he shook his head and smiled. 'Is she, by God. Well, well. It's a wonderful life, isn't it?'

Oliver didn't open the folders until he had poured himself a large duty-free Scotch and was settled comfortably in an armchair in his hotel room. He propped up his feet on the bed, lit a cigarette, set Pond's reports aside without even glancing at them and turned immediately to the photocopied newspaper clippings.

The first photograph of Oona took his breath away. Her eyes dominated in cold newsprint, as they did in life, staring evenly out at the world, too open, too knowing. Too unforgiving. Oona might have been only eleven years old at the time, but those eyes must have unnerved a good many people when she forced the country to sit up and take notice.

She was so far ahead of him.

Her hair was surprisingly short in the picture, trimmed in a *Rubber Soul* mop-top, the fringe neatly parted in a tight inverted V in the middle of her forehead. It was quite thick and full but nothing like the mane she now possessed.

Oona's face was younger, but not much. The Oona he knew had hardly aged in ten years, in spite of all she'd been through. It was a personal snapshot, not a police or newspaper photograph, Oliver realized. She looked as if she had applied a bit too much make-up to her face. Her lips were rather dark and full, her eyes shadowed. A girl trying to look like a young woman, and she still had that quality today. The photo had probably been taken at a party or some other such occasion.

The rest was suddenly uninteresting to Oliver and he quickly scanned the contents of both folders. Details, details, but none of them essential. He didn't care if the home secretary had had a hard time deciding what to do with Oona. Oliver could go back over all that some other time, but he could see that Mr Pond had given him an accurate and thorough summary of the case.

He turned again to the first photograph of Oona.

Oliver gazed at the grainy black-and-white image. He wanted to cry. She was so beautiful. She would be perfect for him, the ultimate Myra. If only they had met at the right time, if only a few things in his life were different, and in hers. If only this and if only that, fuck fuck fuck fuck fuck it.

Was it too late?

You know me, Oliver thought, but now I know you, and nothing will ever be the same. You never had a proper father, but that wasn't the real problem. It was your mother, wasn't it? She was never there for you, even when she was there. Everything else in that household was probably bad enough, a kind of swirling chaos of pain and fear, hatred and need, but your mother was the centre of gravity, the black hole at the heart of it all.

That's why you used the word mother so many times and in so many ways in your psychic rants. They were only marginally about me or Carrie, or the O'Donnells. They were really all about you and your mother. I know, love, I know.

Oliver forced himself to stop grinding his teeth. He took a long drink of Scotch, drained the glass and poured another. He felt as if an iron bar had been removed from somewhere inside his chest, a dead weight he'd been carrying around all his life. Oona was like him. She knew.

It was different but the same. Oliver's mother had *always* been there, suffocatingly omnipresent. He had watched her slowly wear down his father, sanding him away like a piece of wood until there was nothing left but dust. It was just the little things, the million daily little things that cumulatively add up and make human life intolerable. The only justice came when his father's heart finally gave out – on the M5 at 110 m.p.h.

Oliver's mother had died at the same time. He liked to think that, somehow, the old boy had done it on purpose.

But the price was too high. No man should have to yield his life to escape. Why did his father stick with her? Why not just leave, separate, divorce? Had it been for Oliver's sake?

No. Please, no.

You're so beautiful, he thought, staring at the photograph. Oona had been out for more than three years now. So why have you stopped? It's Roz, your surrogate mother. Roz had Oona trapped in that psychic racket. Scream for a bit of affection, bleed for the money we live on. And beat your brains out because Roz won't let you do the one thing you want to do and need to do and *like*. She even has you convinced you're helping people. It's that much easier to sell torture and slavery if the victim actually thinks there's a point to it. But it was sick, that's all.

How could he kill her now?

Oona, if I could save you would you come with me?

Be my my my my my Myra?

He couldn't stay in. This information made him restless and excited. Oliver had a burger at a place down the street and then continued on to the Edgar Wallace pub, just off the Strand. He'd read a number of the Wallace thrillers and mysteries when he was about twelve or thirteen – his father had had a whole shelf of them. They would probably seem simple and rather silly now, but at that age Oliver had fallen in love with the image of a vanished London conveyed in the books. It was the London of the 1920s, by turns glitzy or grey, gaudy or drab, swathed in cold wet fog. A London somehow always exotic, and wonderfully dangerous.

Forty miles and a lifetime away from the house in Aylesbury, where he'd been raised by a quiet stamp-collecting accountant dad and his – and his dad's wife.

Oliver had been dreaming of London for years, long before he finally got to the city. And it had been great for a while, but then New York drew him. Perhaps that had been the mistake. He could move back. Carrie would do it. But then what?

He had a wife, work, a range of business activities, a whole life – apart from himself. It was dangerous to imagine he could somehow scrap all of that – with Oona? – and merge with himself to be reborn, complete and fully realized. No, no. That way was the path to chaos and collapse. He could kill them all if he had to – Carrie, Marthe, Becky, Roz and even Oona. That would be an astonishing feat. But a greater admission of failure was hard to conceive.

And what would be left of him then? His true self, pure and supremely unconstrained? Or nothing at all?

The Edgar Wallace was somehow comforting, as always, but too quiet just now. Oliver finished his pint and caught a cab to the Miranda club. It was quiet there too, but the usual late-evening crowd was starting to drift in. Soon he would be able to feel at peace in their midst, blurred and anonymous.

Perhaps Marthe was the best he could hope for, after all. A ferocious lover, not a placid wife. A partner in lighting up the dark, who shared his monumental secrets. Marthe had a talent for it, no question. But there was something missing in her. She was not the perfect Myra.

He knew what it was. Marthe was too much like him. Unique, different if not special, talented, bright, *sui generis*. In sum, she was not ordinary enough and never would be.

That was what made the real Myra Hindley – and the barbaric child-killings, the Moors murders, that she participated in some thirty years ago in Manchester with her crabbed little pea-brain of a man, Ian Brady – so fearfully compelling, so significant in the annals of crime. Myra was as ordinary as a block of wood but she had gone all the way down to the bottom of the deepest trench in the deepest part of the deepest ocean, where all of the great transactions in the secret agenda of the true soul are conducted. Myra had been there. She knew.

Oliver sipped his drinks, smoked his cigarettes, and watched the dancers stripping. A fair crowd for a week night. He felt a growing sense of confidence and certainty. He was touching down, feeling solid ground beneath his feet again, and it was good. He was lost in the club, the crowd, the babble and music, the bodies and heat, the joyful pointlessness of it all – all of which, for reasons he never understood, made him feel safe.

Alone, later in his hotel room, he took out the photograph of Oona. Slum goddess of the far north. Oliver could love her, she was perfect: ordinary but fearless, damaged but pure. Oh, yes, he could save her, and love her, and they could go on to write their own occult history between the lines of life. But that was only a dream. A connection missed. The beautiful terrors never to be achieved. Oliver's heart ached. Too bad. But fuck fuck fuck it all anyway. Oona had challenged him.

'This floor is cold.'
   'Why not?'
   'What do you mean, why not?'
   'It's a floor. All floors are cold.'
   'A mattress would help.'
   Marthe snorted. 'Too soft.'
   'Well, some extra blankets, then.'
   'If you want.' Obviously she didn't.
   'I love you,' Oliver said.
   'Jerk-off.'
   'Fuck you, bitch.'
   'Yeah, yeah.' Bored.
   'Shit-eating cunt.'
   She smiled. 'Yes?'
   'Why am I being nice to you?'
   'Because you're stupid. Asshole.'
   'Arse.'
   'Stupid.'
He pushed the second vibrator into her, ramming it with the heel of his hand. Marthe winced and let out a squeal. 'This is your *arse*,' he said, slamming it again, forcing another yelp from Marthe. 'Understand? Not your ass, your arse.' She was down on her belly, hips raised. He reached under to make sure

the other one wasn't going to slide out. Then he crawled around, kneeling in front of her. He grabbed her by the ears, twisting her hair, roughly yanking up her head at an uncomfortable angle. 'You were saying? Eh? What were you saying, cunt?'

'Faggot.'

He almost slapped her. 'No, no,' he said, grinning.

That annoyed her. 'English faggot.'

All right, bing, a little slap, a teaser. Then another one, harder, and again and again, and so on, until he forced her mouth open and she loved it. Ram on.

He liked her purple eyes. Marthe had taken to using coloured lenses ever since that time he came on her face and it burned her right eye so painfully she had had to go to the doctor. Burning the eyes was not a very good idea.

The body, yes. Later he would kiss her scar tissue. Three horizontal lines burned into the skin between her tits. Six more down the lower left side of her back. Four on the right shoulder and two on the sole of each foot. Oliver had done them, branding Marthe with the fire of love. She liked it – no, she loved it. The searing, the stink, and then the splash of Cristal to purify the wound. But where next? Perhaps the back of her neck, or the soft skin behind the ears. Just above her bush, or maybe beneath each tit. There were so many possibilities. Marthe would choose the site. It was her body; it was her rite.

He always felt strangely sad when the time came. It wasn't because he cared. He did, but not very much. Oliver felt that it had something to do with the underlying tidal sadness of life itself. The usual thing.

He was already rehearsing the phone call.

The fucking floor was so cold. He pushed up from the ratty blanket and poked Marthe. Enough of this dozing in the post-fuck haze of temporary respite. The energy was coming back to him now and he needed to move, do, make happen.

'Are you ready?'

'Sure, why not.'

Oliver picked up the knife as he got to his feet. He took a few steps to the chair where Becky was bound hand and foot, waist and neck, the ball gag tightly in place. Her eyes were open wide and she looked like a manic animal. Oliver hadn't seen her blink once since she got there. Quite right, too.

Marthe got in place on her knees in front of Becky. Oliver knew exactly where to slide the blade so that it went in quickly, straight to the heart.

Becky-Becky Something-Something.

Marthe gasping and chirping in the spray.

Oliver went to the telephone and tapped out a long series of numbers. Bing bing pop bang click click click ding dong. To his great delight, the voice that answered was Oona's.

'Oi,' he said. 'Do you know me?'

Hesitation. 'Oliver?'

'Very good. I take it you're all rested and recovered now, after your recent ordeal.'

'How's Germany?'

Oliver laughed. 'You tell me.'

'Someone is dead.'

Good. She knew, but she didn't know.

'You seem to be functioning quite well.'

'Who is it?'

'It would be easier to list the living.'

'What do you want?'

'Is Roz there?'

'No.'

'Great. This is for you alone.'

'What?'

'Do you understand? You alone.'

'Yes. What is it?'

'I know all about you.'

A very long, very gratifying pause at the other end.

'No.'

'Yes. It's quite a story, isn't it? The whole world would love to know. But I can save you from all that. We have to talk. In person. Alone.'

At Swim

Oona hung up and looked down at Roz. 'He knows.'

Roz had a dab of shaving cream on her nose. 'And I suppose he wants you for himself.'

'Something like that. But he's got it all wrong.'

'That doesn't matter.'

'He wants me to meet him at Heathrow.'

'You can't go there. I'll see to it.'

'But I want to.'

'Don't be a fool,' Roz said. 'You couldn't do it. You have no idea how to negotiate with a man like that.'

'You mean any man.'

'You mean you care?'

Oona shrugged. 'No, not really.'

'All right then.'

'Roz.'

'What?'

'Don't go.'

'Better than waiting for him to come here.'

'Don't leave me alone.'

'Only for a day or two.' She kissed Oona's belly. 'You'll be fine, you know you will.'

'Not alone, please.'

'It'll be all right. You'll see.'

'No, no, no . . .'

'Ah. You want his wife to stay with you.'

Oona smiled.

'It doesn't feel like it's over,' Carrie said. 'It's been a while since the last event, but I don't have the feeling that I have

260

come through something and understand it.'

'Because it's unfinished.'

'I think so,' Carrie said. 'That must be why.'

'I'm sure you're right.'

'What does it all suggest to you?'

'We do this through you,' Oona said, looking sad. 'What do you think it could mean?'

'At first I thought it was about my father, or Oliver. But the next events didn't have anything to do with them.'

'No?'

'Until our last session with you,' Carrie said. 'Then, what you were saying matched the previous incident. I heard my father speak again, but most of it seemed to be about Oliver.'

'Yes.'

Carrie frowned. 'Was it something that happened in the past or something that could happen in the future? Was it literal, or metaphorical? A warning, in general terms.'

'It could be just as it seems.'

'Can you tell the difference?' Carrie asked.

'Sometimes.' Oona lit a long thin cigarette and took a sip of her vodka. 'You know inside.'

'I don't.'

'Maybe you do.'

'Oona, I'm just not sure about it.'

'What did Oliver say to you after the last session?'

'Oh.' Carrie looked embarrassed. 'He said that some of the things you said were lines from songs by Morrissey, and maybe the Sex Pistols. And that Mr O'Donnell had told him that some of it came from a book by Sir Walter Scott.'

Oona laughed. 'I bet they're right. What else?'

'He said that he'd been to India before we were married, and he had an argument with some man, but that's all there was to it. He never went to those places you mentioned.'

'He really was in Bombay.'

'Yes.'

'Do you think the rest of what he said is true?'

'I don't know.' Carrie looked quite forlorn. 'No.'

261

'Neither do I.'

'But if he did something terrible, that was a long time ago. What could it mean now? Why would it come up at all?'

'The past is always part of the present,' Oona said. 'It's always with us. It's not something separate.'

'I know,' Carrie responded. 'I do understand that. But how does that part of Oliver's past connect with me, now?'

'What kind of a man was your father?'

'He was a good man. A good husband, a good father, a man of kindness, humour, intelligence.'

'Was he honest?'

'Totally,' Carrie said. 'He hated politics, but he believed in the importance of public service, and in all the years that he worked in the diplomatic corps he never compromised his integrity or took advantage of his position. In fact, it probably hurt him in a way because, aside from one brief period in London, he never got the plum postings he should have had.'

'Was he there for the family?'

'Always, no matter how busy his schedule might be. If he was needed at home, he found a way to be there. Birthdays, or school events, all the things you want your dad to be there for, he was there. Never missed one that I can think of.'

'Sounds like you were very lucky.'

'We were. My mom was great too – she still is.'

'Is that right.' Oona crushed out her cigarette and reached for another one. 'Let's stay with your father. What I'm getting at is, the qualities you associate him with in your mind are love and faithfulness, integrity, goodness – things like that.'

'Yes, that's right.'

'And your father meant a great deal to you.'

'Oh, yes. Yes.'

'All right,' Oona said. 'When you began to experience these strange events, the very first image you perceived was?'

'My father.'

'And the one thing you understood him to say was?'

'Something about Oliver.'

'And how did your father appear to feel on the two occasions when you saw him?'

'Unhappy. Sad. Sorrowful. In pain.'

'Okay, good.'

'But we've been over all this before,' Carrie said. 'What's it supposed to mean? That the ghost of my father was warning me about Oliver, in some way?'

'Maybe we shouldn't think of him as a ghost. Maybe he was a kind of language for you, like the lines from songs or books were for me. He was your image of goodness and truth, and he appeared to you in sorrow and pain, bearing the name of your husband. You have been trying to tell yourself something.'

'You think I imagined all that?'

'No, no, no.'

Carrie was upset now. 'I was knocked down and strangled the last time. Was that a hallucination?'

'No, those things were real,' Oona said. 'But they're real on different levels and in different ways. They will lead you to an inner truth. Inside you.'

Carrie gazed bleakly at her. 'What truth?'

'Are you a happy woman?'

Carrie was about to answer with something predictable. Yes, she was happy in some ways, unhappy in others. That's the way it is with people. Nothing is ever perfectly good or perfectly bad, and blah blah blah. But Carrie stopped herself. She looked down at the bedcover she was picking at with her fingers.

'No ...'

'When was the last time you were a happy woman?'

'I ... I don't know ...'

'Okay,' Oona said. 'It starts there.'

She liked Carrie, liked her very much. Carrie would make a good mother, if she ever got around to it. Why on earth did she waste her time designing rooms for rich idiots? The money was part of it, but that wasn't much of a reason. It was what Carrie did, to express and define herself. As if an East Side apartment suite were more creative and definitive than a child.

Ah, well, people find their way, somehow. But as much as she liked Carrie, she couldn't feel sorry for her. Carrie had plenty of time. She could save her life thrice over and still find new opportunities and new futures, new happinesses.

Oona had seen so many people like that. They came to her to have the truth revealed, for help and guidance. They lacked only the wit to see around the scariest corners inside of themselves. Too bad, but that was everything.

Their lives crowded in on her. They killed her, but somehow always kept her alive to crush her and kill her again, and again. The truth about being Oona is it's impossible to live, impossible to die. This is the truth, ha ha, poor me.

Oliver was in love with her. Or *the idea* of her. This was the corner Oona could not walk Carrie round. Carrie would have to find her own way, if at all.

Men always want the one thing they can't have. No one could have her. Ever ever ever. The price was too great.

Carrie came out of the bathroom, wearing a long flannel gown, prim but somehow fetching. Victorian? This is what I can't ever ever ever have. But the rest was nearly better, the comfort, the closeness, the warmth. Carrie was a good person.

'You didn't look at my scar.'

'Oh, I never even noticed it.'

Carrie sat down beside Oona and leant close. Minty breath, clear skin, bright eyes, lovely clean lady. Hold me. Carrie ran one finger across Oona's forehead.

'See it?'

'No.' Perplexed. 'I don't.'

'I'm cursed with quick healing, among other things.'

They both laughed.

'Well, that's good,' Carrie said. 'I'm glad. That was such a terrible thing. Do you remember how it happened?'

'My mind's a blank on the end of that session.'

'Probably just as well.' Carrie brushed a wisp of hair off to the side of Oona's head. 'Do you still think it's coming back to you or—'

'Oh, it is, sure. I get little tremors and flashes every day now. It'll be all the way back soon enough.'

Carrie stroked Oona's cheek. 'Oh, Oona . . .'

Oona was not in the mood for pity. 'Roz told me that I put on quite a show.' She laughed as soon as she said it.

'It was terrible to see, and for you.'

'Maybe I'm only kidding you.'

'What do you mean?'

'Maybe I really like it.'

'Oona, you couldn't.'

'No?'

'Not the way you suffer. I've seen it.'

'You could be wrong.'

Carrie shook her head. 'You're joking.'

'I don't know if I am,' Oona said. 'That might be the part I never let on to myself. That I like it. You know?'

'You like helping people. That part of it. But not all the pain that comes with the voices and visions. You might like what comes out of the process, not the process itself.'

'You may be right. Carrie?'

'Yes?'

Oona composed a mischievous grin on her face. 'What would you do if I asked you to kiss me?'

Carrie answered with a tolerant smile, 'I'd kiss you.'

Oona, you can be surprised. 'You would?'

'Yes.'

'Go ahead, then.'

Carrie put her hands on Oona's shoulders, and her lips moved just past Oona's lips to kiss her first on one cheek and then the other. Carrie pulled back a couple of inches, but kept her hands on Oona's shoulders. She smiled warmly.

It was all rather slow, gentle, touching. Sweet, in a way. 'I feel like de Gaulle.'

Carrie laughed. 'What?'

'I saw a movie with some fellow kissing de Gaulle like that. It must be the European method, right?'

'You could say that.'

'On the other hand, it's not French-kissing.'

'No, it isn't.'

'How does a man French-kiss a woman?'

'He puts his tongue in her mouth.'

'Does she do the same to him?'

'She can if she wants.'

'Would you kiss me like that?'

'Do you want me to kiss you like that?'

Oona nodded once. Carrie kissed her. It was lingering, but not too long. Warm, soft, gently exploratory.

'Why'd you do that?'

'Because you wanted me to,' Carrie replied.

'What else would you do if I asked?'

Half a beat. 'Whatever you want.'

'Why would you do anything like that?'

'If you want it and need it . . .'

'But why?'

'Because you're very special and—'

She didn't hear the rest. Oona could feel the blood humming in her own veins. Darkness flickering at the furthest corners of her vision. Wind swirling against the window glass. The ceiling turns colours for you, and faces appear in the grain of the paint. Voices speak to you and in you and through you. They say you are so special, so very special. You have a gift, a talent. You are so special they will do anything for you.

They will love you to death, and back again.

See? It's never any good.

'Oona.'

'Yes?'

'What do you want me to do?'

After a long while, Oona said, 'Hold me, please.'

When Oona awoke early in the morning, Carrie was right next to her, propped up on one elbow and looking at her. Spooky. She wasn't used to anybody being a step ahead of her like that. But Carrie immediately smiled lovingly at her and Oona began to enjoy the feeling of cosy intimacy in the grey light. In a way, it was what she had wanted – someone, this someone, to be with her all night long and be there with her in the morning.

'I always wake early in a strange bed.'

Oona smiled and stretched. 'My bed's not so strange.'

'Not any more.'

Oona crawled onto Carrie, who let herself sink back into the pillows and mattress. They hugged, and Carrie held her, and Oona nestled her face beneath Carrie's chin, kissing her neck lightly. She was suddenly desperate for this warmth, this flesh. Oona's fingers trembled as she undid the buttons on Carrie's nightgown. She buried her face between the breasts, nuzzling them, touching them with her lips and tongue. Carrie held her as a mother would a hungry infant, and for a few moments Oona began to lose herself in a warm, enveloping fog of serene acceptance.

'Oh, shit.'

'What—'

They both sat up. Carrie felt the wetness on her chest, and then saw all the blood. Oona held her hand to her face, as blood trickled out between her fingers.

'Nosebleed,' she burbled in alarm.

'Lie down on your back.'

Carrie dashed off, and was back in a few seconds with a cold wet towel. She used part of it to wipe away the blood, and then pressed it gently to Oona's nose.

'Just hold it there.'

'Shit.'

'Don't worry, it's not bad,' Carrie said comfortingly. 'The air-conditioner, probably. It makes the air very dry. I'll get some ice to wrap in the towel.'

'No.'

'What?'

'It's not the fucking air-conditioner,' Oona said, trying to focus on her anger to keep from crying. 'It's not that. It's me and my fucking talent. I can feel it in my skin. I can feel it in the roots of my fucking hair. Oh shit shit shit.'

Carrie sat down beside her and stroked her forehead. 'Look, it's stopped already.'

'Doesn't matter.'

'It was nothing, Oona, just a little nosebleed.'

'*I hate it!*' Oona screamed, the tears coming now. Her body jerked and twitched, and her eyes blinked furiously.

Carrie sat closer to her on the bed and stroked her forehead soothingly. 'I'm here, don't worry. You'll be all right.'

Carrie helped, being there. Oona felt herself easing out of it. A brief contact, that's all it was this time. Hello, hello, remember me? Your lady friend can't save you.

They heard the front door open, then close.

Footsteps on the stairs.

It was late in the morning. Carrie had prepared a breakfast of coffee, juice, eggs, toast and grilled cherry tomatoes. Oona felt a little better. Tired, lazy, but calm. Carrie was talking about going out for a drive that afternoon. The Litchfield hills or something. Countryside, anyway, not many people about. Oona had no idea and didn't care one way or the other.

'A lot of movie stars live up there, you know.'

'Like who?'

'Dustin Hoffman, Meryl Streep, Richard Widmark—'

'No way! I love him.' Ooh, God, yes, to be killed by Richard Widmark. That'd be tops. 'Think he'll be home?'

Carrie laughed. 'Not to us.'

Carrie was talking about the Litchfield hills, the Hamptons, some such thing. Oona half listened, half talked. She poked the remote but couldn't find anything on television. Where's Richard Widmark when you need him?

The door, the footsteps.

Roz walked into the bedroom and sat down in the small chair beside the dressing table. She was wearing shorts and a light sleeveless summer blouse. She looked at them.

> *'Tis hard for such to view unfurl'd*
> *The curtain of the future world.*

> *Yet – witness every quaking limb,*
> *My sunken pulse, my eyeballs dim,*
> *My soul with harrowing anguish torn—*

'Roz,' Oona said, faintly. A day too soon, wrongly dressed for someone who'd just come off a jet plane.

'Hi, Roz,' Carrie said. 'You're back early.'

> *Nor sought she from that fatal night,*
> *Or holy church or blessed rite,*
> *But lock'd her secret in her breast,*
> *And died in travail, unconfess'd.*

Pockets of blackness opened up inside Oona, and she began shrieking hysterically, great jagged sounds ripping out of her as she rocked and bounced uncontrollably on the bed.

'*OH NO NO NO NO NO HINNY DON'T GO DON'T LEAVE ME—*'

'Oh, Lord,' Carrie said, as she turned to Roz. 'Can you give me a hand with her, Roz, it's—'

Carrie cried out as if she'd been wounded. She saw the same thing Oona saw – Roz looking so sad as she sat in the chair, Roz blurred and distorted, Roz disappearing. Gone.

PART III

23

Oliver wasn't surprised to open the door and find Roz standing there with a cold, thin smile on her face. This was what he had had in mind all along. Oona and Roz wouldn't want to set foot in England so he reckoned they would either ignore him or try to gain an edge by confronting him in Munich. They obviously didn't think they could risk ignoring him. So. Excellent.

'Where's Oona?' he asked immediately.

Roz shook her head in disbelief. 'You think I'd let her hop on a plane and come all this way? Oona isn't allowed in downtown New Haven most of the time, and never on her own.'

'Why not?'

'You don't understand anything, do you?'

Oliver led Roz to part of the loft where there were several chairs and a sofa, the closest thing to a social area. He saw no reason to be polite with her; she was merely an obstacle, soon to be removed. Perhaps Oona was parked at a local hotel.

'I know everything,' he said, as he perched on the arm of the scuffed Naugahyde sofa. 'I know all about the two of you.'

'I doubt that very much.'

'Then why did you hop on a plane and come all this way?' he asked, mimicking her words. 'Why bother?'

'I want you out of our lives.'

'And how do you propose to accomplish that?'

'It works both ways,' Roz told him. 'We know about you, Mr Spence, and you've got more to lose than we have.'

'Oh, really?'

'A lot more, I would say.'

'Have a seat, Rosalind.'

'No thanks.'

She stood a couple of yards away from him. Smart slacks and blouse, a light summer blazer. She had a tight grip on the Gucci handbag hanging from her shoulder – too tight. Roz looked rigid and tense. Oliver liked that in other people, it always made him feel more relaxed.

'What is it you think you—'

'You're a murderer, Mr Spence,' she cut in. 'You should be put away for the rest of your life.'

'Then why haven't you notified the authorities?'

'You'll undo yourself sooner or later.'

'You have nothing to tell anybody, Roz,' he said, scornfully. 'Mumbo-jumbo about something that supposedly happened in Bombay a long time ago? Knowledge that came in a seance? That would make a great story. The press and television people would be all over it, doing follow-ups on the pretty child-killer who got off easy, moved to America and became a successful medium.'

There was hate in her eyes. He liked that too.

'If necessary, we'd face it.'

Oliver laughed. 'What I know about Oona is fact, Roz. What you know about me amounts to nothing.'

'What do you want with her, anyway?'

'I fancied her. She feels the same about me.'

'Whatever gave you that idea?'

'She told me so,' Oliver insisted. 'Before we all went into the back room for that session, she whispered in my ear.'

'You do have a problem reading other people.'

'I don't think so.'

'Believe me, Oona doesn't fancy you.'

'She may not fully realize it herself yet,' Oliver said, with a trace of annoyance.

'Ah, so that's how it is.' Roz seemed more at ease now, and that was foolish, but her manner was starting to irritate Oliver. She glanced briefly at the surroundings. 'I waited for your lady friend to go out. Will she be long?'

'No.'

'Does she know—'

'Marthe doesn't care. About anything.'

'I might've guessed. Birds of a feather.'

'Where's Oona?' he demanded curtly.

'Far from here, in good hands.'

Shit. 'My wife is with her.'

Roz didn't care for that. 'Forget about Oona.'

Oliver shrugged. 'I can't. She has a way of getting under your skin and into your life, and then you want to get into hers. Oona's very special.'

'Not the way you think.'

'You don't know her, Roz,' he said. 'That's rather sad, not knowing your own sister. Half-sister, whatever. The truth is, I know Oona far better than you do. I understand her.'

'Get out of our life.'

'You could have told me that on the phone. Are you staying for dinner, Roz? Got a room booked in town, have you? Or do you want to kip here for the night?'

'You've been warned.'

'Warned about what?'

'Is Becky still here? Or did you dump the body?'

'Becky?'

'Becky Wade-Wellman.'

When Oona had mentioned Becky on the phone, Oliver had been startled for a second. Becky was current. In England people would soon be looking for her, if she wasn't already a missing-persons case. Oona had come up with the name and the connection to him. It was not evidence of anything but it could be used to make Oliver the subject of official scrutiny, and that would be bad.

However, Oona wouldn't tell anyone on her own. Oliver could handle Oona. Roz was the threat, as he had known all along. He stared calmly at her and saw no fear in her eyes – another good sign, because it was a mistake.

'That rings a bell,' he said blandly. 'Did I hear something on the news about somebody with that name?'

'No, you told Oona about her all by yourself.'

'Oh, yes. How *does* she do that?'

'You still think there's some trick to it? When you come to Oona, she begins to *know* you. After that, just the sound of your voice tells her more. You have no idea what kind of power you're dealing with, Mr Spence. Oona is genuine. She has a tremendous talent. That's how she does it.'

It quickened his heartbeat to hear that. If it was really true, then Oona was much more special than he'd thought. Oliver wanted her, he had to have her, in some way, at some level. What *couldn't* they do together? They were kindred spirits in a shitty world, and he couldn't bear to let her slip by without trying to make something happen between them. Oona had challenged him to his face, and he loved her for it. It said everything.

Roz feared the awful media attention he could bring on them, but that wasn't the greatest threat Oliver posed. Roz was afraid of losing control of Oona. She knew that if he came between them she'd be left out in the cold. Alone. Not a happy prospect, not much of a future.

Oliver smiled to himself. But, then, look where Roz was now. Alone. Here. No future at all.

'Funny, but I thought it was you who killed that little girl in Scotswood. That maybe you put the blame on Oona and have been making up for it to her ever since.'

'I was the only one who loved Oona, and cared for her,' Roz responded. 'Always have done. I'm the one who's kept her alive, or she'd have found a way to get herself killed by now.'

Hello. Did Oona honestly mean those provocative remarks she had made about his killing her? Perhaps so. Oliver didn't quite know how to factor this idea in yet, but he found it fascinating. Would he kill Oona? Perhaps, but not before they wrote a passage of secret history together.

'I visited her all the time,' Roz continued quickly. 'I was the only one who did. I saved and prepared and made arrangements so that when she was finally released she'd be able to start a new life in a new country. She could do something to help people, she could use her gift in a positive way. You don't know anything about it. You have no idea.'

'Why did she do it?'

'Do what?' The belligerent cow.

'Kill a child of four.'

'She was a child herself, she didn't mean it.'

'That's not true, and you know it,' Oliver said. 'You know the real reason she did it, don't you?'

'Leave off,' Roz replied angrily.

You can't say it, Oliver thought, feeling gratified. It was because Oona was like him. Oona did it because she wanted to and needed to and liked it. Even at the tender age of eleven. He'd come late to it, much later. She was so far ahead of him. She'd been forced to stop for a while, but Oona was like him.

By Christ, he could love her. The image of Oona's face swam in his head, Oona as she was today and Oona as she was in the old newspaper photo – the dark hair, the heart-shaped face, the eyes that knew so much. His slum angel. Visionary. Goddess.

This was so convenient, really. He would take great delight in disposing of Roz and saving Oona – how often had she alluded to somebody saving her in her psychic riffs? That was what Oona wanted and needed: saving. She was brilliant and gifted, but she was a wild child with little understanding of herself. Direction and focus were called for, and Oliver could provide it. He might have to give up his wife for this, Marthe certainly, but he could see how the prize was worth even such a high price. You can find bright and beautiful women. They're all over the place, and each one of them may be a gem. But Oona was a true discovery.

'Roz.'

'What?'

Oliver stood up and went slowly to her. She didn't back off or show any fear. He slipped the leather strap off her shoulder and tossed the handbag onto a chair. He ran his fingers down the underside of the lapels on her blazer, deliberately brushing the back of his hands across her breasts.

'I don't want to hurt you.'

'I think you do, Mr Spence.'

'You have lovely fair skin,' he said, stroking her cheek and letting his hand trail down her neck. He slid his fingers under her blouse. 'A lovely, lovely neck.'

'I don't like being touched by you.'

Oliver leaned forward until his face was almost touching her neck. Roz remained perfectly still. 'Lovely fragrance,' he told her. 'Joy, isn't it?'

'Joy,' she echoed sardonically.

Oliver gently felt the pockets of her blazer; they were both empty. His hands came to rest on her hips.

'I think I'll touch you anyway.'

'Back off.'

'I don't think so, Roz.'

He put his lips to the base of her neck, the delicate hollow just above the collarbone. Her body shook once but then appeared to exhale. He wouldn't let her move away. He licked and kissed her, his mouth moving up her throat. Roz pulled back her head an inch or two. He looked at her – he saw no anger, no fear in her expression. In a way, she seemed almost curious.

Now, a faint smile. 'Fancy yourself, don't you?'

He smiled back at her. 'Sssh . . .'

He kissed her throat again, and he could feel her body yield slightly in his arms. His hands came up to her neck as he kissed her mouth. She opened it a little, reluctantly, giving in to him step by step. He wrapped her hair tightly in his fingers, another tiny demonstration. With difficulty Roz turned her mouth away from his, and caught her breath.

'You're a bit rough.'

'A bit of rough is just the thing, Roz.'

Oliver held her head still by the hair and began to unbutton her blouse with his right hand. She moved her mouth hungrily and tried to kiss him, but he held her off for a few seconds, letting the desire build. Then he crushed his mouth against hers, backed her to the wall and yanked at her blouse. Roz whimpered faintly, and did not resist.

He let go of her hair and used that hand to reach up beneath her skirt. Tights invariably angered him, but before he could pull them away Roz suddenly bit into his upper lip, the whole left side, nearly as far back as the gums – clamped her teeth into it and wouldn't let go. Oliver howled with pain and rage. Then Roz jerked her head violently away, and a strip of his face was torn off. She spat his own flesh back at him.

The shock to his head dizzied him for a second, but he was so furious that he lunged with both hands at her neck. He dimly saw her hands moving together, and then one of them came up in a pointless attempt to hold him off –

– and he had the oddest sensation: of leaking into himself. He was choking Roz, but his strength was rapidly vanishing. Then he became aware of the pain. He looked down and saw that she had stabbed him with one of those cheap little two-inch paper knives that are barely sharp enough to open a manila envelope – but can puncture flesh. And a lung, he realized. Jesus, he was bleeding into himself. He touched the handle of the knife, sticking out between his ribs, and wondered whether to remove it or not. His knees were turning spongy already. The bitch must have had that toy tucked up in the palm of her hand all the while. Opened it, slipped it right in. Not his heart, but nearly as bad.

Oliver couldn't believe it yet. He glanced back up at Roz, just in time to see her arms swinging around, hands locked one in the other, clubbing him on the side of the face. He went down on one knee, and managed to hold himself there. Roz came closer and casually plucked the paper knife from his chest. She put the tip of the blade to his throat.

'Now you know why I came here, Mr Spence,' she said. Funny bitch, she was half crying. 'I knew this was how you'd try to do it. Better here than have you come for us at home.'

'Fair enough.'

'You're something else, you are.'

'I try.'

'You don't deserve to live.'

'Who does?'

It was hard to find a breath and it hurt too much to speak. Oliver was about out of words anyway – they sounded so distorted and clotted. He wondered what his mouth looked like, and what it would take to fix it. Then he had an image of blood seeping into his left lung and gradually filling it. He would bleed to death, on the inside. That is, he would drown. But slowly. So he had to think carefully and find the right way, while there was still time to save himself.

'The Beckys and Oonas of the world,' Roz answered. 'And all the little girls like them.'

What about the little girl in Scotswood? he thought at once. Didn't she deserve to live? Forgot about her, didn't you? Never mind, best not to ask – even if he could. Roz might react badly and all he wanted was for her to keep talking, buy some time. But she said nothing more. Just stood over him, glaring through her tears, holding the knife on him.

He didn't see or hear Marthe until the last second, same as Roz. She must have come in by the back door and seen what was happening. She flew across the timbered floor, bare feet padding softly. She came up behind Roz, who turned when the sound got to her – too late. Marthe rammed something into the back of Roz's neck. Roz jerked once, then froze, her eyelids flapping. Then they were all moving – Marthe shoving Roz, who fell forward as Oliver tried to turn away. The blade jumped into his throat.

Shit, oh, shit. Such a lot of damage from one chintzy little piece of junk. Oliver eased the knife away from his neck and put his hand over the wound. He lowered himself to the floor, trying not to injure himself further. The hole in his throat felt very large. Missed the major arteries, but too much of his blood was oozing through his fingers.

Marthe dragged Roz onto a tarp, rolled her up in it and tugged it across the room to the sinks. His warrior queen. They would have no trouble disposing of Roz, same as Becky. The acid, the long slow dissolve. That had been Oliver's idea.

Marthe had never heard of George Haigh, the Vampire of South Kensington, who from 1944 to 1949 murdered several people for financial gain and gave them the acid-bath treatment. Only his monumental stupidity had got him caught and hanged. But Haigh had had a certain wit and charm of his own, claiming that he drank the blood of his victims, and, on the day of his execution, issuing final suggestions as to how his likeness should be displayed at Madame Tussaud's.

Oliver slapped the floor with his free hand. It felt like a sheet of rubber hinged at the wrist. Marthe heard him and came. She peered down at him anxiously.

'Are you okay?'

'No,' he uttered, through bubbles of blood.

'Okay, wait.'

She came back a moment later with two towels, and started to pat his hand and neck with the dry one. That only increased the pain Oliver felt, and he pushed away the towel.

'Hey, let me see,' she said, voice flat and calm.

Marthe cautiously peeled his fingers away from his throat to expose part of the wound. More blood foamed out from between his teeth. She made a face and clucked. She took the wet towel and pressed it against his neck.

'Hold it there,' she told him. 'Hold it as tight as you can to stop the blood and close it.'

Oliver did that, but it was no help. He was gulping air but too much blood went into him with it. Marthe stared at his wound and made another face. It wasn't working. Then she noticed, for the first time, the bloody hole in his shirt. She poked a finger through it and felt his other wound. A serious frown.

'Doctor,' he said, the word coming out in a damp red cloud. 'Hospital. Accident.'

It was as much as he could manage to say. They could handle the awkward questions, explain it away as a freak accident. The main thing now was to get him to some help, fast. The opening in his throat was too large, his lung was punctured, he was bleeding to death and drowning, at the same time.

Marthe stood up, thinking. Do something. God save him from women who stop to think. He tried to speak, but all that emerged was a growl and some pink suds. He slapped his hand on the floor again but it barely made any noise.

Grey patches mushroomed across his vision, then disappeared, and were replaced by others. Oliver wanted to lie down, but knew that would be much worse. He held himself together, sitting in a more or less upright position, but his strength was fading.

'Ma – Ma – Ma—'

Marthe knelt before him. 'What to do?'

Oliver could feel the rage exploding in his face – the only way he could communicate it to her. But she gazed impassively at him and didn't move. He knew. She was thinking it would be too risky and troublesome to deal with the doctors and police, easier just to heave another body into the sink.

Dangerous thoughts.

Oliver could feel the muscles in his face writhing. He must continue. He was the last of the famous international playboys, barely at mid-career. Oona would understand. Too soon to be one for the books. He gave it his best effort, summoning all of his strength, swallowing blood to clear his throat for a few precious seconds, and then geysering a frantic shout.

'It's – not – too – late—'

Marthe blinked, as if mildly surprised. She absently wiped at the red spray on her cheek. Then, just before she got up and kicked his rubbery arm out from under him, his less than perfect Myra leaned forward and smiled sadly at him.

'Oliver, you must be joking.'

24

Laundry detergent, vodka, juice, assorted non-prescription painkillers, tampons, wintergreen bath salts, a bag full of mints and English liquorice. Carrie checked the list: yes, she had everything. It had taken a while because she was unfamiliar with New Haven, and Oona's handwriting was tricky to read.

Oona had hardly spoken a word since that ghostly apparition of Roz. The incident. They had both seen it, no mistake about that. And poor Oona had been hysterical for hours afterwards, biting her lips, pulling her hair, weeping and moaning – before she finally lapsed into a restless sleep disturbed by occasional plaintive whimpers.

Carrie sat with her through all of it, often holding Oona in her arms, talking to her, comforting her. She knew that Oona was convinced that Roz was dead. Somehow, somewhere.

When she woke up the following morning Oona had seemed calm, subdued and lost in herself. Her skin was pale, and cool to the touch. She ate a little and drank some hot tea. But she seldom spoke, and mostly just sat in bed, looking vacant.

'It'll be all right,' Carrie told her.

'It won't ever.'

'It doesn't have to mean what you think.'

'But it does.'

Roz didn't return home that day or the next. There was no phone call from her, explaining why she was late. Oona had told Carrie that Roz had gone away to take care of some family matter. She hadn't said where, but she did tell Carrie that Roz would be back by – yesterday.

This morning Oona gave Carrie some cash and a list of things she needed, and asked her if she would go out for them.

They had to talk seriously. Carrie wouldn't return to New York and leave Oona by herself, but she couldn't stay in New Haven indefinitely. If there was still no word from Roz . . .

The apparition had fooled Carrie completely. Roz had looked and acted so real. There'd been no sense that she was witnessing another psychic incident, she didn't have the feeling that *it* was happening to her again – until the end.

The sounds were another difference. Carrie was certain that she had heard the front door open and close, and footsteps on the stairs. So had Oona; they had both looked up at the first sound. When Carrie thought about it, she could even remember the little noises that Roz made as she walked across the bedroom carpet and sat down in the chair by the dressing table. They were everyday sounds, perfectly normal. And wrong.

But the most persuasive aspect of the experience was that Carrie and Oona had shared it. They had both seen the same thing and heard the same noises. They hadn't anticipated it, or spoken of it at all. It seemed to Carrie that psychic incidents witnessed by more than one person must be quite rare, and hard to explain as anything but genuine.

Carrie was beginning to draw her own tentative conclusions. There might be an afterlife or another level of existence, and it may be that some portion of our consciousness continues in that realm – personality, nature, soul, whatever. And it may also be that there are occasional ghostly intrusions from that world into this one, and that particularly sensitive people are more likely to experience them.

But none of that necessarily meant that the intrusions had a purpose or design, that there was a method or process at work, or that whatever happened after death was part of a higher spiritual order. Existence in the next world, to call it that, might be as random, blinkered and mysterious as life in this world. Perhaps the intrusions were just irrational occurrences.

The next step for Carrie was to resolve things with Oliver as soon as he returned home. It would be difficult and painful, but it was absolutely essential. The poisonous doubt that Carrie felt had to be removed, regardless of the outcome.

Roz wasn't back, and Oona was gone.

Carrie immediately sensed the difference. She heard Oona's music coming from upstairs, the usual stuff, but the door to the front hall closet was slightly open, which looked inappropriate. There was a flatness in the air, a lack of vitality – some force of which Carrie became aware now only by its absence.

A warm summer breeze stirred the filmy lace curtains at the kitchen window. Carrie put the shopping bags down on the table and hurried upstairs. The bedroom was empty, the bed unmade. She quickly checked the bathroom, then Roz's room, and the spare room that was used for storage.

She walked slowly back into Oona's room. She knew that Oona was gone, but she found it impossible to believe. Why? And where would she go? It made no sense. Even if she had received a call saying that Roz was in some kind of trouble, surely Oona would have waited the hour or two until Carrie returned. Carrie would have driven her to the airport if necessary, have helped her do whatever had to be done. Oona didn't drive. She went through the rest of the house and checked the yard, but Oona was gone.

When she went back and looked for them she started to see the signs. Desk drawers left open, a few papers scattered on the green blotter. Bureau drawers not quite shut, a couple of empty hangers in Oona's closet. Oona's pyjamas balled up on the floor beside the bed.

The big room was the same as it had been on the day of their last session. The pillows were still scattered, the bloodstains had never been washed off. The water in the basin had evaporated and the candles had guttered out. What exactly had happened in this place? She'd seen and heard things, remarkable events, but they were still opaque and indecipherable to her.

Carrie touched a blood spot the size of a quarter, a rusty brown scab on the marble. She half expected to receive a

psychic flash, a sudden vision, a glimpse of Oona. But she felt
nothing. She thought of those ancient maps where the coastline
was clearly marked in detail – but everywhere beyond it was
blank, the great emptiness. Sometimes nothing *is* the definition.

'Oona.'

Carrie's voice disappeared at once, as if it had been sucked
into thin air. No resonance, no echo. The house felt abandoned.
Carrie grew angry and fearful. Why are you doing this to me?
It was the worst thing, the least considerate thing that Oona
could have done. Roz had warned her about something like
this.

She wandered into the kitchen, and discovered the note. She
hadn't seen it when she had come in and put the bags on top
of it, on the table. Oona's scrawled handwriting.

> *Carrie*
> *Sorry to go like this but I have to. I wish I did*
> *more for you but I think you'll be O.K. Thanks again*
> *for being so nice to me. You were a big help. We're both*
> *alone now but you'll be OK, I think.*
> *Love, O.*

Carrie walked out of the house and drove back to Manhattan,
where nothing was new and nothing important had happened
at work and there were no messages on the answering machine.
Early that evening she tried Marthe's number in Munich.

'*Hallo.*'

'Marthe Frennsen?'

'*Ja.*'

'This is Carrie Spence. Is Oliver there?'

'*Ja.*'

'May I speak with him, please.'

A short giggle. Carrie heard Marthe speaking away from the
phone. 'Oliver, do you have anything to say to your wife?' She
laughed, and then spoke again to Carrie. '*Nein, danke.*'

'Put him on right now,' Carrie said coldly.

Another giggle.

The line went dead. When Carrie tried again a minute later, it didn't ring at all.

The taxi from the airport skirted central Munich and brought her to a district of dreary warehouses and small factories. The streets were full of lorries and vans. The area was grim enough, but the steady rain made it seem even greyer.

Marthe Frennsen's building looked like a pre-war office, with high windows, muddy brown stone walls and a slate roof. It was stranded by itself at the end of a cul-de-sac, right up against a tall brick wall topped with coils of razor wire. It was the kind of place that had probably been taken over by underfunded artists and musicians, Carrie thought.

She paid the driver and then climbed the wide stone steps to the front entrance. There were no nameplates or cards, only one bell, and mail was delivered through a rusted metal slot in the tall wooden door. Carrie tried the bell. She didn't hear if it rang inside, and there was no response. A second attempt had the same outcome.

Carrie turned the handle and pushed the heavy door. It made a scraping sound on the stone floor, but opened. She went into a small foyer, then through a second doorway. Stairs to the right, and a long corridor straight ahead with rooms off it on either side. The place felt like an old cellar, the air cool and moist, the light from outside diminished by grimy windows.

All the rooms on the ground floor were empty, aside from scraps of litter and a few plastic buckets of varying sizes. The paint hung in spiral tatters from the walls and the ceilings were almost bare, marked with cancerous brown damp patches. The floor itself was strewn with fallen paint, dust and grit. It looked as if the place hadn't been touched since the last occupant departed thirty or more years ago.

The second floor was virtually identical to the first, but a glance out of the back window proved interesting. Carrie saw a car at the side of a cement parking area that was cracked and broken, stitched with weeds. It was an older Audi, with a couple of rust spots. No sign of a new rental that might belong to Oliver.

A small dock had been built onto the back of the house. She figured it was probably for unloading Marthe's supplies. Carrie looked up and noticed a small crane sticking out overhead, above the dock, with a cable and hook. It would have made more sense, she thought, for Marthe to use the basement and ground floor as her storage area and work space, even if it meant knocking out a few walls.

The third floor was a single huge open area, scattered with drums of chemicals, rolls of fabric arranged on wooden racks, and numerous work tables, measuring instruments and cutting tools. A power winch stood at the rear, next to double sliding doors. The machinery looked recent and well maintained.

Other additions included an array of plastic plumbing pipes, a snarl of heavy-duty electrical cables connected to an extensive bank of fuses, switches and breakers, and what appeared to be a dumb-waiter to the top floor.

The ceiling had been reinforced with steel columns situated along the lines of the load-bearing walls on the floor below. So much unnecessary trouble and expense, Carrie thought. The column plates had cracked and punched through the crumbly old plaster on the ceiling, to the floor timbers above. But in other places the plaster was still intact, and Carrie saw several dark stains that had not been caused by dry rot.

It all seemed so dismal and unlikely. It was what you might expect of an amateur inventor, not a serious professional who was developing a product with legitimate commercial potential. Maybe the important work was done on the top floor. Oliver had spoken of the loft, but Carrie had assumed that it was mainly used by Marthe as living quarters. She walked to the front of the building and started up the final flight of stairs.

There was a wide landing at the top, a wooden railing, and a steel door. Carrie knocked forcefully but nothing happened. She hesitated as she was about to knock again. She had a sudden and painful image of Oliver and Marthe in bed, having sex, scrambling into their clothes at a sound from the door. Or not – perhaps they'd just slip into robes and greet her openly; no pretence, no flimsy lies. She didn't know which would be worse.

This is where you learn something about your husband, Carrie thought. And yourself. She felt swamped with diffuse anxiety as she reached for the doorknob. It turned smoothly, the door swung inward, and Carrie stepped across the threshold.

A chemical stench hit her immediately. It seemed to be made up of several different ingredients, by turns harsh, acrid, oily, or as nauseatingly sweet as durian left out in the sun. How could anyone eat, sleep and live with it? Carrie breathed through her mouth, but that only helped a little.

She seemed to be in a maze with no design. There were more tall wooden racks all over the place, but here the textiles were laid out flat on them, as if drying. Items of furniture cropped up at random – a dresser, a dressing table, bookshelves, a dining table, floor lamps, a wine cabinet, wardrobes, free-standing screens and meaningless room dividers – jumbled among the racks, more drums and work tables, tools, instruments and unfamiliar equipment. It was a chaotic non-arrangement of everything in Marthe's personal life and her work. No separation. Carrie understood why Oliver described Marthe as eccentric and a kind of genius – most people simply couldn't tolerate such apparent confusion and disorder in their homes and lives.

There were no windows to be seen in the stone walls, and the skylights overhead did little to dispel the pervasive gloom. She edged slowly down a narrow aisle between towering racks of cloth, passed under a stepladder and went around a corner into a fairly open area with a circle of battered armchairs and a sofa. On the coffee table were the remains of various fast-food meals, crusts of pizza, doner kebabs, burger wrappers, unfinished French fries, rice cartons, soda cups and empty beer bottles. On the dark wood of the floor, a darker stain. Carrie bent down to touch it, and came away with brown powder on her fingertip.

She became aware of certain noises – a steady whirring that might be made by strong fans, some other mechanical droning and music. Industrial rock, driving guitars and drums blended with a variety of sophisticated electronic sounds. Years ago Oliver had had a passing interest in it. Carrie found it oppressive. The music was persistent but not too loud. She couldn't tell where it came from in the huge, impossibly cluttered loft.

Near one wall Carrie found a cubicle containing a toilet and a sink. The bowl was stained with accumulated hard water mineral deposits. A small stack of German newspapers and *Herald Tribunes* on the floor – the *Trib* was Oliver's favourite whenever he was in Europe, she knew. These papers were faded, months old.

A few yards away Carrie came to another clearing. A rug was hemmed in by shelves and boxes containing various personal items. An ashtray full of Disque Bleu and Senior Service butts. A tin canister of snapshots, some lying loose on the rug. She picked up five or six, and looked at them. Oliver and some woman (Carrie realized that she had no idea what Marthe looked like) on the sofa. Sitting, talking, more or less normal – but the young woman was clearly uncomfortable. Next, Oliver and—

The second Polaroid opened black patches in Carrie's vision. The pressure on her chest was so immense it felt as if she would never be able to breathe again. Oliver and the same woman on the same sofa. The woman in torn underwear, flat on her back, Oliver kneeling on her, strangling her.

It was a game, Carrie thought. A nasty role-playing fantasy of sex and violence. Next: the woman half off the sofa, her arms dangling uselessly, Oliver sitting back on his heels. Next: the woman's face in close-up, swollen, cut and bruised, eyes rotated up. Throat slashed, ragged-edged, bloody. The woman was clearly dead. Decapitated, or all but. Not a game.

It was the ugliest photograph that Carrie had ever seen, an appalling image from life too real to abide, a ghastly intrusion that finally shattered for ever the order of things in her world.

And the familiar male hand that held up the young woman's head by the hair was the hand of Carrie's husband. Her Oliver, in whose life she had chosen to root her own.

This charming man.

You'll spend the rest of your life trying to understand, she told herself, why you failed to understand.

Carrie dropped the photos to the floor. She never wanted to see them again. But she needed to see Oliver. She had no words for him, for what he had become, but she had to face him one last time. Look him in the eye, and he will know. The fear inside Carrie vanished abruptly, obliterated by the same scorching winds that swept away all of her doubt and uncertainty.

She moved along the wall. She was starting to get a better sense of the loft's absurd geography. The music was much louder now, and Carrie finally got an idea of where it was coming from. The low mechanical roar in the background was also stronger, but it provided no directional focus.

The temperature went up sharply as Carrie came round a high partition and faced a bank of industrial ovens, all currently in use. Sweat broke out on her forehead and face, and she was about to leave that area quickly when she saw some personal items lying on the floor in a small heap.

A handbag, a crumpled airline ticket, a UK passport. Roz. Carrie knew it even before she picked up the passport and saw the name, the photograph inside. She felt a tremendous sadness, then anger – and not just at Oliver. If Roz and Oona knew the truth about him, why hadn't they told her?

But would she have believed them? Probably not. It was too great a leap, too soon. Carrie remembered Oona telling her that she could help in the process, but Carrie would have to find her own way to the truth. And she had, at last, but the abysmal squalor and horror of that truth was no consolation.

The music roared as Carrie got closer to it. She continued to sweat freely in the awful heat, and the stench in the air was now almost unbearable. Not far from the ovens she found a series of troughs and vats made out of thick, heavy-duty plastic. Numerous wooden rods lay across the top of some of these containers, and several thin strips of cloth dangled from each, soaking in murky liquids. Oliver had mentioned acid baths and rinses, Carrie remembered. The smell was at its foulest here and it stung her eyes and throat.

Carrie found Oliver nearby, in a zinc trough. He was naked and his features were blurred. The fumes burned in her nose. Bits of his flesh floated in the liquid, and Carrie realized he was slowly dissolving in some kind of acid. The tears came, and she clamped a hand over her mouth as her body shook. But was she crying for Oliver or herself? She had lost him a long time ago, she now understood. It stopped after a while, the stifled sobbing, and she felt very still and calm. She felt cold to the bone.

She became aware of the music again, pulsing through the hot and bitter air all around her. Marthe. It didn't matter whether Oliver had died at the hands of Roz or Marthe – Marthe was still there, somewhere, and extremely dangerous. Now all Carrie wanted was to get away from that place and find the police.

But Marthe was just a few yards away, sitting at a workbench covered with hand tools and personal items. Carrie was trying to circle back to the door when she spotted her. She knew it had to be Marthe. Dark hair wildly teased and snarled, a leather apron. She was staring at her face in a small makeup mirror that sat on the workbench. Carrie watched for a moment as Marthe held a thin object – perhaps a carpenter's nail or a needle – with pliers and heated it with a cigarette lighter. Then she rubbed a dab of cream on her right cheek, just below the eye, and carefully pressed the hot metal across her flesh. She gave a short squawk that was all but lost in the relentless music. Her hand didn't waver, and when she was satisfied she put down the pliers and splashed her cheek with liquid from a glass. She looked quite pleased with herself.

Carrie shrank back, feeling ill again. She started to make her way silently through the infernal mess, using the ceiling and walls as a rough guide. She knew the general area where the door was – way back at the other end.

She went a short distance and then found a narrow path that snaked between racks and steel shelves. Before stepping into the aisle Carrie glanced back down it in the direction of where she'd seen Marthe – but Marthe was standing right there.

She grabbed Carrie by the hair and yanked her violently into the passageway. She clapped her hands over Carrie's ears with such force that her head rang and she lost her equilibrium. She seemed to be floundering in thick air. A kind of happy growling sound came from Marthe as she kicked Carrie's feet out from under her, locked an arm under her throat and dragged her slowly towards the workbench area.

Carrie's vision was a confused swirl and she had difficulty breathing. She tried to grab something, but her hand slapped uselessly against racks and shelves. She managed to dig in one heel briefly and push up with her leg, knocking Marthe off balance – but the other woman steadied herself at once and tightened her clamp on Carrie's throat.

Carrie got hold of the edge of a tub, fingers dipping into liquid that burned sharply. Acid. But then it was too late to try splashing it at Marthe, who tugged her into the small open area by the workbench. She slammed Carrie's ears again, and in a shower of swarming images Carrie saw the brown leather apron swim closer to her face, and then Marthe's face zoom in, antic-eyed with glee, three horizontal scar lines on one cheek and the fresh burn wound on the other. Behind the bench, a clump of tall floor fans droned and rotated like giant motorized insect heads.

Marthe hesitated for a couple of seconds, as if deciding to take her time and enjoy this. Calmly she ripped Carrie's blouse and then started to slap her about the face, a sudden flurry meant to keep her off balance more than to hurt her. Carrie took a wobbly step back, grabbed things blindly from the workbench and flung them at Marthe.

But Marthe was in her face again, unbothered, choking Carrie with both hands. There was a smile of casual delight in Marthe's eyes and her mouth moved silently to some unknown language as she bent Carrie backwards, pinning her spine against the hard edge of the workbench. She eased her grip just long enough to let Carrie get a breath, slapped her several more times, and then went back to the slow strangulation.

Carrie knew dimly that she was being used as a toy. Marthe was a veteran at this, and had no fear. It would be so easy to give in and let her life be ended now. I've seen your world. Some world. Keep it. Maybe I'll come back as a ghost to haunt this woman – but no, people like Marthe and Oliver are not haunted by the dead; they're haunted by the living.

Carrie got the plastic mirror in her hand and banged Marthe on the side of the head with it a couple of times. It was enough to loosen her grip slightly – though she smiled, as if amused at the act of resistance. Carrie turned her head, saw something she thought was a gun, fumbled it into her hand and shoved it up into Marthe's face as she leaned forward again. Marthe knocked it to the side with a jerk of her head.

Carrie's blurred vision was quickly disappearing altogether. She rammed the heavy gun at Marthe's head once more, and rapidly pulled the trigger several times.

'Oooooh . . .'

Click, click, click, click – nothing, empty.

But Marthe exhaled loudly, and her hands went slack. Carrie blinked and wiped at her eyes until she could see clearly. Then she discovered that she was squeezing the trigger of a soldering gun. The red-hot element had slid easily past Marthe's eyeball, straight on into her brain.

A faint sizzle, a curl of smoke.

Horrified, Carrie screamed. She dropped the soldering gun and staggered back several paces. Marthe tottered vacantly for a few moments, her mouth and hands still moving slightly. Then she came to a stop, face turned to her chest. Marthe's stalled body sagged to the floor and did not move again.

The gummy air reeked. The fans droned. The music raced and roared. The heat was dissolving her.

Carrie turned and stumbled away.

25

The affair with Heather ended quietly not long after Charley got back to New Haven. He'd called her once from Wisconsin, when he was a little tipsy and very miserable in his motel room on the eve of Jan's funeral. At the wake earlier her relatives had been pretty cool to him. Some, no doubt, believed that Charley should be in jail, charged with murder. It was probably not the best time to phone Heather, but he did. She was careful to say all the right things. So terrible about your wife, it must have been awful, hope you're all right, and so on. Yes, you can call when you get back to New Haven.

Which he did, though it took him a few days. He sat around the apartment, listened to Mahler and Bruckner, sorted papers and some of Jan's possessions, and finally he cleaned the place in a fit of manic energy. Then he slept for thirteen hours and awoke feeling weak and groggy. The world did not look any better to him. It was still his life, and he was still in it.

Heather was just as vague in the second call. She offered a few uplifting platitudes, an all-purpose exhortation or two, and a foggy murmur of indecision when he suggested a rendezvous. She wouldn't say yes and she wouldn't say no. She did say maybe, but when the appointed hour came she failed to appear at Gene's Tap. Probably not the best choice of venue.

Not much of a surprise, really. He was, after all, somebody whose wife had died of a slit throat while alone with him, a fact that was bound to have a cautionary effect on other women. Funny thing: the *New Haven Register* and the local TV news programmes gave only brief and quite restrained coverage of Jan's death. Few of the grim details were made public, although word leaked out by way of cops and newsmen in the know.

The police had certainly pegged him as a murderer, at least for the first twenty-four hours. That, undoubtedly, had been the second or third worst day of his life. The questions, the insinuations, and then the open accusations. Charley bore up very well under it all, he thought. He could have called a lawyer and shut up, but that would only make things look worse. So he answered all their questions patiently, denied guilt heatedly and finally persuaded them when he took and passed a polygraph test. The fingerprints on the knife were Jan's alone, which also helped. The police let him go – reluctantly.

The Brownes had been helpful and supportive, though Malcolm did seem a tad relieved when Charley dropped the summer-school course he had been about to start teaching. Perfectly understandable, a wise move, you need time to heal, to accept your loss and to arrive at closure. Ah yes, good old closure. But it was true that, at odd moments now, Charley felt himself unburdened. That whole phase of his life was over. It was time to pack up and move on, start another life in a new place. Whether you want to or not. Moving on. It's the American way, bud.

He and Jan had done such a thorough banjaxing of their lives that deep and genuine sorrow was now somewhat difficult to dig up within himself. What Charley felt was a kind of detached regret. The last twenty years had been a bad idea in which they had both persisted for far too long. Not entirely her fault, not entirely his, but theirs. And now Charley had no particular desire to trade places with Jan, but part of him, perhaps, envied her in some small way for getting out of it.

Charley crossed the Old Campus and the city green. He ought to make the move to Hamilton soon, take the time to settle in and find his bearings. He could spend the first semester writing his paper on Dunsany and Beckett. He'd also been thinking about one on Dunsany and Calvino – fantasy literature in what Iris Murdoch called the 'crystalline' mode. Clever and

296

sound ideas. He could earn liquor and cigar money by tutoring a few hours a week.

The apartment was pleasantly cool, but stale. Charley got a tumbler and poured some Powers. He put on his beloved Bax, three early tone poems, and settled in his armchair. Great music, fine whiskey, a smoke – the wee pleasures that help us abide.

Charley had barely lit the Honduran cigar when Oona appeared in the archway by the front hall, one hand clamped on the wall as if to steady herself. She had a duffel bag, and let it drop to the floor. She gave him a weak smile. Charley was astonished to see her there, but then felt a swirl of anger gathering within his chest.

'What do you want?'

'I need help.'

'Try the Connecticut Mental Health Center.'

Oona looked around, eyes widening. 'Your wife.'

'What about her?' Charley said in a growl.

Oona was shocked. 'Oh, my God, she's dead.'

'Thank you, Psychic News Network.'

'I'm sorry, I'm so sorry.'

'A mass card in the mail would have done.'

'So's Roz.'

'What?'

'Dead.'

'Roz is dead, is she?'

'Yes.'

'Well, that trumps me.'

'I mean it, Charley.'

'Oh, sure. And I suppose I'm next.'

'No.' Oona sagged a little. 'I am.'

'If you're trying to cheer me up, that's a good start.'

'You're the one. I told you.'

'What one?'

'I always thought it would be you.'

'What are you talking about?'

Oona didn't answer. She continued to look around the

room, her eyes brightly fearful, as if the white ceiling and grey walls were closing in on her. She sagged a little more, her eyes fell shut, and then Oona slumped to the floor. Thin streams of blood were trickling from her mouth and nose when Charley stepped past her to close the apartment door.

'But you haven't even been told.'
'Not officially, but it doesn't matter. I know.'
'You would have heard something,' Charley said.
'If they knew. If they found her.'
Charley shook his head in mild disbelief. He took a sip of Powers and relit his cigar. Oona was stretched out on the sofa, her head slightly raised on pillows. She was light and scrawny, like a child in his arms when Charley picked her up. He stopped the bleeding easily enough with ice and a damp towel.
'Another psychic fantasy,' he scoffed.
'It's true,' Oona said. 'It was like someone reached in and ripped out half of my heart. You don't know.'
'Oh?' Angry again. 'My wife died in my arms. She cut her own throat. Thanks in no small measure to you.'
Oona looked down. 'I'm sorry.'
'Ah, not at all. Think nothing of it.'
'I am,' Oona said quietly. 'We're both alone now.'
'We will be as soon as you leave.'
'I can't.'
'I beg your pardon?'
'I can't leave. I have nowhere to go.'
'You have a whole house of your own.'
'I can't stay there any more.'
'Why not?'
A long pause. 'I'm scared.'
'Of what?'
A longer pause. 'I don't know.'
'Let's go.' Charley put his cigar in the ashtray.
'Where?' A flash of alarm.
'I'll drop you off at Connecticut Mental Health. After that you're on your own.'

'No, no. Charley, please. I've done that scene.'

'Aha. And what did they tell you?'

'That there's nothing wrong with me,' Oona said.

'You need a second opinion, darling.'

Oona laughed. Somehow, things weren't going the way Charley wanted. The spasms of anger he felt were genuine, but they had a way of dissipating as quickly as they came. He didn't like Oona, he wanted to throw her out. But, at the same time, he did sort of enjoy her being there with him. It was the company, and the game she was playing.

'Charley.'

'What now?'

'Can I have a drink?'

'Are you sure you're twenty-one?'

'I think so.'

Charley almost laughed. He brought her a glass of sinfully watered-down whiskey. Some colour had returned to her face. Oona smiled as she took it. You wanted to hate her, you wanted to like her, and the cunning little creature knew it. She patted the space beside her on the sofa.

'Sit here for a minute.'

'Why?'

'I have to talk to you.'

'What else have we been doing?'

'I mean closer. Eye-to-eye talk.'

Charley sat on the edge of the sofa. 'So?'

'You won't make me leave. Please don't.'

'You can't stay here, if that's what you have in mind.'

'Just for a day or two,' Oona said quickly. 'Until I get an idea of where we have to go.'

'We?'

She looked down again. 'Yes.'

'*We* are not going anywhere, and you—'

'Charley . . .'

Tears gushing up in her eyes. He hated this kind of stunt. But those eyes had invisible hooks.

'You can wring your fingers too, for all I care.'

'I'm alone.'

'Who isn't.'

'You need me.'

'Why on earth do I need you?'

Oona sniffed and brushed away a tear. 'Because,' Oona said, her voice nervous and waifish, 'you couldn't save your daughter and you couldn't save your wife.' Now she looked up and gazed at him. 'I'm your last chance. You can still save me.'

What was he doing? Oona meant trouble, one way or another. She could talk like that, she could say things that got under his skin and worked on him – but they meant nothing. It was more of the same blather. She had a huge capacity for poking around the edges of your life, hoping to draw blood. That was the sort of person Oona was: seductive, sly, canny, manipulative.

Throw her out. She has a place of her own to live, and you can't give her the kind of help she needs anyway. Then drive up to Hamilton, Ontario. Find a nice apartment, get your future in hand. Straight away. Lose her. Now. Yes.

Charley stared at Oona, who was dozing on the couch. He had no idea why she'd come to him. He had had no idea about Roz. But he knew one thing. If you think you're lost and alone, you probably are. Oona was lost and alone.

And him with her.

While in the bathroom, he looked at his face in the mirror. Not much flesh tone in that mug. Grey stubble on the chin, to go with the first silvery strands cropping up on top. You have such tired eyes, a tired face. But who was he to judge? He knew some women who'd told him he had bedroom eyes. Meaning sexy, erotic. Charley preferred to accept their judgement over his own, even if he generally felt more tired than erotic. He splashed cold water on his face, brushed a few stray hairs back in place, sprayed his mouth with mint freshener, and returned to the living room.

'Charley.'

'Yes?'

'I'm very grateful to you.'

He hadn't given her a decision yet. 'Why?'

'For letting me stay.'

'Oona, I—'

'But I want to tell you straight, so you'll know.'

'What?'

'Don't try to put your thing in me.'

'Oona, it never crossed—'

'Don't even ask me to touch it.'

'When did you read Sir Walter Scott?'

'At the home.'

Oona was running her fingers along the spines on one of his bookshelves. She seemed a little stronger now and was wandering about the room, looking at things.

'*The* home?'

'It wasn't, really. They just call it that.'

'You mean an orphanage?'

'No. It was the kind of place where they put you when they have nowhere else to put you.'

'Were you in trouble?'

'You could say that.'

'When was this?'

'Oh, a while back.' Oona was growing restless. 'It doesn't matter now. But it wasn't all that bad a place. They had plenty of books, so I did a lot of reading. Makes the time pass.'

'What kind of trouble?'

'I don't know. Trouble trouble.'

'Oona, you must know,' Charley said, gently scolding. 'You might find it helps to talk about it.'

She smiled at him. 'Know what I like about you, Charley?'

'What?'

'You stayed with Jan. You did stay. It might not have been the best thing for either of you but it was the good thing to do. Everybody leaves sooner or later. Even Roz. But you didn't, you stayed with your wife.'

'Jan was not a strong person.'

'You are.'

Charley laughed. 'Oona, I'm probably the weakest man you've ever met, bar none.'

'You have a blind spot about yourself, but I see you in ways you never can. You're stronger than you think.'

'Well, good. That's nice to know.'

Charley was growing uncomfortable. This kind of talk was so ensnaring and it led nowhere. Oona was trying to make him feel better and, thus, more willing to do whatever she wanted. When he asked her anything about herself, she would swing it back to him and his life.

'You joke about it,' Oona said. 'But I was right about you. I was the first time we met.'

Charley ignored that. 'Tell me about your trouble.'

Oona gave him a strange look. She turned to the bookshelf again and moved along it, away from him.

'I saw the worst thing coming at me,' she said quietly. 'So I did the worst thing I could about it.'

'What do you mean?'

'What do you think?'

'Well, you didn't kill anybody. Did you?'

Oona looked at him for a moment, then turned away.

The drink didn't help. It was a long time before he finally fell asleep that night. She took the sofa in the living room and insisted that he leave his door open. Such a fey creature. Oona was not all there in some ways, but was, too much so, in others. Charley lay awake in his bed, trying to figure out what he should do with her.

No doubt there had been some traumatic event in her past. A childhood of abuse, violence, something like that. Murder, even, witnessed more likely than committed. The usual explanations for a disturbed personality. But whatever had happened to Oona years ago interested him less than who she was now. Fascinating in her own spooky way, appealing but at the same time off-putting, the picture of helplessness and yet subtly dominating – oh, yes, Oona was a little wonder. But not for ever irresistible.

He would let her stay for a day or two, three at most. Let her come to her senses. Then he would push her out, gently but firmly. You will know when the time is right because it'll be when you start to like her too much.

He thought he had it more or less worked out, when he heard the noises. Oona. She was crying in her sleep, whimpering as if in response to a bad dream. It grew louder. Bloody hell, it was going to be a short stay if he had to listen to this every night. Louder, then worse. It sounded as if she were choking or gagging on something.

Charley got out of bed and went to the living room. Now he could hear her thrashing about on the sofa, thumping it blindly with her arms. He slapped his hand against the wall to switch on the light. It looked even worse than it sounded.

She was having some kind of seizure. Her body twitched and jerked, and she was grinding her teeth in a clatter. Her eyes were squeezed tight shut. Saliva beaded in both corners of her mouth and then dribbled down her chin. Her fingers clawed at the upholstery, then smacked it wildly, and her head twisted back and forth in a frenzy. Strangled sobs and groans escaped through her clenched teeth.

Epilepsy? That would explain a lot, the visions and voices, the whole mad scene that Oona went through for the customers. It was so obvious – Charley was amazed that he hadn't thought of it before now. But he didn't know exactly what to do for someone in that state. Keep them from swallowing their tongue, right?

He rushed to the sofa and tried to calm Oona – but she was like a wild animal. Charley held her head and tried to open her mouth, but her teeth wouldn't budge. Her breath was hot on his skin and came in tiny snorts. Panic setting in.

'Help,' he said half aloud, to himself. 'Get help.'

Before he could move, however, Oona's hands shot up and took hold of him by the hair. Her strength was shocking. She pulled his head down onto her chest and held it tightly there.

His neck was twisted painfully, and Charley turned the rest of his body on the edge of the sofa to ease the angle. He couldn't pull away or free himself from Oona's grip.

As soon as he stopped trying, and relaxed a little, allowing his head to rest on her, Oona slowly began to thrash and struggle less. The sounds she made lost some of their desperate urgency, and her breaths grew longer and steadier. That's it, he thought, that's the girl. Come on now, come on. That's the way. You're all right now, it's ending.

Oona continued to moan faintly for some time, but her breath eased back to normal and her jaw relaxed. A while later, she let go of Charley's hair, and he slipped away. He didn't realize how scared he was until he went out to the kitchen and tried to pour himself a steadying drink of whiskey. He chipped the lip of the glass with the bottle.

'Too many people.'

'Where?'

'Here,' Oona said. 'All around us in this building, on this street. We're in the middle of a city.'

'Well, yes,' Charley said. 'Sorry about that, but this does happen to be where I live.'

'Too many people. That's what does it to me.'

'I could ask them to move. Clear the entire area for, say, three square miles all around. Would that do?'

'Charley, we have to go.'

'I'm not going anywhere.'

'You have to take me.'

'Sorry, darling.'

'Do you want me to die right here?'

'You're not going to die.'

'I know, it only seems that way.'

'Oona, it's just epilepsy,' he said patiently. 'I'm sure it can be treated or controlled. I mean, I'm not saying it isn't a serious problem. Of course it is but—'

'It isn't epilepsy,' Oona told him flatly. 'They threw that idea out long ago.'

304

'Well, something similar. Something – medical.'

She laughed. 'You still don't believe it, do you?'

'Believe what?'

'That it's real.'

'Oh, it's real enough,' Charley said, 'but it's not the kind of psychic spiritualism you think it is.'

'You have to take me,' she repeated. 'I can't make it on my own. I need you with me.'

'People bother you, but I don't.'

'That's right. I always need someone.'

'Listen, love, I have plenty of things of my own that I have to take care of, arrangements to make and—'

'No, no,' Oona interrupted. 'You have a lot of empty space in front of you right now.'

She stared at him, helpless and sad-eyed, so that he would be forced to think about it. And perhaps think that he was being selfish, that whatever he wanted to do could not possibly be more important than Oona's well-being. Save her the trouble, you can convince yourself that you're the one in control. Why bother to argue about it? Go straight to submission.

'No.'

Oona smiled. 'Thank you.'

'I said no, Oona. Look, I'm going up to Ontario,' Charley told her. 'If you want to come along—'

'First you're taking me – somewhere else.'

'Even if I wanted to, I can't afford to take you anywhere,' Charley explained, with a sigh of exasperation. 'I just paid for a very expensive funeral, you know, and—'

'No problem.' Oona pulled the duffel bag in front of her and unzipped the main section. She opened it wide, revealing stacks of money bound in rubber bands. 'I've got loads.'

'Ah, Jesus. Where did all that come from?'

'People like to help me.'

'There's the phone. Call up one of them.'

'It wouldn't work. It's you.'

'Somehow I knew you'd say that.' Charley stared at her for a moment. 'Where do you want to go?'

Oona frowned, almost cringed. 'Honestly, it's the one place where I can do you some real good. You must believe me, Charley. You must *believe*. It's for you, too.'

He stared vacantly at her, and then he realized what she was saying. Charley's head began to swim. He took Oona by the shoulders and shook her angrily.

'Ireland.'

'That's right.'

'No!'

'Yes, it has to be,' she insisted.

'Are you trying to destroy me?'

'What would you do if I said yes?'

She was feeding off his rage, her eyes glittering, her face vibrant with sensual anticipation. As if she knew that he was so upset he wanted to hurt her just then, physically hurt her – and she was almost eager to see it happen.

Charley pushed her away.

'I'd say fuck off.'

'And if I said I was trying to save you?'

'I'd still say fuck off.'

Oona smiled sorrowfully, and touched his arm. 'Nobody's that strong, Charley.'

That night she cried and talked for more than an hour in her sleep. Oona's voice was as frail as a child's.

'Roz . . . Roz . . . don't . . . no . . . don't go . . .'

Little-girl sobs. Lost and alone. It didn't get any worse than that, it never turned into another seizure, but that was bad enough. Charley sat in a cone of light at his desk, listening to her. It was impossible to read.

Thinking: You're a sorry specimen, you are. Hopeless eejit. If there was one constant in Charley's life it was this: that he had never found a way to say no to a woman. Most of the time, it showed up as an inability to keep his fly zipped. Funny. Now he had no difficulty restraining himself in that regard – Oona was safe enough in his company – but he seemed to be losing the rest of the battle. And he wasn't sure that he cared.

If Roz was home tomorrow he'd turn Oona over to her. But if there was still no sign of her, what then? He couldn't just drop Oona off at an institution like Connecticut Mental Health. He could not do that. Nor could he abandon her at the house in Westville. On her own, Oona was a menace to herself. So he'd still be stuck with her. So he might as well let her do what she wanted.

Besides, he told himself, what have you got to lose? Your life? Your soul? Yes, but anything that matters?

Oona drank before they left the apartment. She drank in the limo to JFK, sneaking little sips from a plastic juice bottle. A few more drinks in the bar at the departure terminal. Drinks all the way in the air. It numbed her some.

'Too many people.'

'You often find them on planes.'

'I should live down there.'

Oona tapped the plastic window, pointing to the vast moonlit floor of clouds far below.

'Up above the world so high.'

'No,' she said. 'I meant the bottom of the ocean.'

'I thought the kelpie was a freshwater fiend.'

'Ah, who's a clever boy?'

'Would you say I'm one of your sensitive ones?'

'No.'

'Didn't think so,' he grumped.

'But I still like you, Charley,' she said, smiling warmly at him. 'I'm really very, very fond of you.'

'Just don't fall in love with me.'

Oona found that amusing. 'Why?'

'Because there's less here than meets the eye.'

She giggled, then started laughing and couldn't stop. She bent forward and put her hand over her mouth.

'What's so funny?' he asked.

'Charley, I know *that*.'

'I was only joking,' he muttered.

'So was I.'

'No, you weren't.'

'No, you're right, I wasn't,' she said, still giggling.

'A bit of shut-up from you would do fine about now.'

'Oona Oona Mamouna . . . Oona Oona Mamouna . . .'

Thump. Charley looked at her. She was all right, for now. She had just bopped her head against the window and was off in a light doze. Tipsy doodle.

He stayed more or less awake for the entire flight, fearful that she might launch into one of her rants. He would whisk her away to the bathroom if that happened.

A few minutes later she rolled in his direction, and rested her face against his arm. She put her hand over his. Her eyes stayed shut, but she smiled sleepily and murmured to him, 'Charley.'

'What?'

'Do you love me?'

'Yes.'

Immediate, and unnerving. But Charley knew at once that in some obscure way it was true, even as it was true that he was not *in love* with Oona. She smiled again and rubbed his arm, although her eyes were still closed.

'I knew it.'

'Why'd you ask, then?'

'I wasn't sure you knew it.'

She woke up, pale and shaking, as they made their approach to Shannon. The drink was wearing off. She was a bit tottery while they waited for their bags, and she struggled to maintain some of her concentration as they went through Immigration and Customs. Charley expected trouble about the money. At his insistence, she had changed a lot of it into travellers cheques, but she was still carrying a suspicious amount of cash. No search, however, and no awkward questions. Two weeks' holiday? Enjoy your stay.

'Thank God for that,' Charley said, as they pulled away from the airport in a rental car. He'd half expected Oona to go into a full-bore spell in the middle of the terminal, spraying people with blood. 'Are you all right?'

'Better.'

'You know, if it happens and you're totally out of control, I'll have to take you to the nearest hospital.'

'Don't do that.'

'I'd have to.'

'No.' Pleading weakly. 'That'd be the worst thing for me, Charley. Just let it run its course. That's all you have to do. Stay close to me, like the other night.'

'But it looks like you're – dying.'

'I never do.'

'You'd better not. Not on my hands, missy.'

They stopped briefly in Ennis to buy some food. They ate it in the car, as he drove towards Galway. Charley was tired, but he seemed to have found his second wind. It felt good to be back in Ireland, as always.

'I should take you to County Mayo,' he said.

'Where's that?'

'North of here. It's very beautiful, but desolate country. There aren't many people about.'

'Sounds great. Like the Highlands.' Oona was sitting low in the passenger seat, her knees propped against the dashboard. 'I'd love to go back to Scotland, but I can't.'

'Why not?'

'Probably cause a stir. The media, and all.'

He thought about it. 'Oona, what actually did happen back then? Get it out.'

'Nothing to tell.'

'I've come this far with you. I have a right to know.'

'I hit her in the head with a brick, okay? She was four and I was eleven. That's all there was to it.'

Oona tried to sound bored and impatient but didn't succeed. She was disturbed, agitated. Charley had difficulty grasping her words for a few moments. Four. Eleven.

'What was – was it an accident?'

309

'I was the accident.'

'Oona, what – why?'

'Now you'll really get me started.'

She reached into the carrier bag on the floor and took out a bottle of duty-free Powers. Charley shut up.

'If I got into bed with you, would you just hug me?'

He smiled. 'Yes.'

'Thanks.'

Oona snuggled up against him. A woman-child in her pyjamas. It was still quite early in the evening, but they were exhausted. They had checked into the hotel just after lunch and hadn't left the room since. Charley had drawn the curtains, as it stayed light outside quite late in the Irish summer.

'Charley?'

'Hmmn?'

'Does it make a difference?'

'No, not to me.'

She snuggled closer. 'Know what I think?'

'I can't imagine.'

'She's inside me. Has been ever since.'

'Metaphorically, you mean.'

'What's that?'

'It means you might be haunted by her, in a way, but they're all your own thoughts,' Charley explained. 'She's not inside you in any true physical or supernatural sense. It means that you're not literally haunted or possessed by a real ghost.'

Oona was silent for a moment.

'No,' she said. 'That's not the way I meant it.'

'Oh, really, Oona. That sort of—'

'Charley.'

'What?'

'If we could find a cottage in Mayo, far from anywhere, near a small village but with hardly any people around, would you live there with me? Would you stay and take care of me?'

'For how long?' he asked warily.

'For ever.'

'No.'

'Why not?'

'Because I'd want to put my so-called thing in you.'

'I've never had that.'

'Ah, that explains everything.'

'I don't see why I should start now.'

'No wonder you're unhinged.'

'Is that what you think? Never mind,' Oona added quickly. 'It doesn't matter. You're doing your best as it is.'

'I know.'

'You never made love like the angels. I can tell.'

'See? You don't know everything.'

'What do you mean? You're not the type.'

'Oona,' he said. 'They're all angels.'

Ravenswood.

Charley held a tall styrofoam cup of coffee with both hands. It was just after six in the morning. They had awakened early, still adjusting to the time change. Oona wanted to go out there straight away. Get it over with first and have breakfast later. Very droll. But there was a kind of sense to it. Charley wasn't entirely awake, his brain felt sluggish, and perhaps that was the best way to approach the ordeal. He parked the car at the kerb, and they sat for a couple of minutes.

'Which one?'

'I'm not sure,' he said. 'Hardly any of these houses were here at the time. It's all built-up now.'

There had been the fateful cottage, plus two or three other widely scattered homes. Rolling land, clusters of big old trees, and the sea view in the distance. One road through the area. It was quite different now. Lines of tidy middle-class houses with tidy little front gardens, the trees mercifully gone, and neatly paved streets winding throughout.

'Come on.'

'Where?'

But she was already out of the car, and Charley followed her reluctantly. They walked up the street and then back down to the car, and beyond it a short distance. He wouldn't be surprised if an early riser spotted them and called the police.

The remains of the cottage would have been razed years ago, and so much landscaping had been done in developing the area that Charley couldn't find a focal point he recognized. He could just see the ocean, far off, but that view of it was more or less the same all along the street, and his memory was imprecise.

'What do you think?' Oona asked.

'I'm not thinking yet.'

'What do you feel?'

'Sleepy.'

'Come here.'

She took him by the arm and started to cross the street, but they stopped near the middle of it.

'Now what do you feel?' she asked again.

'Nothing.'

'It was right here,' she told him.

'No, I don't think—'

'It was,' she insisted. Her eyes were shimmery and dancing, and she smiled as if she were enjoying a secret. 'This is where your house stood.'

Charley looked around. She could be guessing, or she could be right. The road might have been moved. Odd to think that he might have just driven a car through the very space.

'What do you feel now?'

'The same,' he said. 'Nothing. It's all different.'

'Good. That's very good.'

'What do you feel?' he asked.

'I just see grey, like we're standing in a fog.'

It was a clear morning. 'What's that mean? Grey.'

'It means that's all there is.'

'Is something supposed to happen? Am I meant to have some kind of a vision or—'

'No. It's over, Charley. I thought it was for you, but I wanted to come here and make sure. I wanted you to come here and see for yourself. To feel for yourself. You said that you don't believe, but a part of you has always believed and always will. That's why this was so important. I had to get you here so you would know for sure. It's over.'

'Great,' he said. 'But I still don't understand.'

Oona smiled. 'It was about your wife. She had Fiona inside her ever since that day.'

'She felt guilty, of course. We both—'

'Never mind the guilt,' Oona told him. 'It's the loss. Jan survived the fire, but too much of her was lost. She was waiting for Fiona to come back and take the rest of her. To save her, in a way. Charley, a ghost is a form of redemption.'

A mile away, he suddenly pulled the car over to the side of the road and turned it off. For a minute or two he stared ahead blankly. His heart pounded in his chest and he breathed rapidly through his mouth. The sense of Fiona overwhelmed him, he could feel and smell her in his arms. Images of Jan, such a handsome young woman, the woman he'd crossed an ocean and half a continent to marry. Everything had been right – and then nothing was ever right again. All this time, and yet he felt he didn't understand anything of his own sorry life.

Charley put his forehead to the steering wheel, and was dimly aware of Oona's hand on his back. His body trembled and he couldn't think or say anything for a few minutes. He blinked several times and finally turned to face Oona. 'No one's coming back for me.'

'No,' she said sadly.

'Not Fiona. Not Jan.'

'No one.'

'That's for my part in what happened, isn't it?'

Oona stroked his cheek lovingly. 'I'm sorry.'

'This way,' Oona said, pointing south.

'County Mayo is the other way,' he told her, indicating the road to the north-east.

'This way,' she insisted.

They drove for hours, going in wobbly circles, stopping for

a bite to eat, now and then, and to check out every pub they came across. It became apparent that Oona had no special destination in mind, but that was all right with Charley. He felt empty and somewhat detached.

'I expected to feel more,' he told her, when they were in a pub in Lehinch.

'Everybody wants more,' Oona said.

'Or that it would be different,' he amended.

'I warned you about that the first time you came to see Roz. It's never exactly what people want. But that's okay, you're all right now.'

'Oh, am I?' he said sarcastically.

'You'll see. You're one of those who walk away.'

'Is that a good thing?'

'I have no idea.'

The Cliffs of Moher.

'Moher . . .' Oona stared at the sign, her hand on Charley's arm. 'Would you look at that name. I don't believe it. We have to stop here for a while.'

'If you want to see the cliffs, fine. They're spectacular,' Charley said. 'But we ought to find a room for the night first. We might have to try a few places. We can always come back here in the morning.'

'No, I want to see them now.'

'Oona.'

'We can watch the sun set. It's a beautiful evening and it might be pouring with rain tomorrow.'

In Ireland that was a valid point. Charley sighed unhappily but swung the car round. He was tired again, and wanted only to crawl into a bed and sleep. Not yet. A little while later, they parked and hiked up the path to the cliffs.

'Have you been here before?'

'Once, yes,' he replied.

Quite a few people were visiting the scene, but they were widely spaced in small groups along the rim of the cliffs.

Cameras clicking and arms pointing, the usual tourist gestures in evidence. Oona hurried the final stretch.

'Oh – oh my—'

'It's something, isn't it?'

Charley smiled and Oona gaped at the sight. The cliffs of Moher were so stark and dramatic that they almost defied any kind of perspective. Here Ireland ended at the Atlantic Ocean with a 600-foot drop down a virtually sheer rock-face, a huge geological relief map of the aeons before human life, maybe even life itself. At the bottom, the sea crashed against barren stone in a constant storm of churning, pounding waves. There was no beach, no line of earth or sand. Nothing but worn black rocks and the turmoil of the ocean. The cliffs stretched away to the north and south, roughly forming a half-moon arc.

'What's that?' Oona asked, pointing at a ruined building off to the upper right.

'It used to be a tea-house. For the gentry, I suppose. You wouldn't want them to stand around like ordinary folk.'

Oona turned the other way. 'Come on.'

Charley trudged along after her. Oona hiked nearly to the furthest point on the southern end of the cliffs, well beyond any other visitors. She sat down on the heavy grass a few yards from the edge, positioning herself so that she could look at the full range of the cliffs and also watch the sun in its descent. As ever, there was a fair breeze, but the air was mild and clean.

'I'm done,' Charley said, plopping down beside her.

'Isn't it beautiful?'

'Oh, yes.'

They sat in silence for a few moments.

'What does it make you think of?' Oona asked him.

'*The Lark Ascending* by Vaughan Williams.'

'Is that a poem?'

'A piece of music, but yes, very like a poem.'

'Can you hum it for me?'

He laughed. 'It wouldn't be the same.'

'Charley.'

'What?'

'I love you.'

He was going to smile and say something sweetly amusing but he saw how desperate and frightened she looked, and it startled him. The minute before she'd been fine.

'What's the matter?'

'I just wanted to tell you.'

'Do you feel all right? You don't look well.'

'I'm okay.'

'We ought to leave while it's still light.'

'Not yet.'

He kept an eye on her. Too pale, too tense.

'Charley,' she said, a few minutes later. 'You're not scared to be here with me.'

'Why should I be?'

'There were six people in that room, last session.'

She was breathing too fast, her chest heaving.

'So what? Oona, let's—'

'Three of them are dead now. Your wife, Roz and Mr Spence. He killed Roz, but he's gone too. I shouldn't have told her. I should have kept quiet about it and gone myself. That's what he wanted, but he had a different idea about me. Roz wanted to warn him off so he'd leave us be.'

'Wait a sec,' Charley interrupted. 'Would you mind starting over again. I got lost in the credits.'

Oona smiled, but it disappeared quickly. 'Never mind, it's not important now. There's other things I have to tell you. I want you to understand what it's like for me. How people's lives crash into my head. I see them and feel them and hear them. Not everybody and not all the time, but lots of them and most of the time. You know what it does to me, but that's only the outside. It's much worse inside, in my heart and in my head. It tears me to pieces and there's no way I can avoid it, until it runs its course. Until the next time. The drink only helps a little bit, and only for a while, but it doesn't hold. What I go through is real, Charley. You don't have to believe me, you can think it's an illness of some kind. But I'm telling you from inside it. It's nothing anyone knows and it's real.'

'I believe you,' he said.

'How else would I find out you were a good in-fielder but a pretty lousy hitter when you were a kid? I don't know the first thing about baseball, and I don't even know what that means, but it's right, isn't it?'

He nodded again, his throat tightening. 'Yes.'

'Because I get to know things about a person,' Oona went on. 'I can't control it, I can't even find most of the things people want me to find in their lives, their past, their future. But it goes on and on and on, all the time and . . . and . . .'

She seemed lost for a moment.

'Oona—'

'I'm the window.'

'What?'

'I'm the voice.'

'What voice?'

'Lost – the lost.'

'Oona, I'm sure—'

She shook her head and seemed to come out of it. She smiled weakly at him, but then her expression turned serious again.

'Anyhow, the thing is, I have one other thing to tell you about.' She frowned, glanced down at the grass, then back at him. 'You asked me why.'

'Why what?'

'Why I killed Patty Prince.' The wind fluffed her hair, and he didn't notice the pencil-lines of blood that began to well up in her nostrils. 'The little girl in Scotswood. That was where we were living. She was – oh, fuck me.'

The blood washed across her mouth. Charley reached for his handkerchief but Oona backed away from him on the ground, moving like a crab. Her eyes blinked and she shook her head while she wiped at the streaming blood. She sat up on her knees, legs wide apart, and stared at him with a wild urgency in her eyes. He had no idea what to do or how to help her.

'She was a darling, a sweet little thing, and Roz loved her like she was her own, like she was Patty's mam. I was afraid I'd

317

lose Roz, and Roz was the only one I had, she looked after me and saved me time and again. Roz protected me and—'

She couldn't talk for a moment, blood choking her, spraying out of her mouth, her face contorted, her hands fluttering vainly as her body was jarred with successive tremors.

'Don't say anything. Let me—'

Oona waved him off. 'I could see it coming at me. That was the first time I saw ahead. I was going to lose Roz. I couldn't bear the thought. So I did it. The only thing worse.'

Her eyes bulging, with the look of the blind – and streaked now with bright red lines.

'Come on,' Charley said. He felt dazed, unable to take in all he'd heard, but he knew he had to get her to a hospital. She needed help immediately. 'I'll take you.'

'No—' Oona backed away from him again, waving him off as she moved parallel to the line of the cliff. 'I told you, let it run. It's her in me. She's strong, she'll do me.'

'Oona, please,' Charley said pleadingly. 'Let me hold you a while, until it passes. You'll be all right, it'll get better if you do. You know that.'

'You're – not – the – one.'

'What one? Oona, please.'

'You – can't—'

'Oona, let me . . .'

'Save – anybody—'

Oona stood up, swaying like a scarecrow in a stormy breeze. Charley started to take a step towards her but froze. Blood seemed to be coming out of her eyes and ears, her nose and mouth, and it clung to her like a gauzy veil. Like the hazy image of a second person that floated an inch above her skin. Oona let out a barrage of ferocious animal grunts – similar to the noises Jan had made when giving birth to Fiona, Charley remembered absurdly.

He reached for her, but when his hand touched the bloody air around Oona it felt like fire. Filmy stuff that disintegrated as he brushed it on his shirt. He glanced up at her again, and she seemed to be fire itself, a brilliant red glow against the richer crimson of the massive sun. Fire disappearing in fire.

Charley suddenly felt empty, as if all the air had flown out of him and he couldn't breathe. He moved stiffly, angling closer to the edge of the cliff. Oona? But he couldn't speak, and the word died inside him. Oona was no longer there.

Charley looked down, desperate and alone, but all he saw was a boiling mist at the bottom of the cliffs, and the heaving ocean beyond.